HE SEES YOU WHEN YOU'RE SLEEPING

WILLIAM MALMBORG

DARKER DREAMS MEDIA

ALSO BY WILLIAM MALMBORG

Novels

Jimmy

Text Message

Nikki's Secret

Dark Harvest

Blind Eye

Santa Took Them

Crystal Creek

Daddy's Little Girl

The Girl Who Played With the Ouija Board

Josiah

Novellas

Till Death Do Us Part

Don't Go in the Cellar

Short Story Collections

Scarping the Bone: Ten Dark Tales

Copyright © 2024 by William Malmborg

All rights reserved.

No part of this book may be reproduced in any form or by any electronic or mechanical means, including information storage and retrieval systems, without written permission from the author, except for the use of brief quotations in a book review.

This is a work of fiction. All of the characters, organizations, and events portrayed in this novel are either products of the author's imagination or are used fictitiously.

HE SEES YOU WHEN YOU'RE SLEEPING

For all the cats who have blessed me with their company over the years

ONE

"Mommy!" Tabby shouted. "It's Santa!"

Gwen froze at the sudden sight of the fat man in red sitting upon a makeshift throne.

"Mommy! I want to go see!"

"Not now," Gwen said, finding her voice.

"But, Mommy!"

"I said no!" Gwen snapped, heart racing, panic rising.

Tabby started pulling Gwen's hand with all her might, her tiny body trying to drag her toward the display that was claiming to be the North Pole.

"Tabby!" Gwen warned.

Tabby's hand disappeared, replaced by the rough rope that had knotted Gwen's wrists together, the mall around her turning into a family room with pink shag carpet, fluffy couches, a brightly lit Christmas tree with blinking lights, and a roaring fire that she could not see but felt, the heat dancing across her naked backside as she dangled from the beam in the ceiling.

No! No! No!

Screams echoed in her ears, ones that she didn't realize were coming from her own lips.

2

Ian felt his phone buzzing in his pocket while standing in the doorway of the fantasy and science fiction room, his hands struggling to find a spot to set the stack of books so he could grab his phone.

He failed.

The stack of books ended up on the floor.

"Hello?" he answered.

"Ian," a familiar voice said. "It's Sam."

"Hey! What's up?"

"It's Gwen," Sam said. "She's okay. But there was an incident at the mall today and we took her over to the hospital to be checked out."

"An incident?" he asked. "What do you mean?"

"Seems she had some sort of panic attack while shopping and hit her head. She's okay. Tabby is too. Still, I think you better come down here."

"I'm on my way."

3

Sam was waiting by the hospital entrance when Ian arrived, his eyes not seeing her at first given that she was in civilian clothes rather than her uniform, a sudden realization that she must have come in on her day off to help with this situation causing his panic to flare up another notch.

"Where is she?" he asked.

"Room 217," Sam said, turning to lead the way.

Ian didn't need a guide but let Sam lead the way anyway.

"I should warn you," Sam said, stopping abruptly after they climbed the stairs. "She's not happy about the doctor's recommendation that she stay the night."

"No, she wouldn't be," he said, body trying to get around her so he could continue toward her room.

"Ian," she said, hand held out. "It was the Santa display that set her off."

"Oh fuck."

4

"I just wasn't expecting to see him," Gwen said while sitting at the kitchen table, Ian having brought her home from the hospital against the doctor's wishes, two freshly filled mugs of coffee going untouched. "We turned the corner and he was suddenly there, right in the middle of the mall."

"It never even occurred to me that they would already be doing that. It's not even Thanksgiving yet."

Gwen didn't reply.

"Earlier and earlier every year," Ian continued. "It's like Halloween ends at sunset and then boom, Christmas lights, music, and Santa shit."

Tears were rolling down her cheeks.

"Are you okay?" he asked, taking her hand.

She nodded.

"You sure?"

Another nod.

5

. . .

"Why is Mommy scared of Santa?" Tabby asked as Ian put her to bed that night.

Ian froze, unsure how to respond to that.

Tabby waited.

"Some people did some mean things to Mommy last year while pretending to be Santa," Ian said.

"And now I did a mean thing to her too."

"No, no, honey, you didn't do anything mean. Mommy was just surprised. Sort of like that time we were at the pumpkin patch and that scarecrow moved. Remember?"

Tabby nodded. "You dropped the giant pumpkin on your toe."

"I did."

"And you said the f-word."

"Yes, which was wrong of me."

"So Santa was like the scarecrow?"

"Exactly. It scared her because she wasn't expecting to see it."

"But Santa isn't supposed to be scary."

"And neither are scarecrows. Remember *The Wizard of Oz*? That scarecrow isn't scary."

"The monkeys are."

"Yes, but Curious George isn't."

"No, Daddy, he's just silly!"

"See, that is what this was like. Santa isn't supposed to be scary, just like monkeys and scarecrows aren't, but today in this one moment Santa was scary for Mommy, just like the scarecrow was for us at the pumpkin patch, and the flying monkeys are in *The Wizard of Oz*."

Tabby took a second to process that. "Is Mommy okay now?"

"Yes."

"And she won't be scared of Santa next time?"

"Well…next time we see Santa it will be just you and me, okay?"

"What about when he comes down the chimney?"

"We will all be sleeping when he does that."

"Oh yeah!"

"But that won't be for a while. We have to do Thanksgiving first."

"Turkey Day!"

Ian smiled.

6

"Is she okay?" Gwen asked.

"Oh yeah, she's fine," Ian said.

"I'm so sorry."

"Honey, you have nothing to be sorry for."

"I just can't believe I freaked out like that. Especially in front of her. It's humiliating."

"No, it's not."

"Yes," she insisted. "It is."

Ian didn't reply.

"I'm okay now," she said. "You don't have anything to worry about."

"I know."

"I was confused after everything."

"Honey, I know," he said. "Though…"

"What?" she asked.

"Given all the decorations that are about to go up and all the Santa stuff that will be everywhere, do you think maybe we should go see a—"

"No!" she snapped.

"It might be good to simply talk with—"

"No!"

"Okay, okay," he said, holding up his hands.

7

It wasn't real, Gwen said to herself while lying in bed, her mind back in the family room of the Robinson house, body dangling from the beam in the ceiling after being prepared by Jessica, mind and body a wreck from having been chained up in the cellar for nearly a month, the sudden warmth of the family room and the pampering she had gotten before being strung up by the fireplace so that Justin and Jessica could hurry up to bed before midnight a total mind-fuck.

And then...

Not real! Not real! Not real!

Over and over the words played across her mind, their presence having been hammered into her by everyone after the ordeal, various treatments and prescribed pill combinations helping her accept this.

Not real! Not real! Not real!

Hanging for hours, hands purple and lifeless, the red ribbon that had been carefully wrapped around her body completely disheveled from her fruitless struggles, one of the red bows that had been stuck to her nipples having fallen to the floor, the other still clinging for dear life. Some eggnog had also spurted out onto the carpet, leftover from the repeated enemas Jessica had given her during the preparations, stating how eggnog was like Chanel No. 5 when it came to the ruler of the North Pole and how her having been cleansed with it inside and out would help earn her a coveted spot within the castle once she was there while all the other offerings were tossed down to the toy makers.

Not real! Not real! Not real!

She glanced over at the clock on the nightstand.

It was just after eleven.

Leaning over a bit, she looked to see if Ian was asleep.

He was, his body curled up on the cot they had brought into the room several months earlier, her body unable to sleep if he was next to her in bed, all while her mind needed him in the room with her.

Does he mind?

Of course he does.

Shaking her head, she carefully reached into the nightstand and grabbed a pill bottle, one that held capsules that would knock all sense from her and let her sleep a nice dreamless sleep.

8

"Gwen?" a voice said.

Gwen blinked and saw Dee looking at her in the doorway to the small, cluttered office, concern plastered upon her face.

"Are you okay?" Dee asked.

"I'm fine!" Gwen said, voice a bit harsh. Then, a second later: "Sorry. Zoned out a bit. Didn't get much sleep last night. What's up?"

"I'm going to grab some lunch before I start."

"Okay, no problem."

"Want me to bring you something back?"

"Where're you going?"

"Going to try that new noodle place on the corner."

Gwen shook her head.

A few seconds later, the chime on the front door dinged, marking Dee's exit.

Gwen stepped from the tiny office and headed to the counter, eyes looking over at the small sitting area where people could consume drinks and various baked goods. It was empty. The same was true of the rest of the bookstore, the book-lined hallways and various genre rooms quiet, all the paperbacks and occasional hardbacks eagerly awaiting the day when someone would spot them upon the cluttered shelves and decide to give them a good home.

Framed vintage movie posters and other knickknacks were present as well, the former up on the walls serving as temporary decor while awaiting purchase, the latter doing the same only from the shelves themselves, small end tables, podiums, and sometimes the floor itself. A giant globe was the most impressive of these items, one that had recently acquired a Do Not Touch sign after a kid had decided to spin it as hard as he could and got his finger caught.

A few Band-Aids were all that was necessary in regard to medical treatment, yet the mother raised holy hell, threatening lawsuits up the wazoo.

No lawsuits had been filed though, likely because the store itself wasn't part of some big corporate entity that would settle right away to avoid bad publicity. Instead, it was just an independent place that she and Ian owned, one that didn't really make any money yet didn't hurt them financially thanks to them owning the building it was in.

It had been Ian's lifelong dream to own a bookstore, something he had constantly talked about during the early days of their relationship as they both worked themselves to exhaustion on Wall Street, so when the opportunity to take over the antique store his parents owned in his old hometown presented itself, they jumped on it and turned the place into a bookstore, making the dream a reality.

His dream, not hers, though she never really had a dream that she aspired to, so latching on to his hadn't seemed like a hardship at all. Especially after all the drama out east. Still didn't. In fact, she enjoyed being in the store while it was empty, surrounded by the clutter of books and all the other odd items they acquired for resale. It was cozy.

Ian, on the other hand, didn't seem to be enjoying his dream all that much these days and spent most of his time away from the bookstore, tending to things with the various properties they had purchased when moving out here, ones that she originally had managed.

Why this was, she did not know, though she had an idea it was due to everything that had happened last Christmas and all her mental struggles following her escape.

9

Ian sat in the family room of the empty house, eyes staring at the cold fireplace, a dirty stocking with the name Jessica stitched in script still hanging from the mantel where it had been dangling during the final night of Gwen's horrifying ordeal, her body having been strung up as some sort of offering to a Santa that was far from the jolly old elf that most children envisioned.

Dead rabbits had been present as well that night, their lifeless bodies gifts to the demonic reindeer that the siblings believed would be upon their roof while their master was down in the house, assessing the female offering and deciding upon how many presents she was worth—if any.

It was insane.

How anyone could believe such a thing was beyond his comprehension.

The fact that the two had seemed so normal also defied logic, he and Gwen having sat in this very room many times over the years, sometimes to collect rent, sometimes just to visit, Jessica always having some sort of sweet treat she had baked on hand, Justin some new wood carving or mechanical oddity he had created over in his workshop to show them.

Gwen had been their captive during one of his visits with

them, Jessica and Justin displaying sympathy as they listened to how the search was going and how he was doing in his attempts at keeping Tabby in good spirits, the three of them sitting in this very room, his eyes enjoying the cheery Christmas feel they had created, his voice commenting on how it looked like a Hallmark movie, all while Gwen had been down in the cellar, ears likely able to hear his voice as she struggled against the chains that connected her to the stone foundation.

That cheery warm holiday feel was long since gone, all the utilities having been shut off, the boarded-up front windows doing little to keep out the cold November air, the beautiful brightly lit Christmas tree that had stood before those very windows long since dead, its brown needles having somehow gotten scattered about and embedded into the pink carpet.

No one would ever rent this house again, not with the history it now held.

But even if he thought people would move in, he would never put it on the market. Nor would he ever try to sell the land.

What exactly he would do with it, he did not know, but profiting from it following what had happened was most certainly not in the cards.

Dee took a really long lunch, Gwen frowning at the time as the young woman returned, a mental reminder being set to mention to Ian that Dee seemed to feel her start times were merely a suggestion rather than set in stone. She also wanted to mention the wardrobe choices Dee had been making lately. Gwen was no prude by any stretch of the imagination, but the outfits Dee had been wearing these last several weeks seemed a bit too risqué for a quiet bookstore setting. Or really any business setting that didn't involve a stage with a pole.

No dress code was stated when it came to hiring employees to work at the store, Ian having voiced early on that he was tired of putting on what he called *business armor* after all the years on Wall Street and wanted to spend his bookstore years in comfort, which meant hoodies and jeans. How anyone could claim jeans were comfortable was a mystery to Gwen, though she would never argue such a thing. She also did not share his disdain for the attire she had always worn to the high-rise offices, preferring such clothes to the casual outfits that most seemed to enjoy. It actually took quite a bit of effort for her to dress down enough to the point where she didn't look completely out of place while in the bookstore or while simply going about various tasks in town, the so-called "comfortable" clothing items causing her mental discomfort as she went about her daily tasks.

Ian had often joked it was her Gold Coast upbringing that had instilled such troubles and that she had never even known things like jeans, hoodies, and flannel existed until she met him, and while that wasn't true at all, it was true that her family would never have allowed such attire to be worn outside the house. Even inside the house one was expected to dress appropriately after a certain point in the morning and always dress up for dinner, which had caused quite an outrage the first time Ian had stayed with her family during the early days of their relationship since he hadn't packed any ties.

Memories of that visit dominated her mind for several minutes, Dee eventually yanking her attention back to the present when she asked if Gwen had packaged up any of the eBay orders that had come in so that she could walk them down to the post office.

"No, not yet," Gwen said.

Dee gave her a look that pretty much voiced *what the fuck?* before asking if she wanted her to do it.

"No, no, I'll take care of it," Gwen said.

"You sure?" Dee asked.

"Yep." She went back into the office to grab the stack of order confirmations she had printed out that morning, most of them being from a guy outside of Chicago who ordered stuff on a near weekly basis, his reading tastes impossible to pin down given the randomness of his selections. Just the other week he had ordered eighteen *Conan the Barbarian* paperbacks that had been published by Tor in the eighties, while a few weeks earlier it had been six *Doctor Who* paperbacks and a stack of old *Ellery Queen Mystery* magazines. He had also cleared them out of all the *Nick Carter: Killmaster* novels during one buying spree and could always be counted on to grab any *Tales from the Crypt* comics they got in just as long as they were original pre-barcode ones from the '50s. Today's orders seemed to be focusing on old teen horror novels, all being either *Fear Street* or *Goosebumps* titles from R.L. Stine.

. . .

"I don't know!" Dee's voice echoed. "She just went crazy!"

"I'm on my way," Ian said into the phone, all while his mind demanded: *Now what?*

Ten minutes later, he was in the bookstore, staring at the mess Gwen had made, several paperbacks having been torn to shreds in her craze before she had curled up in a corner, hands around her knees as she rocked back and forth, tears running down her face.

. . .

"It's nothing," Dee said, dabbing at the scratches on her arm.

"Are you sure?" Ian asked, horror at what had unfolded dominating his thoughts.

"Totally. It's all good. You just get her home. I'll close up and take care of this mess."

"Thanks."

13

"I'm okay," Gwen said as they drove home, cheeks crusty with salt from the tears that had dried.

"You tore up a book simply because it had a picture of Santa on the cover," Ian said. "And then you attacked Dee."

"I didn't attack her," Gwen said.

"She has claw marks up and down her arm from your fingernails."

"She tried to grab the book from me. It was an accident."

Ian didn't reply to that, the silence heavy as they completed the journey home.

14

"I honestly have no idea what to do," Ian said. "I knew things might get rocky going into the holidays, but freaking out in malls and then tearing up books...that wasn't what I was envisioning at all."

Sam nodded as she contemplated things.

Ian waited.

"I'm really not sure what to suggest," Sam eventually said. "Beyond her seeing someone, that is."

"She won't do that."

"There's no shame in it."

"It's not that. It's just..." He shook his head. "This is PTSD, right? She's suffering from PTSD."

"I'm not a doctor, so I can't say if it is or isn't," Sam noted.

"I know, I know, but it sounds like it, doesn't it? You've had experience with people that had PTSD. This is similar, right?"

"That would be my guess," she said. "Just based on what you've said and the two incidents. And it's not unexpected. Being chained up in that cellar for several weeks, mind constantly filled with that crazy Santa shit they were spewing, and then that night, being raped over and over again by Justin while he was in that Santa suit after being given several eggnog enemas and wrapped up like a gift. Shit, I'd freak out too if I saw Santa imagery without warning."

"Yeah," he muttered.

"She does know that was just Justin, right?" Sam asked. "All that stuff she said initially about it being some sort of fucked-up Santa demon...that's all in the past, right?"

Ian nodded.

"You're sure?" she pressed.

"Totally. She would not be at home if I wasn't."

Sam nodded.

Several seconds came and went.

"You know, I actually thought about skipping Christmas this year," Ian said.

"Skipping Christmas? Like just not celebrating it at all?"

"Yeah, but then I realized that would not be fair to Tabby. Plus, I'd still have the problem of trying to shield Gwen from all the Christmas displays and whatnot, which wouldn't be possible unless she stayed locked inside the house for two months."

"That just doesn't seem practical at all."

"It was pretty dumb, but that's where my mind is at. I just don't know what to do. This is so far beyond my areas of understanding."

"Which is why she needs to see someone."

Ian sighed. "I know, but...I can't force her to do that."

A few more seconds came and went.

"You know," Sam said. "I almost wonder if going the opposite direction is what is needed here."

"What do you mean?"

"Instead of shielding her from seeing Christmas stuff, immerse her in it. Decorations, music, beverages, cookies, gingerbread houses...just go all out on creating a Christmas environment so that she sees it constantly and thus isn't triggered without warning by seeing it when out and about."

Ian sipped his coffee while considering that and then said, "Sort of a face your fears type of thing."

"Exactly. Though, like I said, I'm not an expert in psychological trauma and still think it would be best to have her see someone. But since she won't do that again, being confronted by things while in a safe environment might be the way to go."

TWO

1

"I don't know," Hal said.

"Oh come on, it'll be fun," Dee replied.

"What if someone sees us?"

"No one is going to see us."

"How do you know?"

"Because Ian and Gwen own the place, along with all the land as far as the eye can see, and they're over in Cape Cod or Long Island or somewhere to be with her rich-ass family for Thanksgiving."

"I thought you said they were from around here?"

"Ian is, but not the nutcase. She grew up in, like, a mansion with servants and stuff and can trace her family back to when Columbus landed and celebrated the first Thanksgiving."

Hal chuckled.

"What?"

"Columbus wasn't a Pilgrim and wasn't at the first Thanksgiving."

"Whatever, Mr. History Major," she said, waving a hand.

"The point is, they are gone for a week and no one is out here, so we can totally go inside and see where they kept her prisoner while waiting for Santa to come take her to the North Pole to be his sex slave and make baby elves."

"Jesus Christ."

She grinned.

"Is that really what they believed?" he asked.

"Something like that. And they would apparently leave some poor woman out for him every Christmas Eve. It was like a family tradition or something dating back several generations."

"See, that I don't buy."

"Why?"

"Because if a woman disappeared every year at Christmas never to be seen again, this town would be infamous. All over the world. People would know about this place."

"Duh, they didn't take women from town every year. Gwen was the first time they did that. Everyone else they got from other places way out beyond the state line. It was like a Thanksgiving tradition for them. Some families go out and chop down a Christmas tree after dinner. This one would hit the road in an old VW van and find a woman to bring home."

"Okay, maybe I can see that happening, but what about this: if they really did this every year, then where are all the bodies?"

"Obviously buried somewhere up at the North Pole," she said. "Come on, do you want to see this place or not?"

"No, I don't. I haven't from the moment we left class."

Dee rolled her eyes and led him to the back door.

2

"How do you know the code?" Hal asked as Dee opened the

small box that was attached to the back door, the key to the house within.

"It's the same one they use for the bookstore and their garage door," Dee said. "Probably the same one they use for their ATM too if I could ever get my hands on one of their cards."

"Good way to end up in jail, other than this breaking and entering we're about to do," he said.

"First, this isn't breaking and entering," Dee said while slipping the key into the lock. "They asked me to keep an eye on their house while away, and since they own this house too..." She let her voice fade as the door opened.

"And second?" he asked, eyes darting back and forth.

"I would never actually take any money from their accounts, but if I did, they are so obnoxiously rich that they would probably never even notice the odd withdrawal from time to time."

"See, that's just the thing. Rich people are rich because they do notice things like that. Every penny has to be accounted for. I was watching this show on HBO about Warren Buffett and it said he—"

"Shit!"

"What?"

"It's Sam."

"Sam?"

"A.k.a. the chief of police."

"Ah fuck, I knew this was a bad idea," Hal whined.

3

"Dee, you know better than this," Sam said.

"I know, I'm sorry," Dee said. "I just thought Hal would

like to see the place before heading back home for Thanksgiving. You know, a story to tell his friends."

Sam shook her head.

"Are you going to tell them?" Dee asked, concern present.

"Are you going to try and take a look inside again after I leave?"

"No way, not a chance."

"Okay then, this will just be between you, me, and..." She glanced over at the young man who was standing by an old Saturn. "Hal, was it?"

"Yes," Dee said.

"Between you, me, and Hal."

"Thank you."

With that, Dee headed over to Hal, who opened the passenger door for her before getting into the driver's side himself, the car eventually disappearing behind the overgrown brush that lined the roadways out here.

Sam shook her head, her mind still unable to figure out Dee.

No one in town really could, which was probably why so many ridiculous stories about her filled the void.

Sam thought about some of those stories for a moment and then pushed them aside, the cold air and the unease of being all alone at the Robinson house shifting her focus to the house itself, which she gave a quick walk around.

Nothing seemed amiss.

Then again, nothing had seemed amiss the year before when search parties had been combing these very fields looking for Gwen, the Robinson siblings frequently joining in to help, Jessica's homemade hot chocolate and apple cider always a big hit.

Memories of those cold winter days filled her mind, as did all the comments she used to hear from the various townspeople and her officers on how Gwen had probably walked out on her husband, her inability to fit in with *"us peasant folk"* leading to her running back home to hide among her fellow one-percenters on the Gold Coast of Long Island.

Admittedly, Sam had started to wonder the same thing after the first two weeks, the lack of any evidence pointing toward an accident or foul play making it harder and harder to give credence to Ian's insistence that something sinister had unfolded.

"She wouldn't abandon us," he had often said when venting to her about the comments from the locals, her own thoughts on the matter always held at bay. *"She wouldn't do that to Tabby."*

The rumors about his affair with Dee, which had actually started spreading around town long before Gwen had vanished, hadn't helped things.

A few even speculated that the two had killed Gwen because of her discovery of the affair.

And then came that call on Christmas morning of a crazed woman wearing nothing but a Santa coat pounding on the window of the Chapman place, eight-year-old Billy being the first to see her, his shrieks of terror likely the last thing his parents had expected to wake up to that snowy morning.

No one had even realized it was Gwen at first, the deputy that had responded—already bitter about being forced out on a call that morning—tasering her within moments of arriving upon the scene, handcuffing her, putting her in the back of his patrol vehicle, and dumping her into a cell at the station to stew for several hours until a decision could be made about what to do with her.

Sam herself hadn't learned about the situation until that afternoon when Molly Chapman called her directly, a question on if it was okay for them to head out to their Christmas dinner with the extended family being voiced.

And now here she was, almost one year later, still uncertain about what exactly had unfolded within the Robinson house that cold winter night. Justin was dead, Jessica was missing, and Gwen had given statements that initially seemed like the plot of a direct-to-YouTube horror movie, statements that had eventually landed her in a private mental ward for the rich and famous for several months before her mind was able to process things a bit better and give an account that was grounded in reality. A horrible, twisted reality, but reality nonetheless.

Sam couldn't even say if this was an isolated incident or if there had been previous women brought to and held captive in the Robinson house. Gwen said the Robinson siblings claimed they did this every year, but nothing within the house lent any support to this. Sure, there was a tucked-away area in the cellar where Gwen had been chained up, but nothing within that area provided any evidence of dozens upon dozens of women having been held captive.

And the fields surrounding the property had yielded nothing.

If Justin and Jessica were serial killers, then they had been very good at hiding things during the disposal process. Even the FBI had failed in trying to link them to any of the thousands upon thousands of missing persons reports that were out there.

4

"If this goes on my record, I'm in deep shit," Hal noted. "No law school is going to take a criminal."

"Nothing is going on your record," Dee said, the two back at her apartment over the bookstore.

"So she says, but once she is back at the police station who knows what she will decide to do?"

"Relax. She doesn't even know your last name."

"She has my plate info and with that she can learn everything there is to know about me."

"She didn't even look at your plate."

"Duh, they have cameras in their cars that record everything and she pulled up right behind the car. She totally has it and is probably looking up all sorts of info on me as we speak."

"I highly doubt the patrol cars here have cameras. And even if they did, what is she going to find if she does run a background check? That you once got a B on a history paper because you didn't properly cite a primary source."

Hal gave her a look that was trying to be a scowl but failed. Dee chuckled.

"This isn't funny," he said, failing to hide his own smile.

5

Sam stayed at the Robinson house longer than she had planned after shooing Dee and Hal away, her mind losing itself in a never-ending series of questions on what exactly had unfolded within the house that Christmas Eve night.

No answers arrived.

None ever did.

One thing she was fairly certain of was that Gwen's accounts of things could not be trusted. Not even the ones that she had given after recanting her earliest tales of a Santa demon coming down the chimney in favor of the one where she had killed Justin while he was raping her and fled from the house after smashing a window.

It wasn't that Sam didn't believe this account of the events.

The evidence found at the scene actually pointed toward this very conclusion.

It was that Sam didn't think Gwen believed it, and she

only gave these statements so that she could move on with her life.

6

Dee started to worry that Hal would be staying the night, but then he began to get fidgety after some joyless sex and voicing statements about how he had to leave early the next morning to start the long drive home to his parents' house.

"And I'd hate for you to have to wake up early on your day off and see me to the door," he added after stating his intentions to head out.

"Ah, true that," Dee said, trying to mask her relief.

Nothing else followed, Dee simply walking him to the door, an oversized FBI Academy sweatshirt she had gotten from Amazon thrown on to cover herself against the chill that always found its way into the apartment after dark.

"I'll text you when I get there," Hal said.

"Sounds good," she replied.

A few seconds later he was gone.

Dee stood by the closed door after that, arms wrapped around herself, thoughts on Hal and how she really didn't enjoy their time together at all dominating her mind.

Nothing was there.

No excitement.

No thrill.

Getting together with him felt like a chore, an assigned task, something to endure for a few hours.

This wasn't to say that she didn't have moments of enjoyment with him—they just weren't enough to make her long for his companionship once he was gone.

The fact that he was clearly put off by her fascination with serial killers didn't help things either. That had been a bit of a miscalculation on her part though. She had thought she detected a shared interest from him when they had been working together on a project for their criminal justice class, but really his interest had simply been in getting a good grade on the project, not the killers themselves. By the time she realized this, they were dating.

He didn't even like Netflix's *Mindhunter*, a comment from him on how the show was "too much chatter, not enough splatter" during their second date having been the first sign that she had made a big mistake.

"Some profiler I turned out to be," she muttered to herself and started walking back to her bedroom but then changed her route and headed into the family room instead, a used paperback that she had snatched from the true crime section downstairs waiting on the end table next to her reading chair.

7

Ten minutes later, Dee was staring off into space while the paperback sat open in her lap, the descriptions of an abandoned fallout shelter that a young serial killer had strung up his victims in having shifted her focus back to the Robinson house.

She really wanted to see inside the cellar room where they had kept Gwen while awaiting the arrival of Christmas.

Had wanted to for quite some time now, yet only today she realized the possibility of doing so after it dawned on her that if Ian used the same code for his house and bookstore, then he likely used it for the key box at the Robinsons' house as well.

And she had been right.

She had literally stood in the doorway of the house, ready to cross the threshold, only for Sam to come and cock-block her.

All because they had parked in the driveway.

That had been a big mistake, one she would not make with her own car.

Tonight?
Right now?
No.
Tomorrow.
During Thanksgiving.

No one would be doing any patrols by the house, and even if someone did, Dee's car wouldn't be anywhere near it. Instead, it would be parked in Ian's driveway, her task of feeding their pet rabbits acting as cover while she walked to the Robinsons' house, the distance between the two places just shy of a mile if she cut through the empty fields.

THREE

I

"I still can't believe they haven't found the sister yet," Hailey said. "What was her name? Juliet? Jenny? Jennifer...?"

"Jessica," Sam said.

"Jessica," Hailey voiced, almost as if tasting the name to see if it was to her liking. "And really nothing at all? After nearly a year?"

"Nothing," Sam confirmed.

"That's crazy. People don't just vanish like that."

"What are you talking about?" Paula said. "People vanish all the time. I'm constantly trying to track down deadbeat ex-husbands that don't want to pay child support."

"Yeah, but that's a civil thing whereas this perp literally helped in the kidnapping and torture of a young woman, and maybe the murders of several others. People like that don't vanish unless they have considerable resources, or friends with considerable resources, which these two didn't have." She turned to Sam. "Right?"

"Not that we know about," Sam said. "No living relatives,

no real friends, just locals that they said *hey* to from time to time, and a bank account that was pretty much empty."

"See," Hailey said. "People like that don't vanish."

"Do they know if there were other women yet?" Paula asked, shifting things a bit.

"Actually, no," Sam said. "The feds tried to see if they could link them to any missing persons cases, but nothing came of it. And without any bodies ever being found..." She let that hang in the air.

A few seconds came and went, the three sipping beers and munching on the cheese and cracker plate that Paula had brought to supplement the Thanksgiving meal their mother was making, all offers of helping in the kitchen dismissed.

"Wait, wasn't there a blizzard that night?" Paula asked.

"Yep," Sam confirmed. "Nearly a foot of snow and then once the wind kicked up it was a complete whiteout."

"Well then, I bet she tried to escape on foot and died from exposure."

"And what, Sam and her officers just completely missed a set of tracks leading away from the house?" Hailey asked.

"No, the tracks were covered up by the blizzard. All that snow and wind, probably took ten minutes to erase things. Just like with those two bank robbers over in Hillside a few years back. The Bonnie and Clyde wannabes."

"Wait, what?"

"They waited for a blizzard, robbed the bank, killed everyone inside just to be dicks, and then used snowmobiles to get away."

"Yeah, I know, but how is that connected?"

"It's not, but their tracks were covered by the snow, which is probably what happened that night as the sister tried to get away. And then, once she succumbed to the elements, the snow covered her up too."

"They would have found her body once the snow melted."

"Not necessarily. It's pretty rugged out there. Animals probably scattered her remains before the thaw."

"Ugh."

"It happens."

2

Dee was always amazed at how normal Ian and Gwen's house seemed once inside, the stereotypical rich person persona one would expect given all the digits that appeared before the decimal point on their bank statements disappearing quickly given the cozy, cluttered feel of the rooms within the walls of the large hill-perched house.

Just the fact that Ian had asked Dee if she could stop by every day while they were away to feed their rabbits was another sign of normality—until one saw the living space the rabbits had, which was larger than the living space most humans enjoyed within the average home.

But that was okay.

Using their wealth to turn the east wing of the house into the Shire from the Tolkien novels for the floppy-eared Bilbo and Frodo complete with little custom-built hobbit homes for each was better than what most rich people did with their money. The fact that it wasn't the only fantasy-themed area within the house spoke to how much fun and how dorkish he was. He didn't act like a rich person at all. Far from it, really. Gwen, on the other hand...

Just her outfits alone likely cost more than the average household income, and the little European sports car she drove was so high-end that they literally had to bring it all the way up to the Chicago suburbs to the dealer it had been purchased from to have the standard maintenance done since the mechanics at the regular places most people went to when having their oil changed wouldn't work on such vehicles. Not because they didn't know how, but because the insurance the places carried wouldn't allow it, not at the costs that would be incurred if any damage were done to the vehicle while in their custody.

Ian, on the other hand, drove a pickup truck.

And wore jeans and hoodies.

How the two had ever matched up was a mystery. Well, not exactly, given that they had met in college, but how they made it work given their differences was.

Not that Dee cared since it was none of her business.

Plus their being together and having moved back to his hometown allowed for Dee to have an apartment that she would never have been able to afford if they had decided to charge her the typical rent a place like it would normally go for, and work a job that paid her way more than what was standard for typical retail employment.

And she wasn't the only one that got off easy when it came to paying rents that were far lower than the norm, the two having helped out quite a few of the locals who were struggling with payments during the economic downturns that had plagued the country these last several years by buying up the properties and charging token rents on them.

Of course, not everyone in the community felt that such actions were good-natured, instead viewing them as a money-hungry rich-person scheme to feudalize the town. A few also liked to conjure up rumors, especially about Dee and Ian, ones that were so far from reality that they were almost amusing.

And some that were not.

Like the one about the two having murdered Gwen to keep her from leaving Ian after discovering their sexual escapades during the late-night shifts at the bookstore, the rumors going so far as to lead to her being questioned about why she had bought a shovel from the local hardware store a month before Gwen's disappearance given that she lived in an apartment that didn't have a yard.

That the shovel had been for the October window display of the bookstore called *Dig up a Spooky Read* featuring a shovel, a tombstone, and a coffin overflowing with old horror paperbacks hadn't quelled the suspicions. Her fascination with serial killers didn't help things either, many of the locals finding her interest to be disturbing and unsuitable for a young lady.

In fact, Dee truly believed that if it wasn't for Gwen having escaped her captors, revealing the true nature of the Robinson siblings, she might very well have become the lead suspect in the disappearance, her daily routine eventually involving the obligatory Q&A sessions inside the small interrogation room at the local police station as Sam tried to break her into confessing the crime of passion everyone felt she and Ian had perpetrated.

3

Rabbits fed, Dee headed out the back door and started through the woods and across the fields, the cross-country trek fairly simple given the lack of snow the area had had so far this season. It was also on the warmer side. Not sunbathing weather by any stretch of the imagination, but nowhere near the cold temperatures one would expect of this area during the Thanksgiving holiday. It was pleasant. A far cry from what Gwen had faced on the night of her escape.

And Jessica?

Could she really have fled on foot through the snow?

Though Dee had met the Robinson siblings a few times while growing up, she didn't really know Jessica well enough to make any kind of informed speculation on her ability to flee the scene during a blizzard. One thing she did know: Jessica had been at the bookstore a few days before Gwen had gone missing, stating how she had several boxes of old paperbacks sitting in a back room of the house that they thought the store might like and that Dee should swing by one day to take a look.

The "swing by" had never happened, Dee's car going on the fritz that week, breaking down on her after class one day right in the middle of an intersection and being towed over to Joey's Garage where it sat for over two weeks waiting on parts.

By the time she got it back, Gwen had disappeared and the idea of heading out to take a look at the boxes of books was completely forgotten until one day in January when Dee had remembered the moment and asked Sam if any boxes of books had been stacked up in the Robinson house.

The answer was no.

Dee still got chills thinking about it.

Had she been the original target of the two siblings?

Had they been planning on grabbing her during that visit to look at the books that didn't exist so that they could lock her up in the cellar and then string her up by the fireplace come Christmas Eve?

That answer was yes.

Of this, Dee had no doubt whatsoever.

She had been the intended target, the intended gift for Santa, her body destined to end up buried somewhere beneath the surface of the field.

4

Dee felt a bit like Clarice Starling as she stepped across the threshold of the Robinson house, the old structure having that decrepit feel that Buffalo Bill's house had conveyed in those chilling scenes from *The Silence of the Lambs*. Only no exotic moths were flying around within this house, and Dee would not be saving the day as she shot dead a killer while rescuing the latest victim. Such moments wouldn't even happen once she finally did become a profiler for the FBI, such Hollywood scenarios a far cry from the reality of what those in that profession actually did.

Still, she loved that movie and enjoyed imagining herself as one of the greatest female leads of all time. In fact, she credited the movie itself, and then the book, with her interest in serial killers and her dreams of one day becoming an FBI profiler.

5

The cellar was a disappointment, her mind having envisioned an elaborate dungeon-like area where Gwen and all the prior victims had been chained up and tortured for weeks as the siblings waited for Christmas Eve to arrive. Instead, all she got was a single chain bolted into the stone foundation of a small alcove, one that provided just enough length to reach a discolored toilet that had been installed, a half-used roll of toilet paper still sitting atop the tank.

A holding area, nothing more.

A place to keep the victim until Christmas Eve.

And then what?

The profile she had created in her mind suggested that Justin was a sexual sadist who had an odd Santa fetish embedded into his fantasies. As for Jessica, Dee saw her as a willing accomplice, one that had been conditioned into accepting and helping out with her brother's fantasy much the way Janice Hooker had been conditioned into becoming a willing participant in helping her husband Cameron kidnap and enslave Colleen Stan back in the late seventies.

Only Gwen and the previous victims (if there were any) weren't turned into long-term sex slaves like Colleen Stan but used in some twisted sacrifice-like sexual activity on Christmas Eve.

Nothing in the cellar contradicted Dee's amateur profile, but she still had expected (hoped for) a more elaborate setup. Something with a North Pole theme to it, like Santa's Village meets the Hellfire Club. Instead, she simply got a chain next to a toilet.

But maybe this was how it always was when finally uncovering a serial killer's lair, Hollywood always instilling some over-the-top setup that the perps brought their victims to when in reality they were usually more like this—decrepit cellars (or attics, or back rooms, or storage sheds, or trailers) that stank of mildew and human waste. Places that not only failed to live up to the Hollywood image but also the fantasy that the killer was trying to create, hence the reason they had to kill over and over again as they tried to obtain that ultimate—and unreachable—fantasy goal.

6

Gwen could hear the discussion her mother and Ian were having one room over, and while it wasn't exactly heated, the temperature was clearly growing given that she no longer had to press her ear to the wall to hear the voices.

7

"She's not doing that again," Ian said, voice firm. "Ever!"

"She was getting better," Marybeth replied. "And Dr.

Wilbanks says that if you hadn't convinced her to stop the treatments—"

"Shock therapy!" Ian snapped. "He was doing shock therapy on her."

"It works."

"Not the way that quack was doing it."

"Dr. Wilbanks is not a quack!"

"He prescribed you horse piss during the pandemic!"

"And I never got Covid, now did I?"

"That doesn't mean anything."

Marybeth shook her head. "It worked when she was a teen and would have worked again if you hadn't stopped her treatments."

"It didn't work when she was a teen! All it did was burn away her ability to enjoy—" His voice halted as Gwen stepped into the room, her arms crossed.

8

"I wish you wouldn't argue with her," Gwen said.

"She was insisting that you start seeing Dr. Wilbanks again," Ian replied.

"She can insist all she wants," Gwen said. "It's not her decision. Or yours."

"I know."

"Then why engage?"

He hesitated for a few seconds and then said, "I'm still angry."

"About what?"

"That they were doing that to you. After all you went through. And after what happened when you were a teenager."

"It was my decision to try it this time around."

"But they talked you into it. During a vulnerable moment. And..."

"And...?"

He shook his head. "Nothing."

9

Dee spent quite a bit of time in the Robinsons' house, her mind attempting to make the most out of her entry into the forbidden location. Unfortunately, nothing within could really quell the disappointment she was feeling with what she had finally seen—that was, until she realized this was similar to what serial killers probably felt once they actually did engage in their fantasy.

What was that like for the Robinson siblings?
Once they finally had her strung up by the fireplace?
Once they had dressed Justin up like Santa?

Had it even reached a point where disappointment rushed in to fill the void left by the lackluster realization of the fantasy, or had Gwen's unexpected kick put an end to things before that?

Dee looked up at the beam Gwen had been hanging from that night and then over toward the stone ledge of the fireplace that had cracked open Justin's skull as he was knocked from the small footrest he had pulled over to stand on while fucking Gwen.

One kick.

After a month of being chained to a wall down in the cellar.

One kick, followed by her toes reaching for the footrest so that she could stand upon it to take the pressure off her wrists and start working at the knots with her fingers.

. . .

10

"You know he's having an affair with that girl he hired for the bookstore," her mother said that evening once it was just the two of them in one of the back rooms. "Before your incident, while you were missing, and afterward while you were here being treated by Dr. Wilbanks."

Gwen didn't reply to that, the drink her mother had poured her going untouched as she held the crystal glass in her hand.

"My investigator documented several occurrences when the two would spend a lot of time together in the bookstore after closing, and we have dozens of photos of them embracing each other in ways that are far too intimate for an owner-employee relationship."

"I've heard the rumors," Gwen muttered.

"These are not just rumors, Gwendolyn." Her mother pulled out a file folder. "It's all in here."

Gwen stared at the file folder, one that she had been shown countless times, everything within nothing but circumstantial evidence at best.

"Have you ever wondered why he simply gave her an apartment right above the bookstore?"

"He did not just give it to her," Gwen said. "She pays rent on it just like everyone who lives in one of our properties does."

"Five hundred a month, all utilities included. You should be getting at least three times that."

"It's not Manhattan, Mother," Gwen noted.

"Even so, it is way below market value even for *that* area. As are all the rents on all the properties you bought and are leasing out."

"So what? We have more money than we could ever spend in our lifetime. In two, maybe even three lifetimes. And that community was hit very hard by the recession and then again when the economy collapsed during the pandemic."

A heavy sigh. "*You* have more money than could be spent in three lifetimes, not he."

Gwen sipped her drink.

"Why does he spend so much time in that house?" her mother asked after several seconds.

"What?"

"The one you were held prisoner in?"

"Spend time in it?"

"Almost every day. He goes there and spends about an hour inside. Why?"

"You still have your investigator watching him?"

"I do."

"Why?"

"People keep finding more and more inconsistencies."

"What people?"

"Online. In the investigative groups."

"Mom, no, you've got to stop with those groups."

"Not until we uncover the truth of what happened."

"The truth?" Gwen demanded. "The Robinson siblings were crazy, they abducted me for a twisted Christmas thing, and I got away. End of story."

"So it would seem."

"So it would seem?" Gwen repeated. "What does that mean?"

"Have you considered the possibility that your husband may have staged the entire thing hoping to rid himself of you?"

"That is ridiculous."

"And that is why the sister has never been found. He is now paying her to stay silent. With the crypto accounts he used to use with the whores."

"No," Gwen said. Then, more forcefully, "No!"

"And why have no other bodies been found? Because they were not the killers they have been made out to be. Your husband simply made them an offer to do all this and has now been encouraging the fiction of how these two have somehow been abducting and killing women like you every Christmas for years—something which even the FBI could not confirm."

That's because they were not the ones doing the killing, Gwen thought to herself. *There were no bodies for them to get rid of once Christmas morning arrived.*

"Gwendolyn?" a voice said, concern present.

Gwen blinked at that. "What?"

"Your husband. He just wants your money so that he and that girl and all those whores he used to sleep with can live a disgusting life of sexual debauchery."

"No, that's not..." She stopped herself from finishing what she had been about to say, memories of the various hotel suites and the escorts playing across her mind.

Her mother waited.

"It's late and I'm tired." She stood up. "Please stay out of those stupid investigative groups, and stop having your investigator follow Ian around."

Her mother said something in reply to that, but Gwen didn't catch what it was, her mind too focused on those moments while in the Robinson house, wrists tied to the beam above, the voice of Nat King Cole echoing through the living room as the sound system played "The Christmas Song" over and over again.

FOUR

1

"It's so fluffy," Sam said, running a hand through the fake snow that had been used in various areas of the bookstore to create small yet somewhat elaborate Christmas scenes. "What's it made from?"

"Asbestos," Dee said.

Sam twisted toward her with wide eyes.

Dee was grinning.

"Jesus Christ, you had me for a second there," Sam said. "You know they actually used to use that for stuff like this?"

"Oh, I know. People would pour it all over their Christmas trees. We actually have some old magazines somewhere in here with ads for it. Also ones where doctors are letting women know which cigarettes will help them keep the weight off while pregnant."

"No, for real?"

"Yep."

Sam shook her head.

"I also ordered several different elf outfits to start wearing while working, though they won't be arriving until like mid-December," Dee said.

"All this and elf outfits," Sam said. "How did you do all this?"

"It was easy. I called the company that does all the mall decorations. They came out and did it in a day."

"Wow."

"Ian said to go all out, so I did."

"Yeah, I'll say."

"I just hope it isn't too much."

"How much was it?"

"No, not that," Dee said, waving a hand. "I mean too much as in it causes Gwen to freak out."

"Oh, well, I think that is the point," Sam noted. "Not like in a mean way over and over again, but sort of like an immunization. Expose her to all this in a safe environment so that when she is exposed out in public it doesn't cause a serious problem."

"I know, but...I don't know."

"Yeah, I don't really think it's a great idea either, but..." She shrugged. "What can you do?"

Dee replied with her own shrug.

"Speaking of odd things, the reason I stopped by is I wanted to ask, have you noticed anyone hanging around like they were watching you, maybe following you and whatnot, keeping tabs?"

"Following me?"

"Yeah."

"No, but like what the fuck?"

"Ian called me last night," Sam said. "Advised that Gwen's mother apparently has her investigator snooping around again trying to dig up dirt on you and Ian."

"Oh for fucks sake, will this shit ever end?"

Sam didn't reply.

"I mean, Jesus Christ, it was bad enough everyone in town

thought we were fucking each other and that I had helped bury her. Now I'm being spied on too."

Sam raised an eyebrow. "So..."

"No, I haven't noticed anyone, but I haven't really been paying attention either. Now I know to keep an eye out."

"Okay."

"Though what am I supposed to do if I notice someone following me? Or think they are?"

"Just give me a ring if you do."

"And then what are you supposed to do?"

"Good question," Sam said. "Tell them to get lost, I guess."

"Something tells me that with Gwen's family backing them, it might not be all that easy to send them packing."

"We'll see."

2

The bookstore didn't get many customers that day (or really any day), but those that did enter now carried with them the possibility of being someone that was simply there to spy on her, which added a level of annoyance and surrealism to every encounter.

That was until Dee wondered why anyone would be keeping tabs on her while Ian and Gwen were away. After all, how could they be fucking each other when they were separated by nearly a thousand miles?

Or was there something more to the investigator being here?

Something beyond the possibility of them sleeping together?

Dee pondered this during the slow evening hours but then realized no legit answers would be arriving and pushed away the speculations, deciding to simply ask Ian about all of it upon his return later that week. After that, she made herself a heavily sugared vanilla latte and wandered over to one of the rooms in the back where a shelf of true crime was located, the browsing of the familiar titles somehow giving her solace even though the events described within their pages were horrifying.

Will anyone ever write about the Robinson family?

Is there enough there for a book?

No.

Right now there only seemed to be enough for a brief entry within a book that was made up of several different true crime events, but maybe in time if more was uncovered about the family, their actions, and if bodies were actually found, it might grow into being enough for its own volume.

Is there actually more?

Was it really a yearly thing?

Something passed down through the family, generation after generation?

Once again, she could not answer this, nor could she find any answers to it while simply sitting on a chair in a back corner of the bookstore.

3

Sam saw the private investigator everywhere as she patrolled through the town. It didn't matter if she was in her vehicle, on foot, or having lunch in one of the local diners, everyone she saw that was not a known member of the community became the investigator in her eyes.

And there were quite a few potentials, thanks to the community college over in Hillsborough. Lots of students, lots of teachers, lots of people coming and going throughout the year.

Day after day, it was always on her mind. Not dominating it since there were many things that superseded her promise of being on the lookout for anyone that was snooping around, but always lurking near the surface, ready to knock everything else out of the way when she saw someone that could be the investigator.

Thinking about such things also frequently brought to mind the relationship between Dee and Ian. Both always denied that anything had happened between them, but Sam couldn't be one hundred percent certain of this.

And if she couldn't be certain of this given how much she interacted with them, she could certainly understand Gwen's family having questions and concerns.

Gwen too, for that matter.

4

Gwen had looked in the folder. Not on the first night it was in her possession, nor the second, but on the third—after a bit of a tiff with Ian about how he had once again started provoking her mother by talking about the history of Christmas and all the various pagan celebrations that had been hijacked by the church when creating the nativity myth.

Nothing within the folder actually confirmed that Dee and Ian had been or were having an affair, but they could certainly be used to point one toward such a theory when presented in the right way.

More intriguing to Gwen were all the photos of Ian going into the Robinson house and sitting by the fireplace, the most recent one having been captured a few days before they headed out for the Thanksgiving holiday.

Why was he going there?

What possible purpose could it serve?

Once or twice she could understand, but almost every day for months?

That went beyond simple curiosity.

It also explained why he was spending so much time away from the bookstore. She had never questioned him about what he did during those chunks of time because it didn't really seem all that important, but once she saw the photos, it was all she could think about, which was why she eventually asked him about it while showing him some of the photos from the folder.

5

A winter wonderland was awaiting Ian, Gwen, and Tabby when they arrived home, both a real one, thanks to a fairly significant snowstorm that hit the day before, and the artificial one that Dee had set up within the bookstore.

"Does Gwen know about all this?" Dee asked that evening.

"She knows that decorations were put up," Ian advised, "but not how extensive it all is. Honestly, I had no idea it would be this elaborate."

"It's not too much, is it?" Dee asked, concern coloring her cheeks.

"No, not at all," Ian said, smiling. "I like it. Very cozy."

Dee returned the smile and then said, "Okay, good. I also have the sound system set up with several different Christmas albums. Didn't really know what your thoughts were on types and style, so it's kind of a smorgasbord of stuff downloaded from Amazon."

"I would think a nice variety is ideal, especially so that we don't go crazy from the same style of song over and over again."

"Last Christmas..." Dee began to sing.

"Oh god," Ian cried, hands quickly covering his ears.

"On a more serious note," Dee said. "What the fuck is up with this investigator shit?"

"Ugh, don't get me started on that," Ian said. "It was everything I could do not to lose my shit with her mother after I found out."

"What about Gwen?"

"What about her?"

"What does she think about her mother doing this? And all the rumors about us?"

"First, Gwen knows the rumors are bullshit."

"Okay, good."

"As far as the investigator, she clearly is upset about it and wants it all to stop, but getting her mother to back off is pretty much impossible, especially with her spending so much time in those stupid web sleuth groups."

"Speaking of, have you looked in any of those groups lately?" Dee asked.

"No," he said. "You?"

"I poked around in a few after learning about the investigator."

"Do I even want to know?"

"Most of the groups are simply focused on trying to figure out if there were previous victims and drawing up connections between unsolved disappearances and the Robinson family, which is good because I don't think anyone in law enforcement is really trying to work this thing anymore."

"Okay..."

"But then there are some of the fringe groups where everyone is absolutely convinced you and I staged the entire Santa sacrifice thing, which went afoul, and now you are hiding Jessica somewhere."

"Jesus Christ!"

"Yeah."

"Where do they even get this shit?" he asked.

Dee shrugged.

. . .

6

Gwen did not freak out when seeing the various Christmas scenes on display throughout the store, a simple statement on how it looked nice being the only reaction she produced before heading into the small office behind the counter area to take a look at any financial items that had arrived while away.

Dee looked at Ian, who simply shrugged.

"Whelp, I better get to class," Dee said.

"Back around three today?" Ian asked.

"Yep."

"Okay, sounds good."

7

"I want to go look inside the house," Gwen said.

"The house?" Ian asked, momentarily confused before understanding arrived. "Oh...why?"

"I think it will help me."

"How?"

"I don't know, but maybe seeing it empty and knowing that everything that happened last year is in the past will help keep me on solid footing."

Ian contemplated this.

"I'm not asking if it's okay," Gwen added. "I'm simply letting you know that I want to go look inside the house and will probably be doing it later today."

Ian was a bit startled by the forcefulness of her words but didn't comment on it. Instead, he simply asked, "Do you want me to come with?"

"No," she said.

"Okay."

Nothing else was said, the day passing slowly until it was time to go pick up Tabby from school, Ian taking the lead on that while Gwen waited for Dee to get back from class.

8

Gwen stood outside the Robinson house, toes chilled from the long walk up the driveway, her shoes never intended to be used when mushing through six inches of unplowed snow.

Nothing happened.

She simply stood there in the snow, sun setting out beyond the fields, memories of what had unfolded a year earlier present yet not paralyzing her.

It was weird.

Seeing Santa in the mall a few weeks earlier had caused a fit, as had seeing that book with a creepy Santa theme, but now, standing outside the house where she had experienced everything...nothing.

9

"Daddy, why did you take that out of the trash?" Tabby asked.

"Because I need to check the directions again," Ian said, eyes quickly noting how much milk to add.

"Mommy never pulls the box out of the trash when she is making it," Tabby noted.

"Well, that's because Mommy is a better cook than me."

"Except with cheeseburgers!"

"Except with cheeseburgers," Ian agreed.

"Mommy!"

"Honey, you don't need to—" Ian's voice halted, the sight of Gwen standing in the kitchen catching him off guard given how quiet she had been.

"Daddy keeps taking the box out of the trash," Tabby said.

"Does he now?" Gwen said.

"I told him you never have to do that and he says it's because you are a better cook than he is."

"Well, everyone knows that," Gwen said, smiling at Ian.

"Except with cheeseburgers," Tabby continued.

"What? You love my cheeseburgers," Gwen said.

Tabby shook her head.

"Really?" Gwen questioned, crossing her arms.

"They're like eating hockey pucks."

Gwen lifted an eyebrow and then looked at Ian, who raised his hands in an *I have no idea where she heard that* gesture, which earned a *bullshit* nod in reply.

"I tried calling you earlier," Ian said while giving the pot a stir.

"I turned off my phone."

"Oh."

"You went to the house?"

"I did."

Ian waited for more, but nothing came.

"Do we have any caviar?" Tabby asked.

Gwen gave a puzzled look to Ian and then said, "No, why?"

"I have a taste for it."

"You have a taste for caviar?" Ian asked.

"Uh-huh."

"When did you have caviar?"

"At Grandma's house."

Gwen chuckled and then motioned that she was going upstairs.

Ian nodded and then, to Tabby, asked, "And you liked it?"

"I did."

"And do you know what caviar is?"

"You put it on crackers."

"Yes, but—" The pot suddenly boiled over, milk going everywhere.

10

"You okay?" Ian asked, setting the dinner dishes next to the sink.

"I'm fine," Gwen said, examining the pot he had killed the Pasta Roni in.

"You sure? You seemed very quiet during dinner."

"Did I?"

"Yeah."

"Huh." Then, holding up the pot: "I don't think we can salvage this."

"That bad?" he asked.

She twisted it toward him, the entire bottom nothing but a charred layer of burnt crud.

"Okay, yeah, let's just toss it," he said.

She set it aside and grabbed the first of the plates, scrubbing it for a bit beneath the hot water before handing it to him.

"So—" he started while drying the plate.

"Stop!"

"What?"

"Trying to get me to talk about the house."

"That's not what I was going to ask about," he said, lying.

"Nothing happened."

"Nothing at all?"

"No. Unless you count the fact that I ruined my shoes while walking through the snow to get to the door."

"The snow? Oh, jeez, I totally forgot about that. After I plowed ours...shit, which shoes?"

"The ones from Italy."

"Really? Oh no." He had no idea which ones those were.

"It's my fault really. Once I saw all that snow I should have gone and gotten some boots, but...whatever." She handed him the final plate.

He dried it.

She then looked at the mess on the stove, the milk having left some sort of residue upon the burner. "You get to deal with all that," she said.

"I think we should just toss it as well."

"The entire stove?"

"Yeah," he said. "It and the pot were clearly defective."

She shook her head.

He grinned.

11

Gwen stared at the stocking dangling by the unlit fireplace in the family room, Tabby's name stitched across the front of it.

A box of decorations sat on the floor nearby, one of many whose contents would eventually be displayed all over the house.

"Tabby begged me to put it up," Ian noted as he came into the room. "Claimed that if it isn't up by the first of December then it somehow counts against her or something when Santa is considering her naughty-to-nice ratio."

"Where in the world did she get that idea?"

"Who knows?"

Nothing followed.

"Want me to light a fire?" he asked.

"Yes, that'll be nice."

He did, the aged pieces of pine that he stacked on the rack within soon crackling with flames.

Gwen felt the heat warming her legs and glanced up at the ceiling.

Ian clearly caught this but didn't say anything.

"It looks a bit lonely up there," Gwen said as she shifted her focus back upon the fireplace mantel. "We should add ours."

They did, the three stockings now dangling just beyond the flames.

"Tomorrow I'll pull the rest of the boxes out and then on Saturday we can go get a tree," Ian said.

"That'll be fun."

"Now let's just hope that not having the tree up by the first isn't going to cause any issues."

12

Gwen opened her eyes upon the dark bedroom, sweat oozing from her pores.

In the dream she had been running through snow.

Deep snow.

And the actions had apparently carried over into the actual world given that her legs were tangled up in the sheets.

She took a deep breath.

And then a second.

And then a third.

Moving carefully so as not to wake Ian over on the cot, she untangled herself from the bedsheets and then slipped free from the bed. Less than a minute later, she was downstairs in the family room, staring at the fireplace, the flames from earlier and any warmth they had produced long since gone.

FIVE

1

Val Finley stared at the empty spot within the crook of the large pine tree, a frown quickly dominating his face.

His camera was gone.

Not just fallen, or covered up by snow, but literally gone.

Someone had taken it.

Who?

The husband?

The serial-killer-obsessed employee his mother-in-law thought he was having an affair with?

The local chief of police?

The kids who visited from time to time daring each other to go inside?

Or someone else?

Someone who had yet to appear in any of the photos the various cameras had taken during the last several months?

Someone who knew about the camera and did not want to be seen in conjunction with the abandoned house?

He studied the tracks in the snow while thinking about

this but couldn't ascertain much information from them given that they had been warped from the sunlight that had softened all the edges before everything refroze during the bitter nighttime temperature.

2

Two other cameras that had been positioned at the house to capture photos of Ian and whatever heinous activities Marybeth seemed to think he was involved in were also missing, which meant this clearly wasn't some random person who happened to stumble upon one of the cameras and took it.

Nope.

One missing camera could be explained away as coincidental. Two even, since someone might have gotten curious and walked around all the trees and shrubs to see if there was a second one pointed at the house. But three? Nope. Three missing cameras meant someone had specifically gone inside to remove the third one.

3

"She seems to be doing fine," Ian said. "Though she won't talk about any of it now. Not after going inside the house."

"What was she like while inside?" Sam asked, taking the coffee he had made for her.

"I don't know," Ian said, sipping his own coffee.

"You didn't go into the house with her?"

"No, she went on her own." He added more sugar to his coffee. "I didn't even know until she came home that night."

"Hmm."

"What?"

"Oh, it's nothing."

"Tell me."

"Well, I was there yesterday checking things out, as you know I do from time to time. Keeping an eye on things, trying to glean insight into what might have happened that night in regards to Jessica vanishing." She waved a hand. "Anyway, I noticed tracks in the snow. Lots of them. More than would be made by one person just walking up to the back door."

Ian spent several seconds thinking about that, sipping his coffee. "Maybe the investigator that Marybeth still has lurking around?"

"Maybe."

"Or kids trying to get inside again."

"That's a lot of snow to be trekking through right now for it to be kids on a whim. During summer and fall, totally, but now I've found that most are pretty content with just staying inside playing games."

"All those new PlayStations that have finally arrived," Ian said.

"More like D&D," Sam said.

"D&D? Really?"

"Oh yeah, big time. Actually board games in general. The guy at the game store in the mall was saying demand has been huge."

"I wonder why."

"I think maybe the pandemic was a part of it. All those families stuck inside for months, needing to keep busy. They all started playing board games to pass the time. And now those kids are getting older and are setting up groups with their friends who are getting into really elaborate games."

"Okay, yeah, I can see that."

"And this is all on top of the huge D&D resurgence that began after *Stranger Things* first came out."

"Maybe I should rebrand things here so that the focus is on board games."

"Oh god, no. This place is great. Anytime I need a moment to get away from people so that I can think, I just come here because I know it will be empty."

"Gee. Thanks."

Sam gave him an evil grin.

"Speaking of getting to think things over," Ian said. "Any luck on figuring out who this private investigator actually is?"

"No, sorry."

"You'd think someone like that would stand out like a sore thumb in a small town like this, but I guess we do actually get quite a few strangers through here, what with the interstate to the east and the college to the west."

"That we do."

4

Val sat in a local diner that he visited every time he came to town, eating a meatloaf sandwich, thinking what his next steps would be, if any, the time spent working this thing having failed to yield any connections between Ian and the two siblings that had kidnapped and terrorized Gwendolyn for several weeks before her escape.

He and Zoey had looked everywhere, digging up everything he could find on Ian, following every lead Marybeth's team of online sleuths had uncovered no matter how ridiculous they seemed, and aside from some very poorly written *Lord of the Rings* fan fiction that Ian had uploaded onto various websites under a pen name, the guy seemed like nothing more than an exhausted husband who was doing everything he could to try to help his wife recover from her harrowing ordeal at the hands of the two crazy siblings.

Even the rumored affair between Ian and Dee now seemed like nothing more than small-town gossip, the photos Zoey had captured early on of the two embracing while Gwendolyn was missing simply her trying to comfort him during the trying ordeal.

And yet Marybeth was absolutely convinced that Ian was behind everything, and nothing Val could say seemed to sway her from this conclusion.

Thus the cameras.

First up at the cabin in Maine that Ian and Gwendolyn owned to see if Jessica Robinson was hiding out up there, his body having slithered through the brush for hours one night getting them positioned perfectly to snap photos of anyone who came and went through the front and back doors, and then some at the Robinson house itself after the cabin had yielded nothing but curious forest critters moving about within the range of the photo-snapping motion sensors.

Initially, he had simply had the front and back doors covered, just like at the cabin, but then he had planted a nanny camera inside after discovering that Ian spent quite a bit of time within the house—only to realize that the poor man did nothing but sit in a chair by the cold fireplace while there, possibly meditating upon the horrors that his wife had faced.

These photos still did not sway Marybeth. In fact, they somehow confirmed to her that Ian was behind everything, which meant she wanted Val to continue with his investigation rather than focus on what he was supposed to be doing for her firm—uncovering information on various companies that would have impacts upon their market values so that her company could continue making informed decisions on how best to line the pockets of their investors.

But now the missing cameras gave him pause.

Could he have missed something?

Had Ian taken them down so that something could unfold

within that house as the anniversary of Gwendolyn's ordeal grew near?

Or maybe not Ian.

Maybe someone who everyone had written off as having died out there in the wilderness, her body scattered by the elements.

5

"Dee says some of the more extreme web sleuths think I'm hiding Jessica somewhere," Ian said.

"They've thought that for a while now," Sam said.

"Really?"

"Oh yeah. It was right around May when they started sending tips in about that."

"Tips?"

"It's still an open investigation, so..."

Ian nodded just as the chime on the door echoed, three young adults filing into the bookstore.

Sam stood. "Speaking of open investigations, I should be heading back to the station."

Ian stood as well. "Want a refill before you go?"

Sam looked at her coffee for a moment and then shook her head. "I'm good." She started toward the door but then stopped and asked, "Oh, hey, do you have the file that your mother-in-law gave Gwen?"

"Yeah. Well, Gwen does, back at the house."

"Think she'll let me take a look at it?"

"I don't see why not. I'll shoot her a message and then let you know."

"Great."

With that, Sam left while Ian went over to the counter to where one of the young adults was eyeing the menu board.

. . .

6

"Staying overnight?" Zoey questioned. "Why?"

"Someone stole my cameras," Val said.

"Which ones?"

"All of them."

"All of them?"

"Yeah."

"Even the one inside?"

"Yeah."

"Wow." Then, after a few seconds: "They can't be traced back to you, can they?"

"No, it's all good."

"What about when you would reset them after downloading everything? Any chance they got photos of you as you walked away?"

"Well yeah, but my face was always covered."

"You sure?"

"Yeah, totally."

"Because if not, and if someone now has pictures of you inside that house, that's breaking and entering, which is a felony, and you know what that means. Goodbye, license."

"Zoey, it's all good."

A few seconds of silence came and went.

"I still don't understand why you're staying overnight."

"With someone taking the cameras and with Marybeth stressing that things are getting weird, I figure it might not be a bad idea to just take another look at things while I'm here."

"Oh come on, we hit that thing from every angle. Nothing is going on. Ian wasn't behind anything and isn't hiding Jessica somewhere."

"Still, I'm going to stick around a bit to see what's up, maybe figure out who took the cameras."

"Val, come on. Ian and Gwendolyn have probably decided to finally start renting that place out again, or maybe they're getting it ready to be sold and stumbled upon the cameras while inspecting the property."

"Maybe. But I still want to hang around a bit and make sure. Marybeth has always been a really good client, and humoring her now will pay off in the long run once she moves on and starts sending us legit things to look into again."

Zoey let out a heavy sigh.

"How's Baltimore coming?" he asked, hoping to change the focus.

"It's all set. The only thing left to do is wait for the convention to start."

"That's good."

A few seconds of silence, and then she asked, "Where're you going to be staying?"

"Remember that odd western-themed place off of 55?"

"Oh gawd, that place was bizarre."

"Good mini-bar though."

"Yeah, which led to me admiring the toilet bowl all night long."

"Never mix Doritos and tequila," Val said.

"No need to remind me."

He chuckled.

"Anyway, keep me posted."

"Will do."

7

"Why do you want to see the file?" Gwen asked while standing in the doorway, arms crossed.

"Ian asked me to keep an eye out for this private investigator that is snooping around, so I figured that looking at the file might give me a feel for how he is going about his investigation," Sam said, surprised by Gwen's coldness.

"He did?"

"You didn't know?"

Gwen shook her head.

"Huh. He said he was going to text you."

Silence arrived, along with a gust of wind that felt like little razor blades against the skin.

"Ian thinks I'm crazy," Gwen said.

"What? No he doesn't," Sam replied, shaking her head.

"He does. You too. And my family."

"Gwen, no one thinks you're crazy. And what you went through—" She couldn't find the words to complete that and simply shook her head. "Everyone just wants to help you get through this, and having a stupid PI going around trying to dig up dirt won't help with that."

"My mother thinks that Ian staged the entire thing, and that Jessica is hiding out somewhere, living off of the money Ian gives to her."

"You know that's not true," Sam said.

"I know."

Another bout of silence arrived.

"So...is it okay if I see that file?"

"Of course," Gwen said, smiling. "Come on in."

8

Val watched as Dee parked her car in the tiny lot behind the bookstore near a rear door that opened up into a small foyer that he knew gave three options: a stairway to the basement storage areas, a door into the bookstore itself, or a stairway up to her apartment.

After a few seconds, a light went on upstairs in the apartment.

He waited.

And waited.

And waited.

Thirty minutes later, that light went out.

Ten minutes after that, Ian emerged from the back door and headed to his car.

Val followed him, first to the school where he picked up Tabitha, and then to their house where, much to Val's surprise, a police car was parked in the driveway. Ian, however, didn't seem concerned by it and simply parked next to it, Tabitha bouncing out of the car and racing to the door, Ian following in her wake, disappearing inside through the door that Tabitha had left wide open.

9

"Any luck?" Ian asked.

"Actually, yeah," Sam said.

"Oh?"

"Look at this," she said, motioning to a dozen photos of him that were spread out upon the table. "What do you see?"

"Lots of pictures of me being totally unaware that someone was taking photos of me," he said.

"And..." Sam pressed.

"You have them grouped into two sets, but I can't figure out—oh wait, is it by location?"

"Yep. These ones were taken as you pulled into or walked up the driveway, these while you were at the back door."

"Okay, but we already knew the investigator was taking photos of me while there."

"Look at them more closely. What do you see?"

He studied the photos for a few minutes, eyes going back and forth over each one several times, before finally shaking his head.

"Look closely at the ones taken of your truck, and then at the ones of you by the back door," she said, pulling two photos from two areas on the table and putting them side by side. "What do you see?"

"Me driving up to the Robinson house in one, and then me standing at the back door in the other."

"Okay, good, my fears that you might need glasses have been vanquished. Come on, look at them closely. Not at your truck and yourself specifically, but at the background in each of the photos."

He studied the photos for several seconds before shaking his head. "I'm clearly missing something here."

"The backgrounds are always the same. Not the various elements like weather, but all the trees and shrubs and whatnot. Everything is always positioned in the exact same spot."

"Okay?"

"No one is out there taking pictures of you. They simply rigged up a couple weatherproof outdoor cameras that are triggered by motion to take pictures, ones that either have an SD card inside or are connected to the internet and send stuff to the cloud."

"What about these photos?" He pointed to a pile of ones that showed various interactions between him and Dee in the bookstore, usually him hugging her. "You think they rigged up the store with a camera too at some point?"

"No. I'm pretty sure these were actually taken in person back when Gwen was missing. Early on when the private investigator was actually here investigating things instead of whatever this is now with the cameras at the Robinson house."

"But why?"
"I have no idea."

10

Val was still observing the house when the chief and Ian emerged, the chief getting into her patrol car while Ian got into his own. Both pulled out of the driveway, heading west toward the setting sun.

Val followed.

11

"Someone must have taken them down," Ian noted.

"And within the last day or two," Sam added, motioning toward the tracks in the snow.

Ian shook his head in dismay.

"Wait here a second," Sam instructed and started walking toward the bottom of the driveway, retracing their tracks through the snow.

"What are you doing?" Ian asked.

"I just need to check something out."

Ian watched as she reached the end of the driveway, looked around a bit, and then started trekking through the snow to the left of the driveway, her steps careful, her eyes on the snow, but not the snow she was walking through. Instead, she was looking to her right the entire time as she walked up to where each camera would have been hidden, her own phone snapping pictures of the trampled snow.

"So...?" Ian asked.

"I think there have been a couple different visits to where

these cameras were located, some today given how fresh the prints are, and visits either yesterday or the day before given how frozen over those tracks are."

"Jesus, I never would have thought to check something like that," Ian said.

"That's why I'm in law enforcement while you sell used books." She grinned. "Come on, let's go inside."

"Why?" he asked, following her toward the back door.

"I want you to see if anything seems amiss."

"That entire house is amiss."

"Yeah, well, try to see if anything is newly amiss from what it normally looks like."

"Okay."

"We also might be able to see if there are any tracks inside given how wet someone's feet would be after walking through the snow."

"Gwen should be the only one that has been inside since it snowed."

"We'll see."

12

Val couldn't see the rear of the house from where he was sitting due to all the overgrown pine trees that were scattered about the property, but he was pretty sure that Ian and the chief headed inside after investigating the first two camera locations.

Confirmation of this arrived when a flashlight beam appeared within the house, the glow visible through one of the few windows that was still intact.

Though it was a bit risky, Val stepped out of the car and started toward the house, the snow proving a bit troublesome as he charged through it, his body eventually reaching the house and positioning itself beneath the large front window that had been boarded up.

As expected, the voices from within were audible through the thin sheet of plywood.

13

Ian felt a bit odd being in the Robinson house with another person, his near daily visits during the last year always solitary endeavors. Having Sam in there with him made him feel very host-like, and he had to halt himself from acting as if he needed to be showing her around and explaining various areas of the house and what had unfolded in those areas with Gwen during that horrible month of captivity.

One thing he couldn't halt himself from was making a comment on how he still couldn't understand how he had been able to sit in the family room with Justin and Jessica drinking hot chocolate and eating cookies without realizing Gwen was down in the cellar.

"None of us realized this," Sam said.

"Yeah, but I was the only one that was actually inside with them for over an hour, sitting right above where they kept her." He shook his head. "I should have known. I should have felt something."

Sam didn't reply to that.

"And can you imagine what that was like for her? Being chained up down there, hearing my voice, yet unable to get my attention? Being that close and yet it might as well have been thousands of miles away."

"Has she ever spoken about this with you?" Sam asked.

"No," Ian said, shaking his head.

"Then maybe she couldn't hear you up here. Or even if she could hear someone, maybe she didn't know it was you."

"No, she knew," he said. "She and I have never spoken about it, but Marybeth has thrown it in my face several times, which means Gwen has mentioned it to her."

"You know, it might be for the best that you didn't realize she was here during that visit," Sam said. "If you had, you might not have left this house alive."

"Maybe."

"And if you think about it, in the end she did get free and is now back home, so everything worked out. But if you had tried to free her that day and went toe to toe with Justin..." She simply shook her head.

14

"Nothing about the camera inside?" Zoey asked.

"Not while I was listening," Val said, eyeing the liquor selection in his room's minibar. "Before that, who knows, though I don't think so."

"How come?"

"I don't know." He grabbed a spiced rum from the small carton of mini-bottles. "I just didn't get that vibe. Outside, they clearly were there to check out the cameras and seemed surprised they were missing, but inside, they spent nearly an hour simply talking about what happened, Ian dwelling upon the fact that he had failed to realize Gwendolyn was a prisoner in the basement while he visited the siblings, before shifting over to how Jessica probably fled the house after discovering her brother with his head cracked open and Gwendolyn having gotten herself down from the ropes and going out the window, eventually dying from exposure somewhere out in the surrounding wilderness."

"I mean, that is the most logical explanation for things,

though it is still odd that Jessica has never been found, especially if her body is out there somewhere."

"Yeah."

"So now what?"

"Not entirely sure."

"Kind of odd, them going right to the two outdoor cameras but not the indoor one, if, that is, they hadn't actually checked it before you were listening at the window."

"Yeah," he agreed.

"And what drew them to the camera locations in the first place? It sounds like they obviously knew where they were, the outdoor ones at least, yet if they weren't the ones to take them, then how did they find out about them? And who did take them?"

Val had been wondering the same thing.

"You don't think it could have been Gwen, do you?"

"I really don't know, though I would be very surprised if she ever came inside."

"Hmm, yeah."

A knock echoed on the door.

"Oops, that's my pizza. Gotta run."

"Okay, enjoy."

SIX

I

"This one! This one! This one!" Tabby urged while pointing at a tree.

"This one?" Ian questioned, pointing to the tree next to the one Tabby was indicating.

"No! This one!"

"Ohhhhh, this one," Ian said, stepping over to another tree.

"No! Daddy! This one!" Tabby stabbed her finger toward the correct tree. "See! Right here!"

"Ah, this one!"

"Yes!"

Ian turned to Gwen. "What do you think?"

Gwen didn't reply, her eyes staring off at something while steam billowed from the cup of hot chocolate she held in her hands.

"Gwen?"

"Mommy! Do you like this one?"

"Yes," she said. "It's perfect. They all are."

Gwen was right.

The trees that Al had for sale in his lot on the west side of town were always spectacular. Very fresh and full, as if they had just been chopped down earlier that day.

2

An hour later, Ian was holding the tree while Tabby was down below twisting the screws in place, her tiny fingers working carefully to secure the trunk within the stand, Ian's earlier statement to her on how this was the most important task when putting up a tree having backfired a bit given how precise she was trying to be.

"Daddy, one of the screws keeps going sideways."

"That's okay. Just as long as it's tight."

"But the other ones are all straight."

"Let me take a look. Scooch out, okay?"

Tabby came out from under the tree, pine needles clinging to her pigtails.

"I'm all sticky," she noted, holding her arms out in front of herself.

"Me too," Ian said, cautiously stepping away from the tree, hands ready to catch it if it started to fall. "This is a sappy one."

"How's it coming?" Gwen asked, stepping into the room.

"I think we got it," Ian announced after getting down and checking the screws and the trunk. "Tabby did a fantastic job."

"I knew she would," Gwen said.

Tabby beamed and then announced, "Mommy, I'm all sticky!"

"I can see that. Let's get you into the shower before we do anything else, okay?"

"What about Daddy?"

"I will be taking a shower too," Ian said. "But first things first, family hug!"

"No! No!" Gwen playfully shrieked while trying to dodge his wiggling fingers.

Tabby pounced upon her as she did, hands putting two giant globs of sap right onto her butt.

"Ugh," she groaned as Ian then entangled her with his arms, her face scrunching up in disgust as he started pecking her cheek with kisses.

"Now Mommy has to shower too!" Tabby shouted while laughing.

"Yes, Mommy does," Gwen said, giving Ian a *you're in so much trouble* look.

He grinned.

3

"I got nothing," Val said. "Three days of snooping around and the most exciting thing that has unfolded was seeing Dee break up with her boyfriend in the college parking lot."

"Was it pretty intense?" Zoey asked. "A big shouting match and lots of heel stomping and sobbing?"

"No such luck. It was so amicable that the two hugged afterward."

"And nothing new on your missing cameras?"

"Nope. Though if I'm right about them being taken shortly before I went to check them, and if it was either Ian or Dee, as opposed to some random third party that we aren't aware of yet, then chances are good they've held on to them since I've been checking the dumpster behind the bookstore and then the trash bins that were put out last night at Ian and Gwendolyn's house."

"Unless they just drove out into the middle of nowhere,

which is like five minutes in any direction, and tossed them into a field."

"True."

"So, you heading back?"

"Not yet. Marybeth is convinced that Ian is planning something horrible and wants me to keep an eye on things until Christmas."

"Jesus."

"I know, right? The good news is that I made up a ridiculously high Christmas rate thinking she might reconsider, but it didn't even faze her, so that will be a nice chunk of change for us to ring in the New Year with."

"Well, that's something at least."

"How're things looking in Baltimore?"

"So far so good, though speaking of ridiculously high prices, Candy wants twice her previous rate this time around."

"Are you serious?"

"Yep."

"Did she give a reason?"

"Inflation."

Val chuckled. "What did you tell her?"

"I agreed, but I let her know that I better not see any four-hundred-dollar bottles of champagne on her room service tab again."

"Sounds reasonable."

"So, what're you going to do now?"

"Stir up trouble," Val said while looking at the bookstore.

4

"Help you?" Dee asked as the man stepped up to the counter, his eyes glancing up at the menu.

"I'm not sure," he said. "I was told this place has the best coffee around."

"We do. Like no joke, one of the owners is crazy about coffee. We're talking taking trips to coffee plantations all over the world to check out their beans and roastings, samplings and whatnot, like doing that noisy sipping thing with a spoon, all before committing to purchasing. And that's just the beans. Everything behind this counter to brew the coffee is the best of the best."

"Wow, no joke is right." He continued looking at the menu. "What's Blue Mountain Peaberry and is that really the price for a single cup?"

"Okay, so that one is from Jamaica and is like the champagne of coffee. A true Blue Mountain has certifications up the wazoo to be legit and, making it even more crazy, these are peaberry beans, which are in a whole other league from regular beans."

"Wait, are they the ones that are pooped out by some monkey?"

"No, no," Dee said with a laugh. "That's totally different and we don't go for that here due to animal cruelty—a lot of those producers force-feed the civet cats coffee beans while keeping them in tiny cages in order to produce tons of beans due to the sudden popularity. No. Peaberry beans are just a coffee bean that has one seed inside instead of two, which makes for a better roasting experience. They also have to be sorted out by hand since you can't have a mix of regular and peaberry beans roasting together, which really drives up the costs."

"I see," the man said, nodding.

Dee waited a second and then said, "If uncertain, I would recommend the peaberry one from either Costa Rica or Guatemala. Each still has a bit of a higher price than coffee from standard beans, but nowhere near the Blue Mountain prices, and they are both really good. Especially this latest batch of beans from Guatemala."

"Okay, you sold me. I'll do a cup of that."

Four minutes later, Dee was handing over the cup of coffee, the beans having been freshly ground upon order and then brewed in a French press. "Enjoy."

"Thanks, you too," the man said and then frowned at himself.

Dee smiled.

5

Shit, this is good, Val thought while sipping the coffee, a debate on trying a cup of the Jamaican one now unfolding within his mind.

First things first though, he needed to initiate his real reason for coming into the bookstore while Dee was the one working, a question on if it was okay for him to walk around with the coffee leaving his lips.

"Oh sure," Dee said. "Anything specific you're looking for?"

"Do you have a true crime section?" he asked.

"True crime?" she said, enthusiasm blossoming. "Yes! Let me show you."

Val waited a moment as Dee made her way out from behind the counter and then followed her as she led the way through several maze-like bookshelf-lined hallways and rooms, eventually ending in one of the smaller rooms that housed all the nonfiction books the store had acquired.

"It's not the most impressive true crime section, but we do seem to have far more titles than most bookstores, especially those who specialize in new books since true crime tends to go out of print fairly quickly."

"That they do. Milk has a longer shelf life than any of my books."

"Your books? Are you a true crime author?"

"I am," he lied.

"Wow! What's your name? Maybe I've read some of your work. I'm a huge true crime fan myself."

Val gave her the name of an identity Zoey had created for this investigation back when Gwendolyn was still missing, one which had basic background information that could be looked into if anyone did any social media searches. It wouldn't stand up to spy-level stuff that the covert world created when making identities for their secret agents, but it was more than enough for the use he and Zoey had originally planned.

"Hmm, rings a bell," Dee said, eyes starting to scan the shelf.

Val wasn't surprised by the "rings a bell" statement given that the name would ping all the familiar sounds of a very common name within the publishing world, something that always triggered the mind to start a matching process within its memory zones rather than question the legitimacy of the creation.

"What types of crime do you write about?" Dee asked.

"Serial killers."

"Seriously! I love serial killers. Well. Learning about them. Not like sending them love letters or anything while they're in prison." She chuckled. "Which ones have you written about?"

"Oh jeez, I've done books and articles on so many I would have trouble listing them all off the top of my head," Val said. "In my early days I focused on the typical guys. Bundy, Gacy, Dahmer, Manson"—he waved a dismissive hand—"but now I like to focus on the more obscure, less romanticized killers. The gritty ones that the media can't turn into a Touchstone experience."

Dee was nodding with obvious enthusiasm. "Oh my god, yes! I get so tired of them always focusing on those guys. It's like okay, enough with Bundy. We get it. He was a ladies' man that seemed able to charm all those he came into contact with. And if they make one more movie about him I'm going to go nuts."

"Tell me about it. And how about all those documentaries about Jack the Ripper?" Val asked, memories of seeing a Facebook post from Dee ranting about the latest attempts to prove "so and so" was the killer hovering within his mind.

"Ugh, don't get me started. It's all because he was never caught. If he had been, then no one today would even know anything about him or those five murders."

"Totally agree."

"Hmm, I don't see your name anywhere," Dee said, her eyes having scanned all the titles while they were talking.

"I'm not surprised," Val said, pulling a random book from the shelf. "Ah, Israel Keyes. A perfect example of someone most have never heard about."

"Right! I always wonder how long he would have gone on killing people without being caught if he hadn't stupidly used that dead girl's ATM card."

"Oh, I know," Val said, his mind cautioning himself since he really had no idea who this guy was or how he had been apprehended.

He put the book back.

"So, working on anything interesting right now?" Dee asked.

"Nothing specific. I'm kind of just prospecting, looking for situations that might have some '*umphh*,' as my agent calls it, so that she can sell the idea and get me a nice advance. Especially unsolved stuff."

"Ah, I see," Dee said, caution suddenly present.

"You ever hear of the Craigslist Ripper?" Val asked.

Dee blinked, clearly caught off guard. "The guy who has been leaving bodies on the various beaches of Long Island for nearly twenty years?"

"Wow," Val said, genuinely surprised since he figured not many people outside of Long Island itself knew about the ongoing mystery. "You weren't kidding when you said you were a huge serial killer fan."

Dee blushed.

"Anyway, I have been digging around into that for quite some time and have lots of good stuff, and several interesting theories on possible suspects, only there is like zero interest from my publisher. We're talking nothing, nada, zip. Even my agent is being all like, 'Val, come on, you gotta give me something I can work with here!' so I was all like, 'How about a book about that weird serial killer family that was obsessed with Santa Claus that some of the folks around here have been talking about?' And boom, not only is my publisher interested in it, my agent thinks others will be as well and that we could have a bidding war and even maybe a Netflix documentary, which could really push me up into the big times, so now here I am."

Dee didn't reply to that.

"So tell me, do you know anything about this crazy Robinson family?"

6

"Alexa! Play 'Grandma Got Run Over by a Reindeer'!" Tabby shouted.

"No, not again," Gwen said.

"Alexa, stop!" Ian instructed.

Tabby crossed her arms, giving a pouty look.

"Mommy will pick the next song," Ian said, his hands opening another box of ornaments that needed to be put on the tree.

"Maybe a bit of a break with the Christmas music," Gwen said.

"But, Mommy, you have to have Christmas music while decorating a tree," Tabby said, hooking an ornament onto a branch. "It's a rule."

"Honey, that isn't really a rule," Ian said.

"But, Daddy, what if Santa gets upset and then doesn't come to our house?"

"Honey, Santa doesn't get upset over things like that."

"I don't want to be on his naughty list."

"You could never be on his naughty list."

"What about when I asked Aunt Ida if she was growing a mustache?"

Ian tried to mask a grin. "That wasn't being mean, just observant, though you should never ask a lady that."

Tabby seemed deep in thought for a moment and then asked, "What about when I told that joke at school about ghosts having hollow weenies?"

"Nope. No naughty list for that either, though it's best not to tell jokes about weenies in school."

Tabby nodded, seemingly satisfied, but then asked, "How does Santa know who has been naughty and who has been nice?"

"I don't really know," Ian said.

"Does he spy on us?"

"No, I don't think so."

"Do I have to make a list of the naughty things I've done when I go to see him next week?"

"Nope. You just tell him the things you want for Christmas."

"Do you know what Julie asked Santa for last year?"

"What?" Ian asked, trying to remember who Julie was.

"A sister, but instead she got a little brother!"

Ian gave a quick glance toward Gwen.

"Why would Santa do that? Do you think it was a mistake?"

"Honey, let's not talk—"

"I don't think I would want a little brother. A sister would be much better. But if I ask Santa for a sister I might get a little brother instead."

"Tabby—"

"And you can't return a little brother like last year when Santa got me a Playstation game instead of a Switch game. Remember that? And then we couldn't go to the store because it was Christmas, but then you found it on Amazon and downloaded it for me so I could play it, but it was too hard."

"Are there any Switch games you want this year?" Ian asked, trying to keep that direction going rather than baby stuff.

"Mommy, are you going to be here for Christmas this year?"

"Of course she is," Ian said when Gwen didn't reply.

"That's good. Last year I missed you. And then you left again and weren't home until after Easter and Daddy made me wear that dress to church that I hate. You're not going to leave again after Christmas, are you?"

"I think it's time for a hot chocolate break," Ian announced. "Tabby, can you go get some mugs ready?"

"Hot chocolate!" Tabby shouted and zoomed out of the room.

Ian turned to Gwen, who was staring at the fireplace, an ornament dangling from her fingers.

"Are you okay?" Ian asked just as "Grandma Got Run Over by a Reindeer" started blasting from the Alexa in the kitchen.

Ornament still in hand, Gwen left the room.

Ian started to follow but then halted when Tabby shouted a question on if she should start the water boiling in the kettle.

. . .

7

I think the PI is here, Dee texted to Ian and Sam.
Where? Sam asked within seconds.
At the bookstore, Dee replied.
I'm on my way!

8

"You okay?" Ian asked, standing in the doorway of Gwen's home office.

"Yes," Gwen said from a corner chair by an unlit lamp, her knees brought up against her chest while she sat on the leather cushion.

"You sure?"

Gwen shifted her gaze to meet his.

Ian waited.

Nothing followed.

"*Daddy!*" Tabby called from downstairs. "*Dee's texting you!*"

Ian made no move to head downstairs.

"*Daddy!*"

"Go," Gwen said. "Really. I'm fine. Just need a few minutes."

He nodded.

"*There's pie at the bookstore!*" Tabby announced.

Pie? he silently asked himself while turning away from the office and starting back toward the kitchen.

"*Sam says she is on her way.*"

Ian stepped into the family room, his phone having been set on a side table while plugged into the wall outlet to charge. Tabby was leaning over it.

"I'm just reading the screen," she said, previous scoldings for touching his phone and sometimes answering calls when she was younger still ingrained.

"You really shouldn't do that," he said. "With anyone's phone. It's rude."

"What kind of pie is it?" she asked.

"I don't know," he said and lifted his phone to read what had been sent.

I think the PI is here, the initial message from Dee said, the text bubble now at the bottom of the screen.

"Is it pumpkin pie?"

Ian ignored Tabby as he thumbed open the phone and started typing up a question.

"I liked that at Grandma's house. Especially with the whipped cream. But it wasn't fair I only got one piece while Tommy got two."

"Tabby, there is no pie."

"But Dee says there is."

"It's something else."

Tabby crossed her arms, her disbelief with his statement evident.

9

"I didn't really suspect anything at first," Dee said, "but then he started talking about the Craigslist Ripper out on Long Island and how his publisher would rather he write a book about the Robinson family, and I suddenly got this sense that everything he was saying was complete bullshit and simply designed to distract me from the fact that he was trying to gather info on Ian and Gwen."

"But that is exactly what he was doing," Sam noted. "He

flat out told you he was a writer that was working on a book about what had happened."

"I know, but it didn't feel legit," Dee said. "It was too perfect. That transition from Long Island to this was way too smooth. Plus he didn't seem to know that someone has actually been arrested for the Long Island murders, which seems to contradict the idea that he had been gathering up info to write a book about it."

"Maybe it just didn't come up because of the transition to the Robinson family stuff?"

"I don't know," Dee said while shaking her head. "I'm telling you, this guy felt off, almost like he knew exactly what to say to me to get me hooked and talking, first with the true crime stuff, then a very obscure serial killer, my annoyance with the focus on other killers, my love of Netflix documentaries...he kept hitting all the right buttons, almost like he was trying to seduce me."

"Still doesn't mean he is the private investigator. He could have looked you up online after reading a bunch of web sleuth stuff and figured out what exactly he needed to say to you in order to hook your cooperation. Or maybe he is just like you, but instead of taking his interest toward becoming an FBI profiler, he directed it toward writing books about serial killers."

"If he were like me, he would have known about them arresting someone for the Long Island murders."

Sam sighed.

"What? It's true. I was pretty giddy about it last summer when they arrested the guy, as were all the true crime junkies."

"Okay, maybe," Sam said, "That said, I should let you know that we're not even really sure the private investigator is actually in town."

"What?"

"Turns out there were a couple cameras at the Robinson house. Two of them. One by each door. They were motion activated and would snap a photo of anyone who entered the house."

"Are you serious?"

"Yep."

"And no one ever noticed them before?"

"Nope. Looks like they were well placed so that you would only really see them if you knew they were there and went looking for them."

"Looks like?" Dee asked.

"Someone took them down before we went to check them, probably sometime within a day or two given the prints in the snow."

"How do you even know they were there to begin with?"

"The pictures from the private investigator file. A quick look at them made it pretty obvious that the cameras were in fixed positions."

"So they were simply collecting photos of Ian going into the house?"

"Yep."

"And that is why Gwen's family thinks me and Ian are fucking each other and planning to do something horrible to Gwen?"

"I think that is more a result of all the nonsense she reads from those online groups. The cameras were probably there to see if any of that shit was true."

"But then why take them down?"

The chime by the door echoed.

Both looked toward the entrance as Ian entered.

"So, is he still here?" Ian asked, somewhat breathless.

"No," Sam said. "He apparently left shortly after Dee texted us."

"And Sam doesn't even think it was him anyway," Dee added, a tone clearly present.

"I didn't say that," Sam said. "Just that nothing is conclusive."

"A.k.a., you don't think it was him."

Sam rolled her eyes.

"Tell me what happened," Ian said and then listened for about eight minutes as Dee detailed what had unfolded and her thoughts on it.

10

Val watched from his rental vehicle as Sam and Ian showed up at the bookstore, apparently summoned by Dee, who had clearly alerted them to his presence at the bookstore. Now the question was, had she seen through his writer ruse or was she simply concerned by the fact that a writer would be poking around during a time when something horrible was being plotted?

If something horrible is actually being plotted...

He still had no evidence of such a thing, and the fact that Dee had called these two in after his little visit wasn't evidence of anything nefarious going on. In fact, it could have simply been a heads-up that someone was digging into things, something which they were concerned about given how easily Gwendolyn was being triggered into reliving the horrors that she had experienced.

Whatever the reason for her alerting them, he was pleased that she had, his goal of stirring things up a bit having apparently worked.

Now to see what followed.

If anything.

11

. . .

Dee was annoyed by the lack of enthusiasm Sam and Ian displayed following her description of what had unfolded with the writer fellow, her mind still convinced that the man was the private investigator that she had been told to be on the lookout for a week earlier.

Their having failed to tell her about the photos and the likelihood of cameras having been set up around the Robinson property also bothered her.

She thought they were a team in all of this, the three of them working together to try to help Gwen recover from her ordeal while preventing any unnecessary drama unfolding with the stupid investigation her mother was insisting upon.

But no.

Ian and Sam were the team, while she was tasked with keeping an eye out for things that they didn't even take seriously once she reported them.

Topping it off, they didn't even seem impressed by the video she had snagged, her hands having quickly set up the phone to record the man as he came back to the counter, a statement from her asking if he wanted a complimentary refill on his coffee luring him in for his close-up.

The chimes from the front door echoed once again.

Forcing a smile, she looked up toward the door and saw that it was the local mail carrier, one who she was on a first-name basis with and often prepared coffee for to take on the go as he made his rounds.

Today he had a package for her, one that helped brighten her mood following the lackluster meeting about the private investigator.

The elf outfits had arrived.

12

. . .

Tabby was dancing when Ian arrived back home, the Alexa speakers bellowing out the as he stepped into the family room.

"Daddy, what's a whirlybird?" Tabby asked, body rocking out in a way that would leave most adults aching for days.

"It's a helicopter," Ian said, looking around. "Where's Mommy?"

"Basement."

"Basement?"

"Are you going to dance with me?"

"Maybe in a bit," he said, leaving the family room to head down the hallway toward the door that would lead down into the basement.

"You promise?" Tabby called out.

"Promise!" he called back and then took a deep breath before opening the door to the basement.

13

Gwen hurried out of the old coal room as Ian stepped from the stairway into the finished part of the basement, a statement of "That was fast!" followed by "Everything okay over there?" leaving her lips as she pulled shut the rickety door.

"Yeah," he said, giving her a puzzled look. "What in the world were you doing in there?"

"Nothing," she said, forcing a playful ring into her voice.

"Nothing?"

"Well, maybe something," she said, coming up to him, a mischievous grin joining the playful tone. "But you can't see it until Christmas—and only if you're good."

"Ohhhhh," he said, his own playfulness arriving. "And if I'm not?"

"Why do you think I always hide your gifts in the old coal chute?" she said. "Easy to swap out."

"Only there's no actual coal in there these days."

"Ha! That's what you think." She pressed into him with her chest and leaned her lips in to kiss him.

He stepped back, breaking the contact.

"What?" she asked, startled.

"I just..." He hesitated. "When Tabby said you were in the basement I..." He shook his head.

"Thought I was in the corner staring wide-eyed at the old stone foundation mumbling about Santa ass-fucking me?" she asked, crossing her arms.

He blinked.

"I told you earlier, I'm fine."

"I know."

"I just needed to step away for a bit."

"I know."

"I need you to trust me when I say that."

"I do."

She stared at him, arms still crossed.

"Seriously, I wouldn't have rushed off to the bookstore if I didn't."

She considered that and then nodded.

He opened his arms for her.

She stepped back up against him, letting his arms engulf her into an embrace that was far different from what she had been trying to initiate a few seconds earlier.

14

Christmas music echoed throughout the house for the rest of the day, as did the sounds of Ian and Gwen dancing with Tabby, the old hardwood floors squeaking beneath the area rugs as they bounced around to various tunes that were never meant for such activity. Hot chocolate breaks were frequent, the time it took for them to drink down the large mugs a welcome respite for the two adults, who didn't have the same caches of energy that Tabby carried.

Slow dancing eventually took over as the sun set, the glow from the lights on the tree and the various scented candles producing a nice warm romantic feel to the family room, the music theme going from crazy Looney Tunes Christmas music to more traditional, sometimes religious music, an intimacy developing between Ian and Gwen that had not been felt in over a year, one which earned a loud "ewwww" from Tabby as the two kissed at the end of one song.

SEVEN

1

She felt as if her insides were being ripped apart with each thrust, the growing grunts of ecstasy that echoed from the jolly old elf as his red hat jiggled off his head drowning out the once-soothing voice of Nat King Cole.

Blood.

It was suddenly gushing out from her.

She shrieked against the rubber bit in her mouth, her body bucking against restraints as frantic voices replaced the sexual grunts and the music.

Gwen.

Gwen!

"Gwen!"

She looked up at Ian in the darkness, his arms pinning her down to the bed, her own hands twisting, trying to get free, the cream-colored sheets having turned crimson.

"Honey, it's—"

Her right hand slipped free and clawed his face, fingernails digging long jagged furrows through his flesh.

"Fuck!" he cried out, his body quickly backing away as he tended to his wound.

Gwen took the opportunity to throw off the bloody sheets, her eyes seeing a half-formed fetus peeking out between her legs.

"Mommy?" a voice said.

Gwen screamed.

And then Ian was ushering Tabby, who was now crying in terror, from the doorway.

Gwen looked back down between her legs.

The half-formed fetus was gone, yet the blood remained.

She blinked a few times to see if it would return.

It didn't.

She looked back at the bedroom doorway, beyond which she could hear Ian trying to soothe Tabby.

Tears arrived, her face quickly becoming smeared with blood as she tried to wipe them away.

"Jesus Christ," Ian gasped, his body momentarily halting as he stepped back into the bedroom. Then, "Are you okay?"

Gwen started to reply, only to realize it wasn't words that were about to emerge, and quickly ran into the bathroom where she vomited up everything they had eaten for dinner the evening before.

2

Cheek stinging, Ian stared at the bloody sheets, uncertainty on what his next actions should be paralyzing him, all while the sounds of vomiting echoed from the bathroom.

Sobbing followed the vomiting.

Ian went to the bathroom door.

"Gwen?" he asked.

Nothing.

"Gwen, honey?"

"Go away," she said.

Hesitation arrived but then was broken, his body doing what she suggested, arms loaded up with the bloody bedsheets as he headed down to the laundry room.

He didn't actually start washing them. Instead, he simply left them piled in the corner, his next destination being a first-floor bathroom where he took a look at his cheek.

It was bad.

A tube of Neosporin was in the cabinet, his fingers smearing it all over the wounds.

He returned to the bedroom.

Gwen was still in the bathroom, though her sobs had ended.

He quietly stepped to the door and listened.

Nothing.

Hesitation returned, his knuckles poised to knock against the wood but not actually acting.

Movement.

The sound of the shower curtain being pulled back and then water racing through the pipes.

He sighed.

A few seconds later he was sitting on the edge of the bare mattress, uncertainty once again dominating.

3

Gwen spent a long time simply standing beneath the shower spray, the water as hot as could be tolerated, its heat turning the upper part of her body a bright red while down below it sluiced away various areas of blood that could no longer cling to her flesh.

Other areas required the handheld showerhead to be used,

the fierce jet-like spray momentarily bringing back the horror of when Dr. Wilbanks's primary assistant had washed away the evidence of the miscarriage that had begun in the midst of a shock therapy session.

She had screamed at them to stop, but the rubber bit they had put in her mouth during the therapy had stayed in place for the washing, making her words nothing but hysterical gibberish in their eyes. Her wrists and chest had been restrained with padded leather while her ankles had simply been gripped by strong hands, her left one by the second, larger assistant who always played the part of Santa during the therapy.

Nothing had been preserved, Dr. Wilbanks and the assistant simply letting everything be washed down a drain. Later they would claim it hadn't been a miscarriage at all, just a heavy cycle spurred on by the treatments.

Gwen knew differently.

She knew she had gotten pregnant while Santa was fucking her in the Robinson family room on Christmas Eve, her kicks that had eventually led to her freedom coming too late to stop the spurt of seed from swimming up into her.

4

"Jesus Christ!" Dee shouted, startled by Ian's presence in a corner reading chair as she came down into the bookstore to make some coffee for herself. "Oh my god. What happened to your face?"

Ian made an odd shushing gesture with his hands.

"Mommy scratched Daddy," Tabby announced while walking into the room. "Is there still pie?"

"Pie?" Dee questioned, eyes going from Tabby to Ian.

Ian let out a sigh and then said, "Tabby, go back to the kids' area for a bit while I talk to Dee and then we'll go get some pie, okay?"

Tabby zoomed away.

Dee gave him a questioning look.

"Gwen had a nightmare and caught me in the face," he said, voice soft.

"That must have been some nightmare."

Ian didn't answer, which surprised Dee.

Concern followed.

"Is she okay?" Dee asked.

"I don't know," Ian said.

"Is it the decorations?"

"No, well, maybe. But mostly it was..." His voice faded.

"Was what?" she asked.

His hesitation continued for several seconds, and then, after a heavy sigh, he said, "You know how Gwen was convinced that Santa fucked her on Christmas Eve before she escaped?"

"Yeah."

"And that he impregnated her with some sort of evil human-elf hybrid."

"Yeah."

"And how nothing could convince her this wasn't the case. Not the negative test results, not the fact that the police reports detailed finding Justin's body dressed as Santa near the fireplace."

"Yeah."

"And then how she went away to a better hospital for a while after her mother came out to visit and felt this one wasn't up to snuff."

"Yeah."

"Well, she didn't actually go to a better hospital."

"But..." Dee started and then frowned. "She was gone for several months."

"She was at her mother's house."

Dee blinked. "Her mother's house?"

"Gwen was having a rough time in the hospital after her escape. Pulling out her IV, clawing at the staff members, even leaving the hospital in the middle of the night because she thought one of Santa's elves was after her. It was bad. So bad that they restrained her to the bed, which seemed to me the worst thing you could do to a person after they have just spent a month chained up in a cellar, but they said they had no choice. It was either that or she would have to go up to the sixth floor."

"Sixth floor?"

"Psych ward."

"Oh."

"Of course, she ended up on the sixth floor anyway, which is when her mother freaked out because she felt I was up to something in regards to getting Gwen declared legally insane so that I could control all the money."

"Ugh, that's such bullshit," Dee said.

"I know, right? She has always been under the idea that I'm somehow trying to steal Gwen's money, as if the millions I've earned myself don't even exist and I want the billions that she..." His voice faded for a second. "Ugh, I'm digressing." He waved a hand. "So she came out here and whisked Gwen away to her grand estate out on Long Island so that she could rest and recoup, and I didn't stand in the way at all. I just let her go."

"You were at your wit's end," Dee said. "After her missing for a month and all the crazy rumors and then her being in that mental state afterward..."

"Still, I should have known better than to let her go off with her mother like that."

Silence arrived.

"What happened?" Dee asked after several seconds.

"Shock therapy."

"Shock therapy?"

"And not legit modern-day shock therapy. This was like old-school horror-movie stuff where they strapped her to her own bed and continuously zapped the shit out of her brain in hopes of wiping away whatever areas were causing all the Santa delusions. Over and over again."

"Who did?"

"This doctor her mother sees. He is this quack that only treats the ladies in her social circle. And their daughters. Privately in their own homes. They all pay him big bucks to cure them of whatever ails them."

"But...I always thought shock therapy was illegal."

"I did too until I met Gwen. Not only is it quite legal, its use is growing in popularity. And in its modern form it seems to be quite effective in helping with severe depression and other mental disorders that won't respond to medication. It's literally an outpatient procedure."

"Really?"

"Yeah."

"But used the way they were doing it in a home rather than at a hospital," Dee said, her mind barely able to even register this. "That can't be legal."

"With consent it is, and they claim Gwen consented, and she won't say otherwise, so..." He lifted his hands in a hopeless gesture.

"And this is why she scratched you?" Dee asked after a few minutes.

"Gwen thinks she lost Santa's baby during one of the shock therapy sessions," he said. "This is actually how I found out what was going on. She called me in a panic that night talking about all the blood and how they didn't believe her that it was the baby, and that she needed to come back home to protect Tabby because Santa might send elves to take vengeance on her for killing his baby. I couldn't wrap my mind around what she was talking about, but after calming her down a bit, she explained about the shock treatments they were doing, ones that were pretty much the equivalent of hooking a car battery to her brain. After that, I was on the next plane out there and took her home."

"I still don't understand why she scratched you."

"She woke up covered in blood from...well...*it* came early this month, I guess, and she totally freaked out. I didn't know what was going on and was trying to hold her down so she didn't fall off the bed, and she lashed out and got me."

"You think seeing the blood triggered memories of the treatments and the supposed miscarriage?"

Ian nodded.

"And then you came here?"

Another nod.

"Leaving Gwen all alone at home?"

"She told me to go away and I..." Another shake of the head. "She just needs some alone time, I think, and getting Tabby out of there after what she saw seemed like a good idea too."

Dee didn't really know how to reply to that.

"What time is it anyway?" he asked and then glanced at his watch. "Whoa, what are you doing down here so early? We don't open until ten."

"I just came down to get some coffee."

He seemed to process that for longer than was necessary, a simple nod eventually being made.

5

Ian and Tabby were gone.

Gwen realized this fairly quickly after stepping from the shower, body shivering as she slowly walked the empty house.

A note had been left.

By the coffeepot.

Ian had taken Tabby to the bookstore.

Whisked her away from her crazy mother.

Right to Dee.

Who had been like a temporary mother for Tabby while Gwen had been chained up in that cellar, and then again while she was at her mother's house having her brain zapped to oblivion while Dr. Wilbanks had one of his assistants standing over her dressed like Santa.

A temporary wife as well?

Gwen tried pushing the thought away, but it was a stubborn one and refused to budge. Images joined the thought, ones of Ian and Dee in all kinds of provocative positions.

No.

That was not happening.

Ian did not fuck around behind her back.

Not even when she told him he could if he wanted to.

He was loyal to a fault.

6

"You really should go back and be with Gwen," Dee said, handing him a giant mug of coffee.

Ian didn't reply to that, simply taking the mug of coffee and holding it in his hands while it cooled.

"I can watch Tabby for the day while you're there. That way you two can have some actual one-on-one time without the craziness that engulfs everything within her vicinity."

On cue, Tabby came flying into the room and said that the Alexa wasn't working.

"Honey, there is no Alexa here," Ian said.

"Oh." Tabby frowned. "I wanted Dee to hear the whirlybird song."

"The whirlybird song?" Dee asked.

Tabby belted out some of the song lyrics while spinning like a helicopter.

"Oh, oh, oh, I know that one," Dee said, trying to hide her disdain for it.

"You do?" Tabby asked.

"I do, and maybe later we can listen to it, okay? But right now your daddy and I need some grown-up time, okay?"

"Does that mean sex?" Tabby asked.

Dee's eyes went wide while Ian choked on a mouthful of coffee.

"Tabby," he scolded a second later.

"Lindsey says that grown-up time means sex," Tabby said.

"That's not what grown-up time means at all, and I don't want you saying that again, understand?" Ian said.

Tabby nodded.

"Now go back to the kids' area so you can find the next Nancy Drew book, okay?"

"Number twenty-two," Tabby said.

"That's right."

Tabby hurried off back to the kids' room.

"So, grown-up time equals sex in the world of nine-year-olds," Dee said. "Good to know."

"Yeah," Ian muttered and then sipped his coffee.

"I'm guessing Lindsey's a classmate?"

"Probably. She spits out so many names as sources of information that I can never keep track."

7

Gwen pulled her tiny car into the spot next to Ian's truck, concern at what she might see once she stepped into the bookstore keeping her from stepping out of the vehicle for several minutes.

Deep breath.
And another.
And another.
She opened the door and stepped out.

8

"*Mommy!*" Tabby said, voice echoing.

Startled, Dee turned toward Ian, who quickly stood up from the chair he had been sitting in, coffee jostling within the mug as he set it onto a small stand.

Voices reached them, Tabby talking about the Nancy Drew book she was reading while Gwen asked where Daddy was, a comment about grown-up time with Dee being made, followed by, "But that doesn't mean sex."

Ian bolted from the room, leaving Dee alone, uncertainty on what her own actions should be keeping her standing in place.

Then, "Dee?" a voice called.

Coffee still in hand, Dee quickly joined them, a question from Ian on if she could take Tabby upstairs for a bit being made.

"Oh, sure," Dee said.

Nancy Drew book in hand, Tabby slipped by Ian and Gwen to join Dee, the two of them heading out of the bookstore to the rear corridor where a stairway awaited them, one that could go down into the storage areas or up to her apartment.

They went up.

"Why do you live above the bookstore?" Tabby asked as they stepped inside.

"Because I needed a place to live and your mommy and daddy said I could live here," Dee said.

"You don't have a house?" she asked.

"I..." She hesitated. "Did you know this was where your daddy lived when he was a kid?"

"He did?" Tabby asked, her surprise genuine.

"Yep. He and your grandparents lived up here above the bookstore, though back then it was an antique store."

"And now they live in Florida."

"That's right, and your other grandparents live on Long Island."

"We were there for Thanksgiving," Tabby said.

"I know. I went and took care of your rabbits while you all were there."

"They don't eat carrots."

"What?"

"Bilbo and Frodo. Bunny rabbits are supposed to eat carrots, but Daddy says that we have to give them the pellet stuff from the store instead."

"Oh, I guess maybe they—"

"You don't have a Christmas tree?"

"Um, no," she said, her mind having forgotten how quickly topics could change with Tabby.

"Are you Jewish?"

Dee blinked. "Jewish? No."

"Then why don't you have a Christmas tree?"

"I guess I just forgot about it this year."

In reality, she hadn't bothered with a tree in any of the years following the death of her parents.

"If you don't have a tree, then where is Santa going to put all your presents?"

Dee tried to think up an answer to that but then decided to skip it completely and said, "Did you have fun putting up your tree yesterday?"

"Yes!"

"I bet it's beautiful. Lots of lights and ornaments."

"Millions!"

"Millions?"

"And some of the lights twinkle."

"Wow."

"You should come spend Christmas with us. That way Santa can leave some presents for you by our tree."

"Hmm, maybe." Dee's eyes caught sight of the box the elf outfits had arrived in. "Hey, want to see something cool?"

"Yes!"

"Okay, wait here for a second," she said while grabbing the box and starting toward her bedroom. "I'll be back in just a few moments."

9

"I'm so sorry," Gwen said, tears running down her face.

"It's okay," Ian said. "It was an accident."

Gwen wiped at her eyes with a napkin.

"And really it was my fault," he continued, carefully putting his arms around her. "I shouldn't have tried to hold you down like that."

"Not your fault," she said, voice muffled by his shoulder.

His arms squeezed, her own body stiffening a bit, which he must have felt because he quickly loosened his arms.

"No, don't," she said, sensing him about to let go completely. "Keep holding me."

His arms stayed around her.

10

Tabby's eyes went wide as Dee rejoined her a few minutes after disappearing into the bedroom, the elf costume she had donned one that looked completely ridiculous to her when viewed in the mirror with her adult eyes, but seemed magical to those of a nine-year-old.

"You're an elf!" Tabby said.

"That's right!" Dee replied.

"Just like the ones at the mall."

Exactly like them, Dee said to herself, the outfits being from the same supplier that the mall used. "Only I work at the bookstore instead of the mall."

"Does Santa know I've been a good girl this year?" Tabby asked, a very serious tone encasing the words.

"He does, and that's why you will get all sorts of fun presents."

Tabby beamed while bouncing in the chair.

Dee smiled but then saw a large, coffee-table-like book that was sitting next to Tabby on the side table, one that she hoped Tabby hadn't looked at given that it was nothing but crime scene photos, her own eyes having been shocked by some of the images while flipping through it the night before.

"Can we go show Mommy and Daddy?" Tabby asked.

"Not just yet. We will wait until they come up."

Tabby nodded.

"Until then, why don't you tell me all the things you want for Christmas, just so I can make sure Santa is up to date."

11

Ian stared at Gwen as she made them some fresh coffee, his mind having trouble accepting how okay everything now seemed. It felt false. Like the calm within the eye of a storm, one that wasn't going to last very long.

But maybe that was what was to be expected; maybe that was the norm with something like this. And if they could simply get through things this year, next year would be better, as would the one after it.

"What are you thinking?" she asked, catching him off guard.

"That it has been a long time since you made me coffee," he said, the statement completely ridiculous.

"Liar," she said.

He smiled and then rebounded the question to her. "What are *you* thinking about?"

"Honestly, last night. And I would bet money that you are too."

"It's hard not to," he admitted.

"Yeah."

"Do you think we should have waited?"

"Waited?" she asked.

"Until after the holidays to do...*it*."

"You mean like scheduling it on a calendar and saying this is the day that we will start having sex again?" she asked.

"I...I...I guess not. That would have just been weird, and too much like..." His voice faded.

"I think last night was the way it needed to happen," she said after a few seconds. "It was completely organic. Felt right. Natural. And"—she reached out and took his hand—"it was great."

"Was it?" he asked.

"Wasn't it?" she asked, a frown appearing.

"Yes, it was great. Like really, really, really great. I just wasn't sure if you really..." He felt his face turning red. "Since you typically can't really...so you enjoyed it?"

She smiled. "I forgot how cute you get when talking about naughty stuff."

Embarrassment hit, his eyes looking down at her hand rather than into her eyes.

"Yes," she said. "I enjoyed it. A lot."

He looked up and met her eyes once again.

"And if it wasn't for this stupid unwelcome visitor that it ushered in, I think I would have woken you up in a completely different fashion." She made a "come here" gesture with her finger, urging him to lean in.

He did, their lips locking, her tongue probing, and then pain exploded, her nose having pressed right into one of his wounds.

12

"Mommy! Daddy! Dee is an elf!" Tabby said.

"I see that," Ian said, blinking with surprise at Dee's outfit, his eyes struggling to avoid certain areas where the thin fabric had been stretched to the point of no return.

He glanced at Gwen, who was simply staring.

"The ears are just pretend though," Tabby added.

Ian nodded. "I was going to say, I don't remember them being so pointy."

Dee gave a polite chuckle.

"We're going to be heading back," Ian said. "Thanks for watching her for a bit."

"No problem. Anytime."

"When are we going to get some pie?" Tabby asked.

"Right now," Ian said. He turned to Gwen. "The bakery on the corner should be open by now, right?"

Gwen didn't reply.

"I think so," Dee said, jumping in.

"Can Dee come too?" Tabby asked, grabbing Dee's hand and pulling her through the apartment doorway.

Dee stumbled, one hand going to the doorframe to catch herself while the other one tried to tug free of the grip, pulling Tabby back toward her.

"No!" Gwen cried, grabbing Tabby and yanking her away from Dee.

Startled, Ian watched as Gwen backed away, her arms locked around Tabby, who was way too big to be lifted like that, the weight and struggles causing her to stumble backward toward the stairs.

Ian lunged, right hand getting Gwen's shoulder while the other grabbed the collar of her jacket, stopping their backward momentum while forcing them toward the opposite corner, Tabby breaking free and running to Dee while Gwen bounced into the wall, her body sliding down to the floor, tears flowing, her arms quickly wrapping around her knees while her face buried itself.

"Take her inside," Ian urged to Dee while waving a hand toward the apartment.

Dee nodded and guided Tabby inside so that she could close the door on the scene.

Horrified, Ian stared down at Gwen for a few seconds and then got down onto the ground with her, his arms once again going around her in an awkward embrace, her body not resisting this time around.

EIGHT

I

"It was perfect," Zoey said. "She had him in her room twenty-five minutes after sitting down next to him at the bar, and then slipped me his key card within an hour."

"And the laptop?" Val asked.

"Piece of cake. I was in and out. Should know everything there is to know by tonight, and will send everything over to the client tomorrow."

"Excellent."

"What about you?" she asked. "Make any progress with your pointless investigation?"

"Not really, but I did make a life-changing discovery yesterday."

"Life-changing?" Zoey questioned.

"Big time."

"What?"

"Peaberry coffee beans."

"Peaberry coffee beans?"

"Yes, and before you ask, they are not the ones that are pooped out by monkeys."

"What the fuck are you talking about?"

"You've never heard of poop coffee?"

"No! And now I think I'm going to be sick."

"My bad," he said. "But no joke, Dee introduced me to some coffee that is like the best-tasting coffee I have ever had."

"I'm so happy for you," she said, sarcasm heavy. "Wait, Dec introduced you?"

"Yep. I stopped by the bookstore and totally wooed her."

"Wooed her."

"I did."

"Jesus Christ."

He laughed.

"Seriously though, why in the world did you even bother going in there? You trying to move in on her now that she has dumped her boyfriend?"

"Ha! Not a chance."

"Then why?"

"I'm not exactly sure. Figured it might stir things up a bit. See if she knows more than she has let on about Ian and the kidnapping. And maybe the cameras."

"So basically you're bored off your ass and are now trying to create a case where there is no case rather than just sitting around for a month in the middle of nowhere collecting the exorbitant fee you conned Marybeth into paying us."

"Yep."

"And the results of this were…?"

"A life-changing experience involving coffee."

"Okay, I'm hanging up now."

"Actually, something interesting did happen after I left the bookstore."

"Oh."

"Both Sam and Ian showed up within like fifteen minutes."

"So?"

"Why would she call them right after I left?"

"You think she called them?"

"Why else would they both show up like that?"

"Well, the chief pretty much goes there every day to get coffee and Ian owns the place, so..."

"Ian was spending the day with his family doing Christmas-tree stuff. I spent like forty-five minutes drinking some terrible hot chocolate while watching them picking out the perfect tree. And the chief only goes there for coffee in the mornings, which she had already done, and this was mid-afternoon."

"Okay, it is a bit curious. I'll give you that. But I still don't think some giant conspiracy is unfolding with these three."

"Me either, but it is very interesting that she called them right after interacting with a true crime writer that was going to be writing about what happened last year."

"You told her you were a true crime writer?"

"I did."

"You really are trying to sleep with her, aren't you?"

"Zoey."

"Okay, sorry, but seriously, why? We hit this thing from every angle last year, and then again during the summer after Marybeth discovered those stupid online groups. There's nothing there."

"I know, but something feels off. I can't say what. But it's there."

"Because of the cameras?"

"That's part of it. The rest, I don't really know."

"Hmm...well...just be careful, okay?"

"Aww, I knew you cared."

"And I really am hanging up for real this time," she said.

"Okay, talk to you later."

"Yep."

Call ended, Val once again headed toward the local diner

that he had been eating most of his meals at, one that had felt special during his once-a-month visits to retrieve the camera files but now was already starting to seem dull.

2

"What kind of pie you going to get?" Dee asked.

"Pumpkin!" Tabby announced.

"Oooh, I love pumpkin pie."

"You do?"

"I do. And I'm pretty sure this place has the best."

Tabby processed that for a bit and then asked, "Did we play a mean trick on Mommy?"

"What? No."

"Daddy says last year some people played a mean trick on her and that was why she got scared at the mall. And now she got scared again."

Dee wasn't sure how to reply to this, mostly because she knew that whatever she said could become very significant in the mind of the nine-year-old.

"Santa stuff scares Mommy," Tabby added.

Dee nodded. "It sure does, but soon it won't."

"Really?" she asked.

"Yep. But it will take some—" She stopped, her eyes seeing the Closed sign on the bakery front door.

Tabby saw it too, the disappointed look on her face one that tugged at Dee's heartstrings.

"You know what, this isn't a problem because I know an even better place that has pie," Dee said, turning them back toward the bookstore.

"You do?" Tabby asked, skepticism present.

"I do, but we will have to drive there."

"But you said this place has the best pie in town."

"That's true, but this other place has the best pie in the county, which means it is even better."

"Ohhhhh!"

3

Val sipped his coffee from the chipped cream-colored mug and grimaced, the beverage that had tasted fine during previous visits to the diner now seemingly awful given the quality brew he had been introduced to by Dee. It was like going back to soda with corn syrup after drinking stuff with real cane sugar. It just no longer worked.

Fortunately the food was better, the plate before him sporting a classic diner breakfast consisting of fried eggs, potatoes, bacon, and white toast glistening with melted butter.

A side order of pancakes was present as well, a small metal carafe of warm syrup waiting to be poured over the stack.

4

Dee smiled as Tabby's eyes went wide upon seeing the display case that acted like a semi-border in the waiting area of the diner near the college, its shelves lined with cakes, pies, and cookies of every imaginable type.

"Two," Dee said as the hostess gave her an inquiring look.

The hostess nodded and then looked at her chart before asking if they wanted a booth or table.

"Booth please," Dee said while glancing into the dining area behind the host stand, surprise at how many vacant tables were present arriving. That would probably change soon as the various churches started letting out, their members filtering in, memories of her own family frequently coming here with other church friends for brunch playing across her mind.

"Right this way," the hostess said.

Dee looked over toward the dessert display, her voice summoning Tabby, who skipped over to her, a statement on how they had "soooo many to choose from" echoing from her lips followed by a question on if they were having breakfast too.

"Yep. Breakfast and then pie. Or just pie if you want that for breakfast."

"Pancakes," Tabby said.

"Ah, good choice. I might have some too—" Her voice halted, her eyes spotting the writer/private eye guy from the bookstore the day before sitting in a booth near the kitchen, his eyes seemingly focused on a plate full of food.

And then she bumped into the hostess, who had stopped at the booth that had been assigned to them, a startled "sorry" echoing.

5

Val finished his breakfast, cleaning both plates of food while leaving the coffee pretty much untouched following his first tentative sips, the dark liquid already leaving a ring around the inside of the mug from going undisturbed during the twenty minutes it had taken to consume his meal.

Phone in hand, he thumbed through his social media feeds while waiting for his check, and then went over to his email to see if any updates had come in from any of the other investigations he and Zoey had going, the one she had run in Baltimore being a big one while all the others were more mundane things that had been filtered out to their third- and fourth-tier investigators.

While doing this, he considered his own status and the insinuation from Zoey that he was trying to make something out of nothing with this case.

She wasn't wrong.

Pretty spot on actually.

Yet his own understanding of this would not deter him from continuing to keep an eye on things here, the fact being he could not simply sit in the motel room collecting a fee.

If Marybeth was going to insist he continue with this investigation, especially after she had agreed to his ridiculously high Christmas fee, he would continue investigating, even if it all seemed like a waste of time.

Plus, he felt like there was a very slim chance something was going on, and thus he wanted to be in a position to act should that slim chance become a reality.

If he wasn't in position, if he failed to intervene in something that unfolded because he was simply kicking back in his motel room pounding back liquor from the mini-bar while collecting a ridiculously high fee, that would be the end of his career. The end of the firm itself.

And even if it weren't an end to things, it would be something he couldn't live with, a regret that would plague him for the rest of his life.

6

"I'll be right back," Dee said as Tabby continued to color in the various objects on the "kid" placemat that had been put before her, the red crayon one that looked ready for an early retirement after a lifetime of use and abuse by tiny fingers.

"Okay," Tabby said without even glancing up, her tongue caught between her lips as she focused on her masterpiece.

Slipping from the booth, Dee quickly made her way to the

front of the restaurant, pausing a moment at the door to make sure the writer/private eye guy wasn't standing just outside of it for some reason. He wasn't. Instead, he was looking at his phone while walking toward a car, his fingers eventually retrieving a set of keys from his coat pocket.

Dee thumbed open the video camera app on her phone and then held it at her side while slowly walking toward the far end of the lot as if going to a car, the camera angled in such a way as to capture the license plates of all the cars she was walking by, all while noting to herself that given its location in the parking lot, she could have simply snapped a photo from the booth itself given the large window they were sitting next to.

Then again, she had had no idea which car he would be going to, so this had been the best option.

Plates with pancakes, bacon, and sausage were waiting on the table when she returned, Tabby having already soaked her stack with warm syrup.

Between the two plates was the "kid" placemat that Tabby had been working on with the crayon while they waited for their food, Dee realizing that Tabby had not been coloring in the various objects that had been printed upon it. Instead, she had flipped it over to the blank side and drawn a Santa with a happy face.

"I made it for Mommy," Tabby said when Dee asked about it. "So she can see that Santa is nice and that she doesn't have to be scared of him."

"Oh, honey," Dee said, reaching a hand across the table to touch Tabby's shoulder, moisture actually appearing in her own eyes. "That's so sweet."

Tabby beamed while slicing into the pancakes with her knife, fork ready to spear the giant hunk of gooey goodness.

Sadness followed.

Tabby was clearly being impacted by all the drama that

was unfolding, and not just the incidents that she witnessed. She was absorbing everything.

7

Pancakes consumed, Tabby ordered her piece of pie, which earned an "is that okay?" glance from the waitress.

Dee nodded at the glance and then said, "With whipped cream, right?"

"Yes!" Tabby declared.

"Anything else for you, hun?" the waitress asked.

"No thanks," Dee said.

The waitress gave a nod and headed off to get the piece of pie.

Dee pulled out her phone.

"What are you watching?" Tabby asked after a few seconds.

Dee hesitated and then said, "Remember earlier when I had to go outside for a bit?"

"Uh-huh."

"That was because I'm investigating someone and I had to get video of them and their car, which I secretly did with my phone without them knowing."

"Just like Nancy Drew," Tabby said.

"Yes."

"But Nancy Drew doesn't have a phone because she is from the olden days."

Dee smiled at that.

"What is your mystery called?" Tabby asked.

"What do you mean?"

"The one I'm reading next is called *The Clue in the Crumbling Wall*."

"Oh, right. Ummm...mine is called *The Mystery of the Mysterious Writer*."

"Can I help you solve it?"

Dee hesitated.

"Please!"

"Okay, but you have to be very sneaky and careful so that the mysterious writer never knows what you're doing."

"Okay."

"The mysterious writer drives a blue car. So anytime you see a blue car I need you to write down where you saw it and at what time. I'll be doing the same thing. We will then compare notes and mark on a map all the places the mysterious writer visited."

"I'm going to need a secret notebook," Tabby said, a very serious tone appearing.

"We can grab one from the bookstore," Dee said.

"And a secret hiding spot for it so we don't get caught."

"Yes," Dee said, trying not to chuckle.

"The basement has lots of hiding spots."

"Basements usually do."

"That's where Mommy hides things."

"Oh," Dee said, hesitation arriving as she debated giving that thread a pull. Then, "What kind of things?"

"Weird cameras."

"Weird cameras?"

Tabby nodded. "And a scary DVD."

"A scary DVD?"

"Of Santa hurting Mommy."

8

For lack of a better idea, and hoping to score a good cup of coffee after that disgusting stuff from the diner, Val headed to the bookstore, only to find that it was closed, which was odd given that it normally would have been open for an hour by now.

Adding to the oddity was that Gwendolyn's little sports car was parked in the rear area in the employee/resident parking area for the building, while Dee's rusting sedan was nowhere to be seen.

Typically this would mean that Gwendolyn was running the shop while Dee was at school, but given that it was Sunday and the store was closed, the car being there made no sense.

Unless Gwendolyn was there and had simply forgotten to unlock the door?

Heading back around to the front of the building, he stepped up to the store window and pressed his face to the glass, his eyes able to scan the small cafe-like area and the coffee counter before the chaotic mess of oddly placed bookshelves and randomly setup Christmas decorations beyond blocked his view into the deeper regions of the store.

A sound behind him.

He turned just in time to see a patrol vehicle rolling to a stop in one of the angled parking spots in front of the bookstore.

Start walking away?

No.

That would simply seem odd given that they had clearly seen him with his face pressed up to the glass. Plus, he had a feeling he knew what this was. The chief had stopped by for her regularly scheduled cup of morning coffee.

Now the question was, would she be surprised by the door being locked?

9

. . .

Sam eyed the man that was standing by the display window as she stepped out of her patrol vehicle, one who had been peering inside the bookstore for several seconds as she rolled up.

"Everything okay?" she asked.

"Yeah, just trying to figure out if they're open," the man said.

"Oh? They should be." She walked up to the front door, eyes noting the Closed sign. "Huh, that's weird."

"My thoughts exactly," the man said. "Was thinking maybe they forgot to unlock it or something, but it doesn't look like anyone is inside."

Sam walked up to the display window and peered through the glass.

Lights were on near the counter, lights that would only be on if someone had flipped the switch in there.

She pulled out her phone and called Ian.

Voicemail.

Next she tried Dee.

This call was answered, though not by Dee. Instead, a voice said, "Dee's phone, Tabby speaking."

"Tabby?" Sam asked. "It's Sam. What are you doing with Dee's phone?"

"Dee's driving," Tabby said.

"I see. And where are you guys?"

"We were at the bookstore, but then Mommy got scared because of Dee being an elf and then Daddy threw her against a wall, so we went to get some pie, and now we are—"

Dee's voice was saying something in the background about the phone.

"But you're driving," Tabby said, voice still near the phone.

A second later, "Sam?"

"Dee," Sam said, stepping away from the man who had been peering into the bookstore window. "What in the world is going on? Is Gwen okay?"

"She's fine, though things were a bit crazy this morning."

"Sounds like it. Where are you?"

"I took Tabby to get some pie so that Ian and Gwen could have some time to themselves. We're now on our way back to the bookstore."

"Okay, I'm out front. Let me in once you get here."

"Will do."

Call ended, Sam walked back up to the man, who was still by the display window. "Sorry, looks like the store will be closed for a while. Staffing issues. You know how it is. No one wants to work these days."

"Bummer. They have the best coffee in town."

"That they do, though the bakery down on the corner has some good stuff too and should be open as of"—she checked the phone—"ten minutes ago."

"Guess I will give them a try," he said. "Thanks."

"Yep."

With that, the man started walking down the sidewalk toward the corner bakery, while Sam stood waiting for Dee to arrive, her fingers once again trying Ian's phone, which once again went right to voicemail.

10

Val headed to the corner bakery but didn't go inside, instead slipping across the street to where his car was parked so that he could sit inside and keep an eye on the bookstore, the call the chief had made clearly revealing more than a simple "staffing issue" given the concern that had momentarily crossed her face. The fact that she now stood by the front door of the bookstore, waiting, also told him something was going on.

Five minutes came and went before the front door of the bookstore was opened, the chief quickly slipping inside.

Had his vantage point been better, he would have been able to see who had opened it, but given his angle, such had not been possible.

One thing he was able to see, however, was that the Closed sign was still in place.

11

"He didn't throw her against the wall," Dee explained. "He was trying to stop her from falling backward down the stairs while struggling with Tabby and sort of flung her while twisting her away from the stairs."

Sam nodded. "So, nothing abusive as far as you could see?"

"No, not at all. He was simply trying to save her from falling."

"And then after that?"

"They held each other for a long time while sitting in the corner. About ten minutes later, Ian asked if I could keep Tabby distracted for a few hours while they headed back to the house, which is when our quest for a piece of pie began."

"Tell me again about the scratches on his face," Sam instructed.

Dee sighed. "Gwen was having a nightmare or something and was thrashing around. He tried to stop her from falling off the bed. She scratched him."

"And then he came here with Tabby, she followed, and then the incident upstairs happened where he had to stop her from falling down the stairs."

"Yep."

"Okay."

Nothing else followed for a few seconds.

Then, "How's Tabby holding up?"

Dee considered that for a bit and said, "Honestly, she seems fine."

"That's good. Kids are pretty resilient—or so I've been told." Sam was silent for a moment. "Are you going to be opening the store today, or just kind of chilling with Tabby until you hear from them?"

"Just chilling."

"Probably for the best."

"Yeah."

Sam slapped a knee and stood up. "Okay, I'm off. Thanks for filling me in and setting my mind at ease."

"No problem. You want some coffee to go?"

"Nah, I'm good."

"Let me guess, you're heading over to Ian and Gwen's now," Dee said.

Sam eyed her for a moment and then nodded. "I have to."

Dee frowned.

"Don't worry, I'll play it cool. They won't think you called me to go check on them or anything."

"Thanks."

Sam nodded and then started toward the front door, her eyes spotting Tabby curled up in the display area.

"Hey, Tabby, what in the world are you doing up in there?"

"Working on a case," Tabby said.

"A case, really?"

"Yep. It's called *The Mystery of the Mysterious Writer*."

"*The Mystery of the Mysterious Writer*?" Sam questioned.

"Yep. He's in the blue car over there. See?"

Sam joined Tabby in the display area, carefully maneuvering herself around so that she didn't knock over any of the "Christmas Reads" that had been set up in the winter wonderland scene, and looked out toward where Tabby was pointing.

Sure enough, a blue car was sitting in one of the angled spots across the street, in front of a resale furniture place that would not be open until around noon that day. Same with the barbershop and travel agency on either side of it.

"Hey, Dee," Sam called.

"Yeah?" Dee replied.

"Come here for a second."

Dee emerged from the rear of the store where the two had been talking and asked, "What's up?"

"You have Tabby watching for a mysterious writer in a blue car?"

"What?" Dee asked, her attempt at momentary confusion a complete failure. "Oh, that's a bit of a game we're playing."

"It's like Nancy Drew, just not in olden times," Tabby added.

"I see," Sam said. Then, thinking about the man who had been peering through the storefront window earlier, asked, "You still have the video of the writer from yesterday?"

"I do."

"Let me see it again."

Dee cued up the video on her phone and handed it over.

Sam watched the short video clip, thumb pausing it at a point where the writer guy was facing the counter. Sure enough, it was the same guy from earlier.

"How'd you know he was in a blue car?" Sam asked.

"Spotted him at the diner this morning and followed him out to his car," Dee said.

"While you were with—" Rather than say her name, Sam simply nodded toward Tabby, who was still up in the display window.

"Yeah, but it was totally coincidental. I wasn't driving around looking for him while with her or anything."

"And that's the same car out there?" Sam asked.

Dee got up into the display area and looked at the car Tabby had spotted down the street. "Looks like it. Hand me back my phone for a second."

Sam did.

Dee worked her thumb on the phone screen and then glanced back out at the car and then back at the phone. A slight nod arrived, followed by, "Yep, that's totally him."

"Okay," Sam said, contemplating things for a second. "Hey, Tabby?"

"Yeah?"

"*The Case of the Mysterious Writer* is over, okay? You did a fantastic job."

"It's called *The Mystery of the Mysterious Writer*."

"*Mystery of the Mysterious Writer*," Sam said. "Got it. We're all done with that game now, right?"

Tabby looked up at Dee, who gave a nod.

"We can figure out a new mystery to solve now, okay?" Dee said.

"Okay. But first we need to celebrate with a hot fudge sundae."

"Hot fudge sundae?" Dee asked. Then, "Oh, right."

Sam gave an inquisitive look toward Dee.

"Nancy Drew," Dee said. "That's how they always ended the books."

"Ah, okay."

12

Val wished he had a camera with audio set up inside the bookstore to find out what was being discussed, the chief being let in while the store remained closed a very curious situation.

Who was it that had let her inside?

Was it Gwendolyn?

If so, why was she inside with the place closed up when it was supposed to be open?

And where was Dee?

Where would she go on a Sunday morning?

Had she suddenly found religion?

A chuckle echoed within his mind, followed by Zoey's voice once again chiding him for trying to turn all of this into something it wasn't.

And then the chief was leaving the bookstore, only she did not get into her car. Instead, she started across the street, her steps angling her toward where he was parked.

"Fuck," he said to himself, momentarily considering and then quickly dismissing the possibility of trying to drive away.

She arrived at his driver-side window, his body having repositioned itself into the driver seat, a realization that he should have gone into the bakery for a cup of coffee so that he could hold the cup up as a prop being made.

"How's the book coming?" the chief asked.

"Book?" he asked.

"The one you told Dee you were writing about the Robinson family?"

"Ah, that book."

"Yes, that book."

"I think the young lady—Dee, you said her name was?—is mistaken. I simply said I was *thinking* about writing a book about them."

"Just thinking about it?"

"That's right."

"And have you made a decision yet?"

"I'm not sure. It is a very interesting situation. Lots of questions being asked in various groups online. Were they really serial killers, or was it just a one-off thing—a sudden snap with reality that led to the abduction?" He paused to see if she would say anything, and when she didn't he added, "And then there are the other theories, ones involving the husband and a bookstore employee. Were they behind everything so that they could eventually pursue their relationship without the threat of losing out on all the wife's money? Could that be why the bookstore employee suddenly called the husband to the store following the sudden appearance of a writer who was snooping around asking questions? Actually"—he put a finger to his lip as if in deep thought—"she called both the police chief and the husband to the bookstore after that, which makes things even more curious given that the chief of police and the husband used to be an item before he headed out east, where he eventually met and fell in love with a young lady named Gwendolyn, wouldn't you say?"

"I'd say speculation like that could easily lead to lawsuits that would ruin a writer's future."

"In this day and age, lawsuits tend to have the opposite impact. In fact, the notoriety could be the breakthrough my career needs to launch me up into the big leagues."

"Good luck with that."

"Want to tell me what happened this morning?" he asked.

"What makes you think something happened this morning?" she asked, clearly caught off guard by the question.

"Oh, I don't know. Bookstore is closed, yet someone was clearly inside and let you in. And now you're out here, asking my purpose for being here when a few minutes ago you had no idea who I was, which means someone clearly pointed me out to you from within the store." He gave an exaggerated pause. "Very curious."

"Curious indeed," she said. "I suppose I should be a bit more careful in how I approach things given your investigative skills. Tell me, where are you from? I'm picking up a bit of an East Coast accent. New York maybe?"

Val smiled and said, "Oh, look at the time. I best be off. I really did just stop by here for some coffee, but since it doesn't look like they are going to be opening anytime soon, I'll just head back to my motel and start my writing for the day. Give my best to Dee, her lover, and his wife."

. . .

"What's wrong?" Dee asked, her heart still racing from the sudden pounding Sam had made against the bookstore door a few minutes after leaving.

Sam didn't reply right away, her legs simply taking her over to one of the chairs in the cafe area so that she could sit down.

"Sam?" Dee asked, concern now present.

"I need some water," Sam said.

"Water? Of course."

Dee grabbed a bottle from the little cooler behind the counter and brought it over to her.

Sam twisted the top off and took a long swig.

Dee waited, body eventually slipping into a chair across from her.

"That writer guy—if he really is a writer—knows way too much about things and is paying way too much attention to all of us for this just to be a whim."

"I told you," Dee said.

"I know you did."

"So, you think he might be the private investigator?"

"I'm not sure on that yet, but I'm going to certainly look into him. Find out everything there is to know."

NINE

1

"I don't want to talk about it," Gwen said.

"We have to talk about it," Ian replied.

"I just panicked a bit."

"You almost went down the stairs," he said. "With Tabby in your arms."

Gwen simply stared out the windshield, lips tight.

Just Dee.

Dressed like an elf.

Nothing more.

"And this morning you clawed my face because of a dream," he continued while signaling for a turn.

Just Dee.

Not a real elf.

She wasn't taking Tabby.

"I was just trying to protect her," Gwen said, voice soft.

"From what?" Ian demanded.

"One year he took our little sister," Jessica had voiced while

sitting with her in the cold cellar room. *"Mommy was so upset that she started hitting Daddy."*

The car came to a stop.

Gwen blinked.

They were home.

Ian said something.

She turned toward him, eyes noting the emptiness between them.

"Where's Tabby?" she asked, panic building.

"She's with Dee," Ian said.

Elf!

Taking Tabby!

"No! No! No!" Gwen cried, hands fumbling with the seatbelt catch.

"Honey! Stop!"

The seatbelt released, her hand quickly reaching for the door latch.

Something gripped her wrist, a shackle of some kind, pulling her.

Toward the fireplace.

Legs kicking.

No! No! No!

She fought, arms flailing, fingernails clawing.

Something shattered, pain exploding up her right arm.

Cold air.

It suddenly enveloped her.

She tried running away, only for her feet to go out from under her.

Thunk!

Bright flashes of light exploded all around her.

A voice.

Calling her name.

She began to crawl, warmth spreading across her face.

Pain arrived, and then nothing but darkness.

. . .

2

Voices.
 All around her.
Then a bump, her body bouncing.
Someone cussed.
She blinked.
A figure was standing over her but not focused on her, their face looking somewhere beyond her.
Santa hat!
They were taking her to the North Pole!
To Santa and the toymakers.
No! No!
She tried to grab the person, her fingers feeling odd. Almost lifeless.
Another attempt.
This time her action got the person's attention.
It was a woman.
She looked down at her, concern present.
A dull throb.
In her head.
And her arms.
She tried taking a breath, only to start gagging.
Voices once again were echoing, as well as other sounds she could not place.
And then she saw Ian.
Or thought she did.
He was following them.
Why?
Had he given her to them?
Was Mother right?
No!
No!
No!

She started kicking, her legs working better than her arms.
More voices.
Shouting.
Something cold touched her upper arm.
Alcohol hit her senses, followed by a brief sting.
And then she was floating away.

3

Val wasn't sure what he would discover—if anything—by driving to Ian and Gwendolyn's house, but seeing a driveway full of blood wasn't what he had been expecting.

It started in the center of the pavement and then trailed over to a small snowbank along the right edge, the pattern looking as if someone had suffered some sort of devastating impact in the center of the driveway and then crawled to the snowbank, blood oozing the entire time.

After that...

No answers arrived.

The blood trail simply ended there on the small snowbank.

Anyone home?

He rang the doorbell several times and then pounded on the door until his knuckles felt ready to burst, all to no avail.

Next he walked around to the right of the property and took a peek into the garage through the window.

Empty.

He went back to his car and sat in it for a while.

Blood on the driveway.

Gwendolyn's car at the bookstore, which was closed.

A chief who seemed concerned about something while being let into the bookstore that was closed, only to come out a few minutes later to confront him while parked across the street.

Something had clearly unfolded during the morning hours. Something problematic.

And he had no idea what it was.

4

Sam bolted from the bookstore to her car, a *whoop whoop* of her siren alerting anyone on the street that she was backing up, and then gunned it toward the hospital, which was a good fifteen-minute drive even with the lights and siren clearing the way.

Memories of another drive to the hospital flowed into her mind, that trip a bit more harrowing given that snow had been falling, the lights and siren pointless on the empty roads, her main concern being the slick surfaces that could easily put her into a ditch.

She had had Gwen in the car that day, her realization of who the crazed woman in the holding cell was after getting the odd call from the Chapman family resulting in her quickly ushering Gwen into her car and heading to the hospital, a frantic call to Ian being made while on the way.

No snow was falling during today's race to the hospital, though the surfaces were slick, the county being very frugal with its use of salt this season given that they had gone over budget last season and thus didn't have enough money in the budget to stock the amounts that they were expecting to need. She also did not have Gwen in the vehicle this time around, nor had she been the one to call Ian, the roles seemingly reversed given that he had called her about the situation and then was the one to race to the hospital with a crazed Gwen in the car.

"Move! Move! Move!" she shouted at the cars that were

failing to yield fast enough for her, the slick roads likely to blame as they carefully eased over to the gravel shoulder.

Ian had given her no details on why he was taking Gwen to the hospital, his voice simply stating there had been an incident in the driveway and that he wasn't going to wait for emergency responders to arrive.

Dee had been standing near her during this call, her own panic growing as she heard the one-sided conversation. Questions had followed as Sam hurried from the store, questions that Sam did not answer. Instead, she had told her to stay with Tabby until further notice.

5

Ian didn't realize he was covered in blood until he met up with Sam outside of the emergency room, her gasp at the sight of him as well as the questions on if he was okay and what happened causing him to look down at himself.

"It's not mine," he mumbled, taking off his jacket, the shirt beneath blood free. "Gwen broke her nose."

"Broke her nose?" Sam asked. "How?"

"She slipped on some ice while getting out of the truck and smashed her face along the doorframe," he said.

Sam stared at him, the look one he had seen before back when she was trying to assess whether he had had anything to do with Gwen's disappearance.

Annoyance followed until he remembered the claw marks across his face and how this all must look to Sam.

"This"—he motioned to his face—"was something else."

"Tell me," Sam said.

Ian did, leaving nothing out, the words flowing from him without pause, starting with waking up to her screaming, to being scratched, to the incident by the stairs above the bookstore, to the sudden panic in the truck that had caused her to slip on ice, to his struggles in getting her back into the truck and racing to the hospital.

Exhaustion hit.

Hard.

He took a seat.

Sam stayed standing for several seconds, clearly processing what he had just told her and what her response should be.

He waited.

"This isn't good," she said.

Ian chuckled. Not with humor, but simply as an odd type of agreement.

"I know," he added.

"She needs help," Sam said.

Ian nodded.

"Like serious legit help from trained professionals," Sam continued.

"I know, but..."

"But?" Sam questioned, crossing her arms.

"One thing at a time. We'll focus on the nose for now and then figure out what to do."

Sam didn't reply to that.

Ian silently sighed.

If they could just get beyond Christmas. Things would be better. Once the holiday came and went and they had ten months of normality before the next holiday onslaught, she would be fine. They all would.

His phone buzzed.

It was Dee. Again. She had called him several times during the last half hour—ever since his call to Sam about taking Gwen to the hospital.

He considered that for a moment and then asked, "Were you at the bookstore when I called you?"

"I was," Sam said. "Stopped by for some coffee."

He nodded.

"That was when I discovered the store was closed, which surprised me, but then Dee let me in. Along with Tabby."

"So you already had a pretty good idea of how fucked-up today had become," he noted.

"I did."

6

Dee tried calling Ian five times following Sam's abrupt departure before giving up and dropping herself into a reading chair, thoughts on trying to text him instead being vetoed.

She would simply wait for him to call. Or to text. He would have to at some point. After all, she had Tabby with her.

Speaking of...

She pushed herself up from the chair so she could go check on Tabby. No concern or worry was present as she strolled the various bookstore rooms looking for the nine-year-old. It was simple curiosity. And maybe a desire not to be alone at the moment, thereby making it less likely that her mind would dwell upon all the craziness that had unfolded that morning.

Tabby was in the fantasy room, sitting on the floor beneath a framed piece of Frank Frazetta artwork, a notebook in her lap, pencil in hand, the yellow Nancy Drew book she had found earlier sitting on the floor, seemingly discarded.

"Whatcha doing, Tabs?" Dee asked.

"Adding notes to the case we're working," Tabby said.

"We're finished with that case."

"But Sam came back inside and said that the mysterious writer was spying on you and that she is going to try to learn everything she can about him."

Dee nodded. "She did say that, didn't she?"

"Uh-huh," Tabby said.

Dee wasn't sure where to go from there.

"Why is he spying on you?" Tabby asked.

"Well, you see, that's the mystery I was trying to solve," Dee said.

"It is?"

"Yep," Dee said, nodding. "He has been sneaking around asking questions and being very *mysterious*, which is why our case was called *The Mystery of the Mysterious Writer*."

"Sam said he might not really be a writer."

Dee nodded. "Sometimes people say they're writers when they really aren't to cover up the real reason they are asking questions."

"She said he might work for Grandma."

Oh jeez.

"Why doesn't Grandma like my daddy?" Tabby asked.

"What makes you think she doesn't like your daddy?"

"I heard her talking to Mommy while I was playing in the wardrobe during Thanksgiving."

Playing in the wardrobe, Dee said to herself. *Because of course she would be. Probably looking for a doorway to Narnia or something.*

"She said you and Daddy wanted to get rid of Mommy and take all her money so that you can have lots of sex, which made Mommy angry because she says that you and Daddy don't do that."

And never will.

"I see," Dee said, once again unsure if she should try to press for more info. Then, *fuck it*. "What else did you hear?"

"Grandma wants me and Mommy to live with her so that Mommy can get better and I can go to a proper school. But I like my school. I have lots of friends, and have my singing group, and Mrs. Patrick lets me draw in my art pad when I finish with my times tables."

"Did you know I had Mrs. Patrick in the third grade as well?"

Eyes wide. "You did?"

"Yep."

"Wow. She's *really* old."

Dee chuckled. "So it sounds like you don't really want to move back to Long Island and live with your grandma and go to a different school."

"No way, José!"

Dee hesitated once again and then asked, "Did your grandma say anything else? Maybe more stuff about me and your daddy?"

"Like what?"

"I don't know. Anything?"

Tabby thought for a second and then shook her head.

"What about your mommy?" Dee pressed. "Did she say anything about me and your daddy?"

"No, she just got upset because Grandma started showing her pictures."

"Of me and your daddy?" Dee asked, the earlier comment about pictures of them still hovering in her mind.

Tabby frowned. "No. I think these were whores."

Dee blinked. "The what?"

"Whores."

"Whores?"

Tabby nodded.

Dee did not know what to make of that, the word one she never expected to hear from Tabby. "Your grandma was showing your mom pictures of your dad with whores?"

Another nod.

Her phone buzzed.

Ian.

Finally.

She stepped out of the fantasy room and answered it with: "Hey, what in the world is going on?"

"I'm at the hospital," Ian said. "With Gwen."

"I know. Sam was here when you called her. What happened?"

"She fell while getting out of the truck. Broke her nose."

"Oh fuck, is she okay?"

"Yeah, but she'll be in the hospital for a while and I need to stay with her. Do you think you can watch Tabby for the rest of the day?"

"Of course, no problem."

"And if you want to take her to the house and watch her there, might be easier given that she has all her stuff there."

"Okay, yeah, I'll do that."

"We can just leave the bookstore closed for the day."

"Okay, yeah, that's probably best."

Nothing else was said, the call coming to an end.

Dee stared off into space for a moment, marveling over all the craziness that had sprung up, and then shook herself back into the present and returned to the fantasy room.

Tabby was still sitting on the floor, notebook in hand, though she was no longer writing anything.

"I have a question," Dee said. "These pictures of your daddy with the whores. Are these hidden in the coal room too?"

Tabby made a face and then nodded.

Dee considered that for several seconds and then said, "Change of plans. We're going to head back to your house for the rest of the day."

7

"Alexa, play 'Whirlybird'!" Tabby shouted within seconds of stepping through the front door, her body spinning with excitement as the song began echoing from the nearest speaker, arms out like a helicopter, hands coming dangerously close to a vase with a cheerful flower arrangement that stood upon an entryway table.

Oh god, Dee said to herself.

She had completely forgotten about Tabby's earlier enthusiasm for one of the most annoying songs ever created, and the possibility of it being played over and over again once they were at the house.

This led to thoughts on how long she would be here.

All day?

Overnight?

The second one didn't seem likely given that the hospital wasn't that far away and Ian would probably be booted from the place once visiting hours were over, yet the possibility was still one to consider.

Not that it would be a problem.

She had stayed overnight several times in the past without issue.

Tonight would be no different—if it came to that.

Would they actually keep Gwen overnight?

For a broken nose?

Dee had no idea on that one, her only experience with broken bones having been when she fractured her left pinky on the playground at school during an intense game of Four Square.

That had been an in-and-out type of thing, one that didn't even require a hospital room.

"Dee!" Tabby called. "Come see the Christmas tree!"

"Okay!" Dee replied.

She made her way to the family room.

"Wow!" she said. "It's huge!"

"I helped put it up," Tabby advised, a look of satisfaction on her face. "Daddy held it while I screwed it in."

"That's a tough job."

"I got all sticky. Daddy did too. And then we attacked Mommy and made her sticky."

Dee grinned, mind picturing the prim and proper Gwen

getting all gooey from sap. Why this amused her, she did not know, but it did.

"Have you ever played find the pickle?" Tabby asked.

"Um..." *What the fuck is that?* "No, I don't think I have."

"Daddy taught it to me."

Oh jeez.

"On Christmas morning there will be a pickle ornament on the tree and whoever finds it first gets an extra present."

"Ah, I see."

Tabby went to a side table and picked up a small ornament that, sure enough, looked like a tiny pickle. "On Christmas Santa hides it, so we have to remember to leave it where he can see it. But today we can hide it ourselves and then try to find it."

"Oh, okay."

"We can't open any presents yet though," Tabby said, looking down at some of the gifts that were already waiting beneath the tree, a sense of longing and anticipation present.

Dee had a feeling discussions about getting to open things early had taken place at some point in recent days. Probably a few times actually.

"Do you want to hide it first?" Tabby asked, holding out the pickle.

"How about you hide it first so that all I have to do is find it, and then after that I will know how to play and can hide it for you."

"Okay." Genuine excitement appeared. "You need to leave the room."

Perfect! "Shout to me when you're ready."

Tabby nodded.

Dee left the room, heading straight for the basement stairs, mind trying to recall if she had ever even been in the coal room before.

"Ready!" Tabby called before Dee even made it to the stairway.

"Are you sure?" Dee called back.

"Yes!"

Dee sighed and returned to the family room.

Fifteen minutes later she asked, "Is it even on the tree?"

"Uh-huh," Tabby said, grinning.

"What happens if I give up?" Dee asked.

"When Daddy gives up I get to stay up for an hour after my bedtime."

"An hour?" Dee asked, skepticism dominating her voice.

Tabby nodded.

"Well, I probably won't be here for your bedtime, so we will have to think up something else, okay?"

"Okay!"

"Now, where is it?"

Tabby pointed to the top of the tree, which was way beyond her reach.

"Up there?" Dee questioned. "How?"

"I tossed it like this," she said, demonstrating her tossing skill.

"Oh, sneaky, sneaky, sneaky."

Tabby beamed.

Grabbing a chair, Dee got up so that she was eye level with the top of the tree and sure enough, the pickle was resting in a little crook of short pine branches.

"I never would have found that," Dee said, stepping back down from the chair, tiny pickle in hand.

"That's because you underestimated me," Tabby declared.

"I did. Now let's see if you can find it when I hide it."

The answer to that was yes.

Within seconds.

Of course, Dee wasn't trying to hide it all that well, but even so, she didn't make it as obvious as it must have been given how quickly Tabby discovered it.

"Okay, this time around, I have to make a phone call, so you go ahead and hide it and when I'm done I will come to the doorway, ask if you're ready, and if you are, I will then try to find it."

"Perfect."

Phone in hand, Dee headed from the room, this time making it all the way into the basement without issue, the phone having been tucked back into her pocket.

8

Gwendolyn's little sports car was still parked in the small lot behind the bookstore, all while the store itself was still closed.

No Ian.

No Dee.

And the chief's car was nowhere to be seen on Main Street, which now was alive with Sunday activity.

Indecision gripped him.

Something odd was going on.

Something that had upset daily routines and kept the bookstore closed well into the workday.

Something that involved bloody sheets tossed into the corner of the basement laundry room as well as blood splattered all across the driveway.

Fuck it.

He opened the back door that led to the rear hallway of the building, which allowed one to access the employee-only doors to all the various businesses on this side of the street, as well as the basement storage areas for those businesses, and—most important for him right now—the stairways to the various apartments up above the stores.

He headed up to Dee's and knocked on the door.

No answer.

Less than a minute later, he was inside, the old door one that could easily be slipped with a credit card while twisting the knob—something he had discovered last winter when she was still an unofficial suspect in the disappearance of Gwendolyn.

9

Despite Dee's frequent explorations of the house while babysitting Tabby or taking care of the rabbits, she had never once been inside the old coal room located at the far end of the cellar, the narrow unassuming door into the room one that she barely remembered seeing even though she must have glanced at it dozens of times while down here watching old DVDs with Tabby, the main finished part of the cellar being the only TV area of the house that had a DVD player hooked up.

The coal room itself was cold and uninviting, the old stone walls reminding her of the cellar in the Robinson house, the only significant difference being that no toilet had been randomly installed in a corner alcove.

A single bare bulb dangled from the ceiling, one that was fairly bright yet somehow didn't do much in regards to illuminating the room itself, the shadows clinging to their areas as if able to repel the light that tried to clear them rather than yielding to it.

The old coal chute was up against the wall on the right, one that she realized sat in an area beneath the garage, which was a part of the house that clearly had not been present at the time when coal was delivered on a regular basis to keep things warm during the winter.

Not much light made it into the coal chute after she pulled open the large iron door, the flashlight app on her phone quickly thumbed on so she could peer inside. No coal was present these days, the coal chute itself no longer having access to the outside world given the garage that had been built over its original delivery point, but there were several items within, the most noticeable ones being gifts that had been wrapped. Ian's name was on all of them, the sizes making them seem like they were hardcover books of some kind. A DVD sat next to the presents. It was in a paper sleeve that was simply labeled with the word "Treatments." Not far from the DVD was a basic manila file folder that also had the word "Treatments" on it, one that sat atop a leather binder with the name "Allied Investigations" printed in the center.

Dee opened it.

Several pictures were inside, each one depicting Ian with a young well-dressed woman in a bar or restaurant setting. Attached to each photo with a paperclip was a sheet of paper listing the woman's name, age, contact info, and the escort company she worked with. Beneath these were notes documenting all the various locations the two were spotted at, each one ending with a statement that declared *No Sexual Activity Observed* along with the investigator's printed name and signature, which was always Valentine Finley.

One of the woman pictured looked familiar to Dee, though she couldn't pinpoint why. Knowing this would bother her until she did figure it out, she took a photo of the woman and all the info that was listed for her. After that, she went ahead and did the same with all the women in the file.

No sexual activity observed...

This note held firm in her mind as she tucked the folder back into the coal chute, a question on why exactly Ian had been seeing these women if sex was not the reason going unanswered.

Next she opened the Treatments folder, its contents nothing but page after page of scribbled notes that she could not really make out. Her ability to read cursive was not all that great to begin with given that she had never had need of the skill after learning it in grade school, but even if it was up to snuff, she would have had a difficult time deciphering what had been put upon these pages.

Folder closed, she tucked it back into the coal chute atop of the Allied Investigations folder, and then, with the DVD in hand, left the coal room and walked over to the TV setup in the finished part of the basement, her eyes having to do a quick search to find the clickers that were necessary to work the TV and DVD player.

Once those were secure, she popped the DVD into the player.

No menu was present, the DVD simply jumping right into things.

10

"Elf costumes?" Zoey asked.

"Yeah," Val said. "And not just one or two, but several, and in two different sizes."

"Hmm."

"And she has only opened and worn one of them, which seems odd."

"Why does that seem odd?"

"If you had ordered a whole bunch of elf costumes, or really any costumes or clothing items, wouldn't you try them on once they arrived?"

"You're thinking they may not all be for her? That she bought some for someone else?"

"Exactly."

"That someone else being Jessica," Zoey said.

Val hesitated. "I don't know."

"But you do know. We both do. They are not hiding Jessica anywhere. It's just not possible."

"I know, but that still leaves a question on why so many

different elf costumes in two different sizes were ordered," he said. "Who are they for?"

"Maybe she simply ordered different sizes just in case one size didn't fit right. Ordering things like that online can be tricky."

"But why order them in the first place? And why were they paid for by Ian?"

"How do you know Ian paid for them?"

"The receipt was still in the box and the credit card listed was the one Ian has linked to the store."

"They listed the credit card number on the receipt?"

"No, just the last four digits. The rest was x'd out, but those last four digits match the store card we have on file."

"Okay. So Dee used the store card to order these elf costumes."

"Which means Ian had to know about her ordering them."

"Maybe they're for work. She'll be dressing like an elf while making coffee and cashing people out. Stores do stupid things like that for the holidays and you did say the place is completely decked out with decorations."

"True."

"And maybe the second set in the different size is for Gwendolyn. After all, she works there too."

"Not a chance," Val said.

"Yeah, okay, I don't see her wearing an elf costume. Not after what happened."

"Which brings me back around to why in the world would Dee be wearing one?" Val said. "Jessica often dressed like an elf whenever she was tormenting Gwendolyn, so Dee dressing like that could totally freak her out."

"Hmm."

"And even if Dee was ignorant of the elf outfits Jessica wore, Ian wouldn't be, and he clearly knows about the purchases, so..." Val let his voice fade, not really needing to complete the line of thought.

"Okay, yeah, that is a bit messed up."

"Big time."

"I still don't buy that Jessica is involved in anything that is going on right now, or that Ian had anything to do with what happened last year."

"What if he wasn't involved last year, but then realized how much better off he would have been if she hadn't escaped?" Val suggested. "Let's face it, his life has not been a good one since her return, what with her constantly freaking out in various places and all the crap he obviously gets from her family and random people who are influenced by all the crazy things that are suggested online. Probably why he deactivated all his social media accounts."

"Hmm, Marybeth did suggest early on that he might be trying to have her committed to a mental hospital in order to get control of all her money," Zoey noted.

"Right! And Dee herself told me that it was Ian's idea to put up all the decorations, which seems really odd to me. And then he dragged her along to pick out a Christmas tree the other day, which she clearly was not enjoying, and from what I've seen when looking through the windows of their house, it's pretty well decked out with decorations too, almost to the point of looking like it belongs in one of those stupid Hallmark Christmas movies."

"Hey now, don't be dissing the Hallmark movies."

"My bad."

"Seriously though, you might be onto something here."

Val grinned.

"Have you checked out the hospital?" she asked.

"No, not yet. That's my next stop."

"Let me know what you find out."

"Will do."

Call ended, he tucked the phone away and took a sip from a bottle of water he had on hand.

After that, he started toward the hospital, his mind starting to play over options on how to find out if Gwendolyn, or someone else from that household, had been admitted.

11

Dee had seen some god-awful things over the years thanks to her fascination with serial killers and attempting to understand their sick and twisted mindsets, but none of that could compare with the horror of what she witnessed on the TV screen in the basement as the DVD revealed its contents.

Even with the TV muted so she didn't have to hear the cries escaping from around the giant rubber gag they had put in Gwen's mouth as she lay strapped to the bed, Dee could barely stand to keep her eyes open, the silent visuals of Gwen's naked body arching up against the restraints while a figure dressed like Santa stood over her unlike anything she had ever seen. The fact that Gwen pissed herself while undergoing this, the glisten as the urine ran down her leg as her body was arched upward upon the bed, only added to the horror.

And this was only the beginning, a quick pause of the screen showing a progress bar that noted she was only a few minutes into a DVD that went on for nearly two hours.

12

Sam had known Ian her entire life and was pretty sure he wouldn't do anything to hurt Gwen, but given the things she had seen during her time in law enforcement, especially with domestic situations, she had to leave room for the possibility that he had snapped and that Gwen's injuries were not caused by a simple slip on some ice.

But had he been the aggressor?

The marks on his face from earlier clearly showed that Gwen had attacked him at some point, and then given Dee's statement about what had unfolded on the landing by her apartment, there was a chance that Gwen had freaked out once again, which had then resulted in Ian striking her in the face as some form of self-defense.

Though he probably would have told her this if that had been the case. After all, he had been very forthcoming about everything else.

He also did not have any marks on his hand, though a single blow to the face would not necessarily leave wounds upon the hand that delivered the blow.

She needed to talk to Gwen.

Hearing from her what had unfolded that day, starting with the scratch marks on Ian's face, would be a big step toward understanding what had unfolded, especially if her story matched up with the various statements Ian and Dee had made.

Talking to her right now was not possible though given the pain medication she had been given, so she gave the hospital instructions to call her once Gwen was ready to talk.

In the meantime, she was running down the plate info on the supposed writer that she had spoken with outside the bookstore, her hope being to get an identity from the rental agency before the day was out so that she could know for sure whether he was just a writer or was in fact the investigator that Gwen's family had looking into things.

What she would do with this information once she had it, she did not know. Her options as a law enforcement officer in regards to his actions were limited unless she could somehow prove he had been inside the Robinson house, which she doubted. But just knowing who he was would be a step in the right direction.

. . .

13

Gwendolyn was checked into the hospital, having been admitted through the emergency room. Val learned this by simply asking at the admitting desk, past experience having taught him that most people in such positions would give out information without even really thinking about it, which was exactly how things played out here.

Facial trauma.

Brought in by her husband.

Injuries considered serious enough to be hospitalized overnight rather than treated and released.

No information on the cause of the facial trauma was offered and most likely not available on the screen the guy was looking at, so Val thanked him and started making his way into the hospital, another inquiry at the main information desk providing him with Gwendolyn's room number up on the third floor.

An elevator bank was not far from that main information desk, Val riding one up and taking a left once it opened.

Ian was actually in the hallway talking to a young lady in a lab coat, his right hand frequently running through his hair.

Val started toward them, his plan being to walk by them and the hospital room Gwendolyn was in, slowing his steps as he did so that he could get a simple visual. Later, once Ian was gone, he would come back and see if he could get a look at her chart, which typically would be near the door or hooked onto the bed.

Ian glanced his way as Val approached.

Val stopped, startled.

Ian looked like he had gone toe-to-toe with a tiger, one side of his face bearing red gouges that glistened with what was likely freshly applied disinfectant.

Shaking away the shock, Val started walking once again,

his eyes glancing in through the open doorway of the hospital room.

Bandages covered Gwendolyn's face.

Knowing this was all he would get at the moment, he continued the rest of the way down the hallway, eventually veering off to the left where another elevator awaited, this one leading down toward the area where the cafeteria would be.

He took the elevator down and made his way back to the emergency room and out the doors, his goal this time being to find Ian's truck, which he figured would be somewhere near the emergency room entrance.

He was right.

It was three rows back from the main doors of the emergency room.

Other spots had opened up near it, his own rental vehicle pulling into one of them so that he could keep an eye on it and see when Ian left.

14

Dee could not get the horrors of what she had seen from the *Treatments* DVD out of her mind as she went about the evening activities with Tabby, guilt frequently arriving because she could tell that despite her outward projections of being interested in whatever it was they were involved in, Tabby knew it was not actually the case.

The fact that Tabby had found the DVD at some point and watched it was also heavy upon her mind, a debate on if she should try talking to her about what she had seen going unresolved as the hours ticked by.

"When are Mommy and Daddy coming home?" Tabby eventually asked.

"Soon," Dee said.

"That's what you said *hours ago*," Tabby pointed out.

The *hours ago* part of that statement was an exaggeration, but the rest was true. Dee had said this. And not just once but a few times that afternoon, the question becoming more frequent as the sun neared the western horizon.

And then Tabby started crying.

"Oh, honey, it's okay," Dee said, arms out.

Tabby crashed into her, face buried into her chest, tears flowing to the point of soaking through her sweatshirt.

This went on for several minutes, Dee simply holding her as she bawled her eyes out, her lips occasionally offering up soothing statements that didn't seem to have any impact, Tabby's own lips moving from time to time but the words too muffled for Dee to understand.

"Do you want me to call your dad?" Dee eventually asked.

Tabby pulled away from her chest and nodded, hands wiping at her tear-streaked face.

Dee pulled out her phone and called.

It rang several times before going to voicemail.

"Hey, it's Dee. Please give me a call," she said.

Tabby stared at her, bottom lip quivering.

"It's okay. He's probably in an area where he can't answer the phone," Dee said. "He'll call us back any second."

"Can you try Mommy?" Tabby asked.

"Okay," Dee said.

Voicemail.

Dee disconnected the call.

"She's not answering either?" Tabby asked.

Dee shook her head.

"Can you send her a message that says I miss her and hope she comes home soon?" Tabby asked.

"Okay," Dee said.

Together they typed up the text and sent it, Dee adding an impromptu picture that she took of Tabby after telling her to go stand by the Christmas tree.

Her phone buzzed.

Ian.

"Hey, I just tried to call you," Dee said. To Tabby: "It's your dad."

"Daddy!" Tabby shouted.

"Tabby says hi," Dee said, switching the phone to speaker mode.

"I heard," Ian replied.

"Daddy, are you coming home soon?" Tabby asked.

"I'm on my way," Ian replied, voice echoing from the phone.

"Yay!" Tabby shouted.

Thirty minutes later, Ian was walking through the front door, two pizza boxes and a bag of crazy bread from Little Caesars in hand, Tabby nearly knocking the food from his hands as she pounced upon him with a tear-filled hug, Dee coming to the rescue with outstretched arms to secure the food.

"Is Mommy coming home?" Tabby asked after a few seconds.

"Mommy has to stay the night," Ian said.

Tabby frowned at that.

"This pizza smells so good, doesn't it?" Dee said, trying to distract Tabby. "Let's go eat some before it gets cold."

"Okay," Tabby said, no enthusiasm present, though she did dive into a slice once it was in hand.

"It's been a bit of a rough day," Dee noted once she and Ian were out of earshot of Tabby.

"Really?" he asked, face sinking.

"Yeah, more so during the last two hours."

"I suppose that's to be expected. She's been up ever since this"—he motioned toward his face—"happened, and with all the back and forth between the bookstore and then the stuff on the stairs by your apartment..." He shook his head and sighed.

"How's Gwen doing?"

"Broken nose," he said.

"Fuck."

"Yeah. Face-first right into the bottom edge of the doorframe." He let out another sigh. "But of course everyone thinks I punched her right in the face."

"They said that?" Dee asked.

"No, but I can tell it's what everyone's thinking."

"Not me," Dee noted.

"Thanks."

Of course, this was because she had seen him and Gwen shortly after she had clawed his face, so she knew firsthand how far removed the two incidents were from each other. Had that not been the case, had she first seen them together with their injuries, she probably would have wondered about Ian's explanation as well.

"Anyway," Dee said, "I think I better head home. Finals week and I'm not ready at all."

"Want to take some pizza with you?" he asked.

"No, I'm good."

"You sure?"

"Yeah."

"Okay. Thanks again for today. For everything." He pulled some bills from his pocket.

"No, no," Dee said, waving them away.

"No, I insist," he said, trying to hand them over.

Dee wouldn't take them, stating how they were like family to her and were already far too generous, what with the job and the apartment and helping her out with her car whenever it crapped out on her.

Ian nodded, hand slowly putting the cash back into his pocket.

An awkward silence arrived.

"Tomorrow then, after finals," Ian said.

"Yep. Should be back around four."

A hug followed and then she was walking out to her car, feet mindful of any ice that might be present.

15

Val retrieved the chart that had been tucked into a plastic sleeve-like slot near the hospital room door, left hand snapping several photos of it with his phone before tucking it back into the slot.

Following that, he stepped into Gwendolyn's room and snapped several more photos of her bandaged face.

No one paid any attention to him while he did this, the hospital staff simply going about their duties while friends and family members of the patients in the other rooms said their goodbyes as visiting hours came to an end.

A food cart was making the rounds as he left the room and headed toward the elevators, a question on if Gwendolyn would be eating anything from one of the pink trays entering into his mind.

Or would they simply keep her sedated on whatever IV cocktail they had going, thereby allowing her body to go undisturbed while in the early stages of the healing process?

No answers arrived.

One thing he did know, treating a broken nose was mostly a process of making sure the airways stayed clear, so unless surgery was required to piece things back together, one was usually treated and released.

Keeping Gwendolyn overnight seemed extreme, unless they feared complications arising. Either physical or mental. Or a safety issue. Did they worry about sending her home with a husband who may have been lying about how the injury unfolded? Or had Ian been the one to insist she stay overnight?

Back at his motel, he called Zoey and filled her in on what he had learned so that they could brainstorm a bit.

"Breaking a nose during a fall?" Zoey questioned. "That doesn't seem right. People typically fall backward on ice, not forward, and if they do fall forward, they break their fall with their hands."

"My thoughts exactly," he said.

"So, he punches her in the face, she crawls around on the driveway, gushing blood from her broken nose, he then gets her into the truck and drives her to the hospital." She paused. "So when did the scratches to his face happen? Did he punch her because she scratched him, or did she scratch him because he punched her? And if it was before he punched her, what led to her scratching him?"

"Couldn't have been right after, not with all the blood on the driveway. She clearly went down and crawled to the snowbank."

"Maybe she attacked him while driving?"

"Not while driving," he said. "Scratches were on the left side of his face going down toward his nose, so she would have had to be facing him when she did it."

"Okay, maybe he got on top of her after punching her, after she crawled onto the snowbank, and she managed to swing up her hand and claw him."

Val thought about this for a few seconds and then said, "I think the scratches came first. Maybe they were arguing in the driveway about something, she claws his face, and then boom, he punches her, she goes down, gushing blood, and he then brings her to the hospital."

"You know, given that her car is at the bookstore, maybe everything started there, maybe some sort of confrontation which resulted in them heading home together rather than separately, they then start arguing once they are back home in the driveway, and then boom, she claws him, he punches her."

"And where is Tabitha during all this?" Val asked.

"Maybe at the bookstore? With Dee."

"Hmm."

"And you said that the chief showed up. Maybe whatever unfolded at the bookstore was disturbing enough that Dee called her after Ian and Gwendolyn left. Giving her a heads-up or something."

Val shook his head, which Zoey obviously could not see.

"We're missing something," he said. "I don't know what, but something."

"Maybe," she agreed. Then, "You know who you need to talk to if you could get her alone?"

"Who?"

"Tabitha."

"Tabitha," he said, almost as if taste-testing the idea.

"Yep. Kids always know more about what is going on than the adults around them realize, and they often are much less cautious about spilling what they know."

"Yeah, but getting access to them is much tougher than getting info at a hospital or glancing at a chart, especially if the two of us are going to have a little chat about what happened today," he said.

"True, but that's why you're making the big bucks—so you can figure out how to make tough things like that happen."

Val didn't reply to that.

"Anyway, I gotta run."

"Okay, talk to you tomorrow."

"Yep."

Call ended, Val took a seat on the bed, thoughts on Tabitha and how he might go about getting her alone so the two could talk playing across his mind.

16

. . .

Gwen could hear the whispered voices beyond the open doorway, the recent visit of a young man to her room to check something having jarred her awake. Confusion had followed for several seconds before fading away, disjointed memories of what had unfolded during the day displaying themselves across her mind's eye.

Was that today?
How long have I been here?
What if Christmas has come and gone?
No!
No!
No!
She needed to get back home.
She needed to get to Tabby.

The room started spinning as she pushed herself from the bed and tried to stand, her body crashing into something that was next to her and then into a wall.

A tug on her arm.
Ropes.
The fireplace.
Santa.
Taking me to the North Pole.
No.
Not me.
Jessica.
And this year...

Horror arrived, her screams echoing throughout the entire third floor.

TEN

1

"She had a very bad night," Ian said, a yawn punctuating the statement while also attesting to the fact that he too had gotten very little sleep.

"How bad?" Sam asked, hands around a Styrofoam mug of hospital coffee.

"Ripped out her IV while getting out of bed and then crashed into a wall, all while screaming." He shook his head. "She clawed two nurses while they were trying to help her, one right across an eye. They literally had to knock her out with something, a sedative of some sort. Stuck her right in the butt while four or five guys held her down."

"Jesus Christ."

"And now they have her restrained to the bed, with wrist and ankle cuffs and some sort of waist strap."

"No!" She put a hand to her mouth. "Are you serious?"

He nodded. "I about lost my mind when I saw that. Screaming at them to release her, threatening legal action up the wazoo, until they had security come up in force, saying they would remove me from the hospital if I didn't calm down."

Sam took his hand, squeezing it.

"They want to move her up to the psych ward again for seventy-two hours of observation," he said, eyes glistening as tears welled up.

"Maybe that's for the best right now," Sam said.

He pulled his hand free. "It would destroy her."

"Ian," she said. "Look at what has happened during the last twenty-four hours, and all the stuff that happened during the last month. She needs help. Professional help. You do too."

His eyes went wide. "Me?"

"Not for your own mental well-being or anything, just to help you with what is unfolding. To help take some of the burden off of your shoulders."

"I'm fine," he said.

"You're not fine. Far from it."

"We just need to get through Christmas. That's all. After that, things will be better."

"Then why not have help getting to that point? Professional help. What about that place she went to last year? The fancy one her mother recommended."

"No!" he snapped.

Startled, Sam stared at him for several seconds before saying, "She seemed better after that."

"No," he said again, only this time it wasn't a shout.

Sam continued to stare, not yet trusting herself to speak.

"Did you find out anything more about Dee's writer guy?" he asked, shifting things.

She shook her head. "Rental agency stonewalled me."

"Really?" he asked. "Why?"

"I don't know. Sometimes people give you info, sometimes they don't. It all just depends on who picks up the phone. And since I stupidly announced that I was the chief of police…"

"I would think that would make them more willing to give you information."

"Maybe fifty years ago, but now with all these cop shows, everyone is always *warrant! warrant! warrant!* the moment you mention you're with the police."

"Is it true?" he asked. "Should you have a warrant for requesting info like that?"

"If I want to force them to give me the info then yes, but if I'm just asking...not so much. A warrant in this type of situation is really for their protection should they eventually be confronted on why they provided customer information to someone like me."

"I see." A few seconds came and went. "So, will you now try to get a warrant?"

"I don't really have cause for one since this isn't an actual investigation. At least not an official investigation that is being looked at by the department."

Ian nodded.

Sam sipped her coffee. "Ugh."

"It's really bad," he said, chuckling.

"Now you tell me."

"Gwen has spoiled us."

"Big time. I used to be able to drink the most vile sludge imaginable without issue. Now..." She pushed the Styrofoam mug away.

"Same," Ian said.

"So..." Sam started and then hesitated. "What are you going to do?"

"I don't know. I guess I'll just go in there once they're done with her bath, spend the morning with her, see how she is, and then take her home."

"And if she is still freaking out and having these crazed moments?"

Several seconds came and went.

Sam waited.

"I really don't know," he finally said.

2

Gwen clenched her fists as the nurse started running the wet cloth over her bared flesh, remembering Jessica with the soapy rag and discolored wash bucket kneeling before her in the cellar, scrubbing away the grime that somehow kept finding her skin as she sat chained to the stone wall, a *tsk, tsk, tsk* sound frequently leaving her lips.

The nurse didn't make any *tsk* sounds while washing her, but she did hum a Christmas tune, one that felt like a drill bit going into her skull each time she hit one of the high notes.

"No eggnog," Gwen muttered as the nurse pulled her gown away from her legs and pubic region.

A momentary frown crossed the young woman's face, followed by an overly enthusiastic smile and comment about how they didn't have any eggnog on the floor, but that if she was still around during Christmas they might be able to sneak her up a mug.

"No!" Gwen shrieked, arms yanking at the restraints.

Startled, the nurse backed away, washcloth dripping lukewarm water across the bed and floor.

"Hey now, no more of that," the nurse said after a few seconds. "Unless you want to go up to the sixth floor."

Gwen knew about the sixth floor, the hospital having put her up there for several weeks after her escape from the Robinson house. She didn't want to go back. Not this year. Not now. Not when she needed to get home so she could be there to protect Tabby.

Eyes closed, she took a deep breath.

And then a second.

And then a third.

"Are you going to be calm now so I can finish?" the nurse asked, voice stern.

Gwen nodded.

Resoaking the washcloth, the young woman returned to her task of bathing Gwen, who turned her head away and stared at the wall as her pubic region was scrubbed.

"We're going to have to take care of this tangled mess before bringing you upstairs," Jessica said, curling some of Gwen's pubic hair around a finger and tugging. *"Santa doesn't like a hairy bush."*

"NOOOOOOOOOO!"

Water splashed as the plastic washbasin was knocked from the small table, the nurse nearly tripping herself as she scrambled away from Gwen's bucking body.

Others were in the room.

Some simply gawking, some shouting instructions, one filling a syringe, another dabbing her arm with a small alcohol swab.

"No! No! No!"

A sting as they jammed the needle into her arm.

"Nooooo..." Her voice faded, a blissful cloud-like realm encasing her.

3

Ian heard the shouting and bolted up from the table he and Sam were at, feet taking him toward Gwen's room, which already had a crowd of people around the open door.

Sam was right behind him, her voice trying to calm him down as he shoved his way into the room, people protesting his actions.

A hand grabbed him but could not keep a grip.

"Hey!" someone cried. "Give that back!"

"You can't take that!" another screamed.

Ian got into the room, body nearly crashing into Gwen's hospital bed.

Two staff members were at the bed, one checking Gwen's vitals while another was quickly covering her lower body with the bedsheets.

"Everyone out!" Sam shouted.

Another voice issued a similar command.

A few seconds later, the room and doorway were cleared of everyone but Gwen, a doctor, Ian, Sam, and the supervisor of this floor.

"People were in that doorway filming," Sam snapped at the supervisor.

"Her screams brought visitors from other rooms," the supervisor noted.

"You better find all the phones and delete the footage before it leaves this floor because if any of it is uploaded online this place will face the biggest lawsuit it has ever experienced," Sam said.

"We don't have the authority to look at phones or have people delete anything."

Ian was staring at Gwen during all this, who was out cold. "Is she okay?" he asked.

"Vitals are good," the doctor said. "She'll be out for a while though."

"How could a simple bath lead to this and why wouldn't they just let her take a shower?" he asked, voice raised a bit.

"We talked about this earlier and explained the policy following any incidents where a patient assaults a staff member," the supervisor said. "And now we're going to have to move her up to the sixth floor."

"No," Ian said.

"We are not equipped to deal with this type of situation, and the disruption to other patients will not be tolerated."

"I'm taking her home."

"Ian," Sam cautioned.

"No," Ian snapped. "Stop. I've made up my mind. How soon before I can take her home?"

"Sir, I have to advise against that," the doctor said.

"I don't care," Ian said. "I'm taking her home."

"You'll have to sign a waiver stating you understand that you're discharging her against hospital recommendations."

"Bring me the fucking waiver," Ian said. "Right now. And a pen."

No one moved.

"Now!" Ian shouted, spittle flying.

The doctor held up his hands and said, "Okay, I'll have them draw up the paperwork."

With that the doctor left, along with the supervisor.

Ian looked at Sam, who stared back at him, concern dominating her features.

"Any idea whose phone that is?" Ian asked.

Sam gave him a puzzled look and then glanced down toward her right hand, seemingly startled by the pink phone. "Fuck, I have no idea. I just saw them trying to film everything and grabbed it from them."

"Did they actually get anything from in the room?" he asked.

"No idea, but..." She disappeared into the tiny bathroom, the sound of something splashing into the toilet reaching his ears. "Oops."

Ian turned back to Gwen, eyes taking in the pitiful sight of her shackled to the bed.

Tears arrived.

"Jesus Christ," he said, wiping at his eyes. "Why is this all happening to us?"

"I don't know," Sam said, despite the question having clearly been rhetorical.

"We were happy," he said, turning toward her, wiping his eyes a second time. "I mean, honestly happy. We had worked out all the stupid stuff from the past, we were away from her family and all the stress of Wall Street, we had the bookstore and her coffee imports, and were getting ready to get her set up with an actual coffee company, and then boom, the fucking Robinsons try to gift her to a demonic Santa Claus and totally fuck her up."

Sam simply shook her head.

"I mean, Jesus Christ." He ran a hand through his hair and then made a fist. "I just want this to all be over. For us to be back to normal."

"It will be eventually," Sam said.

Ian nodded and then reached down, fingers hovering over Gwen's cheek for several seconds before he committed himself to a gentle caress.

4

Val was surprised at how quickly he was able to convince the people in the school office that allowing him to speak with Tabitha was in everyone's best interest, the statements he made about concerns of abuse within the family followed by pictures of Gwendolyn in a hospital bed with a "broken face" that he had printed from his phone at a kiosk at a local drug store the day before having startled them into pure compliance with his request.

"I will also need a staff member to be present during my interview with the young lady to comply with Illinois code 87c, thereby protecting all those involved from any complaints one may try to file," he said, the code one he made up on the spot.

This final bit seemed to seal the deal, Mr. Rhodes, the assistant principal of the school, leading him to what he called a *quiet room* where he, Val, and Tabitha could speak.

"Unless you think it should be a female staff member that sits in on this?" Mr. Rhodes questioned, voice unable to conceal his unease.

"No," Val said, waving a dismissive hand. "This is not that type of interview. We are just assessing the situation that resulted in her mother being hospitalized with the broken face on Sunday. Nothing at this time indicates any ill actions toward the child in question."

"Oh thank goodness," Mr. Rhodes said with a heavy sigh of relief.

A knock echoed on the door, which was already partially open, a young lady poking her head in. "I have Tabby here," she said.

"Ah, yes, very good," Mr. Rhodes said, standing. "Bring her in."

Val stood as well and watched as Tabitha was ushered into the room, a look of concern on her face given that she probably was very confused and startled by being summoned to speak with the assistant principal.

"Hi, Tabby, please have a seat," Mr. Rhodes said, and then, likely having noticed the look of concern as well, added, "You're not in trouble or anything. This gentleman here simply has some questions to ask you."

"Okay," Tabitha said, taking a seat, eyes darting back and forth between the two several times.

"Hi, Tabitha, my name is Valentine," Val said, reaching out a hand to shake, her tiny hand hesitating for a moment before reaching out and completing the greeting. "How are you today?"

"Are you named after Valentine's Day?" she asked.

"Sort of. I'm named after the guy who Valentine's Day is named for," he said. "What do you think of that?"

"I thought Cupid started Valentine's Day," she said.

"Well...Cupid is a big part of it too."

She frowned.

"Anyway, everyone just simply calls me Val," he said. "And I'm guessing everyone calls you Tabby?"

She nodded. "Except my grandma. She calls me Tabitha."

"I see. Is this the grandma that lives on Long Island? Your mother's mother?"

"Yes. We went to see her for Thanksgiving. She lives in a giant house right on the beach. But she didn't let me go swimming and said I had to wear a dress while there, which is stupid."

"You don't like dresses?"

She shook her head, the jeans and flannel shirt she currently was wearing somewhat of a testament to this.

Val smiled and said, "Tabby, I wanted to ask you some questions about yesterday."

"About the mysterious writer?" she asked.

Val blinked. "No, um...well, maybe? What mysterious writer?"

"Me and my friend Dee are working a case. It's called *The Mystery of the Mysterious Writer*. He drives a blue car with a palm tree on the license plate. I keep notes on when he is spying on us."

"Hmm, wow, okay. I think we will get back to that in a little bit. First, can you tell me about what happened with your mother yesterday?"

"She got scared because Dee was dressed up like an elf."

"Why did that scare your mommy?"

"Because some people did mean things to her while pretending to be Santa and now she is scared of Santa and his elves and sometimes Christmas stuff."

"And what happened when she got scared by Dee dressed as an elf?"

"Daddy threw her against the wall."

Mr. Rhodes let out a gasp.

"But not to be mean," Tabby added.

"Oh, then why did he throw her against the wall?"

"Because she almost fell down the stairs so he had to grab her, and when he did he threw her against the wall."

"Is that when your mommy scratched his face?"

"Noooo, that happened when they were sleeping."

"Did you see it happen?"

Tabby nodded. "I went to see what was wrong and it was gross because they were naked, and then Mommy scratched Daddy. We then went to the bookstore with Dee, and then Mommy came too, and then she got scared because Dee dressed like an elf, and then me and Dee went to go get pie, and then Mommy went to the hospital."

"Do you know why your mommy had to go to the hospital?" he asked.

"She hurt her nose."

"Do you know how?"

"She slipped on ice on our driveway. It's really slippery. I always walk like a penguin so I don't fall."

"You didn't see your mommy fall though because you were with Dee, correct?"

Tabby nodded. "We were getting pie and working on our mystery."

"Do you spend a lot of time with Dee?" he asked.

"Umm, sometimes."

"What about your daddy? Does he spend a lot of time with Dee?"

"They work together," Tabby said.

"What about when not working?"

"Umm..." She shook her head. "No, not really."

"Are you sure?" Val asked. "They don't spend time together when your mommy is working?"

Another shake of the head.

"What about last night?" Val asked. "Did Dee stay over while your mommy was gone?"

"You mean like a sleepover?"

"Yes."

Another shake of the head. "She went home after we ate some pizza. And then Daddy started crying, but pretended he wasn't crying and said it was bedtime even though it really wasn't. And then he cried a lot while in his bedroom, which made me sad too."

"How do you know he was crying in his bedroom?"

"I can hear through the vents."

"Ah, I see," Val said. Then, after a few seconds, "Do you listen through the vents a lot?"

Tabby didn't reply, but the look on her face told him the answer was yes.

"It's okay," he said. "I'm not going to tell anyone if you do. This is a safe space."

Tabby considered that for a moment and then nodded.

"What kinds of things do you hear though the vent?" he asked. "Are they ever arguing or fighting?"

"Sometimes," Tabby said.

"And what do they argue about?"

"*The Lord of the Rings.*"

"*The Lord of the Rings?*" Val questioned.

"Yep. Mommy thinks the movies are better than the books."

"I see," he said. "Do they argue about anything else?"

"Ummm...Grandma stuff."

"Grandma stuff?"

"Grandma wants Mommy to come stay with her again, but Daddy says no."

"Oh. And what does your mommy want to do?"

"She doesn't know."

"And what about you? Would you like to go live with your grandma?"

Tabby shook her head and said, "No way, José!"

"Tabby," Mr. Rhodes said. "We don't say the name José like that."

"Sorry," Tabby said.

Val looked over at Mr. Rhodes for a second and then back at Tabby, mind struggling to figure out what to ask next.

"My mommy isn't crazy," Tabby said abruptly.

"Oh, did someone say she was crazy?" Val asked.

"Lots of people. Maria showed me on her phone what everyone was saying, and then her friends were saying bad things about Mommy. I tried to tell them about the mean stuff that was done to her, but they all just laugh at me and make crazy faces."

"These are girls in your class?" Mr. Rhodes asked.

"Yes, except Ginny, who is in Mrs. Pitts's class," Tabby said, nodding.

"I'll speak to them after we are done here, okay?"

"But then they'll think I'm a tattletale." Concern appeared on her face, one that looked almost ready to burst into tears. "Can I just show them the video instead?"

"Video?" Mr. Rhodes asked, looking over at Val.

"What video is that?" Val asked.

"The one of Santa being mean to Mommy," Tabby said, hand wiping at her eyes, which had started to mist up.

"There's video of it?" Val asked, startled.

Tabby nodded. "In the basement."

"And you've watched this video?"

Another nod and then she burst into tears. "I didn't know it was bad stuff," she said between the sobs. "I was just looking to see if I could find any Christmas presents and looked in Mommy's secret spot."

"It's okay," Val said. "You didn't do anything wrong, and we won't tell anyone."

Tabby looked at him, tears still falling, lip quivering.

"What I do need you to do though is to tell me where exactly this video is, okay?"

Tabby nodded, wiped her eyes and then nose with her sleeve, and began telling him about the basement and where the old coal chute was located.

. . .

5

Dee dropped her test into the tray on the professor's desk and left the quiet classroom, concern getting the better of her as she made her way toward the school parking lot given all the trouble she had had with this particular final, her inability to sleep the night before coupled with a very unsettling discovery she had made online shortly before the final was to begin having destroyed what normally would have been a well-prepared and focused mind.

The *Treatments* DVD was to blame, the scenes that had unfolded on the basement TV screen having implanted themselves within her mind, which had then led to a series of nightmares that she had not been able to recover from, her body bolting up with a gasp around three in the morning. Sleep would not return after that, and honestly, she wasn't sure if she would have welcomed it if it had, not if it put her right back into the nightmares she had been experiencing.

By the time the sun was rising upon the horizon Dee had drank two entire pots of coffee, the beverage consumed while attempting to get some last-minute studying done for the upcoming math final.

Nothing from the pages of her notebook or the textbook would register, her mind constantly returning to the scenes from the DVD.

Thinking a change of scenery might help her focus, Dee headed to school three hours earlier than was necessary and planted herself in a cozy corner area in a third-floor study room that she loved, one that had some windows that looked westward over what seemed to be an endless sea of prairie grass. In reality, that prairie grass disappeared less than two miles away where it bumped up against a large rest stop for those traveling northbound on I-55.

More coffee was consumed while attempting to study, vile

stuff that had been brewed in the cafeteria. No amount of cream or sugar could make it palatable, yet she still sipped away at it until nothing but a few strands of congealing coffee crud remained.

The relocation to an academic environment did not help in dislodging the horror of the DVD from her mind, the pages of her notebook and textbook still not registering as she went from one equation to the next, so eventually she gave up on the endeavor and simply stared off into space for a while before pulling out her phone in an attempt to pass the time, several really difficult levels of an Angry Birds knockoff game dominating her focus until her frustration with one stage got to be too much. After that, she thought about trying to study for a third time but knew that would be a hopeless endeavor, and before she even realized what she was doing, she was thumbing through the pictures of Ian sitting with the various escorts, questions on what exactly he had been up to with them once again echoing within her mind.

Google searches followed, Dee plugging in their names one by one, the results varying with each search, her only real goal at the moment being to kill time before the final was to start since she knew that looking up the woman themselves wouldn't really give her any insight into why Ian had been seeing them. Some of the women were still active in the escort scene, their names pulling up pages that had been designed to sell sexual services without specifically stating they were selling sexual services. Other names didn't link to anything within the escort world, likely due to how common the names were. A few of these women with common names were found when the escort site itself was plugged in; others were not, given that some of the sites were no longer active. One by one she went through the photos and their info sheets, the start time of her final drawing closer and closer until eventually she got up and started making her way toward the classroom where the final was being administered, her thumb plugging in the next name from the photo spread as she walked.

Had she glanced at the search results while actually walking she probably would have halted abruptly in the middle of the hallway, but given how close she was to the classroom and the fact that the door was already open, it wasn't until she was in a chosen seat halfway down a row near the far wall when she actually looked back at her phone.

A gasp followed, one that was loud enough to cause the professor to raise an eye and look her way before looking back down at whatever they were working on. As for Dee, she now realized why this one particular escort that Ian had been photographed with looked familiar to her. She had been the most recent victim of the Craigslist Ripper out in Long Island, her remains having just been found a year earlier after having vanished back in 2018.

6

An hour came and went before Gwen began to stir, a groggy question on what happened alerting Ian to her consciousness. Panic followed, Gwen's realization that she was shackled to the bed causing her to start bucking against the leather restraints, tiny cries escaping her lips, ones which threatened to grow louder and louder as the last remnants of the sedative faded away.

"Gwen, honey," Ian said, leaning over her. "It's okay. We'll have those off in a moment. Just hold tight."

His words seemed to do the trick. Or maybe it was simply the sight of him standing over her. Whichever it was, she stopped struggling, though her body remained tense, fists clenched, arms clearly ready to try to break free at any moment.

"We're going to go home now that you're awake, okay?" Ian said, his words slow and gentle, all while his heart was racing. "I just need to let a nurse know so we can release you and get you down to the truck."

"Tabby?" she asked, voice barely audible.

"She's fine," Ian said. "She's at school."

Gwen gave a slight nod.

"I'm going to go get a nurse now, okay?" he said.

Another nod.

Ian hesitated for a moment, eyes on Gwen, and then quickly turned himself around and darted into the hallway.

A few minutes later, Ian was waiting in the hallway while Gwen put on the clothes he had brought her, the awkwardness of handing her the bag while she sat on the edge of the bed in the hospital gown rubbing at her wrists having caused him to simply make a comment about stepping out to give her some privacy.

Not long after that, he was pushing her down the hall in a wheelchair, the hospital having insisted upon the use of the chair, which Gwen did not protest. Instead, she simply got into the chair and let herself be rolled down the hallway to the elevators and then from the elevators to the hospital exit, where Ian parked her near the doors while he went to go get the truck, his steps hurried, not wanting to leave her alone for too long.

"You hungry?" he asked as they drove away from the hospital.

She shook her head.

"You sure?"

A nod.

Silence arrived, one that Ian struggled with as he stared at the road, hands tight on the wheel, eyes occasionally glancing over at Gwen, who was picking at the edge of a bandage that covered the spot where the second IV had been placed after she had ripped out the first.

Ian wanted to say something that would get Gwen talking, but he simply did not know what words to use. He worried about setting her off, though he wasn't sure why exactly this was a concern. She seemed fragile, which was odd given that he had never viewed her in this way before. At least not until after the events that had unfolded last year.

Just relax, he told himself.

Yesterday had been crazy. For everyone, but more so for her, and it would take time to resettle.

But resettle into what?

Maybe Sam is right.

We need help.

The silence stayed in place for the entire drive, Gwen's focus going from the bandage on her wrist to something out beyond the horizon, her eyes seemingly glued to the window until they finally turned into the driveway and came to a halt before the garage.

This is when she freaked out yesterday.

And then slipped on that patch of ice.

Ian had added tons of salt to the driveway last night, doing it after dark once Tabby was in bed, his own body unable to even contemplate the idea of going to sleep.

He had put so much down that the ground literally crunched beneath their feet, the outside temps too cold for it to actually do any deicing. But at least it gave some traction.

"I'm going to make us some coffee," Ian said once they were inside, Gwen having walked into the entryway with an odd hesitation that he could not understand at first.

And then he realized she was staring at herself in the mirror.

"They say the worst of the swelling should go down in a few days, maybe a week..." His voice faded as she turned away from the mirror.

He watched her take off her coat and hook it onto the rack.

"Do you want me to get an ice pack ready?" he asked.

She shook her head. "I'll handle all that."

He wanted to protest that decision, to insist that it was no trouble and that he wanted to take care of her, but realized that was exactly the opposite of what was required here. "Okay."

"What coffee are you going to make?" she asked.

"Hmm, not really sure," he admitted. "What are you in the mood for?"

"Whatever you make I'm fine with," she said.

He nodded and headed into the kitchen to get some water going in the kettle, and then went to the coffee cupboard to see which one he wanted to make, the whole idea of making coffee having been an attempt to get Gwen talking, but once again silence had settled in.

7

Gwen heard the coffee grinder going as she stepped into the family room, body halting for a second as she studied the fireplace and then the Christmas tree, thoughts on what might unfold come Christmas Eve playing across her mind.

Screams.

Her own, as they hauled her up into the air by her wrists, her legs kicking back and forth, trying to find something—anything!—to set her weight upon.

Nothing was there, her kicks fruitless, as were her screams.

No one but the Robinsons could hear her, and they would not be moved by her pleas. She had learned this within days of being put into the cellar.

"Honey?" a voice said.

Gwen turned and looked at Ian, who was standing a few feet away from her, two mugs of coffee in hand, the right one held out a bit farther than the left.

"Thank you," she said, taking the coffee in her cupped

hands and moving toward the sofa, where she took a seat.

Ian joined her.

Silence once again, the only sounds those of them carefully sipping their coffee, testing the heat until it dissipated enough for them to take actual mouthfuls.

Gwen contemplated the taste, the maltiness and a lingering chocolate aftertaste confusing her at first until she realized this was a blend from a fairly new coffee roaster in Hawaii.

She voiced the name of the coffee blend.

"Bingo," Ian said, clearly impressed.

"This one is best with a little spritz of vanilla syrup," she noted.

"Want me to go add some?" he asked.

"No, no, just making conversation," she said. "I remember being unsure on if I was going to start offering this one while over there sampling it until I tried it with a shot of the vanilla at the recommendation of the owner's son, who was being very secretive when mentioning this given his father's unyielding opinions on how one should drink their coffee. It was quite the rebellion, though one that was necessary since it did actually lead to me making an offer." She chuckled. "Do you remember that trip?"

"I do," he said.

"Our last vacation before all the *drama*," she said.

"While you were tasting the coffees I was trying to teach Tabby how to snorkel, which did not go so well."

"She was too young," Gwen said.

"Yeah."

"I was impressed though. You went into the water and stayed in there for a long time trying to teach her, and then continued going into the water with her anytime she wanted to go to the beach, which was pretty much every waking minute."

"Well, I wanted her to enjoy herself and have a good vacation, especially after being cooped up inside the house for so long during the pandemic."

"I liked how you pushed your fear of the water to the side so that it didn't impede her enjoyment—that you would do anything for her."

He nodded and then sipped his coffee.

"That's what being a parent is all about," she continued. "Doing anything for your children, whether it be making happy memories for them or protecting them at all costs."

"It is," he agreed.

"He took our mother," Jessica had said. *"Because he didn't like the gift Mommy and Daddy offered that year. And then the next year he took our little sister."*

Gwen had been sitting in the cellar as Jessica talked about this, a chain connecting her neck to the stone wall, horror and confusion still dominating her thoughts when contemplating why the two had grabbed her and put her into the cellar.

Jessica had actually spoken to her a lot about Santa and the gifting process, a very apologetic tone frequently present given the horrors that would be in her future once Santa took her with him to the North Pole. Horrors that Jessica was now experiencing due to Gwen having escaped.

"Should I make us a fire?" Ian asked.

"Not just yet," she said, blinking away her thoughts on what Jessica might be enduring, if she was still alive. "Let's just sit here for a while. It's nice and peaceful."

"Okay," he said, putting an arm around her.

Gwen snuggled into him, pulling his arm tighter, all while fears began playing across her mind on what might happen that Christmas Eve.

Would Santa come to the house simply wanting a gift from them, or would he be there to take out vengeance on her and the family for what she did to him that night while hanging from the beam?

If it was just a gift, would he accept it or reject it?

And if the latter, would that mean he would take her instead?

Or Tabby?

Or both of them?

8

Ian had not been expecting Gwen to snuggle up against him and fall asleep, though it did not surprise him once it happened given how stressful her last twenty-four hours had been. His own eyes were heavy with exhaustion after everything as well, though he knew he would not be falling asleep, his body not positioned properly for it to happen at that particular moment. Had he been up for several days, he might have been able to pass out, but not with the current moderate level of exhaustion he carried. It just wasn't enough for that to happen.

So he simply sat there with Gwen curled up into him, a brief period of discomfort given how his body was angled against the armrest being slowly worked out as he ever so gently shifted himself.

Gwen's arm shifted a bit with his movements, exposing the inside of her wrist, which still bore marks from her struggles against the restraints that had held her to the hospital bed.

She had been rubbing at those marks when he walked in with the coffee earlier, though he didn't think she realized she was doing it. She had engaged in similar actions following her escape last year, though the marks back then had been much more severe, the ropes they had hung her up with having chewed away several layers of flesh while also bruising the surrounding tissues.

Fortunately, she had not been hanging long enough for the

nerves and tissues in her hands to die, rendering them permanently useless and requiring amputation. Such would have happened if left like that for several days, though according to Dee she probably would have asphyxiated before that at some point given the strain hanging like that would have put on her chest and lungs.

"Probably why her memories of that night are so fucked up," Dee had said. *"Her brain wasn't getting enough oxygen while hanging there, resulting in her drifting in and out of consciousness, and likely hallucinating."*

Information from the web had been shown to him as well, Dee's fascination with serial killers having resulted in all kinds of twisted rabbit-hole-like explorations.

"Hanging like that is similar to being crucified," she had added, and then went on to explain in horrific detail how crucifixion actually asphyxiated a person as their strength gave out, the position designed so that the victim had to keep lifting themselves up a bit by pressing against their nailed feet so that their lungs could suck in air. *"Now, if the Romans were feeling merciful, they would actually cut the hamstrings of the victim after nailing them up to the cross, making it impossible to press downward against their nailed feet, thus not allowing them to get their body into the upward position required to take a deep breath, thus suffocating themselves quickly rather than over a period of days."*

Ian had simply stared at her for several seconds after this, her enthusiasm when detailing such things somewhat disturbing. The fact that she had had her hair in pigtails that day had only added to how weird it was for such gruesome subject matter to be leaving her lips. But that was why he adored her. She subverted conventional impressions and didn't care what anyone thought, but in a way where she also didn't care if people knew that she didn't care, which would show that she did care. Nope. Dee was one of those who honestly didn't give a damn about how people viewed her.

"The rack actually asphyxiates people too when used properly, though during the long journey toward the eventual asphyxiation one suffers the agony of having just about every joint, ligament, muscle, and bone pulled—" Dee had continued, only for Ian to cut her off with an upraised hand, which had caused her to grin.

Now, sitting there on the couch, he wondered about these things and whether Gwen's hanging in that family room by the fireplace for several hours had caused her to hallucinate what it was she had claimed to see, her mind projecting some sort of demonic Santa over the Santa-dressed Justin as he raped her over and over again that night—all after spending nearly a month chained up in the cellar being fed nothing but eggnog and Christmas cookies, and then being given an eggnog enema.

Of course, this thought led him to wonder what it was that Justin and Jessica believed. Did they truly think that a demonic Santa arrived every Christmas Eve? One who Justin gave life to as he donned the Santa outfit he always wore while portraying a more traditional Santa at the mall every year, all while Jessica donned one of her elf outfits? If so, how would something like that come about?

And how did they seem so normal?

This last question was one that always bogged him down, mostly because it inevitably led to him questioning how it was he could sit in the family room of the Robinson household without realizing Gwen was down below in the cellar. How could he sit there eating Christmas cookies with them while listening to Christmas music, their gentle words soothing him as they offered reassurances on how everything would be okay and that Gwen would eventually be found safe and sound?

Gwen mumbled something in her sleep and then shifted, which caused her nose to press in his chest.

Pain echoed in her scream as she jerked awake, body seemingly throwing itself from him, panic dancing within her eyes.

"Whoa, whoa, it's okay," he said, hands held up.

Gwen twisted toward the fireplace, her arm knocking the coffee mug from the side table as she did, the sound of it shattering upon the hardwood floor filling the room.

"It's okay," Ian continued.

Gwen turned back toward him, blinking a few times, and then looked at her wrists, and then back at the fireplace.

A second later she was reaching up toward her nose, lightly touching the areas beneath the bandages.

"Want me to get you an ice pack?" Ian asked.

Gwen nodded.

Ian got up and headed into the kitchen, returning shortly after that with a ziplock bag of ice in one hand, a broom and dustpan in the other.

"I'll get that," Gwen offered.

"I got it," Ian said. "You just ice your nose."

Gwen did just that, her hands carefully pressing the ice to her face while Ian made a few passes with the broom to gather up the various pieces of mug before scooping it all into the dustpan.

Once that was done, he deposited everything into the garbage can in the kitchen, his eyes noting the time on the stove while doing this.

"Tabby is going to be done with school soon," he said, coming back into the family room.

She didn't reply to that.

"I could probably have Dee pick her up," he said. "Or Sam."

She stared at him.

"So I don't have to leave myself."

"No. Go. I'll be fine."

"I don't think—"

"Go," she said, voice a bit forceful.

Hesitation hit, and then, "Can you think of anything I should pick up on the way that you might need?"

"How about some Vicodin?" she said, giving him a slight grin, one that made her wince.

"If only it were that easy," he said, struggling not to say anything about the pain she was obviously in.

"Honey, go," she said.

"Are you sure you're going to be okay?"

"Yes!" Another wince, the ice pack going back upon her face.

Ian stared for a second longer and then turned to leave.

9

Val stood in the basement of Ian and Gwendolyn's house, listening, trying to figure out if he could make it up the stairs and out the back door without either of them noticing him when he heard what sounded like one of them getting ready to leave the house, their steps upon the hardwood floor clearly heading in the direction of the front door.

Unfortunately, that was also the direction of the stairway to the second floor, which meant they might just be heading up there to get something.

The sounds of the front door opening and closing echoed, followed by the sounds of Ian's truck starting up.

Relief arrived but then was short-lived when he realized that Gwendolyn might still be upstairs.

Heart racing, he waited.

And waited.

And waited.

No other sounds reached his ears.

Go!

He started up the stairs, slowly, feet not wanting to alert

anyone who might still be up there of his presence, the DVD Tabby had mentioned as well as a Treatments folder and a large envelope that appeared to be filled with handwritten letters tucked beneath his arm.

Taking all these items had not been his original purpose when entering the house and coming down here. Instead, he had simply wanted to take a look at the DVD, Tabby noting she had watched it herself in the cozy TV corner that had been set up in the main finished area of the basement, but then they had arrived home far earlier than he had anticipated, which had shifted his focus from watching the DVD to simply escaping the house without being noticed.

Up in the kitchen, he began making his way toward the back sliding door but then paused.

"Alexa, turn on Christmas lights," Gwendolyn said from somewhere within the house.

A few seconds came and went.

"Alexa, turn off Christmas lights."

Another few seconds came and went.

"Alexa, turn on Christmas lights."

Another few seconds came and went.

"Alexa, turn off Christmas lights."

Over and over again, Gwendolyn did this, her voice simply turning on and then off the Christmas lights in the other room.

Why?

"Alexa, turn on Christmas lights."

Val turned and began heading down the hallway so he could peer into the family room.

"Alexa, turn off Christmas lights," Gwendolyn said while kneeling before the fireplace.

A few seconds.

"Alexa, turn on Christmas lights."

All around the room Christmas lights lit up, including a strand that was now in the fireplace itself, the brick interior illuminated with an array of multiple colors.

"Alexa, turn off Christmas lights."

The room and fireplace went dark once again.

"Alexa, turn on Christmas lights."

The room and fireplace lit up.

"Alexa, turn off Christmas lights."

Val watched this for a few seconds and then pulled out his phone to film it as well given how odd it was. Not long after that, he was retracing his steps to the kitchen and then out the back door, a quick sprint around the far side of the house being made, followed by a short jog along the slippery road until he arrived at his rental car.

10

Other parents were looking at him. Ian could sense it while standing outside the school waiting for Tabby to emerge, and then got confirmation of it several times whenever he looked up and caught another set of eyes quickly shifting their focus elsewhere.

Last year at this time the looks were because of Gwendolyn being missing, the thoughts of those around either being ones of pity and sorrow for what he was going through or horror and anger for what they felt he had done, many having already convicted him of murdering his wife.

Now those looks were due to the scratches, which were still very noticeable and would be for quite some time, though some might have also been a result of the various scenes Gwen had made during the last several weeks.

Anger stirred but then faded as children started to emerge from the school, Tabby herself coming out with a group of girls he recognized but whose names he could not place, a sudden realization that he knew very little about those within her little social circle giving him pause.

Does Gwen know any of them?

"Daddy!" Tabby voiced, tiny body slamming into his with a hug. "Is Mommy home now?"

"She is, and she is super excited to see you now that she is feeling better," Ian said, all thoughts and concerns about not knowing anyone in her little social circle quickly fading away.

"Yay!" Tabby said and then, much to his horror, turned and announced across the waiting area, *"My mommy is all better!"*

11

"Hey, Tabby," Ian said a few minutes later while driving. "You don't really have to tell everyone about the things Mommy is going through, okay?"

"But people were talking about her," Tabby said.

"They were?"

"Uh-huh. And Megan had a video of Mommy that she showed everyone at lunchtime."

"A video? Did you watch it?"

Tabby nodded. "Mommy had crazy eyes."

"What?"

"Crazy arms too." Tabby waved her arms up in the air. "Everyone was laughing."

"Can you show me?" he asked, not really understanding what she was talking about.

Tabby shook her head.

"You can't show me?" he questioned.

"It's on TikTok," she said.

"Okay."

"You and Mommy don't let me have a phone or TikTok," she said and started bawling her eyes out.

12

"Where in the world have you been?" Val asked while sitting at the round table in his motel room, the contents he had grabbed from the coal chute spread across the surface. "I called you like three hours ago."

"Christmas shopping," Zoey said, sounding somewhat breathless. "Some of us are finished with our work for the year and don't have a pointless case occupying their every waking moment."

"I'll remember you said that when assigning bonuses with all the extra income this pointless case is bringing in," Val said.

"Yeah, well, we assign the bonuses together, but if that's how you want to play things, then I won't let you in on what I learned from the files of a certain laptop in Baltimore about a certain company that is about to announce its first-ever quarterly loss, one that I'm going to be shorting like crazy as soon as the markets open tomorrow."

"Oh, in that case, all is forgiven."

"Too late," she teased. Then, growing serious: "What's up?"

"I spent the morning talking to Tabitha at her school," he said, pride present in his voice.

"They actually let you in to see her?"

"Yep. I wooed the ladies at the front desk and then smooth-talked the assistant principal into offering me a private room where Tabitha and I talked for quite some time about all sorts of things."

"Nice," Zoey said. "Now the question is, did you learn anything useful?"

"For starters, Tabby is a very clever kid and sees far more

of what is going on around her than most of the adults in her life probably realize."

"Told ya. Kids see everything."

"Big time."

"And what is it she revealed to you?"

"Apparently Gwendolyn herself is the one that took my cameras."

"Whoa, plot twist!"

"Right! She had them tucked in the back of an old coal chute in the basement."

"An old coal chute?"

"Yeah."

"Why?"

"No idea."

"And you're sure it was Gwendolyn that put them there? Not Ian?"

"Tabby says this is where her mother always hides things, and considering there were some Christmas gifts in there for Ian, I'm thinking Tabby's assessment on this being Gwendolyn's hiding spot is pretty spot-on."

"Ian getting anything good?" Zoey asked.

"If by good you mean a signed first edition of *The Hobbit*, then yeah."

"Total yawn, but I'm sure he'll dig it."

"Big time."

"So, find anything else of interest?"

"Maybe," Val said, eyes staring at the DVD that had been sitting on top of the folders, one that he had no way of viewing at the moment.

"Maybe?" Zoey questioned.

"Turns out Gwendolyn had a girlfriend during high school."

"A girlfriend? As in dating?"

"Yep. Found pictures of the two together. Selfies they took. Cheeks pressed together, holding hands, both looking very much in love with each other. Quite a few letters too that Gwen received. Handwritten ones with lots of hearts and smiley faces throughout. I haven't gone through all of them yet, but from what I gather, they were sexually active with each other during their junior year."

"Really? Gwendolyn?"

"I know, right?"

"I can't picture that at all."

"Me either. Though I do have a picture of them together if you want to see it."

"Nah, I'm good. Though..."

"What?"

"Nothing. Was just thinking about how she is married to Ian and the two seemed to have quite a bit of trouble all those years ago."

"It is curious, though this stuff pales in comparison to the other stuff I found."

"Other stuff?" she asked. Then, "What was it?"

"That's kind of why I wanted to talk to you. Do you think you would be able to do me a teensy weensy little favor before heading up to your parents' house?"

"*Valll*," she groaned. "I'm finished for the year."

"It's really nothing crazy and knowing your mad computer skills, you'll probably be able to knock it out in less time than it takes to order a pizza."

"I think you underestimate how quickly I can order a pizza."

"Please?"

"Okay, what is it?" she asked, a sigh punctuating the question.

"Find out everything you can about a Dr. Terry Wilbanks."

Zoey was silent for a few seconds and then said, "Why?"

"I'm not sure exactly, but according to this file folder I

found that is simply listed as Treatments, he spent quite a bit of time treating Gwendolyn earlier this year."

"What kind of treatments?"

"Doesn't really elaborate on that, but several times it mentions failures and—if I am reading this one entry correctly, which isn't easy given how atrocious his handwriting is—it says: *Santa fantasies persist despite repeated treatments. Client gives permission to try the Santa Sex approach.*"

"Santa Sex?" Zoey questioned. "What the fuck is that?"

"That's what I'd like to know, so anything you can find out would be much appreciated."

Another sigh, then, "Spell the name for me."

Val did.

"Any other details I can use?" Zoey asked. "Age? Address? Hospital he—is it a he?—works at?"

"No, but I have some dates, which actually coincide with the time she was staying with her mother earlier this year, so I'm thinking he is likely one of those doctors that works exclusively with the one-percenters out—"

"Holy shit."

"What?"

"I just used my *mad computer skills* to Google this guy's name and the first thing it pulled up was some crazy shit about his having used shock therapy on teens in one of those horrible religious camps where they try to turn gay kids straight."

"Are you serious?"

"Yeah, unless there is some other doctor out there with this exact name."

"Jesus." Val looked at the DVD that he still held, a chill at what might be contained within it slithering through his system.

"Looks like he was also cited several times for giving out fake vaccination cards during the pandemic, as well as recommending various off-the-wall treatments and...*oh my god!* He nearly killed the teenage daughter of a client by pretty much doing the equivalent of waterboarding to her with some horse piss mixture he had created. The girl had Covid symptoms after going to a party and they were trying to get the horse piss mixture into her sinuses and lungs to clear out the virus."

"What the actual fuck?"

"There is an entire Reddit thread dedicated to this one incident, mostly because he got sick right after that and was hospitalized. Nearly died. Was on a ventilator and everything. People were laughing their asses off about it."

"Wow."

"And this would have all been before whatever these treatments were he administered to Gwendolyn, which means that despite all this horrible stuff that is out there about him, Marybeth still brought him in to treat her daughter after all the trauma she had already suffered."

"Well, we have always known Marybeth has a few screws loose."

"Yeah, which is why I said over and over again that you should not go anywhere near this thing after we established that Ian was not responsible for what happened to Gwendolyn. Hell, we shouldn't have gone anywhere near this thing after she tried to have us prove he was having an affair all those years ago, and then again when she was insisting that he was that serial killer out on Long Island."

"Hey, as long as the checks keep clearing."

Zoey didn't reply to that, unless her silence counted as a reply.

"Okay, you're totally right," Val said. "And this will be the last case I take from her."

"I think it would be best if you just packed your things and called it quits right now," Zoey said.

"I can't."

"Why not?"

"Something really fucked-up is going on here, and while it might not be because Ian is up to something, I still would hate to abandon things right now only to realize I could have helped in some way to prevent something terrible from happening."

"What is it you think is going to happen?"

"I don't know exactly," he said, his mind once again visualizing the odd moment he had witnessed earlier with Gwen and the Christmas lights in the fireplace. "But today I saw something that really threw me."

"What?"

"I'm going to send you a video I took of Gwen."

"Okay."

Several seconds came and went.

"It go through?" Val asked.

"Not yet...wait, there it is."

"Okay, take a look and tell me what you think."

Several more seconds came and went, and then, "What the fuck?"

"I know, right?" Val said.

"Christmas lights in the fireplace?" Zoey questioned. "How long did she do this for?"

"I have no idea," he said. "She was still at it when I left."

"I don't really know what to say," Zoey said. "That's just weird."

"My thoughts exactly." A pause. "So, will you be able to do me this one little favor and find out everything you can about this doctor and what might have unfolded earlier this year with these so-called Santa Sex treatments?"

"Yeah, I'll look into it and get back to you. But after this I'm done for the year."

"Agreed," he said. "And thanks."

"Yep."

13

. . .

Gwen stood within the doorway of Tabby's bedroom, the light from the hallway providing just enough illumination for her to see Tabby, her body curled up beneath the sheets, one arm tucked away while another was thrust upward over her head.

Screams echoing, Tabby's tiny wrists locked in child-sized manacles that were linked together by a heavy chain, one that a hideous elf was tugging at as he led her down a corridor to her new home in the bowels of Santa's castle...

No! No! No!

Gwen pressed at her eyes, her knuckles forcing away the imagery, the sight of Tabby sleeping peacefully once again before her.

"I won't let them take you," Gwen whispered. "Not this year. Not ever."

ELEVEN

I

Gwen was in the kitchen with a freshly brewed pot of coffee when Ian came downstairs, the wonderful smell of whichever beans she had chosen followed by his first sips from the giant mug she handed him helping in knocking away the last remnants of sleep that had been clinging to his senses.

"Did I keep you up last night?" Gwen asked.

"No, no, not really," he said, taking a few more sips. "I did notice you tossing and turning a bit though."

"My stupid nose," she said. "You know how I hate trying to sleep on my back, but that is really the only option after breaking your face."

"You seemed to sleep okay in the hospital."

"Yeah, but they had me so doped up that I would have probably been able to sleep on a bed of nails without issue."

"One of the perks of being in the hospital."

"I'm not going back."

"No, no, I wasn't suggesting that, just…" He waved a hand

and took another sip of coffee. "Would be nice if we had some of the drugs they had you on though."

"Now you're talking," she said with a chuckle, which quickly turned into a wince, fingers going up to tentatively touch her nose.

"You okay?" he asked, the question feeling pointless.

"Fine."

He sipped his coffee so that he didn't simply stare at her with concern.

"Remember when your appendix burst all those years ago?" she asked.

"Yeah," he said, somewhat confused.

"You kept noting how one has no clue how many active muscles they have down there until you move around after an operation like that. Well, now I'm thinking the same thing, just with my face."

"Ah, yeah, laughing was bad with that, and that time when I sneezed..." He shuddered at the memory.

"Oh jeez, I didn't even think about sneezing."

"Can you even sneeze with all that packing shoved up in there?"

"I have no idea and think it best if I don't find out."

Silence settled in for a bit after that, Ian eventually finishing and then getting a refill on his coffee.

"Dee have class today?" Gwen asked, breaking the silence.

"Yeah, two finals, I think. So she'll probably be opening the store around two or three."

"Opening? You're not going in today?"

"I figured it best to stay home, what with you being only a day out from your release and all. That way I'm around if you need me and don't have to fend for yourself all day."

Gwen frowned. "I think you should go in."

"Nah, it can stay closed," he said while waving a dismissive hand.

"No, I'm serious. I think it best if you go in and open it."

"Why?" he asked. "Not like it matters all that much."

"It does for appearances."

"Appearances?"

"Being closed for two days wasn't good. A third day will be even worse. Especially with word already spreading about the hospital stuff. Rumors were bad enough before all that, but now they're just going to be getting worse and worse."

"So what? Let them talk."

Gwen stared at him.

"Seriously," he added. "Who cares what people think?"

"It impacts Tabby."

That's true, Ian realized, his mind once again returning to the videos of Gwen that the kids at school were playing on their phones and other smart devices.

Still though, opening the store just so people wouldn't talk felt wrong. Like they were giving in to something that one never was supposed to give in to. A *sticks and stones* kind of thing.

"Might actually be worse if people see my face," he said, instantly regretting the statement since he didn't want her feeling guilty about clawing him.

"People would actually have to go into the store to see it, which we know isn't very likely to happen all that much, whereas a Closed sign is visible from the street and will spur quite a bit of talk."

"Ouch," Ian said. Then, "Why don't you come with me? Be like the old days."

"No, I'm really not up for that at all. At least not today."

"I really don't like the idea of you being all alone right now."

Anger appeared in her eyes.

"I mean, what if something happens? Maybe even a sneeze like you mentioned earlier. It might cause gauze to go into your brain or something."

"Gauze into my brain," she said.

He shrugged.

She slowly shook her head and said, "Seriously, honey, I'll be fine. All I'm going to do today is sit on the couch with a blanket and some coffee watching Hallmark movies." She paused. "But if you really want to stay home and join me, you totally can. I'll curl up on you like a body pillow and then since I'll probably doze off a lot, you can fill me in on all the plot elements I miss."

"You know, there actually is a lot of stuff I need to do at the store today," he said, backing away slowly as if getting ready to make a break for it. "So much work getting stuff shipped out and shelving new books and donating to that Christmas book drive thing...I might be there for days."

Gwen grinned and then let out a very cautious chuckle.

Pain appeared, the glistening in her eyes evidence of this.

Ian waited, concerned.

She waved the pain away. "Honestly, I'll probably just sleep all day. You know how it is, can't sleep when trying to sleep, but once on the couch while trying to stay awake, you zonk out in seconds."

"Yeah."

"Is Tabby up?" she asked, changing the subject.

"Not sure," he said.

"Better go check. Might have to head out a bit early given that dusting last night. No telling what the roads are like."

2

"Daddy, stop!" Tabby shouted.

Startled, Ian hit the brakes, the truck skidding several feet on the icy surface before coming to a halt halfway into the empty oncoming lane.

"What is it?" he asked.

"I need my notebook," she said.

"Your notebook?" he asked. "One for school?"

"No, my other notebook."

"What other notebook?"

She hesitated before saying, "It's a secret."

"A secret notebook?"

She nodded.

"But you don't need it for school?"

"No," she said.

"Then it could probably wait until after school, right?"

"No! I need it now. It's important."

Ian stared at her for a second.

"Please!" she pleaded. "We're still super close."

Super close was right given that they hadn't even made it to the first turn yet after leaving the driveway. "Do you know where the notebook is?" he asked. "So you can be super fast grabbing it?"

"I do," she said, nodding.

"Okay."

Two minutes later they were walking back inside the house, Tabby racing upstairs to get her notebook while Ian announced that they had forgotten something.

No reply.

"Gwen?" he called out.

Nothing.

"Is Mommy upstairs?" he asked Tabby as she came back down, notebook in hand.

"Mommy?" Tabby shouted up the stairs.

Ian winced.

That was not what he had been asking her to do, though the lack of a reply was an answer in itself.

Or was it?

Could she have passed out somewhere during the few minutes that they had been gone?

Had fate brought them back to get the forgotten notebook so they could discover that Gwen needed help?

"Daddy, I was super fast," Tabby said, standing by the door.

"Hang on just a second," he said and began heading up the stairs so that he could check their bedroom and bathroom.

Tabby started to follow him.

"No, no, honey, stay by the door for a bit, okay?" he said, not wanting her to see her mother if she was sprawled out on the floor somewhere.

"Daddy? What's wrong?"

"Nothing, I just need to check some things. Wait there for now so that you're still all ready to go once I'm finished."

"Okay," Tabby said, taking a seat on the bench in the entryway.

Heart racing, Ian checked the bedroom and bathroom, and then all the other rooms on the top floor. After that, he headed downstairs and checked the main floor.

The cellar followed.

Still no Gwen.

She wasn't in the house at all.

Memories of another time when she had been absent from the house upon his return arrived within his mind. Back then he hadn't thought anything of it at first, but then as the hours grew and darkness settled in, worry had appeared, followed by panic.

Worry arrived much faster this time, along with the panic.

Where would she go?

Last year there had been the possibility of her having gone for a walk given that she typically did between four and five miles a day on the streets looping around the fields, even during the bitter cold months, which had been one of the reasons why he hadn't called the police to report her missing right away. This year, she had not been going on walks, and he saw no reason why she would have started again today, not with her busted nose and all the discomfort it brought.

Or had she?

He checked to see if her shoes were by the front door.

They were.

Her boots, however, were missing. Along with her coat.

"Hey, Tabby, did you see Mommy walking outside at all while we were driving?"

Tabby, who now had her notebook open on her lap as she wrote something down, shook her head.

Had Gwen taken an Uber somewhere?

No.

They hadn't been gone long enough for one to come and pick her up.

Thinking about an Uber did lead him to pulling out his phone, however, his sudden panic having kept him from doing the most logical thing one should do when wondering where a person has gone. He called her.

It rang several times before going to voicemail.

Next he sent a text asking where she was.

A "read at 8:03 a.m." note appeared, but no reply followed.

After a few seconds he typed *???* and hit send.

This one was read right away as well.

A dot bubble appeared, then disappeared, and then reappeared.

He glanced over at Tabby for a second to take his eyes away from the dot bubble torment, her tiny hands closing her notebook.

The cover had something written on it in glitter glue.

"*The Mystery of—*" he said, reading the sparkling words.

"Daddy!" Tabby cried, pulling the notebook to her chest. "You're not supposed to see that."

"Oh? Why not?"

"I told you. It's my secret notebook."

"Oh right, sorry.
His phone beeped with a text.
I'm out back on the swing.
Another beep.
To clear my head.

3

Gwen had been about thirty steps into the field behind the house when the text arrived, her body quickly turning and racing back toward the house so she could make it look like she had simply walked out to the love-seat swing they had near the fire pit area, her decision to head out toward the Robinson house so that she could test out her fireplace trap right after the two headed off to school and the bookstore clearly a mistake.

I should have waited.
At least ten or fifteen minutes.
Just to see if they backtracked for anything.

Now, sitting on that love-seat swing, she waited with her phone in hand, hoping that the lie to Ian would go unchallenged.

A text arrived.
Ah, okay.
A second text arrived.
Tabby forgot something.
A dot bubble came after this but then disappeared.
Gwen waited.
And waited.
And waited.
The dot bubble reappeared followed by a text: *And we're off again. Hopefully for real this time.*

. . .

4

"Daddy, am I going to see Dee today?" Tabby asked.

"Today?" His mind shifted its focus from the oddity of Gwen deciding to go sit on the love-seat swing in the cold to Tabby's question. "Um...no, she'll be back before you're out of school. In fact, once she's back, I will be leaving the bookstore to go pick you up from school."

"Oh."

Nothing else followed for a few seconds.

Then, "Why does Dee get out of school before me?"

"Because Dee is in college, which is a lot different from grade school."

"Why?"

"Because it's for adults, and when you're an adult going to school you don't stay there all day. Instead, you just go to your class for an hour or two, which only meets two or three times a week, and then you're done for the day, unless you have another class that day."

Tabby took some time with this, during which Ian once again started contemplating things with Gwen, thoughts on if he should head back to the house after dropping Tabby off at school being considered. A pop-in of sorts just to see what she was up to.

No.

Give her space.

And trust her.

She had been pretty adamant about him going to the bookstore so that she could be alone that day, and if that was what she felt she needed in order to get herself reoriented as the holiday drew closer and closer, then he wasn't going to fight her on it.

"When is the next time I will see Dee?" Tabby asked.

"Um...Friday night, during your Christmas concert at

school."

Tabby processed this for a bit and then asked, "Is Mommy coming to my Christmas concert this year?"

"Of course," Ian said, the question jolting him a bit.

"Okay, good."

Ian kept his eyes on Tabby for a few seconds, the brief exchange nearly destroying him given that it pulled up a memory from last year's concert, one where he had been called into the school at the last minute due to a so-called meltdown that Tabby was having. The reason for this meltdown: Tabby had apparently mentioned that her mommy would finally be home that night because she had promised never to miss one of Tabby's concerts, to which one of the little shits in her class had replied that her mommy couldn't come to the concert because her daddy and his girlfriend had killed her.

"Daddy, are you sad?" Tabby asked.

"No, no," Ian said, wiping at his eyes. "Just my allergies."

"That's what adults always say when they're sad," Tabby noted.

Ian grinned.

Tabby didn't miss a thing.

5

Val watched from his rental car as Ian and Tabby drove by him for a second time that morning, the first time around having apparently been a false start whereas this time around they managed to make it beyond the distant rise in the road and disappeared from view.

Now the question was: were they both gone for the day, or would Ian be returning home to stay with Gwendolyn?

His hope was that Gwendolyn would be left alone, thereby allowing him to observe her in whatever it was she had going on, that moment in the family room by the fireplace with the Christmas lights still at the forefront of his mind.

Movement.

In the field.

Gwendolyn?

What was she doing now?

The closest neighbor was over two miles away, so the chances that one of them would happen to be walking through the snowy field just beyond Ian and Gwendolyn's property line seemed a bit far-fetched, as did the chance of it being some random winter hiker that had parked somewhere along the field for a snowy stroll.

This area did not attract such enthusiasts.

Nope.

So unless some unknown person had been staying with Ian and Gwendolyn, this had to be Gwendolyn herself.

And she was heading in the direction of the Robinson house.

6

Walking through the trees and then across the field through the snow was difficult under ideal conditions, but when breathing through the nose was not an option, it became nearly impossible. Yet Gwen did not let herself falter, her booted feet taking one step after another, an inner voice constantly repeating a statement on how she didn't need to rush. Ian was going to be gone all day, which gave her plenty of time to get there, test what she needed to test, and then come back.

Plenty of time.

No rush.

One step after another.

. . .

7

Whoa! Dee said to herself while staring at her phone while in a study area before her first final of the day, her fingers having stumbled upon an article on Ian and Gwen that she had never seen before, one that talked about how Ian, Gwen, and a redheaded escort named Gillian had sent shockwaves through the investment world after creating a division within their firm that was devoted to helping sex workers invest their money so as to have something to support themselves with once their time within the sex trade came to an end. A photo of Ian, Gwen, and Gillian was at the top of the article, the three decked out in what Ian had once referred to as Wall Street Power Suits.

A paywall prevented Dee from reading beyond the first paragraph of the article, which bummed her out a bit but did not stop her quest to learn more, a Google search with Gillian's name bringing up a treasure trove of search results, some of which were links to Pornhub and other adult sites where her name was a popular keyword, it seemed.

8

Gwen sat on the grimy sofa in the cold family room, staring at the fireplace, the journey to the Robinson house having worn her out far more than she had expected it to, her legs feeling as if she had gone on one of her Covid-lockdown treks around all the overgrown fields rather than simply cutting through them.

Walking, walking, walking.

They had done that a lot during those days, sometimes three or four times a day, Ian often commenting on how they had moved out of the city just in time. Gwen agreed. Their

Manhattan apartment hadn't been a cubbyhole by any stretch of the imagination, but they still would have felt completely on top of each other if forced to spend the various lockdowns in it. Being surrounded by people on all sides also would have felt overwhelming, even with everyone keeping to their own living spaces.

Out here was better.

They had a large house with lots of open land, the three of them all having areas they could escape to within the house if they needed space, as well as places outside they could wander to.

And then one morning Jessica had flagged her down while she was cutting through their old overgrown Christmas tree farm, a statement on needing to talk to her about the rent echoing from her lips.

Gwen had agreed to the talk without any hesitation, knowledge that the last two years had been hard on the Robinson siblings guiding her through their front door...

Ropes pulling her up into the air.
Feet kicking.
Body twisting.
Globs of leftover eggnog spurting from her.
Seconds feeling like minutes.
Minutes like hours.
Hours like...

Gwen closed her eyes and took several deep breaths to calm herself before rising to her feet and walking over to the old Christmas tree, her hands pulling free a strand of lights, dead pine needles raining down with each tug.

9

The rumble of a generator running out in the storage shed near the old workshop was the first thing Val noticed as he walked up to the rear of the Robinson house, the sound feeling completely out of place given how quiet this abandoned area usually was. Footprints were present as well, fresh ones that went from the storage shed to the back door of the house, which was standing wide open, the lockbox that normally held the key sitting on an old porch chair that was partially covered in snow.

Gwendolyn was inside.

Of this he had no doubt.

10

Gwen found the breaker box in the basement and opened it, eyes searching for the transfer switch so she could switch the house electricity over to the generator she had started several minutes earlier.

11

Val quietly followed a set of wet bootprints from the open back door through the kitchen and into the family room, his eyes quickly noting a strand of unlit Christmas lights that had been stripped from the dead Christmas tree and stretched across the room to end in the fireplace, the final few feet wrapped around a single piece of firewood that had been set on the grate.

Reaching inside, he took hold of the firewood so that he could get a better look and hopefully an idea on why Gwendolyn had set this up, eyes suddenly noting a severed endpiece of Christmas light cord next to a pair of wire cutters on the stones that lined the edge.

. . .

12

Gwen flipped the transfer switch and instantly heard what sounded like a small explosion on the floor above, followed by a series of popping noises and then a very vibrant static type of sound that brought back memories of seeing a downed power line dancing in a flooded yard after a summer storm when she was a kid.

13

Val's world exploded, his body feeling as if it had been hit by something that he could not even comprehend, a bright yellow light illuminating everything before a wet popping sensation within his eyes brought darkness.

14

Gwen smelled something awful as she headed back up the stairs, the scent of burnt human flesh easily penetrating the wads of gauze that had been shoved up her nostrils by an ER doctor two days earlier to stem any bleeding that might occur. And then she was vomiting, the unexpected sight of the semi-charred man in the middle of the family room too much for her stomach to bear.

15

. . .

Burnt hair.
Screaming.
Blisters everywhere.
Smoke rising out from between her legs.

Gwen fisted her hands and pressed them into her closed eyes, the sudden, unexpected memory of her very first shock therapy treatment back when she was a teen threatening to overwhelm her.

Deep breath.
And another.
And another.
She opened her eyes.

Smoke still oozed from the body, though not as much as had been present before. Even the smell of charred flesh had seemed to dissipate, though that might have been more a fact of her simply starting to grow used to it.

It works.

This thought arrived without warning.

Today's goal following yesterday's Alexa tests had simply been to see if her fireplace trap would actually produce enough voltage to do damage, her hope being to see a piece of charred firewood in the grate when she came back upstairs.

Following that, she would have tested things with an animal of some sort to see if it could actually kill, but now she knew such a test would not be needed thanks to this unexpected visitor who had clearly found himself in the wrong place at the wrong time.

But who was he?
And why had he come inside?

Crouching down, she started reaching for one of the pockets, the outline of a wallet clearly visible, but then hesitated, her fear about being zapped once again present.

It's fine!

Is it?

Could the body still carry a charge?

16

"Gwen?" Dee asked into her phone while stepping up to the closed door of the classroom where her first final of the day would be taking place, somewhat startled by the fact that Gwen would be calling her. "Everything okay?"

"Everything's fine," Gwen said. "I just had a bit of an odd question for you. One that you're the only person I could think to call that might know the answer."

"Really?" Dee said while trying the door handle, which was locked, the room beyond dark. "Okay. Go ahead."

"When a person is electrocuted in the electric chair, how long do the guards have to wait before removing the body from the chair?"

Dee felt her jaw drop a bit.

"Dee?" Gwen asked.

"Yeah, um, sorry. Caught me off guard."

"Totally random, I know. That's what happens when you get into an argument online with some idiot mouth breather who is now trying to mansplain to me."

"About the electric chair?"

"Well no, electricity in general, but it has evolved significantly from the original topic. Or maybe devolved would be a more accurate way to describe it."

"Ha, yeah, I know how that goes."

"So anyway, my question is back when they would zap people to death in those horrible chairs, were the guards able to touch the body right away or did they have to wait a while so they didn't get zapped themselves? Like, would the body hold a charge that was still dangerous?"

"No. Once the electricity was turned off, they could touch it right away without issue," Dee said. "One thing they couldn't do was an autopsy. For that they would have to wait at least an hour."

"An hour?" Gwen asked. "Why's that?"

"Because the inside would be too hot from being cooked."

"Oh, I see."

"Guess the first doc who did an autopsy found that out the hard way when he cut into the body and got scalded by steam or something, though why exactly they even felt the need to figure out the cause of death on someone who they had just witnessed being electrocuted is a mystery to me."

"Yeah, that does seem odd."

"I'm thinking it was probably so they could try to understand exactly how it killed so they could make it more streamlined, especially since the first few weren't all that successful in regards to being humane. In fact, one of the earliest attempts didn't actually kill the person with electricity. They kept throwing the switch, but every time they shut it down he was still alive. It was actually one of the electrodes that finally did the trick, though only because it got so hot that it burned through his flesh into his body, eventually cutting right through the spinal cord."

"Oh god!"

"*Oh god* is right. Witnesses to it were noted as saying something to the effect that an ax would have been much quicker."

"An ax?"

"For beheading."

"Oh."

"They also discovered that the eyes would explode when being electrocuted, which is why hoods are used. Can you imagine, all those people sitting down to watch a guy get zapped only to then find themselves splattered with eye goo? How horrible would that—" Dee realized other students had joined her in waiting by the locked door, many of whom were staring at her with disgust. "But...that is probably more than you needed or wanted to know."

"A bit," Gwen said.

Dee saw the professor coming down the hallway to open the door so that they could begin the final. "Anyway, I gotta run. But if you ever need to know anything else about the electric chair, or any other forms of execution, give me a ring."

"Will do," Gwen said, though based on the tone of her voice, no such call would be happening anytime soon.

17

Stupid! Stupid! Stupid! Gwen said to herself while disconnecting the call with one hand and pulling the wallet free from the body with the other, thoughts on how Dee would probably tell Ian about her odd inquiry into the electric chair now dominating her mind.

Then again, getting herself zapped while in the middle of the Robinson family room by the body of a person she had accidentally killed while testing a fireplace Christmas-light trap would not have been ideal.

She opened the wallet and looked at the ID.

Valentine Finley.

Her mother's private investigator.

One that she had actually met face-to-face many years ago back when her mother had hired him to find out if Ian was having sex with any of the escorts they managed money for. The answer to that was yes, he was, though not in the way her mother envisioned.

And if she had seen what it was that was really unfolding...

Gwen grinned for a moment but then refocused herself on the task at hand, returning the wallet and ID to one pocket while pulling his phone free from another.

Thumbprint access? she wondered after seeing that the phone still worked.

Disappointment followed.

The hand was fried to a crisp, thumb included.

Whatever prints had once been there were no longer present.

Left hand?

She tried, but that thumb did not open the phone.

18

A half hour later, Gwen was in the middle of the field pushing the body into one of the many holes that had been dug by the various law enforcement teams earlier that year as they tried to see if any bodies had ever been buried by the Robinson family, the *thunk* as it landed muffled due to the snow within. Following this, she took a seat in the trampled snow, her exhaustion at getting the body to this point far more strenuous than she had envisioned it would be when exiting the house with it.

The snow was to blame.

Dragging a large body across a regular field gone to seed would be tough enough; doing it when there was nearly a foot of snow on the ground that would bunch up in the crotch area of the body as if the groin was some type of snowplow...that was just beyond ridiculous, the situation forcing her to stop every few feet so she could bend over and scoop out the accumulation.

But now that task was complete.

Next up was covering it, which meant she had to go get some bags of dirt since the soil itself was frozen. Four or five bags probably. After that, she would scoop more snow atop the area so it wouldn't be all that visible from a distance and then await another snowfall so that everything would be smoothed out—or at least look that way when viewed from a distance.

With any luck the body would go undisturbed all winter long, and then come spring, vegetation would start to grow, a mix of weeds and prairie grass completely masking things. It was perfect. Or at least it seemed perfect.

If any law enforcement agencies ever came back out here to do more digging, the body would probably be found fairly quickly by the dogs they used. By then though Tabby would be safe and whatever evidence she had left on the body would be long since decayed.

Or would it?

She had no idea on this and thus had no business even speculating upon it. Not when she had so much she still needed to do—both today in cleaning up the mess she had unexpectedly made in the Robinson house, and then preparing for Christmas Eve itself during the next several days so that she could be ready to set her fireplace trap that night after everyone went to bed.

Would it actually work?

Clearly the trap would kill a full-grown adult, but what about Santa?

Could he even be killed?

What if this just made him angry and he decided to wreak havoc upon everyone in the house after that?

19

"I'm actually surprised by how much better it looks," Sam said, her fingers on his chin as she turned his face so the light illuminated the wounds. "If I hadn't known the scratches were only two days old, I would have thought it had been at least a week."

Though he knew Sam was not one to blow smoke up his ass, Ian struggled to believe this particular observation. It just didn't seem right.

"I'm not saying it isn't noticeable or anything," Sam added as if sensing his thoughts while releasing his chin. "You're still going to frighten old women and young children if you go near them. But it certainly is healing much faster than I would have anticipated."

"Well that's something," he said, the sensation of her fingers lingering upon his flesh.

"What are you putting on it?"

"Just Neosporin."

"Really? Wow. They should hire you for commercials. Like real-time ones where Gwen scratches you on camera and then they do a time-lapse of how fast it heals."

Ian gave a slight shake of his head at this and then quickly rubbed at his chin with his forearm in an attempt to dispel the last of the lingering finger sensation.

"Or maybe I'll be the stand-in for Gwen if she doesn't want to be on camera," Sam added, holding up her hand as if it were a claw.

"Oh jeez."

"Seriously though, keep doing what you're doing and I bet come Friday night those scratches will be barely visible."

"That might not be such a good thing."

"Why not?"

"Because then everyone will simply focus on Gwen and her bandaged face."

Sam was silent for several seconds after that. "Well, me and Dee will be there for moral support should things get awkward. Speaking of Dee"—she cocked her head to the rear of the store—"sounds like she has arrived."

Ian listened but didn't hear anything. "Think so?"

"Cop ears," she said. "I've honed all my senses to the point of being nearly superhuman in my crime-fighting abilities."

"Ah," Ian said. A comment on how those "honed" senses had totally failed when it came to locating Gwen during her month of captivity nearly leaving his lips.

20

"Oh my god, Gwen's mother about lost her mind after this article was published," Ian said, laughing.

"Really?" Dee asked, taking her phone back.

"Big time."

"Did she not know what you two were doing within her own firm?"

"Oh she knew, and she loved the money we brought in, but she hated the headlines it generated. This of course made Gwen even more eager to give interviews and go on talk shows dedicated to investing. She would get so giddy knowing the drama it would cause. It was hilarious."

"Wow." Dee could not picture Gwen being all giddy about anything. Or working alongside escorts—even after seeing the photo of her alongside Gillian. "How come?"

Ian shrugged. "I'm not entirely sure. Those two have always had a very complicated relationship. I think it probably stems from the fact that Marybeth put her into a boarding school for most of her childhood and then pretty much forced her into working finance within her own firm, and while Gwen was actually really good at it, it wasn't something she had ever aspired to, so her being able to make tons of money for the firm while working with men and women who made her mother uncomfortable was like a huge win for her."

"Wow," Dee said for a second time.

"And of course, like most things, it was all my fault."

"What? How?"

"Gillian"—he nodded toward the phone—"was the very

first escort we worked with. Well. I worked with. Though Gwen joined me fairly quickly once things started to snowball. It was kind of funny actually. You know the old '80s movie *Trading Places*?"

"Um...is that the old movie with Eddie Murphy and the *Ghostbusters* guy? I never can remember his name."

"Dan Aykroyd."

"That's it."

"Anyway, in that movie Jamie Lee Curtis plays a prostitute who mentions at one point that she has been putting all her money in T-Bills that will allow her to retire in five years. Gillian apparently saw this scene one night and was intrigued and decided to find out what T-Bills were."

"Which are what exactly?" Dee asked.

"Treasury Bonds."

"Ah, okay." That didn't really clarify anything for her, but she let it slide.

"Not long after that she was hired as entertainment at a party being thrown by a bunch of Wall Street hotshots where she started talking with a young guy about investing who thought her attempts at discussing such things was hilarious. He and some of his buddies poked fun at her all night while she serviced them and eventually suggested she see me, thinking it would be a great office gag if I unexpectedly realized I had a prostitute at my desk wanting to set up investments, one who thought I managed a special hedge fund just for sex workers."

"Jesus. What a bunch of douchebags!"

"Totally, though the joke ended up being on them because not only had Gillian learned quite a bit about investing, she also had tons of money on hand thanks to Bitcoin, which she had adapted early on as a payment method and then converted into cash during one of the early price surges. We're talking six figures, all just sitting in a bank account. Had those guys at the party known this, they never would have let her go, but they were dicks that simply wanted to poke fun at her before poking themselves into her."

"Not you though."

"Nope. I simply helped her find places for all that money, places that ended up doing very well for her, which naturally caught the attention of others in her field who she recommended to me, and before I knew it, Gwen and I were running a division within the firm that focused solely on escorts, strippers, porn stars, and dominatrixes."

"That's incredible," Dee said. "Like legit incredible. I'm also now totally picturing you in a nice wood-paneled office with leather furniture and a fireplace, a huge desk, dressed in one of your Wall Street Power Suits while a bunch of scantily clad women in stiletto heels come and go, which I'm guessing is really far off the mark and so cliché that I'm almost hating myself for even thinking it."

"That would have been hilarious, but yeah, totally off the mark. In the beginning I didn't even have an office, just a desk in a tiny cube in the bullpen that couldn't even see any windows. And the only women who ever dressed like that when coming to the firm were not sex workers at all but this group of stupidly rich trust-fund brats who all wanted to be influencers on the web and were spending way too much money and frequently demanding access to the principal of the funds their parents or grandparents had set up for them, which in most cases wasn't allowed because those who had set up the funds were wise enough to know that they were raising dumbasses who couldn't be trusted with money."

"Ugh, no thanks."

"Yeah, I'm so glad Gwen and I didn't have to deal with them."

"I'd be right there with you. If given the choice, I'd always pick working with the sex workers. Their success with money would feel way more deserved. Plus investing their money when they're young is really smart because that career is not one that can last very long."

"Gwen and I felt the same way. And the fact that we eventually got to run our own division was kind of awesome."

"I bet that just totally bugged the shit out of Gwen's mother."

Ian chuckled. "The best part about all of it was that creating the specialized division within the firm was initially her way of quarantining all of us into our own area so that we didn't sully the rest of the firm and the clients, but given the amount of money it was bringing in, money that was suddenly seen as newfound untapped wealth by all the other firms, it brought even more notoriety to the firm because everyone else began to copy it and create their own 'red light districts' within their firms that specialized in money from the sex-worker industry. We were seen as groundbreaking within the financial world, the ones that paved the way into uncharted territory. Only no one else was ever able to achieve the same type of success since all the women in those industries always wanted to work with me and Gwen."

"How come?"

"Gillian always said it was because Gwen and I treated them as equals and with respect. That was a big deal within their world, especially given how most of society views sex workers. We also were very quick to right any disrespect showed toward the women by our team members. Gwen actually butted heads with HR about this once after she found out one of our team members was actually demanding blowjobs from the women and threatening to withhold their money if they refused. A young lady named Crystal secretly filmed him making these demands and went to Gwen with it, who then showed it to HR. They suggested letting the employee quietly resign. Gwen, however, said nope and made sure everyone in the firm knew why he was being fired and had security march him out to the street with a cardboard box filled with his stuff.

The best part of that spectacle was that he had this stupid little cactus plant balanced on top of everything that had a very phallic look to it, and it kept poking him in the face as he walked out."

"Shame! Shame! Shame!"

"Ha! Exactly. Minus the bell and the nudity."

"Probably for the best."

"He actually tried to sue the firm for wrongful termination, which was a huge mistake because despite never wanting any publicity, Gwen's mother threw all the power of her legal team into the lawsuit while also having her investigator dig up dirt on him, which made it so he not only totally lost the lawsuit, but also found himself unable to get a job with any other firm. His wife also scored big in their divorce since most of the dirt Marybeth's investigators uncovered on him somehow made its way to the wife's lawyer."

"Nice!"

"Gwen and I were quite tickled by all that."

"So what happened?"

"What do you mean?"

"Seems like you two had a good thing going out there and were on your way to becoming superstars in the financial world, and then boom, you suddenly leave it all behind to move out here to run a used bookstore."

Ian didn't reply.

"Not that I'm complaining or anything since I love this place, and my apartment, and being able to go to school without any financial worry, but still, seems like quite a big change, one that not many people would take."

And right after one of the women you likely worked with and might have also been fucking disappeared, she said to herself.

Just a coincidence, another voice inside her head countered. *They've caught the guy responsible for those murders.*

But they haven't linked him to all the bodies.

Ian continued his silence, though it didn't seem like it was due to not wanting to answer. More like he was trying to figure out the best way of answering.

Dee waited, discomfort at the silence arriving as her mind continued its debate on if Ian could be responsible for some of the bodies that were found out there on Long Island.

"This might sound odd, but we just weren't happy," Ian eventually said.

"What do you mean?" Dee asked.

"Me and Gwen," he said. "Neither one of us was feeling very fulfilled with our lives. Don't get me wrong, we loved each other and Tabby and were really happy with the success we had and the opportunities it brought us, but we also both felt completely exhausted with it all and way too close to her mother's authority."

Dee wasn't sure how to respond to that.

"We also realized that if we wanted to make a big change with our lives, one that involved completely uprooting ourselves, it was a perfect time to do it given Tabby's age."

"Her age?"

"Yeah, she was only in kindergarten at the time, so we felt it wouldn't be too difficult of a move for her, whereas with first grade and beyond, moving to a new school would be tougher."

"Ah, okay, I get that."

"And it seems to have worked. Tabby loves her school, which I think is a way better environment for her than what was awaiting her out there. Going to the academy in the city we originally picked out where all the children of the crazy rich attended just wasn't something I was ever comfortable with."

"How come?"

"Not sure. I think maybe just the idea of her being surrounded by very privileged people who might not fully appreciate what they had or the fact that they had lucked into their existence when so many others around the world are struggling didn't sit well with me."

Dee nodded.

"And Gwen actually agreed with me on that one, which was a bit of a surprise. I figured she would have been upset by my thoughts on that given that it was pretty much a criticism of her upbringing, but no, she thought I had a very valid point."

"Probably why you two clicked so well back in college."

Ian nodded. "Probably."

21

"Daddy, what street is this?" Tabby asked, yanking him from thoughts on Gillian and all the incredible threesomes he and Gwen had with her—threesomes that he had not initially realized were actually an attempt by Gwen to see if she could reignite some of the sexual excitement that had been present during the period of time prior to her and her girlfriend being discovered together in a disused wing of the boarding school they both were students at, and the horrible shock treatments that followed.

"What, honey?" he asked, even though he had totally heard the question, his eyes looking out the window for a few seconds to reorient himself.

Robinson house.

They had just passed it on the left while coming up to the turn that would put them on their own street.

"I asked what street is this?" she repeated.

"Route 6," he said, his mind suddenly wondering if she was noting where the Robinson house was and whether that meant she knew what had unfolded within it last year.

They had never told her where all the bad things had

happened, or what those bad things were, but in today's world that didn't really mean anything. And if kids were showing her videos of her mother freaking out while shackled to a hospital bed, chances were good she had been given details on what had happened.

Well...speculation on what had happened since many of the details had never been made public.

Eggnog enemas...

A diet of candy canes, Christmas cookies, hot chocolate, and more eggnog...

Christmas music playing twenty-four seven...

Being fucked while hanging by the fireplace...

Ian shook the thoughts away, his mind unable to even fathom the full horror of what that had been like to experience day in and day out, followed by what had unfolded on Christmas Eve itself.

22

"Alexa, turn on Christmas music!" Tabby shouted while racing down the hallway toward the family room. And then, once in the family room: "Alexa, turn on Christmas lights!"

23

Gwen shrieked as an image of Santa emerging from the fireplace played across her mind, Christmas music echoing, the electricity that was supposed to kill him doing nothing but tickle him, all while Tabby screamed *"Mommy!"* over and over again as two elves began putting her into a giant sack, one that was already overflowing with struggling gifts that had been given to Santa that year.

"Gwen!"

She opened her eyes upon the charred face of the investigator, his body looming over her as his fried vocal cords and burnt tongue spoke her name.

Water hit her in the face.

She blinked.

Ian was standing over her, the now empty water pitcher in his hand, concern dominating his face.

Tabby stood behind him, looking terrified.

Christmas lights illuminated the room while Christmas music was echoing from the speakers.

"Mommy?" Tabby questioned, clearly frightened.

Gwen couldn't form the words of comfort that were needed, not when the imagery of her being put in the giant wiggling sack was still so prominent within her mind.

"Honey, go to your room for a bit," Ian said.

Tabby didn't argue.

24

"Sorry," Ian said while handing Gwen a towel from the bathroom. "I couldn't think of anything else to do."

Gwen mumbled something unintelligible while dabbing at her face.

Ian hesitated.

On the wall-mounted TV a Hallmark Channel Christmas movie was playing, one that had been muted at some point prior to his arrival back home with Tabby.

Gwen continued dabbing at her face and then touched the bandages that were holding her broken nose in position.

"Is it soaked?" he asked.

"Not really," she said, fingers continuing their investigation.

Ian watched this, unsure what to do.

Gwen patted the cushion next to her on the couch.

He sat.

Neither spoke for several minutes.

"Another nightmare?" Ian eventually asked.

"Yeah," she said.

"About Santa?"

A nod.

"Want to talk about it?" he asked.

She shook her head.

"You sure?" he pressed.

A nod.

Ian didn't reply to that.

"It wouldn't help," she said, clearly sensing his thoughts.

"It might."

"No."

Ian bit his tongue.

She reached out and took his hand. "It's getting better," she said.

"Is it really?" he asked, unable to mask his doubt.

"Yes," she said, both hands now holding his hand. "Please trust me."

He gave her a pained smile.

25

"Mommy's okay," Ian said while stepping into Tabby's room. "She just got scared while waking up."

"Because of the Christmas stuff?" Tabby asked.

"A little bit," he said.

"You splashed her with water for the Christmas tree."

"I did, but not to be mean. Sometimes splashing water like that helps when someone is scared and freaking out."

"Why?" she asked.

"I'm not really sure," he admitted.

Tabby took some time with that, eventually nodding as if passing a judgment of acceptance upon his statement.

26

Snow flurries began falling during dinner, which then turned into snow showers as the evening hours progressed, Ian eventually taking a look at the weather app on his phone while he and Gwen were standing by the window watching it fall, a statement on how it looked like they would be getting three inches that night leaving his lips.

"Just like my wedding night," Gwen said.

"It didn't snow on our wedding night," Ian replied.

Gwen gave him an evil grin.

Understanding arrived. "Wow," he said, shaking his head. "Just wow."

Gwen chuckled. "Sorry, couldn't resist."

"No, no, it's all good," he said. "I just never realized you had been married before me. I thought I was the first. This is quite a surprise. And to now know how tiny he was..."

"Ha," she said and then grimaced while gently reaching for her nose.

"I still can't believe they didn't send you home with any painkillers," he said after a few seconds, feeling helpless. Then, "Want me to get you the ice pack?"

She shook her head and then removed her fingers from her nose area, hand trailing down until it was on the windowsill. "My poor car is going to be totally covered in snow."

"Your car..." he started. "Oh jeez, I totally forgot about your car."

"Me too."

"Tomorrow I'll see if Dee or Sam can pick me up so I can then drive it back after work."

"Nah, I'll just come with you in the morning and bring it back myself."

"Think you'll be okay to drive?"

"Should be. As you just noted, they didn't give me any painkillers to take home, and whatever was in my system from the other day has to be totally gone by now."

"True."

Nothing else was said for several seconds, the two simply gazing out the window.

"I'm sorry about earlier," Gwen eventually said.

"Earlier?" he asked. "You mean when you woke up on the couch?"

A nod.

"You don't have to apologize for that," he said. "You just got spooked."

"You seemed upset by it," she noted.

"I did?"

"You were so quiet during dinner and then afterward while watching TV."

"Oh, that had nothing to do with what happened on the couch."

"What then?"

He hesitated.

She turned to him. "What is it?"

"Nothing really. Dee just caught me off guard with something today that brought up old memories, ones that took me a while to shake."

"Oh?" A bit of concern was present. "What memories?"

"Ones about Gillian."

"Gillian," Gwen said, clearly surprised. "Really? Wow. Been a while since we talked about her."

"I know."

"So, what brought it all up?"

"Dee apparently stumbled upon an old article. The one that had the picture of the three of us standing with our arms crossed in front of the bullpen."

"Oh god, I remember that. Talk about a pain in the butt. I never thought taking a simple photo would be such a hot mess."

"Hot mess?" he asked.

"Yeah. All the wardrobe stuff. Before the photo."

Ian gave her a questioning look.

"Did I ever tell you about all that?" she asked.

"No, nothing."

"Huh," she said. "Well, things got a bit ugly before the photo shoot. Mostly because of Gillian."

"What'd she do?"

"Nothing. She was totally cool. It was the magazine people. The photographer apparently assumed Gillian would show up looking like a woman in an office-themed porn video rather than a classy businesswoman, and they were quite insistent that she change into something more risqué for the photo shoot."

"Seriously?"

"Yeah. They actually had a screenshot from one of her old website ads that showed her in a frilly red corset with garters hooked up to silk stockings, and asked if she could change into that and wear her blazer over it but nothing else."

"What? Did they think she had stuff like that at the office that she could change into, or that she carried it with her wherever she went?"

"Who knows?" Gwen said.

"Unreal," Ian said. "Were they like that with you too?"

"No, well, not to that extreme. They had a few suggestions

that would give me a more seductive look, but after firmly saying no to several of their suggestions I started simply waiting them out with silence, which eventually got the message across."

"Where was I during all this?"

"In your office. They clearly didn't care what you would be wearing as long as it was a suit of some sort, and simply brought you out for the photo. They did make sure you were front and center though, and standing a bit closer to the camera than me and Gillian so that the photo gave a male-in-charge vibe."

"Is that really why they had me in the center?" he asked.

"Totally."

"Jesus."

"And at that point I really didn't feel like making a fuss over it after all the wardrobe stuff, so..." She waved a hand in the air.

"I had no idea about any of that."

"It was all so stupid that I didn't really feel like bringing it up after all was said and done," she said. "Plus, we weren't talking all that much at that point, so..."

Ian nodded.

"Are *those* the memories seeing the photo dredged up?" she asked.

"Yeah," he said.

Several seconds came and went, the only sound that of wind blowing outside.

"Well, don't dwell on it too much," Gwen eventually suggested. "That's all behind us."

"I know," he said. "It's just..." He shook his head. "Are you happy?"

"Happy?" she asked.

"Here? With me?"

"Of course."

Ian didn't reply to this.

"Ian," she said. "I love you. And Tabby."

"I know you do, and I love you. Tabby does too. But... well...you know what I mean."

"I do," she said.

"And?"

"I really don't like talking about all of this."

"I know. I'm sorry."

"It's okay."

"I just wish..." Another shake of the head followed by a sigh.

"It is what it is," Gwen said after a few seconds. "Nothing anyone can do about it. They destroyed that part of me. *Burned it away* as you often say. I've long since come to terms with it."

27

Gwen stayed by the window for quite some time after Ian left the room, thoughts on Gillian and how she had stupidly tried to recapture everything she had lost as a teen after her first experience with the shock therapy treatments filling her mind. First with threesomes that she claimed were an attempt to spice up their sex life, and then, when that didn't seem to be working, she had started secretly seeing Gillian alone, her hope being that if Gillian posed as her girlfriend from back then, complete with a genuine uniform from the boarding school, something might reignite the passion and pleasure she used to feel before the first series of shock treatments had torn everything from her.

It hadn't.

The shock treatments her mother had forced her to endure as a teen after she and her girlfriend had been caught together had effectively destroyed her ability to experience any sort of pleasure when it came to sex. Men, women, it made no difference.

Not that Ian had realized this for the first several years that they were together, her ability to act the part of a satisfied lover worthy of an Academy Award, it seemed.

Though once he did learn of this truth...

After Tabby had seen a very naughty text from Gillian on her phone screen...

She shook the memories away, her focus returning to the snow that was falling beyond the window she was standing at.

Would it be enough?

To mask all her tracks and cover up the disturbed area where the private investigator's body was buried?

If not and someone found it...

Horror at what had unfolded in the Robinson house earlier that day arrived once again, though not in regards to her own fate if everything was uncovered, but the fate that Tabby would be faced with given that, if arrested for what she had done, she would not be there to set up and activate her Christmas light fireplace trap come Christmas Eve, which in turn would lead to Tabby being taken by Santa to the North Pole, where she would endure horrors beyond imagination.

TWELVE

1

Tears began spilling from Gwen's eyes as she pulled the last strand of tape from her face, the flesh beneath where the splint had been resting these last several days tingling as it was finally uncovered.

Next came the gauze wads that had been shoved up her nostrils, globs of crusty snot-laced blood coming free with each one.

Not long after that, Gwen emerged from the master bathroom and headed to her walk-in closet where her evening ensemble was waiting, the tears and snot-laced blood having been cleared from her face with several tissues that were now wadded up in the wastebasket.

2

"Last year you didn't wear a tie," Tabby noted as she and Ian waited in the entryway for Gwen to come down so they could head to the school.

"I didn't?" Ian questioned, eyes glancing up the stairway.

"Nope."

"Hmm."

"It was because Mommy wasn't here. You only wear ties when Mommy makes you wear them."

Ian glanced up the stairs again, indecision on if he should go check on Gwen to see if she was okay getting the better of him.

"Why does Mommy make you wear a tie if she knows you don't like them?" Tabby asked.

"She doesn't make me wear them," Ian said. "She just sometimes likes me to wear them when it is a special occasion, which is what tonight is."

"But last year wasn't because Mommy wasn't with us and we were sad," Tabby said.

Ian wasn't sure how to reply to that, the statement catching him completely off guard.

"And now this year we are happy!" Tabby said, her face bright with that happiness.

"We are," Ian said, leaning in to hug her.

"Mommy!" Tabby shouted.

Ian turned and looked up the stairs, surprise arriving.

"Your nose is all better!" Tabby said.

"It is," Gwen replied as she stepped off the final stair and made her way to where they were waiting.

Ian stared for several seconds, not sure how he felt about her having removed the bandages this early since it totally went against what the doctors had recommended.

Then again, his having taken her home several days earlier went against what the doctors had recommended as well, and nothing horrible had happened as a result.

"Ready?" Gwen asked.

Ian didn't reply.

Gwen gave him a look.

"I'm ready!" Tabby announced, wrapping a thick scarf around her neck and then donning her mittens.

Ian looked down at her and then back at Gwen, smiled, and said, "You look beautiful."

She smiled, but then let out a slight grimace while dabbing at the area beneath her nose.

Ian frowned. "You okay?"

"Fine," she said, looking at her fingers. Relief appeared upon her face. "Let's go."

3

Dee felt an unexpected sense of sadness as she stood in the main lobby of the elementary school, memories of her own plays and concerts, and the parties afterward that her parents would host hitting her in a way that she had not expected.

She wanted to bounce back and relive those days.

Not to redo them, or to change anything. She simply wanted to experience them once again.

But such was not possible.

And even if it were, the results probably would not be as satisfying as one hoped they would be.

Such was life.

A voice called out her name.

She turned.

It was Sam.

"I almost didn't recognize you," Sam said.

Dee smiled and said, "I barely recognize myself."

It was a lie of course. For the sake of small talk. In fact, Dee was pretty sure Sam was guilty of it too. She had had no trouble recognizing her.

"I have exactly two outfits for dressing up," Dee continued. "Happy formal, and somber formal."

"Which one is this?" Sam asked.

Dee pretended to scoff.

Silence settled, during which Sam looked around, making as if she were taking in all the holiday decorations the school had put up.

"This place just does not change," Sam noted.

"I was thinking the same thing, though for me it has only been like twelve years, not fifty like you."

"Wow. Fifty? That's it. Starting tonight you won't be able to cross a street without getting a ticket."

Dee laughed.

"So, how do you think tonight will go?" Sam asked.

"What do you mean?"

"With Gwen."

"I think it will be fine."

Sam didn't reply.

"You don't?" Dee asked.

"I'm just nervous. Ian says things have been fine since she came back from the hospital, but he has said that quite a few times since her escape last year, and then boom, something freaks her out and she has a total meltdown. Or panic attack. Or whatever you want to call it."

"Well, everything is pretty holiday neutral in here. No Santa stuff. No actual Christmas stuff really. And I'm sure the songs have been modified so as to be winter themed rather than Christmas themed. So nothing that will really trigger anything."

"Good point."

"But I totally get being nervous. I hate being embarrassed for people and if she has a blowup, especially if it's in the middle of everything..."

"Exactly."

Silence arrived once again, the two watching as parents

and family members of the students who were participating in the holiday concert entered the front lobby of the school, many with siblings and cousins of the students, who clearly had no desire whatsoever to be here.

4

Zoey was in a foul mood as she pulled into the parking lot of the El Rancho motel, the past twenty-four hours having taken quite a toll on her as she left the cozy comforts of her parents' house up in Boston to come here to this small town located three hours south of Chicago.

All because Val had gone silent on her.

She had tried to ignore it, her mind telling herself over and over again that this was Val's case and that she was finished with her own cases for the year and had no obligations whatsoever in regards to making sure everything was okay after sending him all the horrible information she had learned about Dr. Wilbanks, especially not when her mother always went above and beyond in making the holidays incredibly special, the list of holiday activities that she and her sisters would take part in with their parents in a house that looked like it had come out of a Christmas movie always bringing about a magical childhood-like feel that most adults could never recapture or experience. And yet here she was, back in this ridiculous motel that sat just off I-55, her mother's tear-streaked face and quivering lip a constant companion as the guilt of her sudden departure refused to vacate her mind.

Should have stayed.

Should have just enjoyed myself.

That had not been possible though.

Not with the level of concern that had been flowing.

Everyone in the house had started to sense it too, her two

sisters noting that she seemed to be growing more and more anxious with every check of the phone, which she had been doing every couple minutes during all the various activities, her mother asking her what was wrong over and over again, Zoey finally revealing everything to everyone.

Suggestions on calling the motel to leave a message with Val were made, and then when she noted that she had already done that, they had suggested that she call the local police to send someone over to the motel to do a wellness check, Zoey shaking her head and explaining that the police in that area might be involved in whatever had unfolded given that Ian had dated the chief of police while in high school.

Involved in what though?

This question had been echoing in her mind ever since Val had failed to acknowledge the information she had sent him the other day, every direction her mind went with the question quickly taking on a sense of absurdity given how ridiculous each theory was.

Nothing rang true to her, the various theories she came up with seemingly as far-fetched and ridiculous as all the ones Marybeth had concocted within her own mind and used to justify investigations into Ian.

And yet something had clearly happened.

Val would not go silent on her like this. That just wasn't how the two did things. In addition to being business partners, they were also best friends, ones who pretty much talked on a daily basis even when there was nothing to really talk about, so even with her declaration of being finished with things for the year, and his agreement to that, they would still have been communicating with each other.

Of course, her family did not grasp this at all, their minds unable to understand that their lives were entwined beyond the office to the point where they would sometimes simply say *hey* to each other just to say *hey*, the single word able to convey more information when used between themselves than full-on sentences were able to convey between other people. Simply put, they were soulmates, just not in the sense that most people envisioned when picturing two people that laid claim to such a thing.

It was this inability to grasp the relationship between her and Val that drove her older sister to stand firm and refuse to move her car so that Zoey could get her own car out of her parents' driveway, Zoey eventually having to summon an Uber, all while her sister screamed at her about how she was ruining Christmas.

Zoey didn't disagree with the shouts.

Twice while at the airport waiting for her flight to Chicago she had summoned and then canceled Ubers to take her back to her parents' house, and then once she was finally at O'Hare she nearly bought a ticket to go back to Boston after she was informed by a stressed-out employee behind the counter at the rental agency that they had no more cars, her reservation having failed to actually hold a vehicle for her, and that she was now on a first-come-first-serve waiting list with several other angry customers who were lingering around the counter area, many looking ready to become violent.

One hour and several phone calls later, she was in another Uber heading out to a rental location in Naperville, their promise of having a rental car for her having only been a half-truth given that they had secured a car over at a location in Winfield that they were having brought over to her at their location, Zoey barely able to control her frustration while voicing dismay at how she could have simply been dropped off at that Winfield location if she had known the car was up there. The response to this from the rental counter person was that Zoey never mentioned her destination flexibility when setting up the reservation an hour earlier, and that if she had they would have connected her with that location.

Another two hours came and went before she was in that rental car, her relief at finally being in control and able to move freely keeping her from voicing comments to the rental employees on how Winfield was only eight miles away and that it seemed unthinkable that it had taken them two hours to cover that distance with the rental vehicle.

Now, sitting in that rental vehicle, one which had naturally thrown up a check engine light not long after she had gotten onto I-55, she stared at the office of the El Rancho motel, thinking how she could totally be in her parents' house right now, building gingerbread houses while eating cookies and drinking hot chocolate, all while classic Christmas songs echoed from the sound system.

Anger followed.

She was going to find out what had happened to Val, and when she did, she was going to make whoever was responsible pay for fucking up her holiday.

5

Gwen struggled to keep from touching the area of flesh beneath her nose while making small talk with Dee, Sam, and one of Tabby's teachers, a sensation of fluids dripping out a constant companion while standing in the main foyer, one which she knew was all in her head since no fluids were ever present whenever she did actually touch that area of flesh.

A hand tapped her shoulder.

She jerked her head toward whoever had touched her.

It was Ian, who had been standing by her side the entire time yet somehow felt as if he had disappeared at various moments.

"Tabby was asking if it's okay for her to go show Dee her classroom before having to head off to her music area," Ian said, all while a look asked: *Are you okay?*

"Yes," Gwen said, smiling. She turned to Dee and Tabby

and repeated her consent, her lips tightening a bit when she saw Tabby reaching for Dee's hand so that she could lead her down the hallway, Dee's hand returning the grip.

"She is so good with Tabby," Sam noted.

"She really is," Ian replied.

Gwen wasn't a fan of this line of discussion and looked away, eyes glancing over everyone who was present within the foyer, studying some of them, trying to recognize who was who from various get-togethers over the years, but failing.

Her eyes shifted to the decorations.

No real Christmas feel was present, the lights that were up and wrapped around various trees that had been erected looking more like what one would see year-round inside of a hotel lobby, with a bit of a winter theme thrown in.

"Gwen?"

Gwen turned toward Ian once again. "Huh?"

"I said I think we should go grab some seats so we can all sit together."

"Ah, yes, very good," she said and then looked toward the direction Tabby and Dee headed off in.

"Dee will know where to find us," Ian said, clearly noting her gaze, though not what she had been thinking.

Seating concern was not present at all. Instead, Gwen had suddenly generated a horrible image of Dee handing Tabby over to some elves who had been sent down from the North Pole to collect her due to Santa having learned about her plans to shock him in her fireplace trap.

6

"I didn't really want to show you my classroom," Tabby admitted after they rounded a corner in the hallway. "It was just a ruse so we could go over some stuff I have learned in our investigation."

Dee had no idea how to reply to that, the absolute seriousness that Tabby was conveying with her statement making it almost impossible not to chuckle. "Oh...I see. That was a very clever *ruse*."

Tabby beamed.

"So what is it you have learned?" Dee asked.

"The mysterious writer's car has been parked on Route 6 for four days, not far from the bad house where Mommy was last year."

Dee's eyes went wide. First at the mention of Route 6, and then even more at the realization that Tabby knew the Robinson house was where everything had unfolded last year.

"Are you sure?" Dee asked.

Tabby nodded. "It's the blue car with the palm tree license plate that you showed me."

"And you're certain it has been there for four days?"

"We drive by it every day on the way to school and back again, except one day when Mommy came with us because Daddy went a different way because of the snowy roads."

More like so they didn't drive by the Robinson house while Gwen was in the car, which Gwen probably totally knew was the reason they went a different way given that none of the roads in this area were ever good after it snowed.

"I can show you all my notes too once we are back home," Tabby added.

"Okay, we'll do that for sure. But right now I think you better get to your music room so you're not late for the show."

7

Zoey spent very little time in her motel room once she had

access to it, a quick inspection while walking toward the bathroom her only real activity before leaving the room and heading down to the one that Val had been staying in.

A knock went unanswered, as expected, and her attempt at peering through the window was stymied by the blinds, which were drawn tight.

Next she studied the lock.

No electronic keycards were used here, which was for the best since those were difficult to get around. Picking the lock was an option, but one she would rather not engage in at the moment, her thinking being that snatching the manager key from the wall behind the front desk would be much easier than risking a picking. First things first though, she tried her own key, thinking (hoping) that it might be similar enough to disengage the lock. Once in the keyhole, it would not turn, but giving it an upward thrust while torquing the doorknob to the right did the trick, the lock disengaging with an audible *pop* sound.

Nothing had happened to Val in the motel room itself.

She had figured that would be the case while still at her parents' house given that things would have started to smell fairly quickly if he had been killed within, the thin walls and proximity of the room to the main office making it so it would have been noticed even with the world's most unenthusiastic and detached staff running things. Plus most motels along the I-55 route between St. Louis and Chicago had an unspoken policy of looking into the rooms once a day, even if a Do Not Disturb sign was on the knob given the frequency of bodies being left in rooms during the mob era that had plagued both cities up until recently.

Val always lived out of his bags while on the road, never using the dressers or closets for anything, the room a testament to this as she looked around, the second unused twin bed acting as a holding place for whatever he wasn't currently wearing. Thankfully, his *toss it anywhere* attitude did not extend toward empty food containers, the only exception to this being a lone soda can that had been set near the TV. Everything else, which likely would have consisted of pizza boxes and other takeout items from all the different food joints near the exit, had been discarded somewhere beyond the room.

A file folder and various pieces of paper that likely came from within it were scattered about on the round table that stood in the corner of the room. Val's laptop was also present, the screen dark given that it had likely been unused for two days. On top of the laptop keyboard was a plastic DVD case, the DVD itself having the word "Treatments" written on it with a Sharpie.

Val had not mentioned finding a DVD, just the treatment notes.

She shifted her gaze toward the TV in the room. No DVD player was present, and Val's laptop did not have a CD drive that would allow for a DVD to be played, which meant he had probably not been able to view anything on it yet.

Her own laptop wasn't equipped either, but that wouldn't be a problem. Portable DVD players were not all that hard to come by. She would simply have to find a Walmart or Target that was open and voilà, she would have a really cheap portable DVD player that she could use.

8

Because the grade school did not have an actual theater, the gymnasium itself had been turned into a makeshift theater with a portable stage erected on the north side near a set of doors that would be used by the students to come into the gymnasium and mount the stage from the rear steps. Beyond the stage itself, folding chairs had been set up in rows that initially were neatly arranged but soon became disjointed as people shifted the chairs a bit in an effort to give themselves a perfect seat for what was supposed to be a fifty-minute holiday concert.

It only lasted fifteen minutes.

Gwen, however, was not to blame for this.

Instead, a family over on the right side of the seating area apparently grew upset about the songs having been modified from traditional Christmas-themed songs to winter-themed songs that owed no allegiance to any specific holiday.

Grumbles turned to shouts as others in that area tried to shush the family, the angry vocalizations quickly drowning out the singing from the stage, which was soon halted by the music teacher who had been conducting the students.

"Fuck," Sam muttered as things turned physical, the sounds of metal chairs crashing into other metal chairs as people were shoved joining with growing shouts and screams.

Soon the entire gymnasium was in an uproar.

"Where's Tabby?" Gwen demanded as Ian tried to clear away some chairs that were blocking them from being able to get to the stage area, which was seeing its own brand of chaos as teachers tried to usher the panicked students from the stage while various parents who were not part of the growing fight tried to shout over the teachers to get the attention of their own children.

Some of these parents even began to climb up onto the stage itself, which spurred other parents to do the same, all while others hurried around to the rear where the students were being led down the steps, which created its own problem as their adult-size bodies forced their way up the steps, knocking away any child that was not their own, the stage eventually collapsing.

"Tabby!" Gwen and Ian both shouted as they raced toward the collapsed stage.

"I got her," a voice called out.

It was Dee, her right hand clutching Tabby's as she led her away from the stage area toward Ian and Gwen.

Tabby had a look of terror on her face, which was soon buried into Ian's chest as he hoisted her into the air while walking toward a set of doors that Dee pointed out, one that no one else seemed to be aware of at the moment.

These doors led to an office behind the gym that the gym teacher used, as well as a stairway leading up to an area that had a small window overlooking the gym. Beyond this stairway was a storage area and then a hallway that went to the left, one that had a double-door exit leading to the rear of the school.

Bitter cold air was awaiting the group as they emerged from the school, none of whom had their coats, which had been draped over the metal folding chairs and forgotten during the madness that had ensued. Car keys were with two of those coats.

"I'll go get them," Dee announced.

"No, no, you stay here with them," Ian advised, setting Tabby down next to Gwen, who quickly knelt down and put her arms around her crying daughter, his suit jacket quickly going around them for a bit of warmth.

A lone siren began to echo in the distance, the flashing lights just barely visible upon the horizon.

"Be right back," Ian said and hurried back toward the doors they had just emerged from, only to discover they were locked in such a way that they could be used only as an exit from the school.

Fortunately, someone opened it just as he was about to sprint around the school toward the front entrance, Ian quickly taking hold of the door before it closed once again and slipping inside.

9

. . .

Portable DVD player secured, along with some Taco Bell that she scarfed down while driving back from Walmart, Zoey returned to her motel room and began watching the *Treatments* DVD.

Horror and disgust followed.

Anger too.

Dr. Terry Wilbanks was a dangerous man. As were his devotees. Zoey had learned this fairly quickly after talking with Val the other day, all the firsthand accounts of what the man had done to individuals at various religious conversion camps that claimed to be able to turn gay teens straight a testament to this.

One account after another had men and women talking about how the doctor had used his own homemade brand of shock therapy on them when they were teens, one that would see them being shocked repeatedly while watching pornographic videos, the doctor believing that if the shocks were administered during periods of stimulation those areas of the brain that were producing the stimulation would be corrected by the electricity.

When such treatment failed, Dr. Wilbanks would move on to what he called his tier-two treatment, which involved shocking the genitals along with the brain at moments of stimulation, one young lady who had been subjected to this treatment while at the camp her parents had sent her to stating that her entire clit had been burned away by repeated jolts of electricity, almost as if she had undergone some type of female circumcision.

When asked about allowing such barbaric treatments at their camps, the church people that oversaw everything advised that even if such treatments didn't actually work as prescribed, they did offer a painful glimpse of what awaited the sinful teens in hell should they continue to engage in their homosexual desires.

As for Dr. Wilbanks, he often claimed that he didn't feel

there was anything wrong with being homosexual, but he would offer treatments to anyone who wanted to rid themselves of such desires, and that all the teens he had treated at the camps had been willing to undergo the procedures in an attempt to better align themselves with their faith and family. Following such statements, he would often advise that his treatments also worked with eating disorders and addictions like drugs, alcohol, gambling, and pornography, and that any negative claims made about him and his treatments were the result of the pharmaceutical companies trying to silence him given the impact his treatments would have upon their earnings. *"They want to keep people sick so that they are lifelong consumers of their products, whereas I cure the problem once and for all."* He even went so far as to claim that the pharmaceutical companies were teamed up with the mainstream media to silence him and anyone who voiced support of his treatments.

Many lawsuits had been filed against Dr. Wilbanks and the religious camps that had hired him, all of which were labeled by the defendants as attempts by the state to persecute Christians. Naturally, this resulted in many religious groups offering support and siding with the defendants. It also gave Dr. Wilbanks quite a bit of publicity, and while his license to practice medicine was revoked, he was still able to make a very good living offering his services in private to those who felt he was some sort of maverick that thumbed his nose at the opposition.

It was terrifying.

Both in that he was still treating people despite his medical license having been revoked, and that so many people out there believed in him and his treatments. It was like *what the fuck?* Why were people so dumb? So gullible?

And then to go so far as to allow their own children to be treated by the guy? She could not even comprehend such a thing, and yet there were dozens upon dozens of online threads about minors who had suffered at the hands of Dr. Wilbanks, all with the consent of their parents, who had hired the doctor. And as if that wasn't horrifying enough, many of those victims were now targets for speaking out against the doctor, his supporters going after them in both the social media and physical worlds, often repeating Dr. Wilbanks's claims that the victims had been hired by the pharmaceutical companies and the mainstream media to discredit the good doctor. One group of devotees had gone so far as to hound a young lady everywhere she went, making it so she and her young children couldn't even leave the house without being confronted, the authorities seemingly unable or unwilling to step in to prevent the harassment.

Videos of this harassment had been uploaded online by the harassers themselves, as if they were proud of their actions, Zoey watching them all with dismay, especially one where the young woman was trying to lead her young children into school and kept being blocked by the doctor's supporters, one of whom was actually shouting to the children themselves about how their mother was a disgusting whore and that she would soon be offering them up as goodies at lesbian sex parties.

At the time of watching these harassment videos, Zoey had only read about the treatments that had been inflicted upon the victims, and while those descriptions had conjured up some horrible imagery within her mind, none of it had actually prepared her for what witnessing those treatments would be like.

Gwendolyn had been tortured.

It was that simple.

Just the first stages of treatment themselves were beyond anything anyone should ever be subjected to, especially when it was being described as a form of medical treatment, but what followed after that first stage was beyond comprehension.

Dr. Wilbanks, having apparently failed to rid Gwendolyn

of her Santa fears while shocking her brain as a Santa figure stood over her, had resorted to having Gwendolyn relive the night of the horror in all its detail, a young woman dressed as an elf administering an eggnog enema to her while she was bound in a cellar-like area, followed by her being strung up by her wrists in front of a roaring fireplace that had been decorated with stockings and other Christmas decor. The Santa figure had then began touching her and thrusting himself against her while she struggled, only to quickly back away whenever some sort of off-camera signal was given so that the jolts of electricity could be delivered to her brain.

Over and over they did this, Gwen's muffled screams around whatever they had stuck in her mouth to keep her from biting off her tongue during the convulsions still loud enough to echo within the motel room, until finally the session came to an end, the voice of Dr. Wilbanks stating that they would likely have to repeat the treatment five or six times during the next two weeks for it to be fully effective, and that they might eventually have to penetrate her sexually with a phallic object for the full memories of what had happened to unfold within her mind so that those areas of the brain could be shocked away.

No such treatments had followed on-screen, the DVD coming to an abrupt end, likely because it was after this particular session when Ian had caught wind of what was unfolding and put an end to things.

Hopefully...

Zoey couldn't even begin to imagine how much more damage would have been caused to Gwendolyn had she been subjected to those further treatments. And knowing her mother had approved of them, and then grew angry about the treatments being halted by Ian to the point where she was convinced he was being purposely detrimental to Gwendolyn's well-being in hopes of her becoming insane...that in itself was madness.

And yet that was the reality of what was unfolding.

Gwendolyn's mother had paid good money for these treatments, as well as for the various investigations into Ian, one of which had now led to Val having vanished.

But why?

What had he stumbled upon that had resulted in someone having decided to silence him?

If it had been something involving Marybeth herself, Val would have told Zoey about the development because it would have meant heading back to Long Island. And even if he failed to mention it, she would have seen charges on their account for the travel expenses between O'Hare and JFK.

No.

Whatever had happened had occurred here. His motel room was proof of this. He clearly had not been planning on leaving anytime soon, the open file folders with the contents strewn about upon the table evidence of his having been in the midst of his investigation.

But where had that investigation taken him?

Keys to the rental vehicle in hand, she headed out to the car to see if she could spot anything while driving around the various areas of town that would have commanded his attention, the first of these being the Robinson house.

10

"Why did everyone start fighting?" Tabby asked as Gwen eased the car out of the school parking lot, her voice barely audible over the roar of the heater, which was going full blast.

"I don't know, honey," Gwen said. "I guess people sometimes get angry over silly things and then decide to ruin it for everyone."

"Was it Ryan's family?" Tabby asked.

"I didn't really see who it was," Gwen said.

"Me either," Ian said.

"We were totally focused on you," Gwen added.

Tabby processed that for a second and then said, "Ryan told Mrs. Lytton that his family would be upset if the songs were too awake."

"Too awake?" Ian asked.

Tabby nodded. "And then Mrs. Lytton said that she hoped Ryan's family would be mature enough not to do something so silly."

"Sounds like they weren't mature enough to do that," Ian said.

"People like that never are," Gwen noted.

A few seconds of silence came and went; then Tabby crossed her arms and said, "I'm mad that they made it so I couldn't sing my song."

"Me too," Gwen said.

"Me three," Ian added. "And Dee and Sam are too. But you know what, Dee is coming over and maybe Sam once they get everything all sorted out at the school, so you can sing your song to all of us. How does that sound?"

"It won't be the same," Tabby said.

"Maybe not, but you know what we have that they didn't have at the concert?" Gwen said.

"What?" Tabby asked.

"Hot chocolate and Christmas cookies."

"And whipped cream for the hot chocolate and candy canes to stir it all in," Ian added.

"And marshmallows?" Tabby asked.

"And marshmallows," Gwen confirmed.

"Yippy!"

. . .

Dee slowed to a near crawl as she drove down Route 6, eyes on the lookout for the car that Tabby claimed she had seen parked near the Robinson house these past several days.

It wasn't actually at the Robinson house.

Instead, it was about half a mile from the house.

So as to not be noticed as they observed the house? she wondered to herself, only to realize that they likely would not have been able to see the house from where the car sat given all the overgrown vegetation alongside the road and the rows of pine trees farther in.

The car itself was empty.

Dee confirmed this after scraping away some of the snow that had crusted to the windows and pressing her face to the glass.

But why park so far from the house?

Was it so they could walk up to the house without anyone realizing someone was snooping around the house?

A quick scan of the ground around the car revealed that this was likely the case, the tracks in the snow easily visible even in the darkness.

No tracks led back from the house.

12

Zoey eased the rental car to a halt at the bottom of the Robinson driveway, her journey to the house from the motel taking far longer than she anticipated given how treacherous the roads were. Ice was everywhere, much of it invisible in the darkness, and while she was no stranger to winter conditions given that she had grown up in New England, she was a bit more accustomed to driving on roads that had been plowed and treated with salt. These roads had simply been plowed. And not very well. Likely one pass on each side during the storm, whatever snow that fell after the initial pass left to melt on its own.

The Robinson driveway itself hadn't even gotten that, Ian and Gwen clearly having decided against tending to this particular property.

Not that she was surprised.

It wasn't like they were going to be renting it out or selling the property anytime soon, if ever, so tending to the driveway would have been a pointless gesture given that it wasn't used by anyone.

In fact...

Zoey thumbed on the flashlight app of her phone to scan the driveway surface to see if anyone had even approached the house from the street.

Nope.

Animal tracks were present. Quite a few actually. But no recent human ones.

This didn't necessarily mean that Val had not run into trouble while at the house. If snow had been on the ground like this while he wanted to secretly investigate the house, he would have done so in such a way as to minimize the obviousness of it, which meant not walking up the driveway itself but approaching from some other direction.

And not just Val.

Others could be utilizing this same tactic to keep from being noticed from the street, the old overgrown Christmas tree area north of the house, the large empty field to the west, the woods beyond both, and the rarely used roads that surrounded it all making it so anyone could approach from just about any direction without being seen.

But why?

Walking through snow was not a pleasant endeavor, which meant that anyone who did decide to approach the house in such a way had to have a fairly significant reason for doing so.

For Val, this significant reason could have been so he could put up new cameras inside the house to see what was unfolding, though if he had gotten new cameras, they had not been purchased in such a way as to leave any electronic trail.

For others, the significant reason would probably be quite devious given the history of the house.

If anyone had actually visited the house.

For all she knew, Val could have simply ended up in a ditch somewhere one night while engaged in this investigation, his car going unnoticed for days as he was stuck inside, succumbing to injury. The area was rural enough for such things to happen, and if snow had been falling at the time, there was a chance his car could have gotten covered both by the falling snow and from a plow unknowingly dumping snow upon it as it cleared the road, making it so it would be quite some time before the car or Val was found.

All while the stupid rental agency continued to charge their card for the car.

13

Dee was crouched down in the snow near the Robinson house, body shivering from the cold as an unknown person stood at the bottom of the Robinsons' driveway, scanning the area with a flashlight.

Though the beam did not reach far enough to illuminate her, or the small pine tree she was near, she still held her breath every time the light was directed her way.

Sam?

No.

Sam was tied up with things over at the school and had noted it would likely be at least an hour before she was able to join them at Ian and Gwen's house. And even if Sam had managed to escape from the school situation sooner than anticipated, there would have been no reason for her to suddenly stop at the Robinson house and scan the area.

Nope.

Ian?

Gwen?

They both seemed highly unlikely as well given that they would have just arrived home with Tabby.

This was someone else.

Someone that seemed very interested in the house yet didn't want to approach it. At least not yet. For now they seemed content with scanning the house over and over again with their light, almost as if they were determined to spot something that they were certain was there but had so far gone unrevealed.

And if it continues to go unrevealed...

If they suddenly decided to come up to the house...

This did not happen.

Instead, the light disappeared as the unknown person switched it off and got back into their car.

Relief arrived but then quickly faded as the unknown person started driving in the direction of the private investigator's snow-covered car, which Dee had parked right behind.

14

Zoey eased her car to a stop behind the two cars that were parked alongside the road, one of which had been there for a while given all the snow that covered it, the other a recent arrival given that there was no snow on it and the hood was still warm to the touch.

Val? she wondered while looking back at the snow-covered car, the out-of-state license plate a pretty significant clue toward it being a rental vehicle.

No rental logo was present though, so she couldn't be absolutely sure about this without looking at a rental agreement, which was probably in the glove box.

One thing she did now know: whoever had been driving this snow-covered car had started walking through the snow toward the Robinson house a few days earlier and not returned, the edges of their tracks having been smoothed out and partially filled in by the recent snowfall. A second set of tracks was present as well, these ones having been created recently by whoever had been driving the second, still-warm car.

15

Though Dee could not specifically see the two parked cars from where she now stood near the Robinson house, she knew the general area they were parked in and had watched as the headlights of the third vehicle came to a stop in that area.

Spotting the footprints in the snow would be next.

Of this Dee had no doubt.

Now the only question was, would they start to follow the tracks or simply look at the two vehicles for a bit and leave?

Dee's gut told her that they would start following the tracks given that they clearly were interested in the Robinson house and whatever might be unfolding near it, which meant she needed to get away from the house and back to her car so she could leave the area, her hope being that whoever this was would simply follow the tracks to the house itself, not the ones that she would now make as she circled back around toward her car.

Or I could circle back around to see who this mysterious person is.

Hmm.

Whoever it was, they were not the private investigator given the lack of tracks back to the car, which meant there seemed to be a new unknown person sneaking around, one who she would like to be able to put a face to since they probably would be poking their nose around other areas as well in the days that followed.

Plus, when push came to shove, she knew that Ian would forgive any trespass she herself made at the Robinson house, especially if it meant being able to point him toward someone else who was trespassing at the house. Someone who didn't belong. Someone who probably was working for Gwen's mother.

16

"I hope she didn't skid off the road somewhere," Ian said.

"I think she would have called for help if she had," Gwen replied.

"Maybe."

"Give her a few more minutes."

Ian nodded.

"Mommy, I think it's ready!" Tabby announced from the kitchen.

"Did the kettle beep?" Gwen asked.

"No, but it's rumbling."

"We need to wait for it to beep."

"It just beeped!"

"Okay, here I come."

Ian watched as Gwen disappeared into the kitchen where a few minutes earlier the two had gotten a tray of colorful mugs ready for hot chocolate, one that would be brought out to the family room once the hot water was transferred into a carafe. Candy canes, Christmas cookies, fudge, and peppermint bark had been set out there as well. Various coffees were also on hand, though Gwen wasn't sure how she was going to go about offering those yet. Originally she had mentioned making a selection that would be put into carafes along with some half-and-half and a sugar bowl, but then later voiced that doing so might be overkill since Dee and Sam were the only ones that were coming.

Another check of the phone.

Nothing.

Unease growing, he decided against waiting a few more minutes as Gwen had suggested and thumbed a text to Dee asking if she was okay.

17

Dee felt her phone buzz with a text, one that most likely was from Ian given that no one else would have any reason to be messaging her this evening.

She ignored it.

Not to be inconsiderate, but simply because she was watching a young woman make her way to the back door of the Robinson house and didn't want to make any movement that might catch her attention.

Who are you?
And why are you here?

18

Zoey followed the first set of tracks to the back door of the Robinson house, all while keeping an eye out for some sort of ambush from whoever had been making the second set of tracks, which had abruptly veered off to the right as if they had decided to walk down the driveway to the street rather than approach the Robinson house.

A trick.

Zoey had no doubts on this.

Whoever had made those tracks had clearly known they were about to be followed, likely from seeing Zoey's rental vehicle coming to a stop near their own car on the empty road, and had made it look like they were veering away from the house so they could loop around it and either watch her from a concealed location or attack her.

If the latter, she would be ready for them.

In fact, she almost hoped for some sort of physical confrontation so that she could subdue the person and put them to the question, her thinking being that anyone who did feel the need to attack her for venturing near this house probably would have information on what had happened to Val.

No one attacked her.

At least not during her journey to the back door, which she now opened without issue, the code on the key box that dangled from the knob one that she and Val had known for quite some time thanks to Marybeth, who had provided everything they would need for accessing any location that Ian might be using as a staging point for whatever nefarious plans she thought he was engaged in.

19

How the fuck do you know the code? Dee's inner voice asked as the mysterious young woman opened the box that held the key and let herself in the back door of the Robinson house.

No answers followed.

Not that Dee was expecting any.

And dwelling upon the question was pointless.

As was staring at the house from her current position near the old shed as the mysterious young woman explored the house, the occasional glimpse of a flashlight within the various rooms that still had intact windows making it seem like she was doing a systematic search of the house.

Go inside and confront her?

As much as she liked the idea of coming face-to-face with whoever this was and demanding answers from her, she knew that doing so could prove to be a big mistake since she had no idea who she was and what she was capable of. Erring on the side of caution, while rarely her preferred course of action, seemed the wisest choice right now, especially given how confident this mysterious woman seemed in how she just walked right up to the house and let herself in.

Decision made, and not without quite a bit of relief given how cold she was, Dee stood up from where she was crouched and quickly began making her way back to the cars, the third of which she took several pictures of so that she would be able to confirm its presence in other locations should this mysterious young woman task herself with snooping around. Following this, she got into her car, cranked the heat, and called Ian, who answered after only one ring.

20

"I'll be right there," Ian said into his phone while looking at Gwen, who was staring back at him, a questioning look upon her face.

"She okay?" Gwen asked.

"Yeah, she just skidded a bit not far from here and needs a bit of a push to get her tires back on the road." He shook his head. "Apparently she has been struggling with it for like twenty minutes now hoping she wouldn't have to call us, but finally realized she would never get unstuck without some help."

"Wow," she said.

"Yeah," he replied, putting on his coat and grabbing some gloves. "Anyhow, I'll be right back."

Gwen nodded.

Ian gave a weak smile and then headed out to his truck.

21

The house had an odd smell to it, one that almost seemed like some dish had been charred beyond the point of edibility, the source of which could not be found. In fact, nothing within the house revealed anything of significance to Zoey, the place looking pretty much the same as it had when she had been inside eight months earlier, the only difference being that the Christmas tree was even more dead now than it had been before. It had also lost its balance at some point and was leaning against the wall rather than being upright in the stand, most of its ornaments having fallen to the carpet along with all the old pine needles. The house was also really cold, whereas before it had been springtime and while it had not felt like a sauna by any stretch of the imagination, it had not been anywhere near this cold.

Back outside on the porch, Zoey once again looked at the set of tracks she had followed from the road.

No other tracks were present.

They led up to the rear of the house, but none left the house.

It didn't make any sense.

Stepping down from the porch, she walked around the house to see if maybe they—Val?—had gone out through a window or something, but once again, she didn't spot any indication of such activity, the snow around the house, up until she had marked it herself, being footprint free.

And then she saw it.

It was a slight dip in the snow, one that couldn't really be seen very well when glancing at it from the porch itself or from the driveway side of the house, but was quite visible now while standing alongside it on this far side of the house.

Something had been dragged into the field, the evidence of this far more pronounced in the area that went alongside the garage that sat behind the house, likely because the structure had acted as a block against the winds that came from the west, thus protecting it from blowing snow.

Once beyond the garage that depression in the snow from whatever had been dragged became harder to see once again due to all the snow that had blown over it, though it was not completely invisible given that she knew what she was looking for.

Footprints were visible from time to time, ones that showed evidence of the person having to pause every now and again in their efforts to walk alongside whatever it was they were dragging. These prints were never smoothed out by whatever was being dragged since they were always off to the right of the direction that was being taken.

Nearly twenty minutes came and went before she came upon an area of snow that had been trampled down quite a bit before being somewhat smoothed over by occasional flurries and blowing snow. Beyond this disturbed area were several sets of prints, ones that had also been slightly smoothed over a bit, yet not to the point where it wasn't obvious that they were footprints. One good snowstorm, or a windy day, and they would probably be gone, but right now they were still visible. Someone had walked to and from this specific area several times, and always from the direction of Ian and Gwendolyn's house, which was just visible in the distance thanks to a glow of Christmas lights.

Zoey stared at that tiny glow for a few seconds before shifting her focus back upon the area of disturbed snow, her mind not really wanting to acknowledge what seemed fairly obvious.

Something had been dragged from within the Robinson house to this spot, something that had the width of an average-sized human body, something that had then been...

Buried?
Right here?
During the winter?

Digging up the frozen ground in this weather would be quite the ordeal, and while it wasn't impossible, it didn't seem all that likely.

That said, there was a mound of snow not far from the trampled area, one that could be a leftover pile of dirt from this area having been dug up.

Only the snow of that mound looked completely untouched, which wouldn't have been the case if it had been piled there the other day while snow was still on the ground.

The mound of dirt beneath the snow was frozen solid.

She confirmed this by scraping some of the snow off it and trying to dig her gloved fingers into the mound itself.

Next she scraped away some of the snow from the trampled area, her eyes quickly spotting a portion of the ground that had clearly been filled in recently given that it was an area of fresh dirt whereas all around it was ground that had frozen field grass beneath the snow.

In fact...

She scraped away some of the dirt, the top layer of which was slightly frozen while beneath it the dirt was still fresh and crumbly.

Something was present about an inch down, something that fluttered a bit in the bitter breeze.

It was plastic.

Scraping away more dirt, her fingers now completely numb beneath her leather gloves, she saw what looked like an image of a tomato, which confused her for a second until she revealed a second and third tomato, and then a carrot.

A colorful vegetable garden display had been printed upon the plastic, which she quickly realized was the remnants from a bag of dirt one would buy from a garden center.

Pulling out her phone, Zoey snapped a photo of this and then took a few steps back and took a photo of the area itself, and then ones of the various sets of tracks leading to and from the area.

Something caught her eye.

Flashlights!

Two different beams!

Emerging from one of the old rows between the overgrown Christmas trees that had never been harvested, trees that she had walked through twenty minutes earlier while following the drag marks through the snow.

They had found her tracks.

And now were following them.

She needed to vacate the area.

Not only that, she needed to get to her car without being noticed.

22

"Mommy, we should have hot chocolate ready for Dee and Daddy when they get back," Tabby said.

"That would be very sweet, only we don't know exactly how long it will take so we better wait," Gwen said, eyes constantly going from her phone screen to the front window.

"After all, we don't want it to be cold when they get back, now do we?"

Tabby pondered this for a moment and then said, "I know! We will just keep the water kettle going so that the water is super hot for them when they come back."

"That's a perfect idea."

"And I'll have the bowl of tiny marshmallows ready too."

"Even better."

Tabby turned, her body preparing to dart down the hallway, only for her to turn back and say, "Mommy, is Dee sad that she doesn't get to celebrate Christmas?"

"What do you mean?" Gwen asked.

"She doesn't have a Christmas tree at her apartment, and no family."

"Hmm," Gwen voiced, unsure how to reply to this.

"We should have her stay with us for Christmas," Tabby quickly added. "That way she will be near a tree and Santa will be able to give her gifts and she will be happy."

Gwen's natural inclination was to oppose this, but before a reply of that nature could leave her lips she started to think about how having Dee here at the house on the night that Santa would return might be for the best because she could use her to add an element to the Christmas-light trap that she had not really considered, one that was quite necessary in the setting of traps: *bait*.

No.

Yes.

Maybe.

"You know what, let me and Daddy think about that for a bit, okay?"

"Okay!"

With that, Tabby turned and disappeared down the hallway, all while Gwen continued to stare out the window, questioning if Ian's statement about Dee getting stuck was true or if something else was going on.

. . .

23

Dee was freezing, and she was pretty sure Ian was too as they silently followed the set of fresh footprints that led from the back of the Robinson house through the old Christmas tree area and into the field.

Ian was in front, guiding them alongside the footprints, while Dee was a few steps behind him, trying to step in his footprints in a fruitless endeavor to keep as much snow out of her shoes as possible despite their having already been subjected to all the snow she had trekked through during her initial journey to the Robinson house.

Step after step they made their way into the field, bodies constantly bombarded by wind gusts that seemed to carry tiny ice particles that stabbed at their faces, Dee's fingers and toes feeling lifeless from the cold.

Ian stopped.

"What is it?" Dee asked, mouth barely able to utter the words in the frozen air.

Ian simply pointed to an area of snow that had been completely trampled.

"Oh shit, looks like they continued from here toward your house," Dee said, motioning toward a set of tracks heading off that way.

"Or maybe not," Ian said, nodding toward a different set of tracks that headed back toward Route 6.

Dee looked at those tracks for a moment and then went over to the ones she had pointed out. "You know what, these ones have been here a while," she noted.

"And these ones look fresh," he said.

"She doubled back on us," Dee said.

"And you're sure it was a woman?"

Dee nodded.

Ian looked toward Route 6 for quite some time after that and then turned back to her where she stood, her body starting to shiver quite a bit now that they were not moving.

"One of us should have stayed by the cars," he said.

Dee mumbled an agreement.

"We better head—" He stopped and crouched down by the ground for a second, examining something.

"What is it?" Dee asked, body doing a little cold weather dance to try to muster up some heat.

"Nothing," he said, standing. "Just some old piece of plastic."

Dee didn't reply to that.

Ian stared back toward the tiny glow that marked where his own house stood for a few seconds, then at the ground, and then back toward the dark area that contained the Robinson house. "Come on, let's get back before we freeze."

"Too late," Dee muttered, trying but failing to chuckle.

24

Zoey made it back to her car without issue, her eyes quickly noting the pickup truck that was now parked behind her rental car.

Ian.

Dee had clearly called him after realizing someone was snooping around the Robinson house, which was interesting. Had Dee called him simply because he was the owner of the house and only a mile or two away, or had she not wanted to get any authorities involved knowing that something awful had happened within the house in recent days?

Just what that awful thing might have been, Zoey did not know, though she was certain that it had involved Val stumbling upon something he was not meant to see, which had then resulted in his body being dragged way out into the middle of the field and buried.

How something like that could unfold was difficult to fathom given that Val was not one who could be easily overpowered and typically was very aware of his surroundings. Adding to this, the house itself did not seem like a good location for any type of ambush, especially when snow was on the ground since it would have alerted him to the presence of someone else in the house.

And then there was the fact that a hole had clearly been pre-dug out in that field, almost as if someone had been expecting to have a body that needed to be buried.

A trap?

Could Val have been lured to the house?

By Dee?

Zoey had always known that Val had a thing for Dee. Nothing specific had made her note this—she just knew. Call it *best-friend intuition*. Maybe with a bit of *female intuition* thrown in.

Not that he would have ever acted upon it.

Not while on a case, and not afterward.

That just wasn't who he was.

And yet he had decided to play a true crime author narrative with her in an attempt to stir things up and see if he could uncover anything, which in turn might have resulted in Dee managing to play him if she had seen through his little falsehood.

Dee was smart.

And clever.

And she harbored some very twisted interests.

Interests that had made it seem very possible that she could take part in murdering another person, especially if she thought herself knowledgeable enough to dispose of a body without it ever being found.

Zoey and Val had learned this fairly early on when digging into her background to see if there was anything there that might indicate her having some sort of involvement in Gwendolyn's disappearance last year, only for these various investigative avenues to be dismissed once the reality of what had happened to Gwendolyn had been realized.

Now she wondered: Had Val been correct in his thoughts that maybe Ian had realized how much better things would have been for him if Gwendolyn had not escaped her captivity? Had Ian enlisted Dee to help him out in making such a thing a reality? Were they slowly but surely trying to drive Gwendolyn so far over the edge that the authorities had no choice but to put her in a padded room for the rest of her days?

Is that what Val had stumbled upon while in the Robinson house?

Something that was being prepared that he should never have witnessed?

Or had Dee lured him there so that he could be eliminated before making such a discovery?

Though why leave the car behind for days?

Even with it parked nearly half a mile from the Robinson house, it still was like a beacon to the fact that something had happened to him at the house.

And why had Dee been at the house that evening?

Actually, she had been at Val's rental vehicle, not the house, and then had been walking a path alongside Val's older footprints, almost as if she had been investigating things herself.

Something wasn't clicking.

Zoey thought about the *Treatments* DVD, the treatment notes, and the video Val had sent her of Gwendolyn instructing Alexa to turn the Christmas lights in the fireplace on and off over and over again, her mind slowly shifting toward a different possibility, one that removed Dee and Ian from being the antagonists in everything and replaced them with Gwendolyn.

What if she already had gone past the point of insanity and did belong in a padded room?

What if Val had been so focused on Dee and Ian, or some other theory, that Gwendolyn had gotten the jump on him?

But why?

What reason could she have for wanting to remove someone who was snooping around the Robinson house?

Was there even a rational motive?

If Gwendolyn was insane and responsible for whatever had happened to Val, the motivation behind it might be so absurd that no one in their right mind would be able to comprehend it up until the moment it unfolded before their very eyes.

25

"That Sam?" Gwen asked.

"Yeah," Ian said while looking at his phone.

Gwen and Dee waited for more, during which Tabby expressed concern about how Alexa kept failing to find the right version of a Christmas song she wanted to play.

"It seems that things actually got worse after we all left, the family that started everything having apparently sent out some sort of communication about what was going on just as everything began to unfold. Several people who were apparently standing by showed up once we were gone and started making all kinds of trouble."

"Are you serious?" Dee asked.

"Yep," Ian said, continuing to look at his phone.

"So they were basically hoping for a fight, which they got."

"Yep."

"Ugh, that's infuriating," Dee said.

"It is," Ian agreed.

"Found it!" Tabby announced.

Nothing else about the disrupted holiday concert was said after that as a Christmas song began to play, one that Tabby insisted everyone sing along to, the room quickly turning into what sounded like a talentless quartet of carolers who thankfully weren't sharing their singing voices door-to-door.

More songs followed, as did the echoing of the four mismatched voices butchering the songs, but that was okay because everyone seemed to be having fun, Tabby's joyful enthusiasm managing to keep all the more serious thoughts on all the various things that had been unfolding from dominating the minds of the three adults.

Of course, those thoughts were destined to return, the ones Ian was dwelling upon arriving shortly after Dee had bid everyone farewell for the evening and headed out to her car.

Not long after that Gwen noted she was exhausted and was going to turn in, Ian deciding to join her even though he wasn't tired at all.

Thirty minutes later, he was slipping free of the bed and heading back downstairs, his mind unable to shake a growing fear that had been present ever since he and Dee had found the trampled area of snow in the middle of the field, an area that he suspected had been one of the many areas that had been dug up by the authorities earlier that year as they searched for bodies that the Robinson family might have buried. All the various holes they had dug had been left open, so finding one of them filled in was quite the surprise. Had that been all he and Dee had found he would have been fine, but it wasn't. Footprints in the snow had been present, ones that clearly headed off in the direction of the house. And not just a single set, but multiple sets, almost as if someone had gone back and forth to that spot several times. However, it was the long piece of plastic that had been half buried in the uppermost layer of dirt that concerned him the most, the image present upon it one he was certain he had seen just a few days earlier while moving things around in the shed to get at the snowblower.

26

Gwen felt Ian leaving the bed, her own body keeping still and feigning sleep until he was downstairs, at which point she slipped out of bed herself and crept to the landing above the stairs so she could listen to his movements and hopefully figure out what it was he was doing.

Whatever it was, she was certain it was connected with his heading out to help Dee earlier, an event that she felt had had nothing to do with Dee getting stuck somewhere.

Instead, Gwen was guessing they had spotted the private investigator's rental car, one which she had been at a loss over on how to hide given that she had accidentally buried the keys with the investigator. At one point she had considered placing an anonymous call to the authorities about an abandoned vehicle on the road, but worried that in itself would likely draw attention to the Robinson house, which she didn't want. Also, placing anonymous calls these days was difficult. Pay phones were a thing of the past, and going out and buying a disposable phone in order to place the call would be noticed given how small the town was. Nope. Short of digging up the body and finding the keys, the best option was to leave the car where it was and hope it went unnoticed until after Christmas, a possibility that she had known wasn't the greatest option.

Ian was leaving the house.

Gwen realized this as the sound of the back door sliding open reached her ears.

Moving quickly now, she hurried to her study at the rear of

the house, the windows within giving her a perfect view of the backyard and field beyond.

From there she was able to watch as Ian made his way through the yard to the shed, her eyes only now realizing how obvious her various sets of tracks were in the moonlit snow, tracks that showed her making several trips back and forth through the trees and into the field.

27

Ian stared at the two remaining packages of dirt in the rear of the shed, his earlier concern confirmed. Not only did the image on the bags of dirt match the image on the piece of plastic out in the field, but he knew there had been at least five bags of dirt stacked out here in the shed given that he had moved them out of the way earlier that month while digging out the snowblower.

THIRTEEN

I

Gwen studied the image of a bundled-up female on her computer screen, one that she had downloaded from the nanny cam that she had found hidden within the old Jessica stocking hanging from the fireplace mantel at the Robinson house several weeks earlier. Initially, she had planned on destroying it and the other two cameras she had found, given that her mother had no right sending investigators to spy on them, but then after thinking about it for a while, she had decided to put the smaller nanny cam back inside the house so that she could see for herself if anything foul was taking place within.

Up until now nothing had been—unless one counted the private investigator getting himself zapped by her Christmas-light fireplace trap.

Gwen didn't.

Annoying, yes.

But not foul.

Or frightening.

At least not after the initial horror of seeing his smoking body in the middle of the family room, a body that she had known she needed to hide.

This tiny bundled-up female, however, was frightening given that Gwen had no idea who she was or where she had come from.

North Pole?
One of Santa's minions sent down to assess things?
To spy on me?

Jessica had frequently talked about how Santa had human-elf minions spread throughout the world to keep an eye on things given Santa's inability to leave the North Pole until Christmas Eve itself. In the beginning of her captivity Gwen had considered this all nonsense but nodded while listening nonetheless since she knew it was probably best to go along with whatever her captors were saying, especially when it came to Jessica, who seemed to carry genuine remorse for what needed to unfold every year and might be persuaded to let her go if Gwen played things correctly.

Such a release never happened, and come Christmas Eve Gwen had learned that everything Jessica had told her about Santa was true. He really was a demonic being that would come down the chimney of those who knew about his true identity, and god help them if they did not have a suitable gift waiting for him.

A demonic being that will now be coming down our chimney come Christmas Eve.

Gwen pushed the thought from her mind, not in a dismissive way, but simply because she already knew this would be the case and didn't need to dwell upon it. Instead, her focus now needed to be on the possibility that one of those human-elf minions of his was here. Watching her. Looking into things. Investigating.

Does she know about the fireplace trap?

Nothing but a lingering smell within the Robinson house

gave any indication that something had happened within, Gwen having wrapped the damaged strand of lights back around the tree. The piece of firewood that had been somewhat charred still remained, but seeing something like that within a fireplace shouldn't be cause for alarm.

This didn't mean the bundled-up female didn't suspect something, the dark pictures that were taken as the camera's motion sensor kept being tripped giving off an appearance of someone who was very inquisitive and seemed to think something was amiss.

And then Ian and Dee had interrupted things.

No pictures of them had been captured, but Ian's actions the night before were a pretty clear indication that he and Dee had been engaged in activities that went far beyond simply getting her car unstuck.

All the footprints in the snow near the private investigator's rental car and the various tracks leading to and around the Robinson house were clear indicators of this. Dee had probably noticed the car and someone snooping around the Robinson house and alerted Ian, who had raced out there to check it out. Little did they realize it wasn't just anyone who was snooping about, but one of Santa's minions, one who must have decided to slip away rather than confront them once they started making their way toward the Robinson house.

If she hadn't done that...

Gwen had no idea what one of these minions was capable of, but she had an idea that they themselves were probably pretty powerful beings. After all, they were conceived up at the North Pole, their bodies half human, half elf; thus they carried with them many of the supernatural elements that the pure beings of the North Pole were endowed with.

They were also evil.

How could they not be when living under the sadistic reign of a demonic Santa Claus?

Just the tiny bit of information that Jessica had been able

to share with her during her days as a captive was enough to paint a picture of an existence that was far beyond any horrors that humanity itself had ever been able to create.

An existence that Jessica was taken to last year.
One that Tabby would be taken to this year.
No! No! No!

Gwen couldn't let herself get overwhelmed with the horrors of what would unfold.

What she needed to focus on was her fireplace trap.

Not the setup itself since she already had that all figured out, but making sure she was actually able to use it come Christmas Eve.

She needed to make sure Santa's minion didn't uncover anything about her plans.

Is she really one of Santa's minions?

Or had her mother simply sent along another investigator after failing to hear from the first one during the last few days?

Gwen contemplated this for quite some time, her mind eventually coming to the conclusion that either way she needed to prevent them from finding out about her plan.

Minion or not, the tiny bundled-up female in the photos could not be allowed to uncover anything.

Gwen also needed more eyes on the Robinson house to see what was unfolding there, a decision to put the other two cameras she had taken from the house back up in their original spots arriving within her mind.

2

Ian was a mess.

Both mentally and physically.

Knowing he would be unable to sleep after venturing outside the night before, he had stayed downstairs in the family room after Gwen headed up, his eyes staring at but not really seeing the TV screen as one unknown program after another played upon it. Sleep did eventually take hold, but it was far from restful, the concerns he had been struggling with while awake following him down into the chaotic landscape of his subconscious where they created a batch of horrifying scenes involving Gwen, Dee, Tabby, and various Christmas-themed corpses.

Sweat covered his flesh upon waking, his body feeling feverish to the point where he considered isolating himself up in a guest bedroom for the day, but then decided against it when the sick-like feelings faded.

After that, he had spent a quiet hour drinking coffee in the small breakfast nook off the kitchen, watching through the windows as the darkness disappeared from the fields with the arrival of the morning sun.

Tabby came down a few minutes after the sun rose, an energetic "Alexa, turn on Christmas lights!" followed by "Good morning!" leaving her lips as she zoomed by him and headed downstairs to her Nintendo area.

Gwen followed in her wake.

Not much was said once she had her own mug of coffee, the words that were spoken being fairly standard inquiries into each other's plans for the day.

Awkwardness was present during this, Gwen clearly knowing something was bothering him but never voicing questions on what it was, for which Ian was thankful because he really did not want to discuss such things with her that morning. Fear was the reason. Fear of what she might say if he asked her about what he had found out in the field.

Had she actually killed someone?

No.

Not just someone.

The private investigator her mother had sent to spy on them.

How?

And why?

Thoughts on going back into the shed, grabbing a shovel, and heading out to the spot in the field came with these questions but were quickly dismissed.

He was not going to go digging up that spot.

Not today.

Not tomorrow.

Not ever.

Nothing good would come of it.

And honestly, if something had happened to the investigator, that was on Marybeth. She was the one responsible for sending the investigator here. She was the one responsible for the horrifying shock treatments. She was the one responsible for all the attempts at separating them.

Anger arrived with these thoughts.

Tears too.

All he wanted was for them to be happy.

Gwen, Tabby, and himself.

Nothing else mattered.

Once they got through this first Christmas—once Gwen realized there was no demonic Santa waiting to come and take her away—everything would be fine.

It was just a matter of getting to that moment.

They were so close.

Just two more days.

Everything would be better after that.

3

Gwen stared at the space within the old coal chute, her eyes struggling to fully process what she was seeing.

Ian's gifts had been opened.

All of them.

The rare first-edition books she had managed to find for him, three of which were signed, having been tossed aside without a care after the wrapping paper had been torn open.

Tabby?

No.

Tabby was a bit of a snoop. Both Ian and Gwen knew this. But she would never go so far as to open gifts that had already been wrapped. Especially gifts that had a name on them.

Things were also missing from the coal chute.

Things she hadn't initially noticed amid all the torn wrapping paper.

All her files were gone, the private investigator ones her mother had given her at various points in an attempt to destroy her marriage, as well as all the ones that contained research she had done into the various myths surrounding Santa, and all the letters her girlfriend Tiffany had sent her.

The treatment folder was missing too.

Along with the DVD of her treatments.

Why she had ever demanded these two items from her mother was a mystery given that she would never open the file or set eyes upon the contents of the DVD, yet demand them she had, the idea of her mother having possession of them never sitting well with her.

And now they were gone.

Taken by someone who likely had a nefarious purpose in mind.

Someone like the bundled-up woman in the photos the nanny cam had captured.

But why take everything?

Gwen pondered this for a moment, but then lost focus on the question when a new one arrived, one that caused fear to begin worming its way up her spine.

How had she gotten inside the house?

And when?

Were Santa's minions able to utilize a chimney the way Santa could, or did they need to access homes through more traditional means like a front door?

This was something that Jessica had never touched upon.

In fact, she had frequently admitted that not much about Santa's minions was known beyond their existence, which was the result of Santa impregnating the women he brought back with him to the North Pole. Some might also have been the result of offspring being produced when the workshop elves were allowed to have their way with the women Santa grew tired of and discarded.

If this was true, which Gwen thought likely, then the offspring that the elves produced with the discarded female gifts likely would be considered less-than the ones that Santa produced with the female gifts, both because his seed had not been used and whatever powers he was able to pass down through his bloodline would not be present within the offspring the elves produced. Unless of course they had originally been created by Santa as well, which would mean his powers had been passed down as well, though in a diluted type of way, thus once again putting them into a less-than position within the twisted societal structure that was in place up at the North Pole.

My baby would have been a direct descendent.

My baby would have had all the powers of a first-generational spawn.

My baby—

On and on this went, her mind being sucked into a realm of thought that was nearly impossible to break free of, almost as if it were some sort of super-max type of prison that had been created within her own head.

4

. . .

"Daddy, after we see Santa can we go find a gift for Dee?" Tabby asked.

"A gift for Dee?" Ian questioned, his mind having drifted elsewhere for a bit as the two stood in the ridiculously long line waiting to see Santa.

"For Christmas," Tabby said.

"Oh, right. Um. Yeah. Of course." He shuffled forward a few steps as someone up ahead took their turn with Santa, his mind marveling over just how many people were here waiting to see the jolly old elf. The mall itself was packed as well, something which he hadn't really considered would be a thing until he had seen the line of cars just waiting to make the left turn into the mall parking lot.

Final Saturday before Christmas, he silently noted to himself. *What were we thinking?*

Actually, thinking had not really played a part, the ritualistic "sitting on Santa's lap" one of those things they had meant to do earlier in the month only for it to get bumped out of consideration each weekend as other things popped up, things involving Gwen and her mental state, until today arrived and Tabby made Ian aware that she still had not gotten to see Santa yet.

And now here they were, waiting in a line that would rival those at Disney World while surrounded by frantic shoppers, many of whom actually had their arms loaded up with bags from the various stores as if they had no idea that one could more easily shop online these days. It was odd.

Now if only they would all go pay a visit to the bookstore, he mentally projected, a silent chuckle following.

Another few shuffled steps toward Santa unfolded, along with a realization that he had just agreed to follow up this little endeavor with one of having to shuffle his way through various stores with Tabby in tow as they tried to find Dee a gift, which then would eventually result in standing nut-to-butt in another line before eventually struggling to get free of the parking lot.

And yet all of this was putting a huge smile on Tabby's face, which made it all worthwhile, especially after all the turmoil of these last several years.

Another few steps forward.

"What kind of gift were you wanting to get Dee?" Ian asked.

"A friendship necklace," Tabby said.

"A friendship necklace?"

"Uh-huh. She would have one and I would have one and it means that we are forever friends."

"I see. Do you know where we would find that?"

"Jenny and Brea said they got them here."

"Did they say where exactly? Which store?"

Tabby shook her head. "I tried to ask, but they said that I didn't have any friends so it would be stupid."

"What? Why did they say that?"

"Everyone says that," Tabby said, her voice very matter-of-fact.

"They do?"

"But I told them that I'm friends with Dee and that she is super cool and could kick all their butts in *Mario Kart*."

Ian smiled at this, though also felt quite a bit of resentment at the statements that had been made to her by the little shits. Thankfully, it seemed Tabby wasn't really fazed by it, and given how genuine Tabby was when it came to expressing herself, he knew this wasn't just her putting on a brave face for his benefit.

Another few steps forward.

"Do you have any other gifts in mind for her just in case we can't find the friendship necklace?" Ian asked.

Tabby shook her head.

"Okay, maybe think about that for a bit. Something like a fun T-shirt or something. Or maybe a crazy coffee mug."

"I will."

"And I'll check online to see if they have any," he said,

pulling out his phone. "Might be able to find one on Amazon if they don't have any here."

Another few steps forward, after which Ian held out his phone to Tabby to see if the necklaces he had found were what she was describing.

"That's it!" she said.

"Excellent. And you know what, if I order it right now it will be here by tomorrow, which will be much easier than trying to figure out which store it was from."

"Okay, but you're sure it will be here in time?"

"Yep." He almost added that if it wasn't they could come back and try to find it here, but then realized that adding an element of doubt about his certainty on it arriving tomorrow would not be good.

Another few steps forward.

Behind them somewhere a child shrieked, followed by a parent telling someone named Kyle to knock it off or else she would tell Santa that he was being naughty this year.

"Santa already knows that," Tabby noted.

"Knows what?" Ian asked.

"That Kyle is being naughty."

"Oh, right."

Another few steps forward.

"How does Santa know who is naughty and nice?" Tabby asked.

"I don't really know," Ian said.

Tabby took some time with this, all while the boy named Kyle continued whatever it was he was doing, the shrieks of one child eventually turning to sobs, all while the mother or whoever it was that was with them decided she had done enough and just let things unfold.

His phone buzzed with a text.

It was Gwen asking how things were going.

He replied back that they were still waiting in line and that at the rate things were progressing, it would probably be another hour before they were finished and heading back home.

5

Gwen wasn't surprised by how long it was taking for Ian and Tabby to see Santa, Ian's initial statement earlier that morning as they were heading out on how it would probably just take an hour something that she had known from the start was nothing but wishful thinking.

A suggestion of getting together for lunch somewhere was made before the text conversation came to an end.

Gwen agreed that would be great and that she would meet them at the pizza place downtown once they were finished, Ian agreeing to give her a heads-up text that they were on their way once they were leaving the mall.

That completed, she tucked her phone back in her pocket and retrieved the memory disk for the nanny cam from her computer, which she stuck back into the device, all while scanning the family room to try to figure out the best location for it to be set. The spot needed to be one that would go unnoticed by Ian and Tabby as they went about their daily activities within the room, while also being one that would actually capture anyone coming and going from the room who was not supposed to be there. An image of the tiny bundled-up woman came to mind as she contemplated this, one who she was certain would be paying more visits to the house in the days to come.

Once that was complete, she would position one of the two trail cameras in the backyard so that she could see if the minion was ever lurking around back there, while the other one would go back in its original spot near the back door of the Robinson house.

Initially she had planned on putting both trail cameras back in their original locations at the Robinson house while returning the nanny cam to its spot in Jessica's old stocking, but then realized the nanny cam would probably be better utilized here at home.

After all, the Robinson house didn't really hold anything of significance now, so it didn't really matter if one of Santa's minions was looking around inside. However, if the minion was snooping around inside the house here, she needed to know this since this was where the trap would be set.

Thoughts on that trap arrived, along with a modification she had been contemplating ever since Tabby had voiced the thought on Dee staying with them for Christmas.

The trap really would work better with bait.

Bait that Santa would not be able to resist giving some attention to once his perverted eyes settled upon it.

Just like with me.

While hanging there.

Thrusting.

Spurting.

Screams.

And then a nasty *thunk* as his head cracked open against the bricks of the fireplace, her sudden kick having sent him flying.

Why had that not ended things?

Why had he been able to get up and take Jessica back with him to the North Pole after her escape?

More important, how long had that recovery taken?

Seconds?

Minutes?

Hours?

Had he stayed sprawled upon the ground while his head slowly knitted itself back together via some form of supernatural regeneration until he was able to get up and continue on with his horror?

Would the same happen once he was electrocuted by her fireplace trap?

How long would it take before all his cooked internal organs knitted themselves back together?

This question led to one where she asked herself how long it had taken her to get free after kicking Santa since that would give her some idea of how long he had stayed immobile, but she could not recall any specific timeframes.

All she really remembered was landing the kick while he was trying to fuck her, hearing the *thunk* of his skull cracking against the bricks, and then realizing the small footrest he had pulled over to stand on while fucking her was within reach of her feet. After that her mind held no memories beyond being really cold and then waking up in a jail cell that she initially thought was within the dungeons of the North Pole.

6

"Did you have fun seeing Santa?" Dee asked while eating a small pizza that Ian, Gwen, and Tabby had ordered for her after their own lunch.

Tabby nodded, but then made a face and said, "His breath was really stinky."

"Was it really?" Dee asked, trying to mask a chuckle.

"Uh-huh!" Tabby said, nodding. "Like rotten cheese."

"Ugh."

"I told him he should eat a candy cane before seeing the next kid."

Dee snorted and then quickly sipped some Coke so as not to choke on the bite of pizza she had just swallowed.

"Guess what?" Tabby said without warning, excitement obvious.

"What?" Dee asked, still struggling a bit with the pizza that had just passed through her throat.

"They had elves there that looked just like you."

"You know why that is?"

"Why?"

"Because we all got our elf outfits from the same place."

"Really?"

"Yep."

"Does that place also send them all the way up to the North Pole?"

"No, the North Pole sent them all the way down to me. Special order."

"Really?"

"Yep."

Dee took another bite of pizza while Tabby contemplated that, the slice she was gobbling up tasting like one of the best things in the world given that she had skipped breakfast that morning and then found herself swamped with customers. It had been crazy. Nonstop people coming into the store, most of whom wanted beverages, though some were also buying books that they found on the shelves, the former making it so the line stayed quite long given that she was the only one behind the counter and could only do one drink order at a time.

More than a few had grumbled at her about this once they reached the counter, one person being so nasty with his statements that Dee voiced back that he had *chosen* to stay in the long line and that he could either place an order or leave, but that being disrespectful and using profanity would not be tolerated. Shock had appeared on that person's face, followed by his quietly placing an order.

Most of the rush had subsided by the time the afternoon hours began, though there were still enough people in the store that Ian and Gwen were now together behind the counter while she ate her pizza in the small break room behind the office, Ian having also advised he would stay with her for the rest of the afternoon to help run things.

"Do elves come with Santa to help on Christmas Eve?" Tabby asked after a while.

"What do you mean?" Dee asked.

"Do the elves come with Santa?"

"You mean in his sleigh on Christmas Eve?"

"Uh-huh."

"I don't really know. Maybe one or two to keep an eye on the reindeer while up on the roof and to help with the toy bag."

"Hmm," Tabby voiced, the wheels within her mind clearly turning. "Do you think anyone ever pretended to be an elf and snuck back to the North Pole with Santa in his sleigh?"

"Wow, that's a good question. If anyone ever did, then they would probably be super cold because the sleigh goes way up into the sky above the clouds and then all the way to the North Pole, which is like a nonstop blizzard."

"But Santa's house is warm. I did a puzzle that showed Santa checking his list and behind him was a huge fireplace."

"You're probably right, but the sleigh itself is still really cold, unless it has some sort of heater built in that we don't know about, though I don't really think it does."

"Why doesn't Santa get cold?"

"Umm, I think he is probably used to the cold since he lives up at the North Pole. Even with his giant fireplace. And he has that fluffy beard and the really warm coat."

"My mom took his coat."

"What?"

"Santa's coat. After she escaped from the bad house where Santa was being mean to her. She took his coat to stay warm while outside in the blizzard."

"How do you know about that?"

"Kids at school talk about it."

Dee nodded. "I think the coat your mom took wasn't actually Santa's coat. It belonged to the person pretending to be Santa that was doing mean things to her."

Tabby chewed her lower lip a bit while considering that.

"The real Santa wouldn't do mean things like that to her," Dee added.

"You're right," Tabby said after a few seconds. "The real Santa is nice. And he doesn't have stinky breath."

Dee smiled at that and took another bite of pizza.

"And he's magic, which is why he can fly in his sleigh and visit all those houses and not get burned up by fireplaces."

"Exactly."

"But only on Christmas Eve."

"That's right."

"What happens if he doesn't make it back in time?"

"What do you mean?"

"If Santa doesn't make it back to the North Pole in time. Like if he gets stuck in a house."

"Hmm, I never really thought about that. Maybe it's like in Cinderella. The magic only lasts until midnight."

"And that's why he can only come out on Christmas Eve."

"Exactly."

7

"His breath was very stinky," Tabby was saying. "But that's because he isn't the real Santa, just one of Santa's helpers so he doesn't eat cookies and candy canes all the time like the real Santa."

Gwen nodded along with this, her knuckles white as her fingers squeezed the steering wheel, mind trying to focus on the slick road and getting home rather than the various images and memories that Tabby's excited voice was conjuring up.

Santa's breath had been grotesque.

She remembered that clearly.

The scent oozing up into her nostrils and polluting her senses as he salivated upon the flesh beneath her right ear, his cold dirty hands squeezing her breasts while his engorged penis thrust itself up between her legs.

"The real Santa can only come out on Christmas Eve," Tabby continued. "That's why he has so many helpers that dress like him. Because he can't leave the North Pole until Christmas Eve."

Gwen blinked away the memory, only for a sudden scene of Santa standing before her to appear, one where his right hand was clutching a link of chain that connected two manacles that were secured around Tabby's tiny wrists.

Three more turns.

Three more streets.

"Dee says he is like Cinderella. He can't stay out after midnight. And if he does he will be in trouble because all the magic will disappear."

Magic will disappear.

After midnight.

The chime of a grandfather clock striking the hour echoed in her memory, one that she had heard over and over again while dangling from the ropes in the Robinson family room.

Had it ever struck midnight?

Or just each hour leading up to it?

She couldn't say for certain one way or the other, just that it had chimed several times shortly before Santa had arrived. Her mind had been in a complete daze during those moments, the pain of hanging from the ropes so intense that she could barely process anything beyond it.

"Mommy!" Tabby shouted just as the tires on the right of the car started to bounce over something.

Gwen twisted the wheel to the left, trying to get them back on the road, the snow that now gripped the tires not wanting to release its hold, a slight cry escaping her lips as she fought with the vehicle.

The tires broke free, the car now twisting across the road toward the opposite side, a ditch awaiting beyond the pavement.

They did not go into it.

Instead, they twisted around, car nearly doing a full 360 while in the middle of the road, her hands having had the wheel turned so far to the left while trying to get free of the snow that it was almost as if she had turned into the skid like one was supposed to.

A horn gave a double tap as someone neared, not in anger, but more of an "are you okay?" honk, the words also voiced once the person was pulled up alongside them.

Gwen nodded while saying something about being fine and waved them away.

"Mommy, what happened?" Tabby asked.

"We just skidded a bit on the ice," Gwen said, her heart thumping against her rib cage.

"You're bleeding," Tabby said, her voice way too calm for what had just happened.

"Am I?" Gwen asked just as she tasted the blood on her lips.

She looked into the mirror.

Blood was trickling from her right nostril.

No pain was present.

She dabbed at it a few times.

"Don't tilt your head back," Tabby advised.

"What?" Gwen asked.

"Bobby got a bloody nose at school once and one teacher told him to tilt his head back, but then another told them that was wrong because he could choke on the blood and die, so the other teacher checked on her phone and found out that was right. You're never supposed to tilt your head back."

"That's good to know," Gwen said. "I'll make sure not to do that."

Pinching her nose shut with the fingers of one hand, she used her other hand to get the car angled correctly on the road and then slowly continued down the street.

A few minutes later, they were walking inside the house, the blood from her nose having already stopped, which meant it was probably just a burst capillary or maybe a scab that had come off up within.

8

Zoey had thought for sure the car was going to go into the ditch, but then watched with amazement as the driver turned into the skid rather than trying to turn out of it like so many people did, which allowed for the car to simply spin itself around rather than going off the road.

It wasn't until after all of this had unfolded and she was pulling alongside the car to check if those inside were okay when she realized it was Gwendolyn and Tabby.

A few minutes earlier she had been at their house looking for clues, a search of the shed out back to see if there were any bags of dirt within that matched the strip of plastic from the one that she had partially dug up in the field having turned up nothing.

This didn't mean anything though, especially when tracks in the snow confirmed that someone had gone back and forth several times to the trampled spot in the field where the plastic had been found, the spot where she was sure Val's body was buried.

Most of those tracks were a few days old, but one set had been fresh. So fresh that she had been able to see all the markings from the sole of a boot in the bottom of the print when bending down for a closer look.

Pictures of that print were now stored in her phone, along with all the other photos she had taken during this endeavor.

Unfortunately, nothing she had documented really proved anything. It was just circumstantial.

That was why she was going to dig up the spot.

That night, once it was dark.

Or just call the police.

No.

She didn't have enough to warrant police involvement, especially not when the officers involved would be under the command of someone who was good friends with Ian.

That just wouldn't work.

Not just yet.

She needed more.

She needed a body.

Once dug up, she would be able to point the police toward its location, the body itself likely holding clues as to what had happened and who was responsible.

Ian?

Gwendolyn?

Given the tracks back and forth to the shed, as well as the ones that went back and forth from the house to the shed, Zoey had no doubt whatsoever that one of them was responsible.

What she could not figure out yet was why.

9

Gwen could not stop thinking about what Tabby had said in regards to Santa losing his power after midnight, and while she wasn't completely convinced that the midnight hour was the exact moment, she was convinced there was a specific time somewhere between midnight and the dawn hours when Santa needed to be back at the North Pole or else he would be in serious trouble.

After all, if there was no such time limit, why did he only come out on Christmas Eve? Why not whenever he felt like it? And why hadn't he come after her during her most vulnerable moments for the pain she had caused him?

A time limit being imposed upon him answered those questions.

It also brought about a new one.

What happened to him if he did not get back in time?

Would he be stuck here?

Powerless?

Unable to recover from whatever wounds she inflicted upon him this time around?

No certainty was present with these thoughts, but they did give her hope. She also realized she might have to do more than simply zap him with electricity. That might work for subduing him but likely wouldn't keep him subdued long enough to run out the clock. Not if his body had been able to heal a cracked-open head in time for him to kill Justin, grab Jessica, and return to the North Pole.

She would have to do more.

Once he was zapped and unable to move for a period of time she would go to work on his body. She would give him wounds that would require further healing time. Wounds that he would not be able to recover from quickly enough to get back home.

Ian had an ax out in the shed, one that he had used when cutting down a dead tree in the rear of their yard during the pandemic, and then chopped up for firewood.

Come Christmas Eve she would have that ax by the fireplace, ready to be used once Santa's body was on the ground, momentarily paralyzed from the electricity.

. . .

10

"That might have been the busiest I have ever seen it," Dee said as Ian was closing things down for the evening.

"I think it was," he replied. "And totally unexpected."

"Maybe word has finally spread and this will be the new norm."

"God, I hope not."

Dee laughed.

"And…I'm out," he said a few seconds later.

"Okay, see you tomorrow," Dee replied.

"Yep."

"And thanks again for the pizza earlier."

"Hey, no problem."

Silence settled over the store as Ian headed out, Dee hanging back for a bit to enjoy the calm of the darkened store, the book-crammed shelves and the lingering scent of various coffees always soothing to her.

She would not be hanging around for long though.

Not when she wanted to check something out, which was why twenty-five minutes later she was pulling into the dark parking lot of the El Rancho motel, eyes on the lookout for the car she had seen the night before on Route 6.

11

Zoey's trip to the local hardware store had been a test in patience, her inquiry into if they sold bags of dirt for vegetable gardens having been met with confusion. Not in the question itself, but in why she would want to plant a garden during the winter. Nothing she said to the guy running the store seemed able to settle his confusion, the man going on and on about how she really needed to wait until spring to start a garden, which always resulted in her stating that she wasn't planning on starting the garden yet, she simply wanted to see what the dirt options were for when she did.

Eventually it was revealed that they didn't have any dirt on hand since it would be foolish to stock it when there was no use for it during the winter. Following this, she grabbed a basic shovel from the aisle that sold such things, one that she feared would bring about even more confusion and statements on how she couldn't start a garden just yet as she neared the counter, but thankfully was rung up and cashed out without comment.

Shovel secured in the trunk, Zoey navigated the dark streets back toward the motel, where she planned on changing into clothes more suitable for creeping around unseen in a dark winter landscape, at which point she would head back out to the Robinson house and into the field to dig up whatever it was that had been put into the freshly filled hole.

12

Dee circled the El Rancho parking lot four times before deciding to head off to the second of the three motels that were in the area near the I-55 exit that one would use if heading to town, her eyes having failed to see any cars that matched the one she had documented the night before near the Robinson house.

Frustration with herself for not thinking to check these motels for the private investigator's car after documenting his license plate last weekend weighed heavy upon her, thoughts on how even an inexperienced trainee with the FBI would probably have known to do that on day one dominating her mind.

But then what? she asked herself while heading toward the parking lot exit.

Confronting the private investigator would probably have led nowhere, the man likely to deny everything she suspected about him. Even putting forth evidence of who he was would have been met with a blank stare, one that would convey the message of "so what?" to her with the knowledge that, despite everything she knew, there was nothing she could do about it beyond being a nuisance to him.

Then again, being a nuisance might have been just what was needed and could have potentially produced results. After all, he had come to town to dig up dirt on Ian that Gwen's mother could use in her attempts to drive a wedge deeper and deeper into their marriage. Dee's continued presence when he was attempting this might have been enough to prevent him from being able to go about his task. It also might have prevented whatever had unfolded at the Robinson house.

What had happened there?

She had sat up for quite a bit of time last night wondering about this very thing, his rental car being abandoned on Route 6 not far from the Robinson house enough for her to suspect that something foul had unfolded.

Or had it?

Could he have simply injured himself and then succumbed to his injuries somewhere out in the field?

Just like Jessica.

Body lost to the elements.

Or had something happened within the house?

Something that had prevented his being able to get out?

A fall down the basement stairs?

Could his body have gone undiscovered by the woman that was snooping around last night?

The basement was very cluttered, the investigators who had been at the house early on having pretty much ripped all the built-in workbenches and shelving units from the walls in an attempt to find out if there was any evidence of the family having been serial killers. Nothing had been cleaned up after their eventual departure, and from what she saw during her visit on Thanksgiving, Ian and Gwen had made no effort whatsoever in making the house livable again.

It had also been dark during the time when the new mystery woman had headed into the house, and even though Dee had spied a flashlight beam from time to time through the windows, it still would have been possible for her to miss a body in the darkness that the light did not penetrate. And given how cold the house was, the body might not have been letting off any type of smell just yet.

Headlights appeared in her rearview mirror, snagging her attention away from her thoughts on what had happened to the private investigator and shifting them back toward her present goal of figuring out where the new mysterious woman was staying.

Slowing to a near crawl, she watched the headlights to see if they turned into the El Rancho parking lot, her mind telling herself that it would be too perfect if they did and that things like that didn't happen in the real world.

A turn signal appeared.

No way.

Go back and take a look.

Dee did, her hands making quick work of a three-point-turn all while her mind kept telling herself that it couldn't be her. It just was not possible. A one in a million chance. Maybe more. And yet stranger things did happen. Especially during these last several years.

The car pulled into a spot on the far left side of the motel, the area one that had almost no cars in it, most of the rooms likely vacant.

Not wanting to reveal herself, Dee had stayed back quite a ways, so she was unable to see who it was that got out of the car and headed into the motel room.

That was okay though since all she needed was to see the car itself.

Specifically the license plate.

Parking her car, Dee pulled up the photo of the plate she had taken the night before, her lips muttering the plate number several times before tucking her phone back into her pocket and stepping out of the car.

A few seconds later she was walking by the car in question.

No match.

Not even close.

13

Hunger got the better of Zoey as she headed back to the motel, a quick stop at a Panda Express near the I-55 exit being made, one that she justified to herself with thoughts on how having some food in her stomach would help keep her warm and energetic while out in the field digging up a semi-frozen patch of dirt.

Back in her vehicle, she fished out an egg roll from her order and began eating it while driving, the item tasting far better than it should have given how powerful her hunger had become once the scent of food was in her nostrils.

A second egg roll was waiting, one that she nearly snagged while pulling into the motel parking lot, but decided against given that she would be inside her room in less than a minute.

14

The next two motels Dee visited had both apparently gone out of business at some point during the last three years, and she had a sudden realization that it had been at least that long since her last journey to this particular area given that the last time she had been on I-55 was when she and her parents were coming back from visiting the Northern Illinois University campus up in DeKalb, which was one of the schools she had been accepted to. She had not wanted to visit the school, her mind set on another university out east, but her parents were somewhat insistent on the benefits of staying within the state and felt that a visit to the school might help sway her into thinking along the same lines. At the time, it hadn't. Her mind was set. She wanted to go to the school out east, which she felt would be a better stepping stone toward her goal of eventually joining the FBI's behavioral unit and becoming a profiler.

Little did any of them realize that such a decision would soon be moot given that a virus was only months away from spreading across the world like wildfire. Now, three years later, it was hard to believe how ignorant they had been in regards to how fast things could change. One moment they were looking at and arguing about various college options, the next both her parents were on ventilators in a wing of the local hospital that she couldn't even visit. A few weeks later, she was an orphan.

And she had not been the only one.

Justin and Jessica had been orphaned as well, their father having died at some point during the pandemic, which had led many to wonder if their estranged mother, who had abandoned the family fifteen years earlier, would finally return. She had not. And given the events that had occurred the previous Christmas, most now realized that the story of her having abandoned the family with the youngest of the three children was probably a lie. Both were likely dead, killed by the husband all those years ago and buried out in the field somewhere.

Why no one had ever investigated that odd abandonment back in the day was something Dee frequently wondered about. Everyone in town had simply believed it when told by Mr. Robinson that his wife and the mother of his children had left abruptly during the holidays and taken their youngest daughter with her. A big part of believing this was likely due to Jessica and Justin confirming the story, many simply assuming the two older kids would say something if foul actions had taken place. They never did and nothing about their conduct while growing up had indicated anything was amiss. That in itself should have been a red flag because having their mother abandon their family with their younger sister should have had some sort of an impact upon them that could be seen by others who interacted with them on a daily (or near daily) basis, yet no changes in behavior or oddities had ever been observed. Even looking back upon things didn't produce anything that could now be viewed as an "OMG that explains it" type of thing, which often happened with other killers.

Had they seen their father kill their mother and little sister?

Had they witnessed some sort of twisted Santa sex situation between the husband and wife that had gone awry?

Had that led to their crazy tradition of giving Santa a female gift to be taken back to the North Pole every year?

Dee contemplated this while sitting in the empty parking lot of the motel, the questions familiar since she had been speculating upon all the various possibilities ever since the horror of Justin and Jessica's actions had been revealed.

Of course, no answers were ever revealed.

None ever would be.

Even if bodies were eventually found, they probably wouldn't yield much when it came to understanding how and why this twisted tradition began.

Speculation was all anyone would ever be able to do.

15

. . .

Though Ian had convinced himself against doing any sort of digging in the spot where he felt Gwen might have buried something (*Someone? The private investigator? Could she really have killed him? Maybe by accident?*), and had gone so far as to discard the extra bags of dirt from the shed that he had spotted the night before so as to not allow for any obvious connections between the filled-in hole and the shed itself, beyond the tracks that would hopefully be covered over with the snowfall that was forecast that evening, he couldn't keep the thoughts of what might have unfolded from his mind, which then led him to start wondering/worrying that there might be some indication/evidence of it within the Robinson house itself.

Concerned, he decided to stop by the Robinson house while on his way back from the bookstore so that he could take a quick look around and see if anything was present within.

And if there is...?

He really had no idea what he would do, which was why he hoped there would be no evidence of anything within.

The private investigator's rental car.

That in itself was quite a big clue that something had unfolded at or near the Robinson house, and while it didn't necessarily mean something foul had occurred, or that Gwen had anything to do with it if something had, it could still lead to speculation given how beacon-like it was.

Not that he could really do anything about it.

Especially since it had already been seen by someone, who had then followed the tracks from it to the house itself.

Someone who Dee said had the code to the key box on the back door.

Who were they?

Dee had pretty much convinced him that the abandoned rental car was that of the private investigator that Marybeth had sent out here, the same private investigator who had been utilized back in 2018 to find out if he was cheating on Gwen with the escorts they managed money for.

Could the woman be an associate of that investigator?

Had the two been out here together since two sets of eyes were always better than one?

Or was the woman one of those web sleuths that Marybeth was always engaging online, one that might have lived close enough to this area to swing out and do some amateur investigative work on her own?

Though how would she have known the code to the key box?

If she actually did know it.

Maybe Dee was mistaken.

After all, she had not been all that close to the woman as she entered the house, a statement on how she had been crouched down in the brush on the far side of the unattached garage having been made to him the night before. Such a position would limit what one could see, so maybe the key box hadn't clicked shut all the way during a previous visit and thus was able to be opened with a simple tug.

If the mysterious woman does know the code though...

He and Gwen used that particular code for everything that required four digits, which meant this woman would have access to the back door of the building the bookstore was in, their house via the garage keypad, and their ATM cards.

Ian's bike lock too, though he wasn't really concerned about that.

But how would she know the code?

Marybeth?

Ian had no idea if Gwen's mother knew the code they used for everything, though if she did know it, she likely would have passed it on to her private investigators so that they had access to all his stuff during their investigations.

Sam also knew it, though she never would have given it out to anyone, especially not some mysterious woman who was roaming around the area, or let it slip out by accident to someone who could then have passed it on to the mysterious woman.

Dee likely knew it as well.

He had never specifically given her the code to the key box, but she knew the code to the building the bookstore was in, and the garage at the house, so she had likely figured out that they used it at the Robinson house as well. She had also probably gone inside the house from time to time to look around given her interest in the macabre, especially when it came to twisted crimes and serial killers. Like Sam though, she never would have given it to anyone. Not intentionally. Someone might have observed her punching in the code when going through the back door of the bookstore.

Or maybe while he was punching it in.

Or while Gwen was.

He had never really felt the need to shield himself while punching in the code given how empty the area behind the bookstore building always was, so if someone wanted to find out the code they could have hidden themselves somewhere back there amid the various dumpsters at an angle that allowed them to see which numbers he pressed.

Or maybe while he was punching the code into the keypad of the garage door at home.

The area around the house was even more isolated and had far more hiding spots that one could crouch in with a set of binoculars. It was also used quite frequently, especially when he and Tabby were coming home since he always parked the truck in the driveway rather than in the garage given how big it was.

Tabby.

She loved to be the one to punch in the code and had to reach up over her head to do it, which meant it would be really easy to see which digits were pressed if someone had a set of binoculars on the keypad while she did it.

Or maybe there were more cameras?

Motion sensor ones that had captured the keypad in use.

All these thoughts and speculations spiraled around within his mind as he let himself into the Robinson house, his eyes glancing around several times to see if anyone was watching now.

No one was.

At least no one he could see.

He also didn't think there were any cameras on him, though he couldn't say for certain.

After last night anything seemed possible.

16

Zoey got a winter weather alert on her phone while heading toward the Robinson house, one that noted a low pressure system was moving into the area and that isolated snow squalls were expected during the next two hours.

Concern arrived.

Snow squalls were no joke.

One minute things would be clear, the next snow would be coming down so fast that it would be a complete whiteout as it fell at a rate of three to four inches an hour, and while she had no fears of what might happen on the roadways given how little traffic there was in the area, she did know that one good squall could erase all the tracks in the field behind the Robinson house and make it impossible for her to find the area she wanted to dig in.

Ten minutes came and went before any snow started to fall, though thankfully these flakes seemed to be standard fare and nothing to worry about at the moment as she pulled up alongside the dark field, her position one that was nowhere near the Robinson house itself given that Ian was currently there, or where she had parked the night before given that Ian might swing by that spot as well once he was done doing whatever it was he was doing at the house, her new plan being to cut across the field from the north until she found the tracks, which went west to east. Once those were found, she would follow them to the disturbed area she wanted to dig up.

If she had judged things correctly earlier while looking at the map she had pulled up on her phone, she would need to walk about a mile before any tracks would be visible. In standard conditions she could probably cover that distance in ten to fifteen minutes, but with the snow that was already on the ground, and the difficulty it would present while walking through it in both the woods and field, she figured her pace would be something like twenty to twenty-five minutes a mile, if not more. Rather than trying to base everything on that guess, however, she simply thumbed open her Map My Walk app, which would tell her the distance covered and vocally alert her to when she had completed her first mile, thereby making it so she would know when she should be coming up upon the set of tracks that would lead her to the spot.

Shovel in hand, she started into the field.

Not long after that, a gust of wind hit, one that was really harsh as it gathered up all the loose snow it could find and hit her in the face with it, the exposed flesh of her cheeks and nose feeling like it was being tattooed with thousands of tiny ice needles.

The wind died down, a calmness arriving.

It didn't last.

Snow began to fall, and it only took a few seconds to know this was not going to be just a few fluffy flakes that glided down upon a gentle breeze. Nope. This was one of the isolated squalls they had warned about, and while the giant fluffy flakes were very picturesque as they fell against the dark rural landscape, it wasn't something she could appreciate at the moment given that she hadn't found any tracks yet and now was racing against the clock as the very thing she had feared when hearing about the potential snow squalls was becoming a reality.

17

I should have done this last night, Ian said to himself as he began working his way through the Robinson house, the flashlight app on his phone lighting his way. *Right after the mysterious woman had been inside.*

But he and Dee had been frozen to the bone given their trek out into the middle of the field as they followed the fresh tracks, so going from room to room throughout the cold, empty house had not been very appealing. Plus, his mind had been processing the sight of the plastic strip from the bag of dirt that had been caught within the freshly filled body-size hole, as well as the various sets of tracks leading back to the house, fears of what might have unfolded in the days prior taking root.

Those fears were still present, but they weren't making the same sort of ruckus within his mind that they had been the night before. He also knew that his fear that Gwen had done something terrible was only one possibility when thinking about all the reasons why the private investigator's rental car had been seemingly abandoned on the road, and a somewhat remote one at that, given that he simply could not picture Gwen killing anyone.

Instead, maybe the private investigator had spent so much time snooping around the Robinson house with an old rental vehicle left out in the cold that the battery had died, which resulted in his partner—the mysterious woman from last night—coming to pick him up in another car. The rental company itself might even be aware of the car having failed and was in the process of getting someone out to tow it, an act that was taking quite a bit longer than it should given how out of the way the vehicle location was coupled with how few tow truck drivers there seemed to be these days.

But why had Gwen gone back and forth to that disturbed area?

And why had there been a strip of plastic from a dirt bag stuck beneath some freshly poured dirt?

He scanned one room after another while contemplating this, the horrifying idea that Gwen might have done something terrible once again getting traction within his thoughts.

No.

Gwen would not kill someone.

What about Justin Robinson?

She had killed him.

Only that had been while fighting for her life.

Could this situation have been the same?

Had the private investigator attacked her?

No. That didn't seem right.

Nothing really did.

And yet something had happened.

Something that had resulted in her burying something out in the middle of the field.

But what?

Nothing within the first-floor rooms answered these questions.

The same was true of the second floor.

The basement was next, his body hesitating for several seconds by the door, the thoughts of Gwen being chained down below and his being totally oblivious to it while sitting up in the family room eating cookies and drinking hot cocoa with the Robinson siblings echoing in his mind.

I didn't know.

I couldn't know.

And Sam was right. If he had realized she was down there, Justin never would have let him leave the house.

It worked out better this way.

Even with all the troubles she was now experiencing.

Time would heal those.

At this time next year all these troubles would seem very distant.

They just had to make it beyond this year.

His phone buzzed.

A text.

From Sam.

It read: *We need to talk.*

18

Zoey was getting worried.

The snow was coming down so hard that she could not see more than a foot or two in front of her, which would not only make it nearly impossible to see the tracks she was looking for (if they were even still visible), but also to know if she was going in a straight line, her hands frequently having to pull out her phone so that she could look at the line marking her route on the Map My Walk app, which would often lead to her having to make a course correction.

Making things worse, she didn't hear the voice from her phone when it alerted her to having walked a mile. Instead, she saw that she had gone a mile and a half when doing another screen check to see if she needed to make another course correction.

Her worry increased when she reached the two-mile mark without spotting the tracks, a thought on turning around and walking back half a mile to see if she had crossed right over them without realizing it being suggested but then dismissed within her mind.

She kept heading south, eyes scanning the ground before

her with each step for any sign of anything that could be a set of tracks going east to west, one of her gloved hands constantly having to wipe snot that was oozing from her frozen nose.

A few minutes later she realized the heavy snow was no longer falling, and that it probably hadn't been for a while now given how quickly snow squalls moved through an area. Nothing but flurries were present, and those posed no problems at all when it came to visibility.

Still no tracks though.

At the three-mile mark she stopped walking.

She knew without a doubt that she would have crossed the tracks by now, which meant she had clearly missed them at some point while walking, likely during the heavy snowfall. Either that or they had been completely erased by the snowfall before she even got to them, which meant that her only chance of finding the spot would be to walk back and forth between the Robinson house and Gwendolyn's house in hopes of spotting the mound of snow-covered dirt the authorities had left behind last spring.

And not just any mound of dirt, but the one that actually had a filled-in hole next to it rather than an actual hole.

This thought led to a realization that if she wasn't careful she could actually fall into one of the many holes that had been dug earlier that year, and if she were really unlucky, break something during the fall that would result in her not being able to get back out and freezing to death during the bitter cold night.

She shivered at the thought.

She was in the middle of nowhere, so if she did get hurt, she would be fucked. It didn't even have to be something as dramatic as falling into one of the holes. If she simply tripped over a buried branch or some stones or something, it could result in her not being able to walk, and crawling all the way back to her car through the snow would probably be an impossible task, her body succumbing to the cold long before she was able to reach the car.

Crawling to Ian and Gwendolyn's house would be better in that particular situation, she noted to herself, only to realize she could not see their house.

While the snow had been falling, not being able to see the house wasn't a concern given that she had barely been able to see anything that wasn't right up next to her, but now that the snow had stopped and the air had cleared, the brightly lit windows of the house should have been standing out against the dark background. And even if they weren't home for some reason and hadn't left any lights on within, the Christmas light display that Ian had put up should have been visible as it created a welcoming holiday glow.

Instead, she saw nothing but darkness as far as the eye could see. And not just in the area to the east where the house should have been when walking from the northern part of the field where her car was parked. She couldn't see any illuminated windows or Christmas lights to the west either. Not even a glow from town was visible, though that didn't concern her quite as much since she had no idea if such a thing was visible from the field given how uneven the landscape was in this area. Lots of dips and rises. Lots of trees too, especially in the area to the south of the field where the road leading to Ian and Gwendolyn's house was, though those probably wouldn't be impeding her view very much given that they had all lost their leaves already.

Something wasn't right.

She had fucked up somehow.

Pulling out her phone and looking at the screen confirmed this, though not right away. As with previous checks of the Map My Walk app, she initially looked to make sure she was going in a straight line, which she had done for the most part, her frequent checks of the phone during the worst of the storm and her course corrections having kept things looking right.

Even scrolling from her current location back to the car showed a fairly straight line, only it wasn't. Not when she zoomed out and looked at the entire map as a whole and saw that at some point early on while crossing through a small patch of woods she had started to veer eastward while walking, and though it was just a slight veer in the beginning, the straight line she had tried to maintain while in the worst of the snow squall had slowly but surely increased how far off course she was, making it so she would never cross paths with the tracks she was looking for. Ian and Gwendolyn's house was also way west of her now rather than being toward the east, which was a testament to how far off track she had gotten. Most horrifying of all, she could have easily continued this way for another five or six miles before hitting the road that Ian and Gwendolyn's house was on given that it angled off in a southeasterly direction for quite a ways before shifting back in a more eastward direction.

All because she hadn't dropped any kind of pin upon the area she wanted to head toward, her mind having brushed off the need of this given that she had felt walking in a straight line from her car would be fairly easy.

Wrong.

Now she did have a pin dropped, though it was on Ian and Gwendolyn's house, her hope being that the tracks from their backyard to the spot in the field she was looking for might still be visible and she could simply follow them from there.

And even if they weren't, she would still be better able to guide herself to the general vicinity of the spot where the filled-in hole had been, the house itself being a sort of rudder as she walked.

19

. . .

"Well no, I was at the bookstore most of the week while Gwen was recovering, but she wouldn't have been going anywhere, especially not clear over to the other side of town," Ian said into the phone while sitting in his car, somewhat miffed that Sam would even consider the possibility that Gwen was the one responsible for vandalizing someone's nativity scene. "Hell, she didn't even have her car for several days."

"Which days?" Sam asked.

"Seriously?" Ian said, aggravation growing. "Sam. She didn't do this."

Sam waited.

Ian sighed. "Monday, Tuesday, and Wednesday."

"Hmm."

"Sam, she didn't do this," Ian said once again. "And you know that a nativity scene wouldn't be a trigger for her at all."

"I know, but quite a few other displays have been damaged recently," Sam said. "Most of them having Santa elements. The Connor house over on Cheshire literally had their Santa figure smashed to pieces a while back, and more recently a witness specifically reported seeing a bundled-up female unplugging and then running away with a light-up Santa figure from the King yard over on Wilson."

"Teenagers," Ian said. "They do shit like this all the time. Remember two years ago? That house on..." He tossed up a hand, nearly hitting his own driver-side window. "I don't remember the street. But those kids rearranged all the reindeer in that one guy's yard so they were all fucking each other."

"Oh, I know," Sam said. "And you're probably right. It's some teens or college students. The trouble is that people are specifically saying it's Gwen after it was noted that it was a female stealing the Santa figure from the King yard the other night, which means I *have* to look into it."

"Well, she didn't have a car until Wednesday evening." *Or was it Tuesday evening?* He couldn't remember for sure which day they had driven to the bookstore together after dropping Tabby off at school. "When was the Santa figure stolen?"

"Tuesday. Shortly after sunset."

"And you're just now learning about it?" he asked.

"Well, like I said, there has been quite an upswing in displays being vandalized this year all over the community. Most aren't being officially reported since most people don't want the hassle. This particular one only came to our attention this afternoon when Carl was following up on another incident that occurred late last night, at which point that homeowner, who was really angry given how much damage his display suffered, noted that one of his neighbors actually saw the theft from the Kings' yard, which hadn't been reported by the King family."

"Then how did they even know about it?"

"People have been talking about it on Facebook. On the town community page. You know we have that Christmas display contest every year, which, by the way, you totally should have entered given how epic your house looks this year. Anyway, everyone has been discussing all the vandalism that has been taking place in the various comment threads, which is where Gwen's name first came up and has now become the focus for quite a few people who frequently post on that page."

Ian let out a heavy sigh. "Well, if that theft was on Tuesday then it certainly wasn't Gwen." *Unless that was the day we actually did grab her car and she did it while driving home.*

But why steal a Santa figure?

Destroying a Santa figure Ian could see given how destructive she had been during the freak-out in the bookstore back in November when she had ripped up the *Fear Street* books that Dee had been holding, though why she would head out to some random house to destroy a Santa display when they had one right in front of the house itself that she saw every day was beyond him.

But taking one from a house?

That didn't make any sense at all.

Where would she have even put it after taking it?

It wasn't in the house.

He was certain of this given that he would have noticed the sudden addition of a life-size light-up of Santa.

And it hadn't been tucked away anywhere inside the Robinson house.

Even in the darkness with just the flashlight app on his phone illuminating things, he was certain he would have seen it.

Though what if it had been there at one point?

What if—

"You still there?" Sam asked.

"Yeah, just thinking," he said.

"About?"

"Just how everyone jumps to suspecting Gwen of something like this. I mean, they have nothing but someone's statement that a bundled-up woman grabbed a Santa figure from some yard, and boom, everyone automatically thinks it's Gwen rather than some bored teenager or someone else who is in the stupid Christmas light contest. It's like, Jesus Christ, why does everyone have such a negative view of her?"

"Well, she is on everyone's mind right now, what with freaking out last month at the mall and then that stuff in the hospital the other day, which sadly spread fairly quickly."

"Yeah, but everyone was saying shit about her even before all this. Back when we first moved out here, and then they really started talking shit when we started helping people out with their homes and businesses."

"You know what they say: *No good deed goes unpunished.*"

"Big time."

"Anyway, I really just wanted to give you an FYI about what people were saying."

Bullshit, Ian thought. *You actually have some suspicions yourself.*

"And if anyone presses me," she added, "I'll be sure to let them know it wasn't her."

"Thanks," he replied, the comment nothing more than an ending statement since he still was annoyed that she had called him.

He also was wondering something.

What if Gwen had destroyed a Santa figure?

Not out in someone's yard like Sam (and everyone else apparently) thought, but one at the Robinson house that someone had put there to be a dick.

In fact, maybe that was why someone had stolen a Santa figure from a yard in the first place. So they could put it over here as a way to taunt Gwen.

Or maybe not even as a taunt, but just because they thought it would be funny to put up a Santa figure at the Robinson house, their minds failing to consider how traumatic that would be for Gwen if she stumbled upon it.

He could totally picture the situation.

Gwen had decided to pay a visit to the Robinson house once again at some point while he was gone, and suddenly stumbled upon the Santa figure that had been set up, freaked out, destroyed it, and then took it out in the middle of the field to bury so that no one would use the action against her.

Someone like me.

He would never actually use something like that against her, but in her mind she might think that if he saw a busted-up Santa figure at the Robinson house, which she knew he visited frequently thanks to that stupid investigator, he might not understand what had happened and insist that she be put into the mental ward on the sixth floor of the hospital again. Rather than risk such a thing, she had decided to get rid of it by dragging it out to one of the holes in the field and burying it, only to realize the mound of dirt left behind by the investigators was frozen and that she needed to get fresh dirt from the shed.

Little did she realize Dee would spot some random woman at the house, which then would lead to him and Dee following tracks to the spot where the destroyed Santa figure had been buried, which then led to him worrying about what it was she might have buried.

Had the random woman been the one to plant it there?
Was that why she had been lurking around the house?
Had she been wondering where the display piece had gone?

20

Zoey saw the glow of Ian and Gwendolyn's house before she actually saw the house itself, the moment of relief at actually seeing something out here and knowing she was truly walking toward her new focal point short-lived as a brutal gust of wind nearly knocked her over, the shovel she was clutching the only thing that kept her upright.

She was cold.

Too cold.

Her toes felt completely frozen, as did her nose, cheeks, and the tips of her fingers, especially those of the hand that was gripping the shovel, previous experience with being out in the bitter cold telling her that quite a bit of pain was going to arrive once she was back in the car and had the heat cranked.

Car.

She longed for that glorious moment when she would be able to hold her fingers against the vents on the dashboard.

Val.
Buried.
Digging.
That came first.

Once she finished that, and had the spot pinned on her phone so that she could lead authorities right to it, she would then be able to enjoy the heat within the car.

Got to find the spot first.

Tracks.

In Ian and Gwen's backyard.

Once she located those all she had to do was follow them.

A faint voice echoed something that she failed to fully register, but later would realize was from her phone as it notified her of having completed another mile.

One step after another, the house ahead of her growing larger and larger, Ian and Gwendolyn's Christmas display quite striking against the black sky, some of it seemingly reflecting off the freshly fallen snow.

A bit of a hill awaited her, one that was very difficult to go up in these conditions, the shovel acting like a brace as she leaned upon it with each step.

A light illuminated her as she passed through the backyard.

Zoey turned toward it, staring, unable to fully comprehend what had happened, all while her feet continued to push through the snow.

No one from the house confronted her, the motion sensor light she had triggered eventually switching off as she moved beyond its range and stepped into the trees that encircled the property.

21

Ian made the mistake of checking out the community Facebook page that Sam had mentioned while asking about the potential of Gwen having been involved in the vandalism of various Christmas light displays, his anger increasing with each comment he read. Everyone was implicating Gwen, it seemed. And not just in relation to the Christmas display stuff. Some were claiming they had seen her lurking outside of windows at various points during the year, her eyes looking glazed over as she stared through the glass at the family members within, lips mumbling things. Others made mention of how Gwen would start to follow them around the grocery store, mimicking their movements and whatnot. It was complete nonsense, and yet others would validate what was being said, the comments beneath these total fabrications filled up with other people who said they had experienced similar things.

People were also talking about Dee and her despicable interest in serial killers, one person making a claim that Dee's former boyfriend had actually broken up with Dee because of how she kept wanting to engage in twisted sex acts while in the Robinson house with him. Others went on to suggest that Ian, Gwen, and Dee engaged in ritualistic threesomes at the Robinson house, ones that involved all sorts of horrifying elements.

Sam was in on everything too, according to the comments, her relationship with Ian back in high school being used by everyone as a launchpad into her culpability in whatever it was the four of them (and potentially others who were unknown at this point) had going on. One person even noted that the state itself was now involved in an investigation into things, and that an investigator had gone to the school to talk with Tabby about all the horrors she might be subjected to by her family and their friends.

Rage erupted within him.

It was one thing to suggest he, Gwen, Dee, and Sam had weird things going on with each other, but to make a claim that they were somehow involving Tabby in whatever perverted ritualistic activities were taking place was going too far.

And to actually post that someone from the state was investigating things?

What the fuck?

Unless...

"Hey, Tabby?" Ian asked a few seconds later. "Can I ask you something?"

"I don't know, can you?" Tabby asked.

Ian blinked, completely caught off guard. "What?"

"That's what Mrs. Patrick says whenever we say 'can I' instead of 'may I,'" Tabby advised.

Memories of a teacher doing the same thing to kids in one of his grade-school classes, himself included, arrived within his mind. He shook his head. "Well, that is a bit silly."

"It is?" Tabby asked, eyes going wide.

Ian hesitated, suddenly realizing he was on dangerous ground because explaining why this this was silly and how both words were fine to use might evolve into a classroom problem if Tabby parroted his explanation to the teacher, which was always a possibility given Tabby's nature. Plus he had an inkling that Gwen might back up the teacher on this one. "I have a question," he said, sidestepping things a bit. "Did someone come to the school to talk to you recently? Someone that wasn't a teacher?"

"You mean the Valentine's Day guy?" Tabby asked.

"The Valentine's Day guy?" Ian asked.

"He says he is named after the Valentine's Day guy, which isn't actually Cupid, though Melissa said I'm wrong when I told her that and that Valentine's Day is because of Cupid."

Ian tried to process that.

"She also kissed a boy on the lips in one of the tunnels on the playground," Tabby added.

"Wow."

"They are going to get married one day."

"So, this Valentine's Day guy. Do you remember what his name was?"

"His name is Valentine. But he says most people call him Val. Just like how everyone calls me Tabby except for Grandma."

Ian waited a second and then asked, "Do you remember what day he came to talk to you?"

"Ummm." She put a finger to her lips. "Monday, because it was right after Mommy got hurt."

"And do you remember what he was asking you?"

"Just questions about you and Mommy and if you two were fighting. I told him you only fight about *The Lord of the Rings*, and that Mommy hurt her face because she fell on the driveway."

Fighting about The Lord of the Rings?
When did we do that?

"I also told him that Mommy is not crazy and that she is just sometimes scared of Santa stuff because of the mean things that were done to her."

"That's good. Now, do you remember if there was a woman with him, or was he just by himself?"

"Mr. Rhodes was with us when we were talking."

"Mr. Rhodes?"

"That's Tabby's assistant principal," Gwen said from behind, startling Ian. "Right, sweetie?"

"Yep," Tabby said.

"And who was it that he was with?" Gwen asked, her eyes going from Tabby to Ian. "Some woman?"

"No, just the Valentine's Day guy," Tabby said.

"His name is Valentine," Ian said. "And apparently he was at Tabby's school the other day to ask Tabby some questions, which this Mr. Rhodes let him do."

Gwen didn't reply to that, though Ian noted a look on her face, which prompted him to give her his own look that hopefully asked: *What is it?*

"Hey, Tabby," Gwen said while holding up a *just a moment* finger to Ian. "In the future, if anyone comes to the school to talk to you about anything, let me or Daddy know, okay?"

"Okay."

"And please don't talk to them until either me or Daddy get there, okay?"

"Okay."

Gwen motioned for Ian to follow her, which he did, the two heading across the house so that they were out of earshot. "My mother's investigator," she said. "His name is Valentine."

"Ah, that's right," Ian said. He had actually learned this several years ago after all the drama with the escorts had unfolded, but then failed to make the connection while speaking with Tabby.

"You were asking about a woman when I walked up," Gwen noted. "What was that about?"

Ian hesitated.

Gwen waited.

"Sam called earlier. Mentioned that there has been quite a bit of vandalism toward holiday displays around town and that during the most recent act a woman was spotted."

"And she thinks it's me," Gwen said, voice showing no emotion whatsoever.

"No," Ian said.

"Then why'd she call you about it?"

"Because people in town think it's you."

A nod.

Another brief moment of hesitation and then, "There also was a woman lurking around the Robinson house last night."

No reply.

"Dee saw her while driving here."

A few seconds of awkward silence came and went before Gwen gave another slight nod and then said, "That's why you went out there. It wasn't because she was stuck."

This time it was Ian giving the slight nod.

"Why did you lie?" she asked.

"I don't know," he said. "I guess I just didn't want you stressing about it."

More silence.

"Sorry," he added.

Another nod.

22

Gwen wasn't really all that upset with Ian for lying to her about the night before, mostly because she had already suspected as much given all the tracks she had seen around the Robinson house earlier that day while retrieving the contents of the nanny cam. Having her suspicion confirmed was a bit of a blow, but that was to be expected and didn't really jostle her.

Instead, her thoughts were on the mysterious female and the newfound possibility that she wasn't just spying on Gwen and her family, but was also responsible for causing damage to Christmas displays all over town.

Would one of Santa's minions really be doing such a thing?

Maybe as a way of sowing even more distrust between her and the community, which could then help to create conflict between her and Ian?

After all, despite what Ian might say, she knew a part of his mind had to be wondering if she could actually be this woman that had been spotted vandalizing things. And honestly, she couldn't fault him for this if he was considering it. Or Sam. Or Dee. Or the people in town. Nope. Not when her various statements early on, and her actions throughout the year, oozed with insanity. Hell, if she were in their shoes she would probably have felt she needed to be pretzeled up into a straitjacket and locked away in a padded room as well.

None of them had seen or experienced the things she had

though, things that one would have to be crazy to believe if they hadn't been witness to them.

She herself had felt this way about Jessica.

Up until the very last second before Santa had appeared in the family room where she was hanging and started fucking her.

Hell, even after everything had unfolded and she had gotten away, her mind had questioned what she had experienced, thinking maybe it had actually been Justin who had been fucking her rather than a demonic Santa from the North Pole.

But no.

Deep down inside she knew what had unfolded.

Nothing anyone could say would change that.

Nor would anyone be able to shake her resolve on what needed to be done.

Santa needed to be stopped.

Once and for all.

Any mother who had witnessed what she had witnessed and knew the threat it posed to her child would do the same.

Of this, she had no doubt.

23

Zoey heard a loud pop and tried jerking away from it, only to realize she was tangled in something that her disoriented mind initially thought was a giant spiderweb but then realized was nothing but a dusty set of bedsheets.

Another pop echoed.

Zoey shifted her gaze a bit, eyes noting the flames within the fireplace.

A memory surfaced, one that depicted her being helped through the snow by someone until they reached the steps leading up to the back porch, her body slipping at one point, her right shin cracking against the edge of the wood. And then she was on the ground, barely able to move, the sound of someone cursing frequently as they tried to get some old matches to hold a flame echoing.

Zoey sat up, eyes darting back and forth.

No one was present.

She looked back at the fireplace.

The flames within were high, the wood that was piled up clearly having been added recently.

Sounds.

To her right.

Shifting again, Zoey looked into the dining room where a wall cutout to the kitchen allowed for her to see a figure within moving about with the aid of a flashlight.

What they were doing, she could not say.

She also had no idea who they were, or what their intentions were, and though it didn't seem like anything sinister was unfolding given that she had been put next to a warm fire after nearly freezing to death, she wasn't going to assume anything until she knew for sure.

A fire poker was on the brick surface near the fireplace, clearly having been used at some point to stir up the flames.

Zoey reached over and grabbed it.

24

Dee was hoping to find something like bottles of water or some unopened cans of soda that had been stored in the cupboards prior to the shit hitting the fan last year, but all she found was a carton of gourmet hot chocolate powder that didn't seem very useful given that the water in the house had long since been shut off. That was, until she saw a fairly solid-looking glass measuring cup that could probably be set near the fire without issue, one that she would fill with snow that could be melted and brought to a temperature that would be helpful for someone who had nearly frozen to death outside.

Adding hot chocolate powder to it might even work, though she wasn't completely sure on that and figured just offering warm water to the female investigator would be good enough, especially after rescuing her from what would have been certain death outside.

Stepping out onto the porch, she used the large measuring cup to scoop up a heaping portion of freshly fallen snow and headed back inside toward the fireplace area, steps careful so as not to make too much noise so that she didn't wake up the woman until after the water was warming.

An arm was suddenly around her throat, squeezing.

Dee let out a cry while trying to break free, the large measuring cup flying from her fingers.

"Who are you?" a voice demanded.

Dee couldn't answer right away, not so much because of the arm that was tight against her throat, but because she simply couldn't find her voice.

"Who are you?" she demanded a second time.

Rather than answer, Dee thrust her elbow backward, catching her square in the gut.

A horrible retching sound followed as the arm against her throat loosened, Dee managing to slip free and then twisting herself around just in time to see the woman swinging something at her with her other hand.

The effort wasn't all that impressive, Dee managing to deflect the object with only minimal pain. Later she realized it was a fire poker, one that could have probably done quite a bit of damage if the woman hadn't still been recovering from her ordeal outside and the blow to her gut.

"Zoey!" Dee snapped. "Chill out."

Hearing her name seemed to take the last of her strength

away, the stunned look appearing seconds before her legs gave out beneath her.

Dee caught her and eased her back toward the fireplace.

"I'm not going to hurt you," Dee said while getting her wrapped in the blankets once again. "Unless you come at me again like that and then I will knock your ass to the ground."

25

"When I couldn't find you at the motel I figured you might be out this way again doing whatever it is that you're doing," Dee said. "Only I didn't see you parked anywhere near the house or over by the other investigator's car, so I decided to loop around to see if you had parked anywhere else this time knowing we had seen your car last night, and boom, I spotted your car way the fuck over on the north side of the field."

Zoey nodded while sipping at the water Dee had heated for her after their little scuffle and then asked, "And then what, you followed me into the field?"

"What? In this weather! Fuck no!"

Zoey stared. "But then how did you find me?"

"It wasn't that hard to figure out you were either going to be heading to Ian and Gwen's house or heading here, and since Ian and Gwen are home right now with Tabby, I figured I'd chill out over here to see if you came this way. And chill is what I did for quite some time while up in an old bedroom that overlooks the field. This place is like a freaking freezer, which is why you are really lucky because I was just about to say fuck it and head back home when I caught sight of you creeping around like a Romero zombie with a flashlight and then saw you go face-first into the snow."

Romero zombie? Zoey silently muttered to herself. Out

loud, she said, "And then you dragged me inside and built a fire?"

"The fire was your idea actually. You kept mumbling about needing to build one. But yeah, that about sums it up."

Zoey nodded and then sipped some more water.

"Your turn," Dee said.

"My turn?"

"To tell me what the fuck you are up to and why. And before you make up some shit about being some sort of true crime writer looking into things in hopes of making me cream my pants with fangirl envy, I should let you know that I took a look through your phone after unlocking it with your thumb, so I know you're partners with that Val guy that Marybeth sent out here who already tried that approach with me and—spoiler alert—failed."

Zoey instinctively reached for her phone while hearing this, one that Dee now held up and waved in the air.

"Lots of interesting things in here," Dee noted. "Especially your photos folder."

Zoey tried to think what was in that folder but couldn't get very far given how cloudy and confused her mind still was.

"You've been in my apartment," Dee said.

What? Zoey questioned to herself and then remembered the photos Val had sent her from within Dee's apartment. Out loud, she mumbled, "It wasn't me."

"Really? Then what's up with all these pictures of the elf outfits I ordered a few weeks back?"

"What's up with having all those elf outfits?" Zoey fired back, her voice growing firmer with each passing second.

"What?"

"All those outfits, and in two different sizes, almost as if some were for you, and some for another unknown woman who hasn't made an appearance yet."

"Unknown woman?" Dee said, seemingly confused. Then, "Oh for the love of God! Is this all that Jessica bullshit those idiots online are talking about? You think Ian is hiding her somewhere and then what, she and I are going to make some crazy appearance while dressed like elves to freak out Gwen?"

"Are you?"

Dee rolled her eyes.

"My thoughts exactly," Zoey said.

"What?" Dee asked.

"All that online stuff about you and Ian being lovers and creating some grand conspiracy to remove Gwendolyn from the equation," Zoey said. "I know it's all bullshit."

"Then why are you out here obsessing over me and Ian, breaking into my place, and sneaking around this house every night, putting up cameras and shit?" Dee demanded.

"That was all Val, who texted me all the photos and videos he was taking," Zoey said and then sipped some more water. "I thought this was all ridiculous and that Marybeth was nuts, and said as much to him on many occasions."

"And yet here you are," Dee said.

"Here I am," Zoey agreed.

"Why?"

"Val went dark on me, which isn't like him at all, so rather than spending the holidays with my parents as planned, I came out here to see if I could figure out what happened to him, and low and behold I discovered what appears to be his rental car sitting out there looking like it has been abandoned for several days. And as if that wasn't alarming enough, there were tracks leading from the car to this house but not away from it, and then drag marks leading to a spot in the field that clearly had something buried in it recently."

"And you think it's him?" Dee asked. "Buried out there?"

"That's what I was hoping to find out before I got all turned around in that fucking storm."

Dee stared at her for several seconds, the look on her face one that Zoey couldn't really read all that well. "When was the last time you talked to him?" she asked.

"Monday," Zoey said.

Dee nodded.

Zoey waited a few seconds and then asked, "What about you? When was the last time you saw him?"

"Sunday. While taking Tabby to get some pie. He just happened to be at a table on the other side of the restaurant."

"You're sure? He never visited the bookstore or anything while you were working this week?"

"Not while I was there, though I didn't really work all that much because this was finals week."

"Ah, right. I forgot about that."

Dee stared at her and then muttered, "Jesus."

"What?"

"It's just creepy as fuck to think that you know my schedule. Annoying too. This town is bad enough with all their stupid thoughts on me, but then to know that investigators from New York are out here keeping tabs on me. It's just totally messed up."

Zoey didn't reply to that. Instead, she said, "Who was working while you were at class? Ian?"

"Um...yeah. Except Monday. He was at the hospital all day with Gwen, so the bookstore was closed until I got back and opened it myself around four."

"Hmm."

"What time was it on Monday when you last spoke to Val?"

"Give me back my phone and I'll tell you," Zoey said, reaching out.

"Fuck that."

Zoey stared at Dee for several seconds, thoughts on springing toward her and knocking her down so she could get her phone back unfolding within her mind.

"Try it, I dare you," Dee said, clearly knowing exactly what Zoey was thinking.

Zoey sighed.

"That's what I thought," Dee said, and then took a second to enter a password on the phone screen, one that she had probably changed after opening the device with Zoey's thumb earlier.

Zoey waited.

"He answer any of these calls you made to him?" Dee asked while staring at the phone screen.

"No, last one where I talked to him would have been him calling me."

"So just after six o'clock Monday evening," Dee said.

"Five o'clock here," Zoey noted.

"What?"

"My phone is still on East Coast time."

"So, five o'clock local time. Do you think he came out here after that?"

"I don't think so. Not that night. He had already been out here earlier that day, so it seems unlikely he would have any reason to head back out."

"So, Tuesday then. He comes out here for some reason, parks half a mile up on Route 6 where no one would automatically question what someone was doing at the Robinson house if they saw his car parked on the road, and then what, you think someone attacked him here and then dragged him out into the field and buried him in one of the old holes that had been left behind by the investigators earlier this year?"

Zoey nodded. "Something like that."

"Why?"

"Why what?"

"Why do you think someone would kill him?"

Zoey thought about that for a long time before shaking her head and saying, "I don't know."

. . .

"Oh, sweetie, I don't think that one is a good idea for tonight," Ian voiced while coming into the room with three mugs of hot chocolate he had just prepared, two with some peppermint schnapps mixed within, one without, all topped with whipped cream and chocolate shavings.

"But, Daddy, this one is my most favorite Christmas movie in the whole wide world and we haven't watched it yet," Tabby said.

"I know, but—"

"It's okay," Gwen said, eyes glancing up from her phone to the movie in question that was now displayed on the screen.

"Are you sure?" Ian asked, genuine concern present as he handed her one of the peppermint-schnapps-enhanced hot chocolate mugs.

"I am," Gwen said, taking the mug and setting it on the coffee table to cool.

Ian eyed her for several seconds before placing a non-peppermint-schnapps-enhanced hot chocolate mug in front of Tabby, a statement on how it was really hot being made.

"I know, Daddy!" Tabby said, the clicker clutched in her hands while she leaned forward to study the steaming mug, her eyes wide with anticipation on how amazing it was going to taste.

His own mug in hand, Ian took a seat on the couch next to Gwen.

"Can I start it?" Tabby asked, her focus shifting back to the giant TV where the movie was waiting to start.

"I'm ready," Gwen said.

"Me too," Ian added.

Tabby hit PLAY on the clicker.

On-screen *The Santa Clause* began.

27

. . .

"This is crazy!" Dee shouted against the wind that was screaming across the fields, her eyes nearly squeezed shut against the icy onslaught. "We're never going to find it. Not tonight at least."

Zoey didn't reply right away, her own face shielded against the wind. Once it died down, she said, "It has to be around here somewhere."

"I know," Dee said, voice only slightly elevated now that the air had calmed for a moment. "But we can't see shit right now and have probably walked past the spot a dozen times without—" Another gust of wind kicked up, this one feeling like the worst one yet. "Jesus Christ!"

FOURTEEN

I

Zoey stared at herself in the bathroom mirror, shock at how red her face was dominating her exhausted mind.

Dee's too? she wondered.

The answer was yes.

In fact, Dee looked even worse than she did, the leather coat and basic gloves she had on when they ventured back outside from the Robinson house the night before in a foolish attempt to try to find the spot where Val had been buried having offered very little protection from the brutal wind.

"Feels like a sunburn," Dee noted while handing her a mug of coffee.

"It does," Zoey agreed.

Nothing else was said for several seconds, the two simply sipping the coffee that Dee had brewed for them down in the bookstore, Zoey quickly realizing why Dee had shot down her idea of stopping for coffee on the way over to her place that morning.

. . .

2

"Think we'll really be able to find it this time around?" Zoey asked as they got into Dee's car to head toward the Robinson house, the old "dig up a spooky read" shovel that had caused so much speculation a year earlier now in the trunk.

"For sure," Dee said. "I know the general area that spot was in, so once we're there all we need to do is look for the mounds of snow that should mark where all the dirt piles are, and then find the one that has been filled in."

Zoey nodded.

"You know, that's another good reason we called it quits last night."

"What do you mean?"

"None of those holes were ever filled in and with that wind and all the snow blowing around, we could have easily fallen in one and broken a leg or something."

"True," Zoey said.

Several seconds of silence came and went.

"You know, that might actually be what happened to your partner," Dee said. "Maybe he simply had an accident out there and died from the cold."

"But then why cover him up with dirt?"

"I don't know, maybe someone freaked out when they saw the body."

"Someone being Gwen?"

Dee didn't reply to that.

"I have one problem with the theory that he had an accident, like falling in a hole or something," Zoey said after a few seconds.

"And that is?"

"The drag marks from the Robinson house to that particular spot."

. . .

3

Gwen opened her eyes upon a brightness that wasn't normal, confusion hitting hard as she propped herself up on her elbows and looked around. The sun was shining in through the windows on the east side of the bedroom.

Normally she was up long before the sun rose high enough to reach the room like this.

Ian too, though like herself, he was still in bed, his body sprawled out beneath the sheets while his arms were holding a pillow to his face, one that had collected quite a bit of drool.

Gwen rubbed her eyes while contemplating some of the things that had unfolded the night before.

Adding peppermint schnapps to hot chocolate was dangerous.

Like drinking liquid candy.

She remembered having three mugs during the movie.

Giant mugs.

The final of which she had mixed herself, the ratio of peppermint schnapps to hot chocolate very lopsided in favor of the peppermint schnapps.

The slight headache she currently had was a testament to this.

As was a fuzzy memory of pulling at Ian's pants while making comments about trying to get a final shot of peppermint from his candy cane.

No memories of actually going forward with such a disgusting act were present, the two likely passing out before anything could unfold. And even if they had attempted anything, she doubted it would have gone very far given that Ian could never perform after drinking, and since he had pretty much matched her drink for drink, chances were good that his so-called "candy cane" had been temporarily out of order.

Blood.

It was on her pillow.

And some of the sheets.

Reaching up, she touched her upper lip.

Crusted blood, likely a result of having bumped herself at some point.

No pain was present, unless one counted the throbbing within her head.

She needed some Advil.

Standing, she headed into the bathroom where she popped a couple pills, her foot finding a puddle of vomit on the floor near the toilet that nearly made her lose whatever was currently in her stomach.

Several deep breaths later, she wrapped a bathrobe around herself and quietly left the bedroom to go see if Tabby was up.

Tabby was, her body curled up on the couch in her Rudolph the Red-Nosed Reindeer PJs while coincidently watching *Rudolph the Red-Nosed Reindeer*, the room around her brightly lit by the Christmas tree and all the lights and other decorations that had been put up.

Good morning greetings were exchanged, Tabby's way more enthusiastic than Gwen's, though Gwen did make an effort to sound enthused herself.

"Mommy, did you know tonight is Christmas Eve?" Tabby asked.

"Is it really?" Gwen replied, even though she did know this.

"Yes," Tabby said and then held up her advent calendar. "See!"

Gwen leaned in to look at the calendar, her eyes taking in all the little open doors that Tabby had found each morning, tiny Christmas-themed images within.

She herself had never had any advent calendars as a kid, nor had she ever really looked forward to Christmas the way most children did. It just wasn't a big deal in her household.

One year she hadn't even bothered going home from school since her mother had been off with a "gentleman friend" in Europe for the holiday.

"Mommy?" Tabby asked.

"Yeah?"

"Are you going to be scared tonight when Santa is here?"

Gwen blinked, the genuine concern that Tabby was expressing nearly bringing tears to her eyes. "No. I'll be okay. So don't you worry. Everything will be fine."

"Okay, good," Tabby said. "That makes me happy."

"Me too," Gwen said.

A hug followed.

I need to bring the ax inside, Gwen thought during the hug. *Right now.*

Before Ian wakes up.

She would tuck it away in the coal room and then bring it up into the family room that evening after everyone else had gone to bed.

A few seconds later, she was slipping her boots on over her bare feet while sitting on the bench by the front door, a decision to go out this way rather than through the back door being made so as not to draw attention and questions from Tabby on why she was going outside.

She didn't make it to the shed, her feet halting the moment she saw the tracks that cut across the yard, ones that had to have been made after the snowstorm had come through the evening before given that all the other tracks in the back that had been made before that storm were no longer visible.

The trail camera.

It was positioned close enough to the tracks to have been triggered by whoever walked through here.

Without another thought, Gwen retrieved the memory disk from within the camera and hurried back around the house to the front door.

. . .

4

The female minion had been in the backyard last night.

And she had been carrying a shovel.

Seeing this, Gwen headed back downstairs to where her wet boots were waiting by the front door, and then hurried back outside, her mind and body completely oblivious to the cold as she followed the tracks into the field to see if the minion had dug up the body.

She had not.

Gwen was a good distance into the field, her eyes burning from the glare of the sun upon the snow as she followed the windswept tracks, when she realized that the tracks went in a direction nowhere near the area where the body was buried, and instead seemed to be on a path to the Robinson house itself.

Questions on why arrived as she turned around and started back toward the house, the bitter cold finally making itself known as she trudged along in nothing but her bathrobe and boots, the stupidity of running out into the field while attired like this hitting hard.

Thankfully, Tabby was still tucked away in the family room watching *Rudolph the Red-Nosed Reindeer*, and Ian still passed out in their bed when she returned, her body shivering uncontrollably as she kicked off her boots before she headed upstairs for warmer clothing.

5

"Anything?" Zoey asked as they stood at the top of the small hill, right hand shielding her eyes from the morning sun, which was intense as it reflected off the snowy field.

"Not yet," Dee said and then pointed toward some tall pine trees. "But that's the northern edge of where they used to grow Christmas trees, which means the Robinson house is about half a mile behind all those overgrown pines." She shifted her finger to the left. "So over that way is where most of the holes should be."

"I can't see anything out there that might be a mound of snow-covered dirt," Zoey said after a few seconds of staring.

"Me either," Dee said. "Though we're probably too far away still, and with this glare we won't be able to see shit from this angle."

Zoey gave a nod of acknowledgment to this and started walking, hands using the shovel as a bit of a brace as she went down the slope.

Dee followed, her steps a bit slower since she had nothing to brace herself with on the downward slope, one which would have seemed like a fantastic find if she was a kid with a sled but now was just troublesome.

And then she slipped.

"You okay?" Zoey asked while helping her up.

"Fine," she said, brushing herself off.

They started walking again, shifting eastward as they did, straight into the glare of the sun.

"So, you and Val," Dee said.

"What about me and Val?" Zoey asked.

"You two a couple or something?"

"Ha!" Zoey laughed. "No way. Just business partners."

"Yet you left what sounds like a very cozy Christmas vacation to come here to look for him."

"So?"

"So...seems a bit much for someone who doesn't have feelings for the guy."

"I didn't say I didn't have feelings for him," Zoey pointed out. "Just that we're not a couple."

"Ah, I see."

"We're friends," Zoey quickly noted. "Best friends. Almost like siblings."

Dee didn't reply to that.

"Plus, he has all the Bitcoin passwords from our nefarious blackmail operations."

"Right," Dee said, her own laugh echoing.

Zoey grinned.

Sadness followed, the grin fading.

Val was dead.

She knew this.

And yet it still hadn't really sunk in.

Almost as if she needed to see the body first.

"You know," Zoey said, trying to shift her mind a bit. "Val totally has a thing for you."

"Me?"

"Yep."

"Why?"

"He never said why exactly and always denied it when I mentioned it, but I could totally tell."

"I see."

Quite a bit of silence followed after that. Awkward silence. Dee clearly not knowing how to respond to such comments.

Or maybe she just didn't want to.

Zoey felt like she knew a lot about the young woman given all the information she had dug up on her through her various social media feeds and school records, but in reality that didn't really give as much insight into a person as one might think.

She also had to remind herself that just because Dee had rescued her from the storm last night, and then had agreed to help her with locating the spot where she thought Val was buried and digging it up, that she couldn't really trust the young woman. Not yet. Not when this could all be some sort of elaborate ploy.

Why rescue me if it is?

Was it simply so she could find out what I might know?

If so, Dee wasn't doing a very good job when it came to trying to learn anything since she wasn't really asking many questions. Even the inquiry into the relationship that she and Val shared hadn't really seemed like an attempt to glean anything. More of a way to pass the time while walking through the snow.

Minutes ticked by, the only sound that of the snow crunching beneath their steps.

"There!" Dee said without warning.

Zoey looked at Dee and then toward where she was pointing but couldn't see anything.

"What?" she asked, eyes squinting against the glare, thoughts on how she would give anything for a pair of sunglasses echoing throughout her mind.

"A snow mound," Dee said.

Zoey stared for several seconds before she saw it, the white of the mound barely visible against the white of the snow that surrounded it.

"Is this the one we're looking for?" she asked while glancing around to see if anything looked familiar.

"Unfortunately, no," Dee said. "But it does mean we are in one of the areas that they focused on when looking for bodies."

"One of the areas?" Zoey asked.

"Yeah," Dee said. "There are three total."

"But this is the one where we were the other night, right?"

"Not entirely sure on that."

"What?"

"It was dark and I was following Ian, who was following the tracks, all while silently cussing about all the snow that was getting into my shoes."

Zoey stared.

"But," Dee continued, "I know I was able to see a glow from the lights that Ian put up around his house, which means we're probably getting close."

"Okay, that's good," Zoey said, pausing for a moment, the

strain of walking through the snow on leg muscles that were already sore from the night before becoming more and more noticeable, especially when pausing.

And we haven't even reached the spot yet.

Unwanted thoughts on having to walk all the way back to the car once they found the body and how strenuous it would be began to play across her mind, ones that she tried to block out, but to no avail.

6

"Hey, Tabby, do you know where Mommy is?" Ian asked as he shuffled into the family room, his mind in shock as to how late he had slept.

"She went to the store," Tabby advised, her tiny body positioned on the floor by the brightly lit Christmas tree, chin resting on her palms as her eyes studied the various gifts that were on display.

"The store?" Ian questioned, a yawn punctuating the statement, one that somehow made the pounding within his skull worse than it was a few seconds earlier. "Did she say why?"

"To get some eggs."

"Eggs?"

"Uh-huh."

"Do you know when she left?"

"Um..." Tabby said while getting up off the floor to go look at the clock on the fireplace mantel, her lips making whispered counting sounds as she studied the numbers on the clockface. "Twenty minutes ago."

Ian nodded while letting out another yawn and then, just to confirm the calculations were correct, said, "So Mommy left when the big hand was on the number three."

"Yes."

"Did she say if she was getting anything else?"

"Nope," Tabby said while giving a very prominent shake of the head.

"Hmm, okay." Ian wanted to ask more questions given how odd it would be for Gwen to go get eggs since he had just picked up two dozen the other day, but decided against going any further with the conversation due to how difficult it was to talk right now.

Instead, he headed into the bathroom to pop some pills for his headache and then into the kitchen to make some coffee.

7

Gwen was not at the store, though she had taken the two egg cartons from the fridge as well as a plastic grocery bag from the trash that she would put the egg cartons in to back up her lie on why she had headed out that morning should Ian wake up and ask Tabby where she was before she got back home.

Two sets of tracks were present at the Robinson house.

Both of which had clearly been made after last night's snowfall.

Could Santa have actually sent two of his minions to keep an eye on her and stir up trouble?

The camera by the back door would give some insight into this.

Disk retrieved, she sprinted back down the driveway to her car where her laptop was waiting.

A popup asking if she wanted to download the contents of the memory disk appeared on her screen.

She clicked yes.

A file folder full of image icons appeared.

She double-clicked the first one.

Dee!

The camera had caught her going into the Robinson house. Why?

More pictures followed, these showing Dee leaving the Robinson house and then returning with someone that she was helping into the house.

It was the female minion that had been walking through the backyard.

Images of the two leaving the house together had been captured as well, the timestamps on these showing they had been inside for nearly an hour.

Doing what?

More important, was Dee actually one of Santa's minions herself?

Or was she simply working with them?

Like Justin and Jessica had been?

8

"Any idea on why they picked these various spots to dig in?" Zoey asked as they found another hole that had been left behind by the investigators, one that once again was not the filled-in hole that they were looking for.

"What do you mean?" Dee asked, eyes scanning the area to see if she could spot another snow mound.

"Like this hole we just found," Zoey said. "Why here and not ten feet to the left or right? Did something pinpoint this specific spot or were they just out here with shovels like a bunch of prospectors digging at random hoping to find stuff?"

"A little bit of both."

"Both?"

"Yeah. So. Okay. I don't really know how much you know

about all the stuff that unfolded around here last spring. I initially assumed a lot given that you and Val were tasked with keeping tabs on Ian and me, but am starting to think maybe that isn't really the case given how ridiculous you felt all of this was at the time."

"A fair assumption," Zoey said.

"Anyway, after Gwen got her head straightened out a bit and told investigators that Jessica had claimed the family had been giving Santa female gifts for over twenty years, Sam tried to get funding from the county to bring in search teams to go over the field with equipment and whatnot to see if they could find spots where bodies might be. The county refused, as did the state, so she was stuck with having to use what little money the town would allow, which resulted in hiring a guy who had cadaver dogs that were so poorly trained they probably wouldn't even be able to find bodies in a morgue." Dee paused to take a breath. "Almost all of these holes are spots that the dogs alerted on, and not a single one of them had a body, which of course led to many people speculating that there never were any bodies to begin with and that Ian had set the entire thing up in order to get rid of Gwen."

"And all that online speculation helped to fuel Marybeth's constant fears that Ian is some sort of diabolical villain that has always had some sort of plot going to dispose of Gwen and take control of all her financial assets," Zoey said.

"Bingo."

A few seconds came and went, the two walking toward a new spot while scanning for mounds of snow.

"What do you think?" Zoey asked. "Are there any bodies buried out here that were gifts to Santa, and if so where do you think they are?"

"I do. They are beneath the pine trees."

"Pine trees? You mean the overgrown ones in the lots behind their house that they used to sell as Christmas trees?"

"Yep."

"That actually seems pretty legit. You ever tell anyone this?"

"Several times."

"And?"

"No one ever took it seriously."

"Why not?"

"I have no idea. And my attempts at seeing if I could uncover any bodies by digging down alongside the trees to get under them was always seen as intrusive by the local authorities, even though they weren't looking in those areas at all."

Several more seconds came and went with the two simply walking.

"I'm like genuinely aggravated about that now," Zoey said. "I mean, Jesus Christ, that actually sounds really plausible, especially given how often they would be planting new trees. It's like the perfect cover."

"You want to know what makes it even more aggravating? Another serial killer not too far from here who was a professor down at U of I was doing this exact thing when burying bodies in his own backyard."

"Seriously?"

"Yep. Only they used peach trees."

"They?"

"He and his daughter."

"His daughter?"

"Yeah. It was pretty twisted actually. He had a daughter with one of the women he kept captive and raised her to think everything he did to her mother and the other women he kept chained up in the cellar was perfectly normal. She actually had her own victim as well, a kid that he brought home for her one day that she thought was her own living doll that she kept in a box up in her room when not in use."

"Jesus Christ, that's really fucked up."

"Big time. And the only reason he was stopped was

because—" Without warning the ground beneath Dee disappeared, her body seemingly sucked straight into the earth.

"Oh my god! Dee!" Zoey shouted while racing up to the hole.

"Fuck," Dee said.

"Jesus Christ. You okay?"

"Yeah," Dee said. "I think so."

"Fuck, you're bleeding."

"Am I?" Dee asked. Then, touching her split lip with a gloved finger. "Shit, I think I whacked myself in the face with the shovel while going down."

"Ouch," Zoey said.

"Speaking of, where the fuck is it?" Dee asked, looking around.

"There." Zoey pointed.

Dee grabbed the shovel and lifted it up so Zoey could grab it and set it outside the hole.

"Now you," Zoey said, reaching down with her right arm.

"Yeah right," Dee said. "No way you're pulling me out of here."

"I can."

"The sides and edges are way too slick, and with the snow up there you won't be able to leverage yourself at all, which means I'll probably pull you right down in here with me and then we'll really be fucked."

"At least let me try," Zoey said. "I'm stronger than I look."

Dee considered this for a few seconds, her eyes shifting between the offered arm and the sides of the hole. "Okay, but if you start to slide in, let go."

"Will do."

Dee was right.

Zoey could not get her out of the hole. Not with how slick the sides were, Dee's boots simply sliding on them when she tried to use the side as leverage. The surface was no better.

Zoey could lean over the side and hold Dee, but she couldn't pull her out, not when sprawled out upon the snowy ground.

"We need a ladder or something," Dee said.

"Where are we going to find a ladder way out here?" Zoey asked.

"The Robinson house. They have all kinds of ladders and ropes in the old barn."

"You sure?"

"Yeah."

"Jesus, I can't even see the house from here," Zoey said, looking westward.

"We're probably about a mile away, but if you just start walking, you'll see it soon."

"Fuck."

9

Ian noted the empty area of the fridge where the eggs should have been while retrieving the carton of half-and-half for his coffee, the trauma of using the coffee grinder to pulverize the beans still echoing within his head.

Never again, he silently vowed in regards to the peppermint-schnapps-laced hot chocolate.

At least not three mugs' worth back-to-back like that.

That had been a huge mistake.

It also was very unlike him, yet at the time he hadn't really considered that, his mind only thinking of Gwen and how the alcohol seemed to be helping her through the movie.

How is she feeling this morning?

Good enough to go to the store apparently.

"Boarding school girls know how to drink!" Gwen had once proclaimed during a party while tossing back a shot of some-

thing that was on fire. Literally. Flames had been billowing out from within the shot glass.

He smiled at the memory.

And then frowned as the brightness of the bulb within the fridge began to get to him, his eyes squinting against the white light as he fumbled out the carton of half-and-half with one hand and closed the door with the other.

A few seconds later he was staring at his milky white coffee, a sudden queasiness within his gut giving him second thoughts on consuming the beverage.

One tentative sip.

And a second one.

And a third one.

Each one stayed down.

A bigger sip followed, the coffee actually tasting really good as it washed out the crud-like acidic peppermint residue that had been clinging to the surfaces within his mouth.

"Daddy, what's *Die Heart*?" Tabby asked from the family room.

"*Die Heart*?" Ian questioned and then groaned at the pain vocalizing that question had created, a hand going to his forehead.

"It says it's a Christmas movie," Tabby added.

Ian frowned for a moment and then let out a slight wince as he stood up and headed into the family room to see what Tabby was talking about. "*Die Heart*?" he asked again, though more softly this time.

Tabby pointed.

Ian studied the screen for several seconds, his squinted eyes struggling to process what he was seeing.

A chuckle followed, one that was unavoidable despite the pain it caused.

"That's actually called *Die Hard*," he said. "And it really isn't a movie for kids."

"But it says it's a Christmas movie," Tabby noted.

"That it does," he said, another slight chuckle leaving his lips. Amazon had the movie listed first up in its Prime Christmas selection. "But it's one for adults only, okay?"

"Okay."

Ian started back toward where his coffee was waiting, but then stopped when he felt his stomach start to rise. A second later he was racing for the bathroom, all the coffee he had consumed earlier coming back up and splashing all over the toilet seat lid, which had slipped from his fingers as he tried to lift it.

10

Dee.

Working for Santa.

Alongside the female minion.

It was all Gwen could think about as she sat on the sofa in the family room of the Robinson house staring at the pile of blankets by the fireplace.

Was Dee a minion herself?

A human-elf hybrid that never really had any family down here?

Or simply a human that had somehow gotten caught up in the horror and was now forced to help Santa so that she didn't end up at the North Pole, her body locked away in the breeding pens so that her womb could be used over and over again in producing new elves.

Just like Tabby would be.

Once Santa lost interest in her.

No!

No!

No!

She wasn't going to let that happen.

She couldn't.

And after tonight that would no longer be a threat.

Santa would be gone once and for all, the various pieces of his body dumped in various holes out in the field once his time away from the North Pole ran out.

If everything went according to plan.

If Dee and the minion didn't ruin things first.

If—

She heard sounds toward the rear of the house.

Someone was opening the back door and coming inside.

Moving slowly, Gwen grabbed a piece of firewood and headed toward the kitchen, her eyes peeking around the edge of the wall cutout.

Someone was kneeling on the floor pulling out an item from between the fridge and the cabinet.

The minion?

Grabbing a stepladder?

So that she could string someone up by the fireplace like Justin and Jessica had done to her last year.

Tabby!

No!

No!

No!

Lifting the piece of firewood over her head, Gwen rushed into the kitchen and brought it down just as the hunched-over figure turned toward her, a cry of surprise leaving her lips as the piece of firewood cracked into the top of her head.

Ian opened his eyes to find Tabby staring at him while wearing a mask that she and Gwen had made during the pandemic a few years earlier, one that had a flower pattern printed into it.

"Daddy, are you sick?" she asked, voice a bit muffled.

"No," he said, a hand going to his head. "Just tired."

"You threw up," she noted.

"I did," he confirmed. "But it's okay. I'm not sick. I just needed to lay down for a bit."

Tabby studied him for several seconds.

"Is Mommy back?" he asked.

"Not yet."

"I need my phone," he mumbled, more to himself than to Tabby, his thoughts being voiced whether they warranted voicing.

"It's downstairs," Tabby said.

"Okay," he said.

He tried to sit up, but then quickly lowered himself back down with a bit of a groan.

Tabby backed up, a look of panic in her eyes.

"Honey, it's okay, I'm not sick. Not in any way that you can catch."

"But you're in the guest room."

"Am I?" he asked and looked around, eyes noting that it was indeed the guest room, one that he had isolated within two different times during the pandemic.

Tabby nodded.

"That's just because it was close to the stairs," he said and sat up, the room spinning a bit, but not to the point of being unable to stay vertical. Or halfway vertical, as was his current position.

Going all the way up to his feet was another story.

"Daddy?"

"Do you think maybe you could bring me my phone?" he asked, putting a hand to his head. "And a soda?"

"Okay."

12

Dee was cold.

Really cold.

The hole she was in no longer bathed in sunlight as it had been when she had first fallen into it, the change of temperature as the light had slithered away quite significant.

Phone in hand, she checked the time, her mind once again noting that Zoey should have been back by now.

What if she has fallen in her own hole?

Indecision plagued her.

13

Tabby stared at the screen of Daddy's phone, which had buzzed with a text as she grabbed it.

It was from Dee.

It said: *Help!*

Another text arrived.

I'm stuck in a hole!

Then a third.

In the field behind your house!

A sound.

Behind her.

She twisted around.

14

. . .

"Mommy!" Tabby cried out with surprise, clearly startled by Gwen having stepped into the family room. Then, "I wasn't reading the screen."

"What?" Gwen asked, momentarily confused.

"Not on purpose," Tabby added. "Daddy went upstairs after throwing up. I was going to bring him a soda since that helps the tummy. I then saw Daddy's phone and was going to bring that to him too when Dee texted that she was stuck in a hole."

"Dee is stuck in a hole?"

"Uh-huh. Out behind the house. But I swear, I wasn't reading it on purpose."

"Let me see," Gwen said, reaching out a hand.

Tabby handed over the phone, a guilty look present.

Gwen took it and looked at the screen for a second, and then thumbed in Ian's password.

"Is Daddy going to be mad at me for reading it?" Tabby asked. "Or what about Santa? Will he take away some gifts now?"

Santa.

Dee.

The minion that had been in the Robinson house and now was in her car trunk.

"*Mommy?*"

Gwen blinked. "No, no, honey, it's okay. But just in case, how about we keep this a secret between you and me? Okay? You never accidentally looked at the screen, okay?"

"Okay."

"And if Daddy asks anything about Dee, you don't say anything about her being stuck in a hole, okay?"

"Okay."

"Now, I am going to go see if Daddy's okay. You stay down here. Once I'm back down, we can start doing that gingerbread house we got the other day, okay?"

Tabby's eyes lit up. "Okay!"

15

"You look terrible," Gwen said, catching Ian off guard.

"I bet," Ian replied, forcing a bit of a smile.

A grimace followed, this from the taste of vomit that was still heavy in his mouth.

"Sorry I wasn't here when you got up," Gwen said. "The store was crazy."

"It must have been," Ian said. "You were gone a really long time."

"It was packed," Gwen said. "Plus I got a phone call."

"Phone call?"

"From my mother."

"Oh."

"Right before I was about to head inside the grocery store." She let out a heavy sigh. "I really should have let it go to voicemail, but..." She shrugged.

"Yeah," Ian said. "Probably best you answered it."

"We talked for like forty-five minutes. Well. She talked, I listened. And by the time we were done the store had gone from being slightly crowded to really crowded. It was like the entire world needed last-minute items."

"But now you're back," he said. "All is right as rain."

"Yep."

"I still can't believe we needed eggs. I don't know what happened to the ones I bought."

"Just one of those things, I guess," she said. "I'm just glad I noticed we needed them before it was too late."

"Me too. And I'm so sorry you had to go out to get some."

"Oh don't worry about it," she said, waving a hand. "I actually think the cold air did me some good. Cleared my head a bit. Speaking of, how are you feeling?"

"Ugh," he said.

"Yeah, you look like *ugh* too," she noted.

"I don't know how you do it," he said. "You had way more than me last night, yet here I'm the one that can barely function today while you've been to the store and back."

"What can I say?" she said with a grin. "Boarding school girl. Raiding the headmistress's supply was literally our favorite pastime. When not having lesbian orgies."

He chuckled.

"Though, honestly, I didn't feel all that great this morning, and would have probably been even worse off if you hadn't helped me purge myself before going to bed."

"What?"

She grinned.

He frowned with confusion.

"You don't remember at all, do you?" she said.

"I must not," he said. "The last thing I can remember was seeing Tim Allen's beard suddenly growing back after he shaved."

"Really?"

"Yep."

"Well then, let's just say I tried doing something to you that resulted in me upchucking all over the floor, which is probably the reason why I didn't have as tough a time this morning as you did."

Ian still had no idea what she was talking about, but then understood when she made an obscene gesture featuring her hand near her wide-open mouth.

"Are you serious?" he asked.

"Yep."

"Oh god, I'm so sorry."

"Nah, I'm pretty sure I initiated it."

Ian didn't reply to that, his mind struggling to contend

with the idea that he could remember nothing of what had unfolded after the movie, especially when his actions apparently involved him shoving his penis down her throat. That was not something he wanted to be engaging in when unable to think about things clearly.

Thankfully, Gwen seemed amused by the entire thing rather than upset, and even went so far as to suggest trying again later without any booze being involved, which really surprised him.

"Oh, here you go," Gwen said, handing him his phone. "It was downstairs."

"Ah, thanks," he said, taking it.

"No problem."

16

Gwen watched as Ian thumbed open the phone, her mind momentarily worried that he would somehow know about her having deleted the messages from Dee before giving him the phone. She had also gone into the settings and blocked Dee so that no more messages or calls would come through.

Relief arrived.

Ian didn't seem to notice anything amiss.

17

Zoey wasn't sure where she was or how she had gotten there, her ability to process her cramped surroundings almost nonexistent given the mildewy sack that was over her face, and the bindings that held her wrists and ankles together.

Something was in her mouth too, a thick cloth of some sort that tasted terrible.

She tried to expel it, but her lips were sealed shut with what probably was duct tape, making it impossible for her to push out the saliva-soaked intruder.

Pain.

A throbbing kind.

It echoed from the back of her head.

Dee.

Is she still stuck in that hole?

Or had whoever struck her in the head gone out to find her?

But who?

And why?

Gwendolyn?

Had she been right about her having killed Val and buried the body?

Had the events of last year and the horrible treatments that her mother had forced upon her coupled with all the sights and sounds of the looming holiday finally caused her to snap?

Or had it been someone else?

Jessica?

Had she really escaped everything last year and come back to wreak her own type of havoc?

No.

Not Jessica.

It couldn't be.

Not after a year.

She would have been seen at some point.

Nausea hit.

Fear came with it.

If she vomited, she would die, choking to death on her own stomach acids because of the gag in her mouth.

Such horrors happened far more often than most people thought.

Especially in abduction situations.

A tickle hit her throat, one that was made worse by the thick cloth that had been shoved within her mouth, a sense of it hovering very near to the area that would cause her to start gagging uncontrollably knocking all other thoughts away, and she struggled to keep her stomach from purging itself.

18

"Chief?" a voice asked while knuckles gave a gentle tap upon the doorframe of her office.

"Yeah?" Sam asked, glancing up from a funding report she had been trying to complete so that she could get home.

Officer Perry was standing in her doorway. He said: "We just got an interesting call forwarded to us from the county about doing a wellness check that I think you might be interested in."

"Oh?"

"There is a family up in Boston that is concerned about their daughter. Said she came here to check on her business partner, who is a private investigator from New York who stopped answering his phone, and now the young woman herself is no longer answering her own phone."

Startled, Sam didn't reply right away, which prompted Officer Perry to ask, "Chief?"

"You have them on the phone right now?" Sam asked. "The family?"

"I do."

"Okay, send it over to me."

19

. . .

The gingerbread house collapsed in upon itself three times before they were able to get it to stay up, the icing that the kit had provided as a type of mortar for the house and all the candy that would be attached failing in its duties until that fourth attempt was made, Ian literally holding the walls in place for twice the length of time that was advised on the box, and then the roof pieces even longer once it was applied.

After that, the only incidents involved pieces of candy not staying where they were placed, much to the frustrations of Tabby, who kept having to scale back her design plans into the realm of practicality.

A small Santa figure had come with the kit, one that Tabby tried to stick on the roof near a Hershey Bar chimney she had made, the figure falling to his death several times upon the spearmint leaf shrubberies that lined a Necco Wafer walkway.

"Mommy?" Tabby asked during one of these death plummets.

Gwen did not reply, her eyes looking upon but not really seeing the gingerbread house that Tabby was working on, her mind dwelling upon the Dee-in-a-hole situation.

"Honey," Ian said, snagging her attention.

Gwen blinked and then looked down at the coffee she had before her, the beverage no longer warm.

"Tabby's asking you a question."

"Oh, what, sweetie?" Gwen asked.

Tabby picked up the fallen Santa from the walkway and said, "In the movie last night Santa fell off a roof and Scott Calvin became Santa Claus by putting on his coat."

Gwen felt herself stiffening a bit. "He did," she said.

"What happens if a girl puts on his coat? Does she become Santa?"

Gwen blinked, memories of putting on Santa's coat after freeing herself from the ropes last year arriving within her mind.

What if that movie was right?

What if I had become Santa after that?

But she had not become Santa.

Maybe because he hadn't been dead yet, just unconscious, eventually coming to and grabbing Jessica to bring back to the North Pole, possibly because she had been the one to revive him.

But if he had been truly dead...

Would she have taken his place, her body twisting itself into some demonic female version of Santa? One that required male gifts instead of female ones?

Or would her body have become some sort of female-male hybrid that had all the different parts so as to be able to keep impregnating the women that were brought back to produce offspring that toiled away in the bowels of the castle?

Beard, breasts, belly, and a giant cock.

The image would have almost been amusing if it didn't seem so horrifyingly plausible, the magic surrounding Santa one that would likely twist a person into some hideous being like that.

What had happened to his coat?

Gwen knew she had been wearing it while in the jail cell after that officer had picked her up, but once in the hospital it had been nowhere to be seen.

Had someone taken it?

An officer?

Sam?

"Gwen? Honey?"

She looked at Ian, who was looking at her with concern, and then over at Tabby, who seemed inquisitive, the Santa figure still in hand.

"I'm—I'm—" She blinked a few times while frowning. "I don't really know, sweetie." She pushed herself away from the table. "I'll be right back."

Ian started to rise as well, but then stopped when she gestured for him to stay.

A few seconds later she was in her office staring at her empty desk, confusion as to where her laptop was dominating her mind for several seconds before realizing it was still in the car.

20

Zoey heard a sound, but couldn't place what it was.

And then another sound arrived, this one a heavy *thunk* that she felt as it rocked the tiny area she was confined within.

Car door.

Being opened and then shut.

Which means...

Trunk!

I'm in a trunk!

"Gwen?" a voice asked. "Are you okay?"

Zoey froze.

Was that Ian?

And the female voice that replied with: *"I'm fine."* Was that Gwendolyn?

Zoey tried to make noise but couldn't move her arms or legs in any way that was effective in making sound, the hogtied-like pose she had been left in one that made it impossible to kick up or down, or to bounce her body around in any way that would cause a *thunk* that could be heard beyond her confines.

Even slamming her head into things as a last-ditch effort before Ian and Gwendolyn left what she assumed to be their garage didn't seem to work, the one attempt she made a complete failure.

Thoughts followed.

All of them focusing on Gwendolyn and how she now knew she was the one that had hit her.

But why?
What the fuck was going on?

21

Ian watched Gwen head upstairs with her computer bag, the hurried comments on how she had left it in her car the other day after visiting one of their properties leaving him somewhat confused because he could not place when that might have been.

Then again, he had been at the bookstore for several days this past week, and then at the mall with Tabby to see Santa for several hours on Saturday, so there was quite a bit of time where her statement could have been plausible.

Plus, why lie about something like that?

"Daddy?" Tabby called from the dining room.

"What is it?" he called back.

"Can you help me make a gingerbread car?"

A gingerbread car?

Concern followed given that he didn't have a clue how to do something like that.

Thankfully, it wasn't as difficult as it sounded, Tabby's vision being a vehicle that was made out of a Hershey Bar that needed to be carefully cut into the shape of a car, one which she would then stick candy wheels on that were made out of peppermint pinwheels.

His help was needed with the cutting, a task that was somewhat tedious once he discovered that even the smallest amount of pressure from his fingers as he held down the Hershey Bar would cause the rectangle pieces to snap off.

"How's this?" he asked after creating what was supposed to be a standard sedan but looked a bit like a flying saucer.

"Hmm..." Tabby said while examining it, clearly not impressed with his chocolate carving skills.

"It will probably look better once you put the wheels on," he noted.

"You're right!" Tabby beamed. "And I'm going to use the red and green icing to decorate it even more so that it is all Christmassy.

"Perfect."

A few seconds came and went.

"Daddy?" she asked.

"Yeah?"

"Can we go Christmas caroling tonight?"

"Christmas caroling?"

"Yeah."

"Is it for school?" he asked, suddenly wondering if they had missed a notice about the activity. "Your music class?"

"No, you, me, Mommy, and Dee."

"Oh, um, I don't know."

"Dee is a really good singer."

"Is she really?"

"Uh-huh. She and I sing all the time when she comes over to stay with me."

"Really? Wow. I did not know that." Questions on what type of songs they were singing began to echo within his mind, a bit of concern present given some of the darker interests that Dee harbored. Then again, Dee was always very good with Tabby and had never exposed her to any of the macabre things she was into—unless one counted the darkly themed Halloween costume she had helped Tabby create for trick-or-treating earlier this year.

"What's so funny?" Tabby asked, clearly catching his slight chuckle.

"Oh, nothing," he said. "I was just thinking about the Halloween costume you and Dee made two months ago."

"That wasn't a funny costume. That was a scary costume."

"I know."

"Then why are you laughing?"

Because, he silently said to himself, *Marybeth freaked out when she saw a picture of it on Facebook and thought we were exposing you to Satanism.* Out loud to Tabby he said, "I was just laughing about how scared some people were when they answered the door."

"Mrs. Lovegrove thought my fangs were real," Tabby noted.

"I remember. She probably still has scary dreams about it." He palmed a piece of candy from one of her bowls while saying this, his movements not stealthy enough, it seemed, because Tabby scolded him and made him put it back.

22

Sam stood in the motel room that Zoey was staying in, her comments a few minutes earlier to the clerk in the front office about needing to do a wellness check on a guest that was staying here having resulted in the clerk unenthusiastically asking for a name, which he looked up and found quickly, and then simply handing over a key to a room with a request that she bring the key back once finished.

Nothing within the room indicated any foul play having taken place, and had it not been for a notepad sitting next to a file folder and some sort of video player on the table, she probably would have called it quits.

Instead, she examined the notepad, which had several things written on it in various places without any real order, almost like a thought journal, the most concerning item being her own name in big block letters halfway down the page along with a comment on how she had been Ian's former girlfriend, which led to scribbled questions on if she still had feelings for him, was having an affair with him, and had helped in burying the body.

Other notes indicated that Zoey was of the assumption that someone in Gwen's orbit had killed her partner and buried him in the field between the Robinson house and Ian and Gwen's house, a search of the area around the Robinson house having revealed what looked to be his rental car sitting abandoned about a half mile from the house itself.

No location of this supposed burial site was noted, though there were questions on what Val might have seen that led to his death, along with a list of theories, most which revolved around Ian engaged in some sort of scheme to drive Gwen crazy.

An underlined note that simply said: *Gwendolyn Alexa Fireplace Christmas Lights* followed by three question marks sat beneath these theories.

23

Try as she might, Gwen couldn't find any online resources devoted to mythology surrounding a female version of Santa Claus, the only thing the search results ever brought up being nonsense about Mrs. Claus and how she always aided her husband by baking cookies, which were cherished by both Santa and all the hardworking elves as they created mountains of toys for all the good little girls and boys.

Adding the word "evil" into things didn't help either, the results either being devoted to Krampus, which had no real bearing on what was truly going on up at the North Pole, or sexy Santa costumes, which were beyond ridiculous, the image that was currently displayed showing an Elvira-like model wearing a skimpy Santa coat that barely covered her nipples, a short red skirt, and knee-high stiletto boots with bells on them.

"No way is she going to fit down the chimney with those boobs."

Startled, Gwen twisted around.

Ian was standing in the middle of her office.

"Oh my god, I'm so sorry," he said, his concern sounding genuine. "I thought you knew I was behind you."

Gwen shook her head while taking a deep breath, one that she hoped would calm her racing heart. It didn't. Even so, she put on a smile and said, "The Christmas music down there is so loud I didn't hear you come in."

"Oh?" he said, frowning, likely because the music wasn't really all that loud and could barely be heard up here.

"Anyway, I totally got sucked down a rabbit hole," she said, motioning toward her laptop, which she then closed.

"It happens," he said. Then, "Everything okay?"

"Yeah, fine," she said. "Tabby's comment. The one about female Santa. Made me curious to see if there was anything out there. Like myths surrounding a female version. But the only thing any of the searches brought up involved sexy costumes."

"That's the internet for you," he said. "Sex, sex, sex."

She nodded and then asked, "How's the gingerbread house coming along?"

"Pretty good. I just finished making her a car out of a Hershey Bar, and now she is putting some final touches on the roof, which is why I came up. She wants you to see what she did."

"Okay," she said, pushing up from the chair.

"She also wants to know if we can go Christmas caroling tonight once Dee gets here," he noted. "Speaking of, have you heard anything from Dee today?"

"Dee? Um. No. Nothing."

"Wonder if she is still planning on coming over tonight?"

"Hmm, I don't know," Gwen said. "I'll give her a call in a bit to find out. So...Christmas caroling?"

"Yeah, totally caught me off guard with that."

"I bet." Then, after a few seconds: "I'm not sure I'm up for something like that."

"I know, same here."

A few seconds of silence followed, neither one wanting to be the one to make the decision on what to do.

"How did she seem while asking about it?" Gwen asked. "Was it something she really wants to do, or just a passing fancy that she'll forget about if we focus her elsewhere?"

"Hard to say," he said.

"Maybe let's just not even bring it up and see what happens."

"Hmm."

"Or, if she does bring it up, suggest something else. Like going to see all the Christmas lights around town. I bet she would love to do that."

24

Sam spent several minutes reading through the first few pages of the treatment notes that were in the file next to the notepad before shifting her focus to the portable DVD player.

Not long after that, she left the motel and started driving toward the Robinson house, the horror of what she had witnessed on that small screen dominating her thoughts as the scenes replayed themselves over and over again across her mind's eye.

25

Tabby didn't mention anything else about going Christmas

caroling, her focus once the gingerbread house was completed landing upon the gifts that were beneath the tree for a while and then upon an old 500-piece Christmas jigsaw puzzle that had been found in the basement.

Gwen joined her in working on the puzzle while Ian got started on his Christmas quiches, the dish one that he always prepared the day before so that they could be simply heated up in the oven the next day while the gifts were being opened.

"Oh wow, you two have gotten a lot done," he said once the two quiches were in the oven, a plate with extra bacon in hand behind his back.

"We did the edges first," Tabby said. "And now Mommy is working on the fireplace while I find all the tree pieces."

"I see," he said. "Doing the edge pieces first is always the best idea."

"That's what Mommy said too," Tabby noted.

"That's right," Gwen said.

"Daddy, what are you hiding behind your back?"

"It's..." he said, pausing dramatically before bringing the plate around for them to see. "Extra bacon!"

"Bacon!" Tabby shouted with enthusiasm and grabbed a piece.

Gwen didn't react right away, and then without warning pushed herself up from the table, puzzle piece bouncing as she clipped the edge with her knee, and bolted from the room, the sounds of the front door opening and closing echoing.

Concerned, Ian set the plate down with a heavy *thunk* and raced outside to join her.

Gwen was on her hands and knees in the snow.

Ian joined her, the socks he was wearing doing little to ward off the cold as they sank into the snow, dampness appearing quickly within the fabric.

"Gwen?" he whispered.

"Go away," she muttered.

"Gwen, come back inside."

"I'm fine, just give me a second."

"Gwen, you're scaring Tabby," he said, an edge to his voice. *And me.*

This did the trick, Gwen allowing herself to be helped up out of the snow, her right arm doing a quick pass over her lips to clear away whatever had been expelled.

Tabby was standing in the entryway as they came back inside, eyes wide, lower lip trembling. "Mommy?" she asked.

"Honey," Ian said while guiding Gwen to the bench near the coats, "why don't you go pick out a present to open for Christmas Eve, and then after that we're going to go look at Christmas lights."

Tabby nodded and left the room.

Ian watched her go and then turned to Gwen, who was staring up at him.

He stared back for a few seconds and then asked, "What was it?"

"The bacon," she said.

"The bacon?" he asked, surprised. He had thought it was something to do with the puzzle.

She nodded.

Ian was at a loss on that.

"I'm okay now," she said.

"Okay," Ian said, struggling to believe this.

26

The private investigator.

In the family room of the Robinson house the other day.

His charred face.

Broiled eyeballs.

Smoking flesh.

Seeing the bacon had brought all of that back to the front of her mind.

She had no idea why. It just did.

With it came renewed concerns on if her fireplace trap really would work with Santa. Would it kill him? Or at least incapacitate him to the point where she could dismember him? Would that finally end things? Once the magic window of time ran out? Was there even a magic window of time?

27

Sam parked behind the snow-covered rental vehicle on Route 6, a quick check of the info she had noted the other day when talking to Dee and Tabby about their *Mystery of the Mysterious Writer* case confirming that this was indeed the vehicle the two had been keeping tabs on, the same vehicle that the rental agency had refused to give her info on when she was attempting to confirm that it was the private investigator who was snooping around as Dee suspected, rather than some random true crime writer who happened upon the area.

Now she knew.

Dee had been right.

Not that it really mattered all that much.

A private investigator snooping around wasn't anything she could put an end to. Not for any legal reasons. Her agreement back when Ian had called during the Thanksgiving weekend to keep an eye out for the investigator one of simply helping to ease the stress Ian had already been facing as the holiday season drew near.

Now, however, things were a bit different. If the private investigator had truly been killed while working whatever nonsense Marybeth had sent him to look into, followed by his partner disappearing while looking into things as well, then that was something she had to look into in an official capacity.

Of course, she had no evidence that anyone had been killed, and it seemed like the partner didn't either, but given the snow-covered state of the rental vehicle, and the insistence by Zoey's family that something had to have happened to her given her lack of contact, Sam felt it was her duty to start looking into things a bit.

Using an ice scraper, Sam cleared away one of the windows so she could look inside the vehicle.

Nothing within looked amiss.

The trunk?

In these cold temperatures a body could go unnoticed within for quite some time, so taking a look inside wasn't something that would seem unreasonable in such a situation. Getting into the trunk would be difficult though given how frozen over the car was, so rather than going that direction right now, she wanted to check out the Robinson house to see if there was any evidence of the investigator or his partner having run into trouble within.

Or somewhere outside the house.

For all she knew, the private investigator had gotten himself caught out in the elements after a misstep and froze to death. As for this Zoey...maybe she had simply lost track of time while investigating things herself and wasn't paying attention to her phone. Or she was ignoring her phone.

One of the family members that had been on the call had clearly not been pleased with Zoey for coming out here during their family Christmas celebration, the other voices on the call frequently trying to stop her from making angry comments while expressing their concerns, so the possibility that Zoey had gotten fed up with her family and wasn't answering their calls was not beyond the realm of possibility.

Back in her vehicle, Sam maneuvered herself around so that she could head down to the Robinson driveway, her mind silently hoping (pleading) that Ian had finally gotten around to shoveling it so that she wouldn't have to walk through the snow on her journey up to the house.

It wasn't shoveled.

Someone had walked up and down it though.

Recently too, since the tracks looked fresh.

Zoey?

Ian?

Gwen?

Dee?

Or just some random person who simply wanted to get a stupid selfie while by the house?

Whoever it had been had gone up and come back, which meant everything must seem okay up there at the house.

Still, she would be remiss if she didn't at least walk up there and check things out. After all, the driveway wasn't the only avenue of approach to the house. The private investigator's abandoned rental vehicle could be viewed as evidence of this, as were all the various people she had stumbled upon during the summer months that had come out here to look around, most thinking they were clever by parking a mile or two away from the house and walking up to it.

28

Zoey struggled against her bonds for what felt like hours, her wrists constantly twisting back and forth in an effort to find some weakness in the ropes so that she could loosen them to the point of slipping a hand free, all to no avail.

Attempting to pick at the knots also failed to yield any results, her numb fingers unable to find any area of give that would eventually cause a knot to fail.

She was stuck.

And in pain.

A lot of pain.

The position she was in was unforgiving, and her struggles had only added to the agony, especially during those moments when she got so frustrated that she tried kicking her feet, which would do nothing but tug on her wrists, which in turn would wrench her shoulders to the point where she was sure dislocation became a risk.

At one point a charley horse developed in her right calf muscle, her leg unable to stretch out to relieve it, her lungs shrieking against the cloth in her mouth while tears erupted from her eyes.

No struggles followed for a long time after that, Zoey simply remaining still in the tight confines of the trunk, her mind drifting in an odd daze where she wasn't even sure of the passage of time.

The doorbell shattered this, though at first she wasn't really sure what the sound was or if it even existed.

Three times it was pressed, the fancy chime sound that echoed throughout the house reaching her ears without fail given how close she actually was to the source.

No one answered the door.

Zoey was not surprised by this.

Earlier she had heard what had to be Ian's truck starting up, and while initially she hadn't been certain if the faint voices she heard out in the driveway were from three people or just Ian and Tabby, an eventual comment of "Mommy, be careful, it's really slippery over here!" confirmed to her that all three were heading out somewhere.

Silence returned shortly after the doorbell chimes had echoed, one that somehow seemed far heavier and more isolating to Zoey than at any point prior.

She was all alone out here in an area that was about as far from town as she could get without crossing over into the next county, which in turn wouldn't put her anywhere near anything for at least six or seven miles. Adding to this was the fact that it was Christmas Eve, which meant that whoever this most recent visitor was, they were likely the last that would be out this way for at least a day, if not more.

Not that she would stay in this trunk for that long.

No.

Whatever fucked-up reason Gwendolyn had for knocking her out and putting her in the trunk, it most likely revolved around that night. Christmas Eve. And unless Ian or Tabby discovered her in the next few hours, she would be at Gwen's mercy.

What about Dee?

Was she still stuck in that hole?

If not, she would be able to bring help, but would that help arrive in time?

Was that what the doorbell had been about?

Had Dee gotten out and come here to check things out?

No.

That just didn't seem like it was the case.

She also realized that if Dee had not brought help by now, then it probably wasn't happening. After all, Dee had a phone, so once Zoey had failed to come back to the hole, Dee would have had no choice but to call for help, knowing she would freeze to death if she didn't. This meant that Gwendolyn had probably done something to her shortly after her own encounter with her in the house, likely by either looking at her phone and seeing the pinned location or simply following the tracks she had made when walking to the Robinson house from the hole.

But why had Gwendolyn been there in the first place?

And would she really have killed Dee?

If so, why was she still alive?

What purpose did Gwendolyn have for bringing her here?

No answer to this was forthcoming, but thinking about it

did spur a fresh attempt at freeing herself, the ropes once again resisting her efforts and causing her nothing but pain.

29

Dee tried calling Ian several times with no luck. The calls just were not going through.

Because of the hole?

Was she too deep for the calls to go out into the world?

Such didn't seem like it should be a problem in this day and age given how advanced the technology was, yet the fact remained, the calls were not going through.

30

Zoey freed her left leg without even realizing it, her renewed struggles following the ringing of the doorbell reaching a point of such ferocity that her boot went flying. Initially, she was horrified by this because despite being in a garage that was attached to the main part of the house, things were getting really cold, whatever heat that seeped into the garage unable to compete with the falling temperatures outside. But then she realized the ropes that bound her ankles had been looped over her boots, making it so she now had a bit of a gap between the coarse rope and her socks.

Taking off her other boot added to this gap, though getting to that point was quite the ordeal, the boot refusing to be kicked off like the first one had, making it so she had to find and untie the knots with her numb fingers, the laces quite tight.

Following this, she worked her legs back and forth as far as the bindings would allow, these attempts putting a strain on her wrists and shoulders that was beyond any physical agony she had ever faced before, her goal being for one leg to hold the ropes steady while the other pulled at the loop and tried to slip free.

Epic fail.

These movements would not produce the desired results.

Next she tried holding the ropes around her ankles with her fingers, her ability to grip them only something she could achieve with the left foot. Why this was, she couldn't say, but after fumbling around in the dark with her hands behind her, this was the conclusion she arrived upon.

And yet that was okay because by pulling on the rope while pressing with that foot, the coarse bindings, which had become slick with blood from the torn flesh her struggles had produced, eventually slipped over her ankle bone, and then, after some more struggling and strain on her foot that produced a pain that would have made the most sadistic medieval inquisitor proud, the rope slipped over her toes.

Two toenails went with the rope, which was why she didn't realize her victory right away, her kicking of the foot to try to minimize the burning pain taking precedent until it dawned on her that she was kicking her foot back and forth while it was extended, which meant it was no longer bent in on itself and held in place by the ropes.

31

Sam called Ian after failing to raise anyone at his house, her surprise at the place being empty having resulted in her sitting in her car for about ten minutes before placing the call.

Voicemail.

She didn't leave a message.

A text from Ian arrived a few seconds later.

It read: *Looking at Christmas lights with Gwen and Tabby. Call you when we get back?*

Sam thought about it for a few seconds, her mind debating whether she should insist on a call now or wait.

She settled on waiting.

If the three were out and about together, that meant things were probably okay with Gwen right now, and she didn't want to spoil that with comments about a missing private eye and his business associate.

Not tonight.

Not with this being the first Christmas after Gwen's ordeal.

Then again, two people were now missing in connection with the Robinson house, people who had been sent out here to keep an eye on Ian in hopes of proving he was responsible for everything that had happened the previous year, which meant she would have to involve Ian and Gwen in her investigation.

But not yet.

Not tonight.

Instead, she would continue to poke around a bit, starting with a call to Dee to see if she knew anything about this Zoey person.

No answer.

Sam tried a second time.

Again, no answer.

That seemed really odd.

Dee always had her phone on her, or within reach, and yet now...

Could she be with someone?

A new boyfriend?

Someone who had gotten all excited about the comments that were being posted online about the twisted fantasies she had wanted to engage in while inside the Robinson house?

Had those comments been legit or just bullshit?

It was hard to say with Dee.

Go see if she is home?

Or go back to the Robinson house and follow the tracks out into the field?

Venturing out into the field right now was not an idea she relished at all, especially now that the sun had gone down and the bitter cold nighttime temperatures had arrived.

Five degrees below zero was the low temperature for the night, and though they had not bottomed out at that yet and were still on the positive side of zero, it wasn't by much, and with the windchill, it felt like they were ten or fifteen below.

Indecision gripped her.

32

Dee missed the call from Sam, the buzz from the call having failed to vibrate all the way through the layers of warm clothing she had put on for this trek through the snowy field. She had also folded herself into a tight ball, arms wrapped around herself, in an attempt to conserve heat.

Once she did check her phone, and tried calling Sam back, she mistyped the password three times before pulling off her right glove and trying again.

This time it worked.

A second later she was calling Sam.

33

Zoey got both her feet free, which was a huge relief both mentally and physically, but then found herself unable to achieve the same success with her wrists. The ropes were simply too tight, and the knots that had been tied were located in a spot her fingers could not reach. It did not matter how flexible she was, or how much pain she could endure while trying to twist her fingers around to get at the knots; they were simply unreachable.

This was okay though because having her feet free meant being able to kick at the trunk lid, which was huge. All she needed now was for Ian or Tabby to come into the garage to get something, and voilà, she would be free after they came to investigate the pounding coming from within the trunk.

What if they don't come into the garage though?

What if they simply come home, go into the family room to watch movies or play games, and then go to bed?

What if the only one that does come to the garage is Gwen?

Despair followed for a few seconds but then was shattered when her inner voice said: *Then I will kick the shit out of her when she opens the trunk.*

Being able to see what she was kicking would help in this attack, so rather than continuing to fruitlessly struggle with the ropes that secured her wrists, she focused on getting the burlap sack off her head.

As with most endeavors, this was easier said than done, especially once she realized that a rope had been knotted around the base of the sack near her throat, which explained why it tugged at her chin whenever she tried to shrug it off with her shoulders.

Trying to work it free by rubbing her forehead against the surface of the trunk failed to move it as well, all while the act itself caused the rough fabric to act like sandpaper across her flesh.

Eventually exhaustion hit, as did a realization that she would not be able to free herself of the burlap sack. Like with the knots around her wrists, it just was not possible to achieve success given the conditions she found herself in.

She would simply have to hope for the intervention of Ian or Tabby, and if the latter, that Tabby went to Ian rather than Gwen after hearing her kicks.

And failing that intervention, she would have to make sure she planted a good kick against Gwendolyn's face without the use of her vision, her target one that she would have to guide her foot toward based on sound alone.

It wasn't the most inspiring of plans, but it was all she had to work with. She also had to remind herself over and over again that if she had failed to free her feet from the bonds, even these potential actions toward escape would be unavailable to her.

Waiting.

Waiting.

Waiting.

A truck engine.

Pulling into the driveway, the sounds of it braking on a slick surface echoing.

They were home.

And just a few feet away.

She began to kick at the trunk as hard as she could, hope that the sound would be enough to be audible beyond the closed garage door filling her.

34

"My god, that wind is getting crazy," Ian voiced once they were all back inside the house, shaking themselves off of whatever snow had hitched a ride upon their bundled-up bodies. "It's like a blizzard out there."

"Daddy, do you think Santa is going to use Rudolph tonight?" Tabby asked.

"For sure."

"That's good."

Gwen didn't say anything during this exchange, her mind only able to focus on one thing at the moment, that being how she would subdue Ian for the evening so that he didn't interfere in what needed to be done, her initial idea of simply crossing her fingers and hoping he slept through everything no longer one that she was comfortable with.

Sleeping pills?

In some hot chocolate?

She always slept like a rock when she downed a few before bed, her mind blissfully free of thought within minutes of swallowing the pills. Dreams were also nowhere to be found when using them, which was apparently a problem, according to stuff she read online, the brain needing the type of sleep that produced dreams in order to function properly, which it was prevented from achieving when the pills were used.

But none of that would matter that evening.

A few sleeping pills with his hot chocolate and he would be out. Though hopefully not while on the couch downstairs watching *It's a Wonderful Life,* which was a likely outcome given how effective that movie could be in putting someone to sleep.

Talk about dull.

And yet she had always looked forward to watching it on Christmas Eve with Ian after their first holiday together given how much fun he had made everything.

Not this year.

She hadn't really looked forward to anything this year beyond being done with the holiday and the tasks it required of her in order to keep Tabby safe for the rest of her life.

Once that was accomplished and the horrors finally behind her, then she could start to look forward to things again, holiday events included.

This didn't mean she wouldn't go through the motions, one of those being sitting down with Ian and Tabby while they watched and enjoyed *It's a Wonderful Life*. She just hoped Ian didn't fall asleep while they watched it because getting him upstairs into bed would be pretty much impossible given how big he was.

The minion.

She really wanted to check on her to make sure everything was as it should be in the trunk, but knew risking such a thing wasn't wise at the moment. Ian had already seen her going in and out of the garage once this evening as she retrieved her laptop, so her going in there again would raise even more suspicions and might cause him to venture in, which could lead to his discovery of the minion.

And making up something about how gifts were in there that he couldn't see wouldn't work very well in keeping him out, not when he knew she kept the gifts downstairs in the old coal room.

No.

She would resist the urge to check on things and only head into the garage once Ian and Tabby were both safely tucked away in bed.

Until then she would simply trust that the bindings she had secured the minion with would stay in place, her own knowledge on how to tie a person properly having come after she had freed herself from three different sets of knots that Justin and Jessica had used on her early in her captivity, each escape attempt always being foiled by Justin.

After that, knots had been positioned in ways that she could not reach, and then switched up for the chain and padlock once Jessica noted that keeping her tightly tied for nearly a month was not practical.

How exactly they had contained prisoners before her was a mystery, one that Jessica only hinted at when asked, Gwen eventually concluding that whatever the old method had been, it had failed at some point, which resulted in their father having been severely injured by a victim before she was once again subdued.

Gwen shook away the old memories and finished taking off her coat, and then sat on the bench to unzip her boots, a comment from Ian on how he would go get them set up for the movie being made, which prompted Gwen to say, "While you do that, I'll get the hot chocolate going, though I'm just going to go change into something more comfortable first."

"Sounds good," Ian replied. "Though FYI, I'll pass on the special peppermint flavoring tonight."

"Ha, yeah, me too."

"What peppermint flavoring?" Tabby asked.

"Oh nothing, Miss Eagle Ears," Ian said and waved her along.

Gwen finished with her boots and then headed upstairs, her lie about wanting to put on something more comfortable simply an excuse so she could grab the sleeping pills from her nightstand drawer.

35

This is bullshit, Sam silently muttered to herself over and over again as she struggled toward the pin-drop destination that Dee had sent her, the wind frequently forcing her to halt all movement as she shielded her face.

And this wasn't anywhere near the severity that had hit the area the previous year on Christmas Eve. That had been a genuine blizzard, the wind gusts reaching over sixty miles per hour at times, all while snow was falling at a rate of nearly two inches an hour. Total whiteout conditions, after what had already been record-breaking snowfall totals during the previous week.

How Gwen had managed to survive once free of the

Robinson house was mind-boggling. It also explained why she had gone south toward the residential areas of town rather than west toward her own house, the horrible weather conditions having probably made it impossible to orient oneself.

As for Jessica, Sam had no doubts whatsoever about the young woman having succumbed to the elements, her attempts at fleeing after discovering her brother dead and Gwen gone having likely found her stumbling around in the semi-excavated areas just beyond the county line north of the fields where the attempts at building a new subdivision had stalled out after the company funding everything had gone bankrupt during the pandemic.

Her radio crackled, the voice on the other end barely audible given the static and the wind.

"Say again," she advised.

More static.

"Say again."

A bit of a voice, then more static.

Sam tried one more time, the old "third time's a charm" saying echoing in her mind while static echoed in her ear.

Fuck it.

The radio simply was not going to reach her out here. Not with the wind blowing all the snow around and the various areas of raised terrain that could cause radio dead zones.

She looked at her phone again just to make sure she hadn't veered off course.

All looked good.

36

Ian felt himself drifting a bit and blinked his eyes several times in an effort to knock away the odd drowsiness that had suddenly appeared. Confusion followed. One moment the scene where everyone falls into the swimming pool had been playing on the giant TV screen, the next George was cheering about having two dollars left in the safe.

He shifted a bit, which caught Gwen's attention.

"You okay?" she asked, voice nothing more than a whisper.

"Yeah, just dozed off for a second," he said.

"Long day. I've been struggling to keep my eyes open too."

He nodded at that and then mumbled something about needing to stay awake, his voice fading away before he could finish the statement. The next thing he knew, Tabby was scolding him for snoring.

"Sorry, honey, won't happen again."

"Maybe some more hot chocolate will help," Gwen suggested.

He agreed.

Gwen headed into the kitchen.

On-screen George was trying to figure out what happened to the eight thousand dollars that Uncle Billy had misplaced.

37

Gwen only added one sleeping pill to this final mug of hot chocolate, the previous mug having had three. Four sleeping pills over the course of an hour and a half. If that didn't put him into a deep sleep for the rest of the night, nothing would, and anything beyond that would probably start to be a risk.

Or would it?

How many sleeping pills could one take before it became dangerous?

Doesn't matter.

He's almost asleep.

Her earlier concerns about him falling asleep on the couch rather than upstairs were still present, but something she felt she could deal with by moving him to a couch in the living room if need be. Though only if she couldn't convince him to head upstairs to bed during the next twenty minutes or so.

38

Zoey got the hood off.

Not that it really helped her while in the pitch-dark confines of the trunk, but still, just having it off was huge because she would now be able to see where to kick once the trunk was open.

When this would happen, she did not know, but anticipated the moment was going to be sooner rather than later given that the transition from Christmas Eve to Christmas Day had to be drawing near.

If that truly is when things will unfold...

Zoey had contemplated this a lot while in the back of the trunk, between frantic bouts of trying to free herself. No definitive conclusions could be made during these periods, but she felt confident that her thoughts on the matter were pretty solid.

All she had to do now was wait.

Actually, it was all she could do.

Waiting.

Waiting.

Waiting.

While sometimes fruitlessly fidgeting with the ropes around her wrists.

39

. . .

Dee could barely make out what was going on up above the hole, the bitter cold and the violent shivers that were racking her body making it so her mind could not process what was unfolding as the bright light illuminated her.

Was it the sun?

Had morning actually arrived?

The light disappeared.

Then reappeared.

Lifting her head, she tried to look up at the source, the small bit of movement as her chin lifted away from her chest bringing about a new source of agony as her muscles all seemed to clamp up. Cold slithered in too.

A voice echoed.

Dee heard the words but didn't grasp what was being said.

The light vanished.

40

Sam tried everything she could to get Dee out of the hole short of getting in it herself and pushing her up and out, all to no avail. Dee herself was to blame, the poor girl chilled to the bone in such a way that she couldn't seem to grasp the help Sam was trying to give her. Even the emergency warming items she dropped down to her went untouched, as did the rope she had tied to a nearby tree and lowered right into her lap.

Requesting help was also a fruitless endeavor, the static she was met with when trying to reach someone on the radio unyielding.

"I'll be back!" she shouted down into the hole.

No reply.

She doubted Dee was registering anything that was going on.

Ian and Gwen's house.

It was her only hope, the tiny glow from their Christmas light display the only spot of color against the darkness.

41

Gwen helped Ian into bed, his voice making a very garbled request that she wake him in an hour once Tabby was asleep so that they could put all the gifts out beneath the tree, ones that Tabby would think were from Santa.

"I will," Gwen said, the lie slipping from her lips without thought.

He was asleep within seconds, his body still clothed, a thought on trying to remove them while he slept and then getting a blanket over him being considered and then dismissed.

Clothed or unclothed, the sleeping pills would keep him asleep well into the morning, his body likely needing to be shaken awake by Tabby, who would be desperately wanting to open gifts.

As for Tabby, she too was struggling to stay awake, her own mumbled statement about making sure to leave cookies and milk out for Santa being made as Gwen tucked her into bed.

Gwen promised she would and kissed her on the forehead.

A few minutes later, she was in the family room, a pair of wire cutters in hand, several strands of Christmas lights that she had squirreled away ready to have their ends snipped off so that the wires were exposed and ready to zap Santa once he came out of the fireplace.

Once this was done, she plugged them into the Alexa wall outlet that controlled the family room Christmas lights and then threaded several strands over to the fireplace, where she wrapped them around the grate and logs. The other strands would be wrapped around the female minion from the trunk, who would be presented as a gift to Santa.

Gwen also considered dumping out some water on the floor and in the fireplace to further enhance the likelihood of Santa being electrocuted, but then feared the water might somehow tip him off before she could instruct Alexa to turn on the Christmas lights.

Now to go get the minion.

42

Zoey found an ice scraper in the trunk, one that she couldn't believe had gone unnoticed for as long as it did given how often she had rolled back and forth.

Unfortunately, it didn't help her get free.

Maybe if she had had more time, it would have, but by the time she found it, and by the time she got it into a position where she could attempt to hook at the knots with a plastic edge, the sound of someone entering the garage reached her ears.

Heart racing, she took a deep breath and waited for the trunk to pop open, her legs ready to kick out at whoever was standing there once it did.

43

Gwen pressed the trunk release button on her key fob and then lifted the lid with her left hand. A second later she was on the ground, her mind unable to process anything but the pain that had erupted within her face

. . .

44

Zoey struggled to get out of the trunk after kicking Gwen in the face, shock that she had landed a blow square into Gwen's broken nose filling her mind.

A hand grabbed her ankle once she was standing on the cold pavement of the garage, her other foot kicking at and stomping on the fingers several times before they would let go, a sense of bone being crushed beneath her heel giving her quite a bit of satisfaction.

And then she was through the door that led into the hallway, heading to the kitchen, where she hoped to find a knife that she could use to cut away at her bonds, her hands trying to reach high enough behind her to get over the lip of the counter so that she could get hold of one of the handles protruding from the fancy knife block.

No use.

Gwendolyn appeared in the hallway, looking through the cutout of the kitchen at her, her face completely smeared with blood, eyes raging.

Zoey yelped into the gag that was still stuffed in her mouth and bolted to the back door, her hands able to twist the lock into the open position without issue.

45

Sam was just emerging from the narrow strip of trees that encircled Ian and Gwen's backyard when she saw someone come stumbling out from the back door of the house and fall face-first down the steps into the snow.

Gwen?

Fleeing from the house in a full-blown evil-Santa-fueled panic?

Lungs burning from her journey through the snow, and legs feeling as if they were ready to snap off with each step, Sam pushed herself toward the fallen figure, the cold air she was sucking in and out feeling like shards of glass as it entered her airways.

46

Another minion!

Helping the one that had fallen down the back steps while escaping!

No!

47

Sam heard a shriek that she momentarily thought was the wind, only to realize someone was bearing down upon her as she struggled to help this mysterious woman to her feet.

Spinning, she got her own body twisted around just as the figure crashed into her, the impact causing her body to be thrown backward all while her right leg stayed stuck in a foot of snow that acted like a shackle upon her ankle, the snap as it gave way echoing up through her body seconds before the pain was realized.

Hands were on her face, pushing her head deep into the snow, one hand fighting against the fingers while the other struggled to find her sidearm, which was seemingly stuck beneath her jacket.

Another cry echoed, and then the weight on her body was removed.

Her hand found her sidearm and pulled it out.

Another hand joined it.

A struggle ensued, one that she could not visually process given how skewed her balaclava had become during the struggle.

A third hand appeared on the gun, this one prying at her fingers.

And then something clamped down on her gloved knuckles, tearing through the fabric and getting at her flesh.

She shrieked into the sodden cloth that was pressed over her mouth.

A wheeze followed, one that caused her nose to try to suck in air through the damp balaclava fabric that covered it.

No air.

She was choking.

All while her fingers were being yanked from the handle of her sidearm, one clearly breaking while the other got twisted until it dislocated.

And then the sounds of something heavy impacting something else reached her ears.

The hands were gone.

The gun was in her control.

Using her free hand, she pulled off the balaclava just in time to see her own flashlight being swung at her, the weighted end of the Maglite smashing into the area between her eyes like it was a nightstick.

48

Zoey threw herself into Gwendolyn twice as the crazed woman

fought with another figure on the ground, but never was able to get the upper hand given how her wrists were bound, and eventually watched in dismay as Gwendolyn swung what turned out to be a flashlight into the figure's face once, twice, and then a third time, each blow sounding like a hammer against a slab of hanging meat.

And then Gwendolyn turned the flashlight upon her, a muffled cry of *no* failing to leave her gagged lips while she also tried to kick with her frozen feet, the weak blow doing little to stop the heavy one that caught her above an eyebrow and opened the flesh.

Blood oozed, mixing with everything that had splashed upon her from Gwendolyn's freshly busted nose, clouding her vision a bit but not before she was able to see the flashlight coming down for a second blow, this one knocking all sense from her.

49

Gwen knelt in the snow for several seconds after smashing the flashlight into the first minion's face, an inner voice urging her to get moving because she didn't have much time. Santa would be here soon and if there was no female figure to catch his attention while Gwen instructed Alexa to turn the Christmas lights on to fry him, then he would simply move on into the house to find Tabby.

50

It was a few minutes after eleven when she finally had the minion strapped into a chair before the fireplace, her now naked body duct-taped in place and wrapped with three strands of the sabotaged Christmas lights.

Now all she had to do was wait.

She did this while on the couch, eyes frequently going back and forth from the fireplace to the clock on the mantel, her lips ready to cry out the command that would electrocute the demonic being.

Midnight arrived.

No Santa.

FIFTEEN

1

Dee didn't know how long it took, or how many failed attempts she made, but she eventually managed to climb out of the hole with a rope that had been lowered down to her.

Hand warmers helped in her accomplishing this, an entire box of them found within a backpack that had been dropped down to her at some point.

Other items were in the backpack as well, all geared toward helping one survive the winter elements if stranded alongside the road in the snow.

Who exactly had provided this stuff to her was a mystery, the last several hours mostly a blur given the frozen agony she had been in.

Not that it really mattered at this point, not when she simply needed to get someplace warm.

Ian and Gwen's house.

2

. . .

Ian opened his eyes, a sense of confusion dominating. One moment he had been on the couch watching *It's a Wonderful Life*, the next he was lifting his head from a drool-soaked pillow.

Shifting himself, he looked toward where Gwen usually slept.

The bed was empty.

Shifting again, he grabbed his phone.

5:36 a.m.

Christmas morning.

Presents.

Did we put them out?

Panic hit.

Tabby could be up any minute and if the presents from "Santa" weren't out around the tree, she would be devastated. This wasn't to say that she wouldn't get any of those presents since they would all be brought upstairs for her, but the "magic" of Santa having brought them while she slept would be gone.

Moving quickly, but quietly, he got out of bed and left the bedroom, feet taking him to the stairs, each step groaning far louder than seemed normal as he went down.

From there he hurried down the hallway and entered the family room, his body coming to a startled halt.

What the fuck?

Gwen was on the couch, her face streaked with blood, while someone was sitting in a chair before the fireplace, naked.

No.

Not naked.

Duct tape and unlit Christmas lights were wrapped around her body, securing her to the chair.

Stepping carefully, he approached, his eyes unable to

figure out who it was given that their head was hanging forward at an odd angle.

He looked at their chest, hoping to see the rise and fall of respiration.

Nothing.

She was dead.

3

"Santa didn't come," Gwen said, staring into the empty fireplace

Ian didn't reply to this.

"I thought he was coming to take Tabby," she added, tears starting to fall.

Ian still didn't say anything.

"I had to protect her," she continued, voice rising, tears streaming. "You know that, right? I had to protect Tabby!"

"Shhh, honey," he said, stepping forward to embrace her. "It will be okay."

Gwen sobbed for several minutes.

Ian held her during this, the position awkward so as not to put any pressure upon her broken nose.

"Who is she?" Ian asked once they had pulled apart.

"I don't know," Gwen said. "I thought Santa sent her."

He nodded.

"How did she get here?"

"She was at the house. Sneaking around. And in the backyard with a shovel. With the other minion."

"Minion?"

"And Dee."

"Dee?" he asked.

"Dee was helping her. On the video. At the house."

"Where's Dee now?"

Gwen frowned.

"Gwen, honey, look at me," he said.

She did.

"Where's Dee?" he asked.

"In a hole."

A look of horror came over his face. "You put Dee into a hole?"

"No, not me. She just said she was stuck in a hole."

"When was this?"

"Yesterday."

Ian didn't say anything.

"We could put her in a hole," Gwen said.

"What?" he asked. "Who?"

"Her," Gwen said nodding toward the woman in the chair. "And the other minion too."

"Other minion?"

"The one outside in the snow."

4

Sam.

Her body was sprawled out in the snow, blood everywhere.

Ian returned to the family room, unsure on what to say or do.

And then he heard the sound of duct tape being peeled away from something.

The body.

In the chair.

Gwen was peeling tape off.

"Gwen, stop," he said, voice struggling to stay quiet so as not to wake up Tabby.

"We need to put her in a hole," Gwen said.

"Gwen."

"So no one will ever find her. And the other one." She peeled off another strip of tape. "No one will ever know."

"Gwen, stop."

She peeled off more tape.

He hurried over to her, right hand taking hold of her.

She shrieked.

And then collapsed against him, crying. "Don't let them take me away." Her sobs grew louder. "Please!"

5

Dee tripped over something as she neared the wooden steps that would take her up onto the back porch of Ian and Gwen's house, her body crashing face-first into the snow.

So close, but so cold.

She wasn't sure she could go any further.

Seconds came and went.

A minute.

Two minutes.

Maybe more.

Get up!

Now!

She shifted a bit, slowly turning herself over so that she could push herself back up onto her feet.

Something was in the snow; the object that had tripped her.

No.

Not an object.

A body.

Partially buried, but not enough to hide it, especially not with all the blood that had oozed out.

Horror hit.

She turned back toward Ian and Gwen's house.

What had happened while she had been stuck in the hole?

What was happening now?

6

"I'm not going to let anyone take you away," Ian said, easing Gwen onto the couch.

Gwen rubbed at her eyes.

"But only if you promise me that you now know Santa isn't real and isn't coming to get you. Or Tabby. Ever."

She nodded. "I know that now."

"Are you sure?" he asked.

Another nod. "I'm sure."

"Justin and Jessica were insane, and it was Justin in the Santa suit that you killed during your escape."

"Justin."

"You know this now, right?"

"Yes. Justin. In a Santa suit. I killed him."

"Okay," he said. "Now, I'm going to get her out of the chair and take her outside. I'll put her and Sam behind the shed for now and then later I'll — "

"Sam?" Gwen asked.

"That's who's in the backyard."

Gwen put a hand to her mouth.

"She wasn't a minion sent by Santa. It was just Sam. Keeping an eye on things. And now she's dead. Do you understand that?"

"I killed Sam?"

"Yes, but it's okay. I'll make it look like this one did." He nodded toward the woman in the chair. "Over at the Robinson house. She killed Sam, and then set the place on fire, and then ... fuck, I don't know yet, but I'll figure something out. For now we just need to get them both away from the house so that Tabby doesn't come down and see any of this. Okay?"

Gwen nodded and watched as Ian began to remove more duct tape from the body, his hands struggling quite a bit.

"Let me help," she said.

"No, no, I got it," Ian replied.

Ignoring this, she joined him at the body and said, "Some of the lights are taped down." She tugged at one of the unlit strands. "See?"

"I see."

She peeled all the tape off the lights and then began unwinding the first strand from around the body, handing the slack over to Ian who began coiling it around his left arm.

First strand finished, she began unwinding the second strand, which was when Ian pointed out the exposed wires sticking out of the snipped end.

"To electrocute Santa," Gwen said.

"What?" Ian asked, clearly startled.

"I cut the ends off all the lights so they would electrocute him when he arrived," Gwen said. "And then I was going to chop him up into tiny pieces with the ax so that he couldn't —"

A sound from the kitchen.

The sliding door.

Someone was coming into the house from the backyard.

Gwen started to turn to see who it was when another sound echoed, this time from the stairway, and then the hallway as slippered feet hurried toward the family room.

Oh no!

Tabby charged into the family room, excited voice shouting, "Alexa! Turn on Christmas lights!"

SIXTEEN

I

Headlines:

Christmas Morning Tragedy: Mysterious Fire Claims Lives of Local Couple
Daughter Narrowly Escapes Flames in Deadly House Fire

Silent Night, Deadly Blaze: Husband and Wife Perish in Christmas Day Inferno
Authorities Investigating Suspicious Origins of Fire; Daughter Rescued by Local College Student

Christmas Morning Horror: Local Couple Killed in Suspicious Blaze, Police Chief Found Dead Nearby
Mystery Grows as Authorities Scramble for Answers

. . .

Third Body Discovered Inside Burned House Bringing Death Total to Four
Authorities Confirm Additional Body; Won't Comment on Identity or Cause of Death

Faulty Wiring or Sabotage?
Damaged Christmas Lights Source of Deadly Blaze; Couple Electrocuted Before Being Burned

Death by Alexa?
New Evidence Suggests Alexa Command May Have Triggered Electrocution and Deadly Fire that Followed

Hero Turned Suspect? College Student's Dark Fascination with Serial Killers Uncovered
A Morbid Fascination with Serial Killers Raises Questions; Online Speculation Rampant

Heroic Rescue or Calculated Crime? True Crime Fanatic's Role in Christmas Morning Fire Under Investigation
Classmate Comes Forward; Claims She Overheard Shocking Phone Discussion About Using Electricity to Kill

College Student's Twisted Interests Lead to Suspicions After Christmas Morning Rescue
Ex-Boyfriend Reveals Feeling Uneasy Within Her Apart-

ment; Mentions Seeing DVD Copy of The Texas Chainsaw Massacre on Display

What Is She Hiding?
"Hero" College Student Refuses to Answer Questions About Twisted Sex Life; Shuts Down All Social Media Profiles

2

"She wakes up every night, screaming, crying, begging for her parents, only to then shout about how she killed them with the Alexa," Marybeth said. "I've tried everything to get her beyond all this, all to no avail, and if she is like this once she arrives at her new school, they are going to send her back to me, which I just can't have." She dabbed at a lone tear that began to crawl down her cheek. "I have no other options at this point. We need to put an end to these horrible memories once and for all."

"I agree," a soothing voice replied. "A child should not have to suffer with such horrors in her mind."

"You've worked with patients this young before?"

"Many times."

"And your treatments help?"

"Always. Those her age respond better to it than those who are older."

"That's very good to hear."

"May I see her?"

"Of course." Marybeth stood. "If you'll just follow me."

3

. . .

Tabby sat on the bed, tears still running down her face from the scolding her grandmother had given her after she had tried to call Dee following the most recent nightmare about her parents being electrocuted.

The sounds of a key in the lock echoed.

Tabby looked toward the door as it opened.

Her grandmother and an older man who was wearing a suit with a bow tie stepped in.

"Tabitha, my dear," her grandmother said. "I'd like you to meet someone. He is a doctor that is going to help you with some of the scary things you've been thinking about lately, okay?"

Tabby didn't reply.

Her grandmother let out a sigh and then motioned toward the man, who stepped forward and said, "Hi, Tabitha. My name is Dr. Wilbanks and today we are going to start doing some special treatments that will make you all better."

ABOUT THE AUTHOR

William Malmborg is the author of the novels *Jimmy, Text Message, Nikki's Secret, Dark Harvest, Blind Eye, Santa Took Them, Crystal Creek, Daddy's Little Girl, The Girl Who Played with the Ouija Board, Josiah* and the novellas *Billy's Blade, Till Death Do Us Part* and *Don't Go in the Cellar*. Future works will include *A Taste of Pain, The Murders at Bootleggers Burrow*, and *Gobble, Gobble*.

Printed in Great Britain
by Amazon